Praise for #1 *New York Times*
bestselling author Lisa Jackson

"Lisa Jackson takes my breath away."
—*New York Times* bestselling author Linda Lael Miller

"When it comes to providing gritty and sexy stories,
Ms. Jackson certainly knows how to deliver."
—*RT Book Reviews* on *Unspoken*

"Bestselling Jackson cranks up the suspense to
almost unbearable heights in her latest tautly written
thriller."
—*Booklist* on *Malice*

"Provocative prose, an irresistible plot and finely
crafted characters make up Jackson's latest
contemporary sizzler."
—*Publishers Weekly* on *Wishes*

Lisa Jackson is a #1 *New York Times* bestselling author of more than eighty-five books, including romantic suspense, thrillers and contemporary and historical romances. She is a recipient of the *RT Book Reviews* Reviewers' Choice Award and has also been honored with their Career Achievement Award for Romantic Suspense. Born in Oregon, she continues to make her home among family, friends and dogs in the Pacific Northwest. Visit her at lisajackson.com.

Also by Lisa Jackson

Illicit
Proof of Innocence
Memories
Suspicions
Disclosure: The McCaffertys
Confessions
Rumors: The McCaffertys
Secrets and Lies
Abandoned
Strangers
Sweet Revenge
Stormy Nights
Montana Fire
Risky Business
Missing
High Stakes

Visit the Author Profile page
at Harlequin.com for more titles.

LISA JACKSON

KEEPING SECRETS

Previously published as *One Man's Love* and *Mystic*

HQN™

ISBN-13: 978-1-335-01797-0

Keeping Secrets

Copyright © 2018 by Harlequin Books S.A.

First published as One Man's Love by Harlequin Books in 1986 and Mystic by Harlequin Books in 1986.

The publisher acknowledges the copyright holder of the individual works as follows:

One Man's Love
Copyright © 1986 by Lisa Jackson

Mystic
Copyright © 1986 by Lisa Jackson

PLEASE RECYCLE
THIS PRODUCT IS RECYCLABLE

Recycling programs for this product may not exist in your area.

CONTENTS

ONE MAN'S LOVE

CHAPTER ONE

CHAPTER ONE

NATHAN SLOAN RACED back into the house and reached the phone by the third ring. He called to his daughter through the screen door, which he hadn't bothered to close. "Cindy, wait for me in the yard! I'll be right there." With an impatient curse, he turned his attention to the phone. "Hello?" he called into the mouthpiece, but there was no answer. "Is someone there?" Irritation gave way to dread. His heart began to pound irregularly, and he tried to listen for any sound that would give away the caller. "Hello? Who is this?" he demanded.

Nothing.

"Hello! Can you hear me?" He waited, his palms beginning to sweat. "Dammit!" Slamming the receiver back into the cradle, he hurried out of the cottage to find that his daughter hadn't bothered to wait for him. "Cindy?"

Maybe the phone call was a trap.

Someone could have been watching the house, called from a remote phone and snatched Cindy. His jaw tightened; a queasiness gripped his gut. "Cindy!" He glanced quickly around the yard, but she wasn't anywhere to be seen.

"Get a hold of yourself. No one knows you're here— only Barbara," he muttered as he ran to the steps leading down to the beach and spotted his child on the white sand.

"Thank God," he whispered, leaning against the sun-bleached rail. His shoulders slumped in relief, and he squinted into the late afternoon sun.

Not far from Cindy was the woman he had hoped to meet for several days, a woman who might be able to help him, a woman by the name of Anastasia Monroe.

Nathan had studied her from a distance, noting the wild disarray of the honey-colored hair that tumbled down her back in soft curls, the smooth slope of her shoulders and the gentle curves of her body, undisguised by her casual clothes.

For the past three days he'd been watching her, wondering how to approach her and, unfortunately, he'd fantasized about her as well, sometimes lying awake at night until all hours of the morning just thinking about her and wondering why she affected him so strongly and deeply. He'd imagined the way her skin would taste, the widening of her eyes as he kissed her, the feel of her lips and the warmth of her body heated with passion. Why? *The forbidden fruit,* he'd rationalized.

Now as he watched her, the wind lifted her wild hair away from her face and wrapped her sundress around her slim legs.

He experienced the same seed of desire that had made his nights unbearable. "Dammit, Sloan, you're letting all this get to you and acting like some horny teenager to boot," he grumbled, but the dull ache of desire raced through his blood, firing a response in his loins just the same.

The woman walking on the beach, Anastasia Monroe, or Stacey as she preferred to be called, was the last woman in the world he could trust with his secret. To become involved with her would be the biggest mistake of his life. He kept reminding himself of those annoying facts as he descended the worn staircase.

THE SAND FELT cool beneath her bare feet as Stacey walked near the ocean's edge, her eyes scanning the tide pools for various treasures that would inspire her young students. She spied a scurrying fiddler crab and carefully captured him with her fingers before dropping him into the bucket of water swinging from her left hand. "I'll make you a star," she promised with a slightly off center smile as the crab lifted his pincers threateningly.

Stacey laughed to herself. "Don't worry," she said. "I'll set you free in a couple of weeks, but in the meantime, fella, you're going to earn your keep."

She continued to walk along the rocky coast of the island as she studied the shimmering pools and squinted at the reflection of the sun on the water. Her feet were callused from two months of beachcombing, and she was so intent in her search of the tide pools that she barely noticed that the hem of her sundress was wet.

"Here we go," she murmured to herself, as she bent down again and this time retrieved a delicate salmon-colored starfish, examined it and dropped it into the oversized bucket.

The sun was warm against her back, and the breeze lifting the sun-bleached strands of hair from her face and shoulders felt good against the bare skin of her arms and legs. As most of the afternoon had already slipped away, Stacey decided it was time to hike back to her cottage near the school where she taught. Thinking of her students, she smiled. So many of them had come so far, overcome so many problems...

She stopped suddenly, and the water sloshed in the bucket as she saw the little girl, all alone on the deserted beach. The blond-headed child hadn't noticed her, so intent was she on digging in the sand. Stacey quickly glanced up and down the beach for the mother, aunt, older brother, baby-sitter or any other kind of guardian who was responsible for the tousle-headed little girl.

Concerned, Stacey walked up to the child. "Hi," she said with a cheery smile meant to disguise her confusion.

No response. The girl kept right on digging.

"What's your name?" Stacey persisted while bending on one knee a few feet from the industrious little excavator.

The child ignored her and continued to scoop up wet sand with a bright red shovel.

Stacey tried again. "Where's your mommy?"

The shovel stopped, and the child lifted her head to regard Stacey with large blue eyes that darkened a little. "Don't got a mommy," she said.

Stacey's heart twisted for the beguiling little girl, though she was slightly suspicious of the story. The child was dressed in bright pink shorts and a white ruffled midriff blouse. Identical pink clips kept the gold ringlets out of her eyes. The little girl was no waif. Someone obviously cared about her. So where was the mother?

Again, almost angrily this time, she scanned the beach. Then she noticed the man, a solitary figure running toward her and the child. He was tall and ran with the easy gait of an athlete. His shoulders were wide, but the rest of his body was lean, and he was dressed in faded jeans and a lightweight sweater with the sleeves bunched over his forearms. His worried eyes were deep set, guarded by thick, black brows as they focused upon the child. His square jaw was set rigidly with concern, but the expression on his angular features was a trained calm—the kind that hinted at an inner wariness—and belied any outward sign of emotion.

"Hello," Stacey said, trying to hide her anger as she

straightened and offered a forced smile. "Is this your little girl?"

With obvious relief softening his worried expression, the man stopped near the child and reached down to pick her up. "Yes," he admitted. "This is Cindy." He glanced fondly at the girl and kissed her wild blond curls. "Can you say hello to Miss—"

"Monroe. Stacey Monroe." *Dear Lord, didn't he realize how dangerous it was for a child to play unattended near the surf?* She wiped her sandy palm on the folds of her skirt before extending her hand toward the stranger.

His fingers wrapped around her hand in a gesture of genuine warmth. "Nathan Sloan." A trace of a smile flashed across his tanned face giving his angular features just a hint of boyish charm that was in direct conflict with the cynical creases near the corners of his intense blue eyes.

"It's good to know that *someone* was looking after Cindy," Stacey said, unable to hide the edge of her voice until she looked again at the child. "And it was nice to meet you."

There was still no response from the little girl. She stared out to sea as if mesmerized, and Stacey began to understand why Cindy's father had let her wander onto the sand where Stacey had been beachcombing. It hadn't been an accident or an oversight on his part. In fact, he'd probably planned it! Stacey's jaw tightened and her eyes grew cold.

"She's…shy," Nathan said as if searching for a better word and Stacey lifted her gaze to meet a secret sadness in his gaze. He looked away and cleared his throat. "And she's also headstrong. We were just leaving the house when the phone rang and she ran off without me." He looked at his daughter in mock anger. "You know you're not supposed to come down here alone."

Cindy ignored her father's disapproval and slid out of his arms. She began digging once again and acted as if the adults weren't present. Stacey knew there was more to Cindy's behavior than timidity. Having worked with disturbed children for eight years, Stacey was able to see the evidence of stress in the small round face.

This Mr. Sloan had probably expected to meet Stacey on the beach. His child hadn't just happened to wander down to the beach alone. Nathan Sloan had arranged it. Stacey couldn't help her anger; the man had *used* his child, put Cindy in danger, to meet Stacey.

As if reading Stacey's mind, Nathan sighed. "She's difficult to handle sometimes," he said, rubbing his chin and staring at his little girl. Cindy had begun to wander down the beach and was out of earshot.

"Probably inherited, I'd guess."

Nathan frowned and his blue eyes, when he looked up, had taken on a seductive hue.

"Look, Mr. Sloan. I know what's going on here," she said angrily, ignoring his smoldering gaze. "You're trying to enroll Cindy in the private school—that's why you're here—on Sanctity Island. Right?"

Nathan's jaw became rigid, but he didn't deny what was so patently obvious. He nodded tightly as he looked at his child. "Yes."

"And you hoped that I'd run into Cindy this afternoon."

"I'd hoped," he admitted.

"And it didn't matter that it was dangerous to Cindy. She could have wandered out in the ocean before I saw her!"

Nathan's head snapped up. "No way. I was watching her—from over there." He cocked his head in the direction of the stairs. "I'll admit that she did get ahead of me when the phone rang. But I didn't plan to have her come down to the beach alone." His expression tightened. "I would never do anything that might put Cindy in any kind of danger." The wariness in his tone and the guarded look he gave her convinced Stacey.

She crossed her arms over her chest and tried to control her temper. "So why didn't you come into the school?"

"I did. Last week. You weren't in. I didn't want to leave a message because I wanted to meet with you in person."

"So you followed me to the beach." she accused.

More times than you'll ever know, he thought. Chuckling at her irritation, he smiled and once again his face took on a certain boyish charm that touched a forbidden part of her heart. "Nothing that sinister. *Really.* I just knew that you walked on this stretch in the afternoons and well, I took a chance that you'd be here."

He seemed honest; the concern he felt for his child appeared genuine. But something about his story just didn't ring true. Telling herself she was entirely too suspicious, she asked, "Why did you want me to meet Cindy?"

"Because of her behavior," he admitted. The lines near his mouth deepened. "Cindy became a different person sometime after her mother's death, just over a year ago. At first I thought her reaction was normal. At least I wanted to believe it. To convince myself, I rationalized that even small children grieve. But..." He frowned and rubbed the back of his neck. "But I'm afraid it's more than simple grief. She seems to be getting worse instead of better. She's regressed to the point that sometimes I need help reaching her." Looking past the cresting waves he sighed wearily. "As I said, I visited the school, but the receptionist told me that Oceancrest wasn't accepting any more children and I'd have to put her on a waiting list."

"That's what I understand," Stacey admitted, frowning a little as she studied the child. "You have to realize that I don't make those decisions—I'm just a teacher."

"Not just a teacher," Nathan interrupted. "The best specialist in this part of the country. You've worked with the Edwards Clinic in Boston and did research for Florida State University before you moved here two years ago. From everything I've read, you're the best child psychologist in the Pacific Northwest."

"I don't know about that," Stacey said, blushing as she laughed quietly and shook her head. "I'd like to know where you got your information. It sounds like you've been talking to my aunt."

"It's the truth," he said bluntly.

Stacey held up her hand in protest. "Look, I'm flattered, but I don't think I deserve all the accolades. In fact, I'm sure I don't!"

"Don't sell yourself short."

"Never," she said, laughing.

"I didn't talk to your aunt. You've earned your reputation."

She blushed a little under his compliment and the intensity of his erotic eyes. "Look, I'm just a teacher."

"And a damned good one."

Stacey avoided his gaze and studied Cindy as the cherubic-looking child returned to play near her father. Staying within Nathan's reach, Cindy examined a broken shell.

"Some people would disagree with your opinion," Stacey thought aloud, her heart wrenching painfully when she remembered Daniel Brown. How dearly she had loved that little boy… Clearing her throat and ignoring Nathan's scrutinizing gaze, Stacey pushed aside the anguish and scandal of the past. "We only have one class for preschoolers." Stacey tilted her head upward to meet Nathan's bold stare.

"And you're the teacher."

"Yes."

Nathan gestured in frustration before making a sound of disgust. His muscles flexed with the strain of trusting a woman he barely knew, a woman with beautiful sun-streaked hair and intelligent hazel eyes that seemed to flicker between green and gold. "Look, I don't like asking for anyone's help," he admitted. "And I'm not crazy about having to plead my case to a woman I don't even know, but, in all honesty, I'm at the end of my rope."

"And you don't like it."

His eyes glinted with a savagery born of desperation. "I like to be in control, Miss Monroe. I don't like the feeling that I have to depend upon anyone but myself."

"Including me?"

"Including you."

Stacey glanced at Cindy before returning her gaze to Nathan's rugged face. Behind the thick dark brows, deep-set blue eyes and angular features was a very proud man. Her spine prickled when she looked into his eyes, and she imagined for a moment that he was lying to her, guarding a secret.

"I'm only asking that you work with Cindy for her sake," he pressed. "She needs you." He shifted his gaze to his daughter. "Cindy, would you like to go to Miss Monroe's school?"

The child ignored him.

"Cindy?"

Again, no response. If anything, Cindy was more remote than ever, to the point that she blocked out her father.

"Cindy, did you hear me—"

"You've made your point," Stacey cut in angrily. "I'll see what I can do. Maybe the school administrator, a woman by the name of Dr. Woodward, can make an exception in Cindy's case and evaluate her. There's always a chance of an opening."

Nathan's taut shoulders relaxed a bit. "That's all I can ask."

"You know, Mr. Sloan—"

"Nathan."

"Okay. Nathan. I don't have the final say in matters like this. If there's no room in the school, well—" she lifted her bare shoulders "—there's just no room."

"I understand."

"But there are other schools—on the mainland."

He grimaced. "Institutions, you mean."

Stacey shook her head. "Not necessarily. It's true that we have a very comfortable, homelike environment at Oceancrest, but that doesn't mean there aren't very reputable, first-class schools in Seattle or Tacoma."

"But *you* aren't in Seattle or Tacoma, are you?"

Cocking her head to the side, she studied him with narrowed eyes. *Why was he so insistent that she work with his daughter?* There was something about Nathan Sloan and his charade of a meeting that didn't quite ring true. "There are other teachers, Mr. Sloan. Good teachers as well as psychologists: Dr. Hale in Tacoma and Maureen O'Brian in Seattle. And then there's—"

"I'm not interested in them."

"So why me?"

His eyes sparked with the same smoldering passion

she'd seen before, unnerving her. "Because I know about you and your background. Without meeting you, I felt I could trust you and I want you to work with Cindy— even if it has to be outside of the school. If you'll work with her individually, I'll pay you directly."

"I only work through Oceancrest," Stacey said firmly, though she was already teetering. There was something about Nathan Sloan's beguiling child that she found irresistible. And then there was the man himself. The secret lurking in his cynical blue eyes mystified and intrigued her. *You're walking on dangerous ground,* she told herself and then promptly ignored the warning. "I'll see what I can do," she said with a forced but confident smile as the wind lifted her hair away from her face and whipped her sundress around her legs.

"I appreciate it." Nathan reached into his pocket and then handed her a piece of paper with a telephone number written on it.

"You really did plan this whole thing, didn't you?"

Nathan's eyes darkened, and Stacey guessed that if it hadn't been for the fact that he was wrestling with his own private hell, that fleeting boyish charm she'd seen before would have softened the hard angles of his face. "Let's just say I hoped I'd run into you." He walked over to Cindy, kneeled and carefully picked up his daughter before turning to face Stacey again. "Thank you." With his precious cargo safe in his arms, he started walking toward the staircase at the north end of the beach.

Stacey watched him disappear up the weathered steps. Folding the small white piece of paper and pushing it into the deep pocket of her dress, she turned, picked up her bucket and headed home.

Twice she looked back over her shoulder, searching for

one last glimpse of Nathan. Both times she saw him standing with his feet planted far apart at the top of the cliff, his daughter in his arms. She could feel his eyes on her back, and she shivered even though the wind was warm.

Nathan Sloan was an interesting, mysterious man, she decided, but then gave herself a mental shake as she climbed the stairs at the south end of the beach. The last thing she needed complicating her life was a man, interesting or not.

"IT'S OUT OF the question," Margaret Woodward said as she dipped her spoon into the small container of yogurt.

Stacey sat before Margaret's ancient wooden desk, her feet propped on one of the short tables designed for young children. "Why?"

"You know why. The school's full as it is."

"But not the preschool class. Remember the Jones boy moved. We have an opening."

"But we must have nearly a dozen kids on a waiting list. It's just not fair to let this man—what's his name?"

"Nathan Sloan."

Margaret pursed her lips and took another spoonful of yogurt before tossing the empty container into the trash basket. "Right. It wouldn't be fair to let this Sloan character's daughter into Oceancrest before the kids who've been waiting for weeks."

"But the girl—"

"I know. She shows some of the signs of depression, depression that can be cured. Unfortunately, she's not alone."

"That's exactly my point!" Stacey exclaimed, jumping to her feet to champion Cindy's cause. "I get the feeling she is alone. No mother—just Cindy and her father, alone on this island—"

"You've got a feeling?" Margaret Woodward looked toward the ceiling and sighed loudly. "Oh, Lord, here we go again. Wasn't it one of your feelings that stirred up so much trouble in Boston?"

Stacey's stomach lurched. "That was a long time ago."

"Nonetheless, it happened. And I can't risk the integrity of this school for one of your 'feelings.'"

"That was a cheap shot, Margaret."

Margaret took off her silver-rimmed glasses and set them on the corner of the desk before looking at the young woman who was more of a daughter to her than an employee. "Yes, I suppose it was. I, more than anyone, know that you weren't to blame for what happened." She looked away from Stacey and waved in the air as if to chase away her negative thoughts. "Okay, forget what I said and tell me about your 'feelings.'"

"Just test Cindy." Stacey stood over Margaret's desk and her hazel eyes were bright with challenge. "Like you do with all the applicants. If it looks like she can be helped easily, then she'll get a chance at enrollment, at least for part of the year. You know as well as I do that most of the children who are waiting to enroll are much older than Cindy Sloan. We wouldn't really be pushing any child out of the program."

Margaret rubbed her chin thoughtfully. "The girl really got to you, didn't she?"

Stacey couldn't deny the immediate fondness she'd felt for Cindy. "Yes."

"And the father?"

"What about him?"

"Did he get to you, too?" Margaret asked kindly.

"Of course not!" But Stacey couldn't hide the telltale blush that crept up her neck. She had reacted to

Nathan—or overreacted to him—more than she would admit to anyone, including herself.

"Hmph." Margaret smiled and shook her head. "I don't know why I let you talk me into these things," she said. "But, after all, it is your class. If you think you can handle another child—"

"I can."

Margaret turned her attention to the phone and pressed the intercom button for her secretary. "Andrea?"

"Yes?"

"Have I got any cancellations this week?"

"Um, let me check." There was a short silence and Margaret's eyes held Stacey's.

"Yes—two. Thursday at three o'clock and Friday at ten."

"Leave them open, will you?" Margaret asked. "I should be testing another child—a Miss Cindy Sloan. She's about—" Stacey held up four fingers "—four or five. Her father is Mr. Nathan Sloan who apparently resides on the island. Stacey seems to think that the child may be severely depressed, and Mr. Sloan wants to enroll her here."

"Okay," Andrea said. "I've got the Sloan girl down."

"Good." Margaret hung up the phone. "All right, Stacey, you win. *This time.* Cindy Sloan is all set to be tested Thursday afternoon at three and again, if I think she needs further evaluation, on Friday at ten."

Stacey smiled brightly. "Thanks."

"No problem," Margaret lied and waved off Stacey's gratitude with a flip of her wrist.

Her spirits buoyed, Stacey winked at the older woman as she left Margaret's office. She strolled down a long corridor to the classroom. In reality, her classroom was several rooms joined together, decorated in bright colors and filled with stimulating toys, books and art or science projects. It had been designed as a warm, creative place that encouraged small children to interact.

She walked over to a bookcase and stared into the large fish tank resting on the top shelf. The fiddler crab was no more hospitable today than he had been yesterday afternoon when she had captured him.

"Just wait," she said, scattering fish food in the water of another tank and watching the eager guppies swim excitedly to the surface. "This weekend I'm going looking for an octopus and if I find one, you'll feel right at home, won't you?" The crab didn't move. "And next week, when the kids come back from vacation, you'll be the most popular guy in the room."

Stacey turned out the lights of the three rooms and locked the door before heading out of the clapboard building. She walked back along a sandy path to her small, weathered cottage perched on the cliffs overlooking the sea. Beach grass rippled in the cool breeze. The air was filled with the smell of the sea and the cries of marauding gulls.

She kicked off her sandals on the front porch and paused to look at the panoramic view of the beach nearly thirty feet below. The blue-gray water was calm, broken only by the kelp floating near the surface and the frothy waves near the shore. Far in the distance, fishing boats trolled along the horizon.

Home, Stacey thought with a smile. *I've finally come home after twenty-eight years of not knowing where it was.* Once inside the cottage, she glanced at the piece of paper near the phone and dialed the number that Nathan had given her.

The phone rang ten times before Stacey gave up and placed the receiver back in the cradle. "Wouldn't you know," she muttered, feeling an odd sense of disappointment as she tossed her dress over the foot of the bed and changed into old jeans, boots and a boat-necked sweater. After drinking a tall glass of iced tea, she grabbed a bucket and a shovel from the back porch and started down the worn path leading to the beach. The tall, dry grass brushed against her jeans, but she didn't notice as she made her way to the weathered steps leading down the cliff.

The beach was empty, but then it usually was. Labor Day was just around the corner but the tourists usually invaded the other, more well-known islands in the San Juan chain. Sanctity Island and the small town of Serenity were off the beaten track and for that Stacey was thankful.

She scanned the white sand in all directions, subconsciously looking for Nathan and Cindy. But aside from a scruffy-looking dog playfully dragging a large piece of driftwood along the shore, she was completely alone.

Hoisting the shovel to her shoulder and letting the pail swing from her fingers, she crossed the dry beach to the wet sand near the water's edge. The tide was out and after a time, she found one small round hole. Quickly she dug into the mire until the shovel was useless, and then she dropped to her knees to dig with her fingers. The escaping razor clam was burrowing deeper into the muck. Stacey pushed her arm into the hole, managed to get her elbow and sweater dirty, but caught her prize.

"One down," she said to herself, placing the golden-shelled clam into the bucket. "And one to go."

She cleaned her arm in the surf and then began poking around the rocks near the shore. Her eyes scanned the darkest crannies of the tide pools, but she didn't find what she was looking for. The small octopuses that lived in the shallow waters of Puget Sound and the strait weren't very common on the shores of Sanctity Island.

"I guess I get to make a trip to Hood Canal after all." Smiling, she pushed her windblown hair from her eyes. "Oh, well, there could be worse things."

On a whim she decided to wade in the chilly water. After tugging off her boots, she tossed them near her bucket and rolled her jeans above her calves before bravely walking into the frothy waves. The cold water made her legs turn red and ache a little, but she loved the feel of the seawater against her skin.

Sea gulls flew over the waves and in the distance, far out to sea, Stacey noticed the colorful sail of a sailboat. The salt air filled her lungs and made her smile. Coming to Sanctity Island had been the best move she'd ever made.

Turning toward the shore, she recognized Nathan and Cindy as they walked hand in hand toward the tide. A black dog was romping beside them, and Nathan compliantly threw an old tennis ball into the ocean. The dog took after the ball like a shot. Stacey grinned, waved and hurried toward Nathan. She was shivering as she approached them, and Cindy eyed her suspiciously before lifting her hands and silently insisting that Nathan pick her up.

Some of the wariness had disappeared from Nathan's sharp features. "You must be out of your mind," he said with an amused smile. "That water is barely above freezing."

"About sixty degress—"

"Right. Just above freezing."

Stacey laughed softly, and her hazel eyes twinkled as she rolled down her jeans. "I guess I've been out of school too long, or the thermometer's changed since I was there. Anyway, the cold water's good for the soul. Exhilarating!"

"Exhilarating?" Nathan's smile widened and he chuckled. "If you say so. I guess I'll have to take your word for it."

Stacey looked into Cindy's wide blue eyes. "I bet you like to go wading, don't you?"

The girl burrowed her head into Nathan's neck, and his smile faded.

Seeing Cindy's reaction, Stacey decided to change the subject. "Speaking of school, I tried to call you earlier. Cindy's got an appointment with Margaret Woodward, the school administrator and psychiatrist, at three o'clock on Thursday and then again Friday morning at ten."

Every muscle in Nathan's body tensed. "Does that mean Cindy will be admitted?"

Stacey frowned and shook her head. "Unfortunately, no. But it's the first step. If Margaret thinks we can help her without overcrowding the classroom, then Cindy can be admitted. I've already said that I would make room for her in my class."

He seemed to relax a little. "It seems that I owe you a big thank-you."

"Not yet. I didn't do anything. Remember, it's not a sure thing."

"I know, but it's a start."

Stacey's gaze drifted to the small girl hiding her face while clinging to Nathan's neck. "Yes—it's a start. Cindy—"

The child didn't move.

"Miss Monroe said something to you," Nathan whispered as he lowered his daughter to the ground.

Cindy refused to look up.

Stacey knelt beside Cindy and reached for the clam inside her bucket. "Look what I found under the sand." She held out the mollusk for Cindy's inspection, but the girl showed no sign of seeing or hearing her.

"Does she tune out frequently?" Stacey asked as she straightened and placed the clam back into her pail.

"Sometimes. Maybe once or twice a day. It can last a few minutes or as long as a couple of hours."

"What else?"

He hesitated and looked out to sea. His sable-brown hair ruffled in the wind and the small lines etching his forehead deepened. "Sometimes—for no reason that I can fathom—she wakes up screaming and crying. She's so frantic that it's all I can do to hold her."

"So she's afraid of something."

Nathan's eyes glittered beneath his thick brows. "I guess so. But I can't figure out what. There doesn't seem to be a pattern to it. Just one night, out of the blue, she'll wake up screaming. I'll ask her if she had a bad dream and reassure her that I'm there, but it might take hours before she'll calm down."

Stacey watched the child quietly playing in the sand. In red shorts and a white T-shirt, a slight tan and rosy cheeks, Cindy looked like any other happy preschooler. "Has Cindy ever been in a teaching program before?"

He hesitated, but shook his head.

"But surely you've had her observed?"

Nathan stiffened, nodded and eyed his daughter as if suddenly concerned for her safety. "When she was a little younger, she saw a psychologist, Dr. Lindstrom in Fairbanks. I was working in Alaska at the time." He plunged his hands into his pockets and shrugged. "Nothing happened." Frowning, he looked out to the sea. "That's why I came to you. I thought you, as a woman, might get through to her."

A premonition of dread stiffened Stacey's spine. "So you arranged the meeting the other day on the beach."

"Yes." He offered a self-mocking grin. "I wanted you to meet Cindy and...well, I was hoping that she would respond to another woman."

"Another?"

Nathan glanced nervously at his child. "She hasn't been around many women since Jennifer's death."

"Jennifer, your wife?"

"Cindy's mother," he confirmed and then, as if the conversation had grown too personal, he quickly picked up his daughter and held her tightly in his arms.

Stacey brushed some sand from Cindy's cheek and the little girl cringed. "Did the nightmares start after your wife passed away?"

He tensed a little and squinted into the horizon, as if lost in thought. "I don't really know," he admitted. "I was away a lot of the time because of my job. I'm a free-lance writer. I'm sure that Cindy had an occasional nightmare, but nothing so bad as the ones she's experienced since Jennifer's death."

Stacey sought his worried eyes and knew there was more to his story, something that he didn't want to discuss in front of the child. *Or something he wants to hide from you,* she thought. "I hope that I get a chance to work with Cindy," she said.

"Not half as much as I do," he said curtly. Then, as if to apologize for his abrupt tone, he smiled. "Look, I'd like to thank you for setting up the interview and evaluation with Dr. Woodward."

"It wasn't a big deal."

"It is to me—and to Cindy. Let me buy you dinner."

"You don't have to—"

"I *want* to."

The invitation was appealing; it had been ages since

she'd been out, but she had to turn him down. She'd learned long ago how to separate her emotions from her work. It had been a painful lesson that had nearly shattered her life. "I don't think so. Why don't you wait until Cindy's accepted into the school's program? Then, maybe we'll all have something to celebrate."

Nathan had to bite his tongue. He felt like arguing. Hell, for more than a week he'd felt like fighting with anyone or anything that might cross him, but he was smart enough to know when to back off. "Fair enough," he agreed, appearing more calm than he felt. Stacey Monroe had that special combination of wit, intelligence and innate sensuality that brought out the worst in him. *So had Jennifer,* he thought coldly and silently vowed to himself that he wouldn't let the hazel-eyed teacher, with the easy smile and intriguing dimples, get under his skin. "We'll see you Thursday," he said as he shifted Cindy in his arms and started to walk away.

"Goodbye, Cindy," Stacey called over the roar of the surf. Though the little girl lifted her head, she didn't respond to Stacey's encouraging wave. If anything, Cindy clung more fiercely to her father's neck.

Don't get involved, Stacey warned herself as she watched the tall man and his child climb the weathered steps at the far end of the beach. *Remember Daniel, and whatever you do, Stacey, for God's sake don't get involved.*

CHAPTER TWO

"WHAT DO YOU know about this Nathan Sloan?" Margaret asked as she stared into the hamster cage and watched the tiny creature climb through the tubes connecting the small glass compartments of its home.

"Nothing." Stacey finished watering the plants in the classroom, then climbed onto a stepladder and began stapling artwork onto the walls.

"Nothing?"

"No. I just met him on the beach."

"And the child—is that where you met her, too?"

"Yep. Hand me that folder, would you?" Margaret gave Stacey the folder containing the bright splotches of red and blue paint on yellow paper. "I told you everything I knew the other day. Cindy's mother is dead—she died about a year ago, I think—and, according to her father, that's supposedly what started Cindy's withdrawal. She's been seen by at least one psychologist, a Dr. Lindstrom, in Fairbanks, Alaska. But I got the feeling Cindy's father wasn't happy with the results. Other than that, I can't tell you much." Stacey lifted her shoulders.

"Nothing?"

Stacey thought for a moment. "Except that it was obvious that Cindy's father would do anything to help his child. He takes her to the beach every day, I think, and gives her a lot of encouragement and support."

"Superdad?" Margaret asked cautiously.

Stacey shook her head and stapled another piece of artwork onto the wall. "I don't know," she admitted, gazing out the window toward the sea. "I just don't know that much about him."

"What does he do?"

"I think he's a free-lance writer, at least he used to be, but I don't really know what he's doing here on the island."

"So all of this is just because of one of your 'feelings.'" Margaret steadied the ladder and looked up at Stacey with concerned eyes.

Frowning slightly, Stacey gave Margaret a disapproving look. "Wait until you meet Cindy. She'll capture your heart."

"Has she already captured yours?"

Stacey stapled the final picture onto the wall with a vengeance. "A little," she admitted.

"And the father?"

Stacey slanted a worried glance at her boss. "I told you, there's not much to tell about him. And stop trying to mother me."

Margaret chuckled softly to herself and checked her watch. "Well, all our speculation about Mr. Sloan and his daughter is about to end. He should be here any minute."

Stacey felt her pulse jump unexpectedly but ignored the gleam in Margaret's wise eyes. "Good. I hope you find it in your heart to let Cindy into Oceancrest."

"It's not my heart that's the problem. It's the facilities and the staff."

Leaning against the top step of the ladder, Stacey offered the older woman a warm smile. Margaret Woodward was more than her boss. She was a lifelong friend.

"I know, but the room is large and I'm the staff; I can handle Cindy."

"I'll see what I can do," Margaret promised, walking out of the room and leaving Stacey to wonder what would happen to Cindy if she weren't allowed to enroll at Oceancrest.

WITH CINDY'S HAND firmly in his, Nathan walked toward the two-story, clapboard building with the neatly-tended lawn. Oceancrest looked no different than any other school. From the exterior there was no indication that two wings of the building were designated for children with special learning problems. Thank God! The more private the surroundings for his daughter, the better.

He felt the apprehension in Cindy's grasp, and she tried to pull free of his hand. "No," she said, tugging backward as they climbed up the two steps to the entrance.

He paused and offered Cindy an encouraging smile. "Come on, pumpkin," he whispered, kneeling in order to look into Cindy's confused eyes. "I'll be with you."

"No!"

"Please?"

"Don't want to!"

Resigned that there was no other way to handle his child, Nathan sighed, lifted Cindy in his arms and carried her through the glass doors of the school.

He couldn't have asked for a more private facility if he'd tried. The fact that Anastasia Monroe—or Stacey—was here made Oceancrest the perfect choice. If only the school administrator, Dr. Woodward, would cooperate and let Cindy enroll, some of his most pressing problems would be solved. But not all of them, he reminded himself grimly, imagining the angry, flushed face of Robert Madison. No, the problems weren't over, not by a long shot. Madison wouldn't rest until he found Cindy. Involuntarily, Nathan's arms tightened around his daughter. He glanced down at his innocent child, vowing silently to himself that he would keep her safe. And away from Robert Madison, no matter what the price.

Trying to disregard his bothersome thoughts, Nathan followed the signs to the school administration offices while Cindy squirmed in his arms.

"We go home now, Daddy!" she demanded.

"Not just yet. I want you to see this school. Maybe you can come here and be with Miss Monroe a few mornings a week."

"No! We go home now!"

"Cindy—"

"We go home now, we go home now..." she wailed, pressing her damp face to his cheek.

"Shh, it's all right," he assured his daughter, wondering if it would ever be. What would happen to Cindy if Stacey Monroe couldn't help her?

Nathan Sloan glowered as he realized that he was out of aces. He'd played his trump card the other day on the beach, and now it was fate's turn. A quiet desperation took hold of him as he considered the final showdown with Madison and considered the fact that he just might lose the only thing that was important in his otherwise worthless life. Clenching his jaw in determination, he marched down the short hallway.

A red-haired woman with pleasant features smiled as Nathan approached the office of the administrator. "You must be Mr. Sloan," she said before turning her attention to the child. "And you're Cindy. My name is

Andrea. Just make yourself comfortable," she suggested, gesturing toward the chairs, "and I'll tell Dr. Woodward you're here."

"Thank you," Nathan replied, his throat tight. The redhead disappeared through a door, and Nathan realized that his hands were damp. His case of nerves was almost laughable, except for the fact that they were the result of his concern for Cindy.

"Daddy, please..." Cindy's round blue eyes, so like her mother's, pleaded with him.

"Hang in there. Okay?"

In a minute Andrea reappeared. "Dr. Woodward will see you in the welcoming room. It's a little different from her office and not quite as overwhelming for the children." They walked into a small room with floor-to-ceiling windows on one side. Tables filled with stuffed animals, puppets and books lined the walls, and the good doctor herself was seated on a plump, pink cushion in the middle of the floor.

"Hello, Mr. Sloan," she greeted as Nathan carried Cindy into the room. "Please have a seat." She indicated another pillow, which Nathan, still holding Cindy, sat upon. "Now, Mr. Sloan," the gray-haired woman began, her shrewd eyes studying the child clinging to Nathan's neck. "I'd like you in here while I try to talk to Cindy and then, once she feels comfortable in this environment, I'm going to ask you to leave. I'll stay here with Cindy, and you can fill out all the medical history, personal history and registration forms in Andrea's office. If Cindy shows any signs of distress, I'll call you and you can come back in . I just want to observe her, see what responses she has to different stimuli, and then I'll talk to you both again. Is that all right with you?"

"Fine," Nathan agreed, but Cindy shook her head in dismay.

Margaret Woodward remained unruffled and folded her hands in her lap. "Good."

For the next few minutes, Dr. Woodward, who insisted upon being called Margaret, discussed the school in general. Her voice was soft and low and though she spoke to Nathan, she continually made eye contact with Cindy. She offered the girl some toys, which Cindy rejected, as she explained why she had come to Sanctity Island in the first place and how the school was growing. After about twenty minutes, Cindy had warily scooted over to the bookshelf and was playing intently with a rag doll.

"Mr. Sloan?"

Nathan jerked his gaze back to the administrator. He'd been watching his daughter.

Margaret cocked her head in the direction of the door and, begrudgingly, Nathan took his cue, leaving quickly and quietly despite an increasing sense of worry. He'd been through hell and back to ensure Cindy's safety, and he didn't trust the child out of his sight unless he knew the person intimately. From what he could discern, Margaret Woodward was a woman who could be trusted, but still he felt the same old tension knotting his shoulders at the thought of being separated from his child.

"She'll be fine," Dr. Woodward insisted as she escorted Nathan out of the room. "If you'd like, you can observe what's going on through the two-way mirror—over there, on the other side of the room." She pointed in the general direction before turning her attention back to Cindy.

Exiting quietly, Nathan stood outside the room, staring through the glass, unobserved while Margaret Woodward tried to communicate with his daughter.

Cindy looked up frantically once she'd discovered that Nathan had gone, but she didn't cry and Margaret continued to talk to her. As far as Nathan could tell, Cindy wasn't responding much, but then she wasn't throwing a fit, either. So far, so good.

STACEY TURNED THE corner near the administration offices and stopped dead in her tracks. Ahead of her, looking through the window of the welcoming room, was the familiar figure of Nathan Sloan. He'd loosened his tie and his shirt-sleeves were pushed upward to the crook of his elbow. His jaw was tight, his shoulders hunched, and he was glaring through the window as if he expected someone to snatch his child from him.

Approaching quietly and looking through the glass at Margaret and Cindy, Stacey said, "She's very good at what she does, you know."

Startled, Nathan glanced in her direction and his gaze immediately warmed.

"But then you probably already know that, don't you?" Stacey persisted. Her round, dark-lashed hazel eyes seemed to look into Nathan's soul.

"I wouldn't have brought Cindy here if I hadn't thought that this was the best possible place for her. Of course I checked out the school as well as Dr. Woodward and you."

Stacey managed a thin smile. "Is that why I feel like someone on the FBI's most wanted list?"

Nathan's sensual lips lifted at the corners. "I suppose I deserved that."

"And more."

With a sigh, he pushed his fingers through his dark hair and leaned a hip against the edge of the window.

"Look, maybe I gave you the wrong impression the other day. I didn't do that much checking into your personal life, or Margaret Woodward's for that matter. I dug deep enough to know that Cindy belongs here—with you."

Stacey blushed and waved off his praise. "Thanks, but it's just my job."

"Is it?" He turned and faced her. One of his thick brows arched. "That's not what I've heard."

"No?" She tried to sound lighthearted. "I didn't realize that I'd gained a reputation for being such a do-gooder."

He leaned back and crossed his arms over his chest. "Actually, that's exactly what I've heard—that you get so involved with your students or patients or whatever you want to call them, that it's hard for you to let them go—"

"That's ridiculous. I never feel better than when a child is happy and well adjusted and fits into a normal home and school environment."

"But it's hard for you to think that you'll never see them again."

"Maybe a little."

"A lot, I'd be willing to guess."

"With some," she admitted, her heart wrenching painfully when she remembered Daniel Brown. "Of course, letting go is the part of being a teacher that's the toughest." Then, squaring her shoulders, she smiled bravely. "But that's what it's all about, isn't it? If I can't let them go, then I haven't done my job." She met his gaze briefly before glancing through the window. "Oh, look—" she pointed at the glass. "—Margaret's got Cindy talking."

To Nathan's surprise and relief, he saw that Margaret Woodward had somehow managed to draw Cindy out, if just a little. The girl was nodding, though still glancing nervously toward the door, her worried blue eyes searching for her father. In Nathan's estimation, the simple communication was a breakthrough.

"Dr. Woodward's got to let her into Oceancrest!" he whispered, his fist balling in conviction.

Though she agreed, Stacey kept her thoughts to herself. There was no reason to give Nathan any false hope. "Come on," she said, noticing the lines of worry gathering at the corners of his mouth. "Let Cindy and Margaret work things out here. You can fill out the registration forms, get a brochure on the school and visit my classroom—just to get an idea of what Cindy will be up against."

"You make it sound like war."

"Do I? Well, it's not quite that drastic, but I won't lie to you. It will be hard on your daughter at first."

"*If* she's admitted."

"One bridge at a time," Stacey said, cocking her head in the direction of her classroom. "Margaret agreed to see her, didn't she?"

"But you said that's no guarantee."

"It isn't. But there's no reason to borrow trouble."

Nathan leaned against the mirror and searched Stacey's gray-green eyes. "Are you always so optimistic?"

"Only when I'm dealing with nervous parents," she said, offering a reassuring smile and trying to ignore the questions in his gaze. She felt her pulse jump under his scrutiny. "Come on."

They walked back to the reception area, and Andrea gave Nathan what looked like a ream of forms. "You can fill these out at home," she said. "Return them to the school tomorrow. If Cindy's admitted, we'll need these records on hand next week when classes begin."

"This is worse than joining the army," Nathan grumbled good-naturedly as he stuffed the folded forms into his pocket and followed Stacey to the preschool classroom.

Stacey snapped on the lights and the three interlocking rooms came alive. A parakeet began chirping, the hamster ran on his treadmill and even the fiddler crab scurried across the bottom of the aquarium.

"This looks suspiciously like a zoo," Nathan commented.

"A little, I suppose. Animals are an important part of helping the children. We have two dogs and three horses in the stable. Some of the older children have the responsibility of caring for the larger animals. Margaret and the rest of the staff feel that children have an innate love and understanding of animals. If human exposure won't help the children, perhaps working with animals will."

Nathan walked around the rooms, picking up books, toys and studying the various creatures. "This would be good for Cindy," he said as he walked over to a bank of windows and looked at the playground.

"Come on, I'll take you outside."

She opened the door and held it for him. "Over there are the stables where the horses are kept. The one meadow is for riding and there's a trail down to the beach for special outings. The preschoolers stay up here, with me, and we play on the slides, swings and monkey bars. In the spring we plant a garden and in the fall we harvest whatever survived through the summer." She pointed to a row of tomatoes and an overgrown hill of summer squash. "Then, later in the year, we might cook with some of the vegetables and, of course, save the seeds for the following spring."

He eyed her speculatively. "You really love working with the kids, don't you?"

"If I didn't, I wouldn't work here."

He placed his arms against the highest of the iron bars and leaned forward to stretch his tense muscles and stare at her. The effect was surprisingly sensual. A hot breeze ruffled his dark hair, and his ink-blue gaze probed deep into her eyes.

Stacey's heart nearly missed a beat.

"So what brought you to Sanctity Island in the first place?"

"Margaret Woodward," she replied. Margaret had been her savior. When her life had fallen apart in Boston, Margaret's offer had been all that had kept Stacey sane. "She offered me a position out here and I took it. But you know that, don't you?"

He frowned a little. "I know how you got here, but I don't know why."

"It was time for a change," she hedged, while looking at her watch. "Maybe we'd better go back to the administration wing. Margaret's probably just about done testing Cindy."

"Good."

She paused as she turned toward the building. "You know that you have a lovely little girl, don't you?"

A sad smile stole over Nathan's features. "Yeah, I know. But it's nice to hear it." For a moment his eyes lingered in the silvery-green depths of hers and Stacey's heartbeat quickened. "Thank you."

Stacey cleared her throat and entered the building. "So what are you doing on the island?"

"I told you that I'm a free-lance journalist, didn't I?"

"Yes."

"Don't tell me you've never heard of me." His midnight-blue eyes glimmered seductively.

Stacey grinned and lifted her shoulders. "'Fraid not."

"Don't worry about it. I do mostly environmental pieces. That's why I'm here, why I was in Fairbanks. Once in a while, I'll do a sports story, or a story on the economy, but not very often. I used to do a lot of sports stuff—you know, who bought whom for how much, drugs and sports, rivalry between coaches, that sort of thing…" His voice drifted off, as if he were speaking about something long dead.

"So what are you working on now?"

"The San Juan islands—the unique climate, wildlife, tourist attractions, that sort of thing."

"And when the article is finished, will you be moving again?" Stacey asked, her thoughts returning to Cindy.

"Not right away. It's a series of three articles," he said. "I also have a commercial fishing story and a tourist pamphlet I'm working on as well as a book about the Native American tribes of the Northwest."

"A big step away from sports."

"Yep. I have more than enough to keep me busy for at least a year."

Stacey relaxed a little even though she wanted to know more about him. There was something about Nathan Sloan that didn't quite jibe. The hardening of his eyes or stiffening of his shoulders when the subject got too personal made her want to know more about him. The simple knowledge that he and Cindy weren't about to walk out of her life as quickly as they had thrown themselves into it was strangely reassuring.

MARGARET WAS OFFERING Cindy a peanut butter cookie when Nathan walked back into the administration wing of Oceancrest school.

The little girl took the cookie from Margaret's hand and then dashed over to her father. "We go home now," she said.

"Yes," he agreed, picking up the child and meeting Margaret's eyes. "We'll go home."

"You have a very bright daughter," Margaret said.

"Thank you."

Stacey had been walking with Nathan and had noticed his quickening stride and the brooding intensity in his gaze as he was reunited with his child.

Margaret glanced at Stacey before turning to Nathan. "And under the circumstances, with Stacey's approval, I think we can enroll Cindy in Oceancrest."

Nathan's face broke into a wide grin and Stacey felt as if a great weight had been lifted from her shoulders. "I'm all for it. I think Cindy will love school here."

"No!" the child screamed, looking viciously at Stacey.

"Thank you," Nathan said, to both Stacey and Margaret.

"Daddy, don't leave me!"

"I won't, pumpkin. You'll only be here a few hours a day. Why don't you come down to the classroom and I'll show you around?" Nathan lifted his eyes to Stacey, silently asking for her agreement.

"Sure. There's a hamster down there who's been very lonely for the past three weeks."

Stacey led Nathan and Cindy back to the preschool classroom and watched as the child, still clinging to her father, discovered the animals tucked in the corners of the room.

"She's going to like it here," Nathan predicted, but the defiant light in Cindy's eyes didn't die.

"Of course she is."

"And I owe you. Big. How about dinner?" Nathan asked.

Stacey shook her head. "I... I really can't—"

"Weren't you the lady that said something about a victory celebration, once Cindy was accepted?" he demanded, his eyes turning an erotic shade of blue.

"I might have said something about—"

"Then it's a date. Tomorrow night."

"I'm sorry, Nathan," she said firmly, "but I make it a practice of keeping everything between the students, parents and myself professional."

"I'm not asking for a lifelong commitment," he said. "Just a simple thank-you dinner." He took one of her hands in his. "Come on, humor me."

"I really *can't.*"

"I don't bite, you know."

"I make it a firm rule not to—"

"Break your rules, just this once. I'd like to talk about Cindy when she's not around to overhear the conversation."

I should be shot, Stacey thought, feeling herself wavering. "Okay," she finally agreed. "I'll come—to talk about your daughter."

"Good. I'll pick you up at seven, if that's okay."

"Seven is fine. I live—"

"On Otter Drive. The gray cottage on the bluff."

Stacey's smile fell from her face. "How did you—"

"I saw you walk up the steps from the beach and take the path to your house."

"I really don't like people spying on me!"

"I wasn't spying," he replied, amused at her sudden outburst. "Just interested." He shifted Cindy to a more comfortable position. Before Stacey could say anything else, he turned toward the door leading outside and called over his shoulder, "I'll see you tomorrow night."

Stacey waved and didn't hear Margaret's soft footsteps behind her. "An interesting man," the older woman commented with a knowing smile. "If I were thirty years younger…"

"Harry would still be alive and you wouldn't be eyeing single men."

Margaret chuckled to herself. "You're right. Is that a polite way of saying keep my nose out of your business?"

"If it was, would you pay any attention?"

"Of course not."

"Then I guess we're both just wasting our breath, aren't we?" Stacey said, turning toward her room.

"Maybe…but take my advice," Margaret suggested. "Don't let what happened in Boston sour you on all men. There are a few good ones left, you know."

"Meaning Nathan Sloan, I suppose?"

"Perhaps." She shrugged.

"You don't even know him."

"I know he cares for that child of his a great deal. You can tell a lot about a man by the way he is around children."

"I think you're overpsychoanalyzing."

"My nature. And I think you're ducking the issue."

"Which is?"

"That it's time for you to go out, kick up your heels a little."

"But not with the father of one of my students," Stacey said.

"Maybe you're right," Margaret reluctantly agreed, chewing thoughtfully on her lower lip. "I know that you've got to be careful, good Lord, I expect you to. But remember: all men aren't like Daniel's father."

"Thank God," Stacey whispered. "If it makes you feel any better, I told Nathan I'd go to dinner with him tomorrow night."

"You did?" Margaret said. "Good." Her expression clouded a little and she added, "Just be careful, Stacey—use your best judgment. Don't get me wrong, I like Nathan Sloan. He seems like a good man. But I don't want to see you hurt again."

"There you go again, trying to mother me! Honestly, Doctor, maybe someone should try to psychoanalyze *you* for a change."

Margaret chuckled softly. "I'm afraid it would be a rather boring case history. And quit trying to change the subject."

"I'm not."

"Good. Then go out and enjoy yourself."

"I'm only going because of Cindy."

Margaret cocked a disbelieving brow. "Sure. Well, while you're at it, try to have a little fun."

Fun, Stacey thought sarcastically as she glanced out the doors and down the concrete walk to the parking lot, where minutes before Nathan had gotten into his Jeep. "You're an incurable romantic, y'know."

"And you're much too cynical for one so young," Dr. Woodward said as she turned back to her office. "You have dinner with that nice young man and enjoy yourself, for goodness' sake! You don't have to get *involved* with him—just enjoy an evening out. Lord knows you deserve one." At Stacey's wry expression, she said, "And for crying out loud, don't act as if it's the end of the world."

"Weren't you the one who warned me about risking

the integrity of the school by stirring up so much trouble with my 'feelings'?"

"Did I say that?"

"Yes! Three days ago! And then again, earlier today."

"Well, I suppose I was being selfish, and you've never listened to me anyway. I didn't expect you to start now."

Stacey laughed as the woman whom she'd come to think of as a second mother marched out of the room. Maybe Margaret was right. It was only an innocent date with an interesting man. What could possibly go wrong?

THAT EVENING, AFTER eating a late dinner and cleaning the kitchen, Stacey walked onto the front porch. She smiled as the warm wind brushed over her face. The night was clear and a thousand stars winked in the black sky.

Far below, the shadowy beach and the dark sea were visible in the blue illumination from the floodlights mounted near the top of the bluff.

Stacey leaned against the railing and stared at the white caps on the ocean. The wind caught her hair and pushed it away from her face as she breathed deeply of the salt-laced air. She loved this island more than anywhere else on earth. In two short years, she'd come to think of it as home.

A movement on the beach caught her eye. Turning, she watched with fascination as a man, hands pushed into the back pockets of his pants, walked along the edge of the water. It was too dark to identify him clearly, but the broad width of his shoulders and his narrow hips reminded her of Nathan. Squinting into the darkness, she convinced herself that the man was, indeed, Nathan Sloan. Stacey smiled to herself and allowed herself the luxury of staring at him from a distance. Watching him walk down the beach made her pulse quicken and without really considering her motives, she slipped on her thongs and headed toward the steps to the beach. At the top of the stairs she stopped, her eyes fastened on the man and another figure hurrying toward him.

Stacey drew in a deep breath and waited. As the other person came nearer, Stacey could see that it was a woman—a tall woman with long, dark hair. She ran to Nathan and threw her arms around him as he returned her passionate embrace.

Stacey's heart lurched. She told herself that she should return to the house, that what was happening on the beach was none of her business, that the man might not even be Nathan Sloan, but she couldn't tear her eyes away from the scene and her feet refused to move.

What did you expect? she chided herself. Nathan Sloan certainly could have a girlfriend, or a lover, *or a wife.* Just because Jennifer Sloan was dead didn't mean anything. Besides that might be a lie. What did Stacey really know about Nathan? Absolutely nothing! Except what he had told her. Everything he'd said could certainly be a pack of lies.

You're overreacting again! she told herself. Just because Nathan met another woman on the beach wasn't a reason to go off the deep end. Maybe the man *wasn't* Nathan.

The couple began to walk up the beach, away from Stacey's cabin, toward the steps at the opposite end of the beach, the stairs Nathan always used when returning home.

Stacey stared in fascination as Nathan and his woman, whoever she was, walked, arm in arm, away from the illumination of the floodlights and disappeared into the night.

CHAPTER THREE

MORNING SUNLIGHT STREAMED through the open windows of the classroom and a salt-scented breeze freshened the air.

Stacey had just finished straightening the books on the shelf in the science corner and was congratulating herself on a job well done when she heard the door open. *Probably Margaret,* she thought with a grin. She turned toward the sound, and her smile froze as she recognized Nathan standing in the doorway. He was wearing soft gray cords and a dark blue sweater. A smile stretched across his face when he noticed Stacey's surprised expression.

"Dr. Woodward is evaluating Cindy. Remember?"

"Oh, that's right." Stacey relaxed a little and tried not to remember the tender scene she had witnessed on the beach the night before. As she had told herself over and over again during the sleepless hours of the night, what Nathan Sloan did with his life was really none of her business. She was his daughter's teacher, nothing more. If he happened to have been on the beach last night with another woman, it didn't affect her.

Nathan closed the door behind him and walked over to the hamster's cage, pretending interest in the fluffy brown creature. "No rats or snakes?"

Stacey smiled. "Not in the cages," she said, unable to bite her tongue.

"Pardon me?"

"They don't tend to get along."

"I suppose not." He straightened. "You know, it took me over two hours to answer all the admission questions."

"All part of the program, I'm afraid. We like to know as much about the children as possible," she said.

"And then some."

"Weren't you the one hell-bent to get her admitted?" Stacey asked.

Nathan's dark brows quirked and he flashed her a disarming grin. "Did I miss something? Are you mad at me?"

"Of course not."

He leaned one shoulder against the chalkboard and slid an appreciative glance up her body. Though she was fully dressed in an apricot sundress, she felt stripped bare. "Then why do I get the feeling I was the last person on earth you wanted to see today?"

"You're imagining things."

"Am I?" His grin widened. "Sounds like I could use some intense psychoanalysis."

"Probably." *Stop it!* she told herself. *You're acting shallow and empty and just like the kind of woman you abhor! You're convicting him without hearing his side of the story. Even if he was with another woman last night, what's it to you? Nathan Sloan is the father of one of your students, nothing more!*

"Want the job?" he teased, and Stacey couldn't help but smile. He was so damned charming, and he seemed to know exactly what to say to disarm her.

"Not particularly."

"It could be interesting—"

"And it could be a disaster. I don't do families, thank you. Let's concentrate on getting Cindy back on track, before we lose our perspective altogether."

"Which is?"

"That Cindy is the only reason we're even having this conversation in the first place," she replied. "Cindy's health and happiness—that's all that matters. It's the reason you're here and I'm listening to you."

He nodded and suddenly sobered. "Speaking of Cindy—I assume that any information I've given the school will be kept in the strictest confidence."

"It always is."

"I'm serious about this." And he looked it. His eyes had narrowed, and his expression had become taut.

"So am I." Puzzled by his change in attitude, Stacey felt instantly defensive of Margaret Woodward's private school.

"And all of our conversations—they'll remain private."

"Of course!" she snapped, unable to hide her indignation. "Oceancrest has a reputation as one of the best schools in the Northwest. None of the staff goes around talking about the students, and the records are kept under lock and key."

"Good." His features softened slightly and he pushed his hand through his windblown hair, as if struggling with an inner battle. "It's just that Cindy's been through so much already…"

Stacey felt herself softening. "I understand. Remember, we want to help her."

"Good." His expression turned thoughtful as he stared at her. "You know, I can't figure you out."

"Oh?" She walked over to the sink and let water run into a plastic pitcher before pretending interest in watering the plants. "What's to figure out?"

"What's a beautiful, talented woman like you doing hiding here on this island?"

She laughed. "That's the oldest line in the book."

"It's not a line."

"Okay. To start off, I'm *not* hiding." She slid a glance in his direction and noticed the skeptical arch of his dark brows.

"You could work anywhere in the world. Why here—in the middle of nowhere?"

"I *like* it here. I guess the middle of nowhere suits me," she added wryly.

"Because it's safe."

She set the pitcher on the counter and turned to face him. "Because it's home! Look, Mr. Sloan—"

"Nathan. We got past the formalities. Remember?"

"Whatever. *I* don't need to be psychoanalyzed."

"So quit digging?"

"To put it bluntly." She sighed in frustration and forced her fingers into the pockets of her dress.

"You're a cruel woman, Anastasia Monroe," he said with a cynical twist of his mouth.

She tilted her face to the side and regarded him silently for a few seconds. "What is it you want from me?" she asked. "You asked me to have Cindy tested; I did. You wanted her enrolled at Oceancrest; she is. You even asked me to go out with you and I, against my better judgment, agreed, although after considerable thought,

I've decided it would be wiser to stay home. So why are you here—"

"Giving you a bad time?"

She relaxed a little and sighed. "I didn't say that."

"You implied it." He rubbed the back of his neck, but his eyes never left hers. "If you want to know the truth—"

"That would be a good start."

"I find you absolutely fascinating."

Stacey's pulse leaped unexpectedly. "I can't imagine why," she said, remembering the painful disaster that had occured when she'd so foolishly fallen for Daniel's father. *Never again,* she'd vowed and intended to keep her promise to herself.

"There are lots of reasons." He noticed the curve of her chin, her trim waist and soft breasts beneath the fabric of her dress. He could even see the small fists balled in the pockets of the apricot cloth and the way her sunstreaked hair brushed across her bare shoulders. "Probably a lot more than I'd like to admit."

He started to advance toward her and her first inclination was to draw away. Instead she held her ground and crossed her arms over her chest, hoping to look and sound totally disinterested.

"Now *that* sounds like a line. If it is, you'd better try casting it off Trinity Bay. You'll have more luck catching something there."

He stopped just short of her, and she could see the questions and wariness in his gaze. "Why all the hostility this morning?"

"I don't like the parents of my students coming on to me, that's all," she lied.

"I didn't get that impression yesterday."

She let out an exasperated sigh. "Well, maybe I've had some time to think and put our relationship into perspective. There's no reason for your 'fascination.' It's very flattering, but completely out of line. Besides, you've already done your research—you know everything about me."

"Not *everything*."

"Close enough," she said with a sad smile. "Look, I've already had one bad experience and it nearly ruined my professional reputation." *As well as my sanity.* "Since then, I've become very careful."

"And cynical."

"Maybe a little," she admitted with a frown.

Nathan found the pout on her lips irresistible. He lowered his head, and his face was so close Stacey could feel the warmth of his breath fan her hair. For a moment she thought he was going to kiss her. Though she tried to back away, her throat tightened expectantly, and her gaze was trapped in the enigmatic blue of his eyes. "I'm not Jeff Brown, Stacey. And Cindy's not Daniel. I won't hurt you."

Every muscle in her body stiffened. "So you know all about that, do you?"

"Enough."

She swallowed hard, trying to keep her voice steady. Painful memories of a boy struggling for his life clouded her vision. *Oh, God, Daniel, I'm so sorry...so sorry.*

"Stacey?" Nathan's voice brought her back to the present.

She drew in a shuddering breath and managed to pull herself together. "If you know about Daniel, then you've got to understand why I can't get involved socially with my students or their parents. My relationship has to be strictly professional." Her gaze met his. "I *can't* let what happened to Daniel happen to Cindy."

"It won't."

"You're right. Because I won't let it. I think it would be best if we just forgot about dinner tonight."

"Nope."

"What do you mean 'nope'?"

"I mean that we've got a date and you're stuck with it, whether you like it or not."

Damned exasperating, that's what he was! "You know, Mr. Sloan. You're coming on pretty strong," she said. *Especially for a man involved with another woman.*

"You're right. I apologize." He stepped away from her, crossed the room and put his hand on the doorknob. "I'll be at the cottage around seven, as we planned." With that, he opened the door and slipped out of the classroom, shutting the door behind him.

Stacey stared after him, not knowing whether to feel anger or awe. "You're an arrogant man, Nathan Sloan. An arrogant, pushy, self-serving bastard!" But she knew her angry accusations were all lies; the love he felt for his child was completely selfless. The contradictions in his character attracted her to the enigma that was Nathan Sloan.

"This is crazy," she told herself as she finished watering the plants and nervously dried her hands on her skirt, "just plain, old-fashioned, hate-yourself-in-the-morning type of crazy!" But though she tried to convince herself that she was making a huge mistake in seeing Nathan again, she couldn't completely stamp out the betraying elation that stayed with her for the rest of the day.

NATHAN ARRIVED PROMPTLY at seven. He helped her into his rather rough looking Jeep and drove the vehicle toward the north point of the island. The restaurant he had chosen was located in the town of Port Smith on the rocky shores of Trinity Bay, about twenty miles north of Serenity.

"Where's Cindy?" Stacey asked, once they were on their way.

"With Mrs. McIver. She's a widowed neighbor who never had any children. She thinks of Cindy as her grandchild."

"And how does Cindy feel about that?"

"She adores the woman," Nathan said. "Mrs. McIver comes over every day for about five hours, so I can work."

"So you lied to me," Stacey said.

"What are you talking about?"

"I thought you wanted Cindy to meet me to see how she'd react to a woman, but she already 'adores' this Mrs. McIver."

"Another *young* woman," Nathan explained with a chuckle. "Mrs. McIver is over seventy."

"Oh."

"Don't tell her I gave away her age."

"Never," Stacey vowed solemnly. "I feel a woman's age is a sacred trust."

Nathan laughed and cast Stacey a charming smile that made her stomach flutter. She hadn't felt so nervous with a man since Jeff. At the thought of Daniel's father, Stacey's soaring spirits hit the ground, and she wondered what had possessed her to go out with Nathan. She was flirting with disaster.

The restaurant was located on the cliff above Skeleton Cove south of the bay. From the vantage point of a table on the deck, Stacey was able to watch the breakers crash against the rocks guarding the cove. In the distance was a solitary lighthouse situated on the northernmost tip of Sanctity Island.

A flickering hurricane lantern shadowed Nathan's angular features as they ate steamed mussels, baked salmon, crab salad and crusty French bread. The conversation was quiet and relaxing, and Stacey found herself smiling over her wineglass as she watched Nathan. His dimpled grin, deep laughter and quiet wit touched a forbidden part of her heart, and she had to keep reminding herself that she couldn't afford to be attracted to him. *You're a fool,* she thought when his hand brushed hers, and she felt a rush of excitement in her blood.

"I owe you an apology," she said, once the table was cleared and they were sipping a final glass of wine.

The breeze picked up, ruffling Stacey's hair and playing havoc with the flame in the lantern.

"For what?"

"Don't act so innocent. You know. I want to apologize for this morning. I was pretty insufferable."

Nathan shrugged. The only sound was the roar of the surf pounding the beach as darkness gathered over the island. "Because of something I did?"

"No," she lied, feeling instant remorse. "I didn't sleep well last night, and I decided that seeing you wasn't a very good idea." At least that much was true.

"Because of Cindy, or because of Daniel Brown?"

Stacey's hands trembled slightly as she picked up her wineglass. "Maybe a little of both. I didn't want to make the same mistake I did with Daniel."

"You won't." He studied the elegant curve of her cheek, the sadness in her wide eyes, the sweep of her dark lashes. "Do you want to talk about it?"

"Not really."

He shrugged again and leaned back in his chair. "Sometimes it helps."

"Not with a perfect stranger."

"Oh, I don't know. There's something to be said about an objective third party."

"I doubt that one of my student's parents would be considered objective. Besides, there's not much to say. Most of the story was reported in the papers," she said with a trace of the old bitterness. "I became very attached to a little boy in one of my classes. He didn't have a mother, and he and I..." She had to clear her throat when she thought about Daniel. All too clearly she could see his innocent brown eyes, his trusting smile. "We had a very special relationship. He was the most lovable child I'd ever met—so full of love, and no one to share it with. Well, no mother at least." Her voice caught. "From what I understand, she ran off when he was only a few months old."

Nathan frowned. "What about his father?"

"When Jeff found out that Daniel and I got along so well, he asked me out. We began dating and...everything seemed—" she looked out to sea, searching for the right word "—almost perfect, I guess. But then nothing ever is."

"You fell in love with Jeff." Nathan's jaw became rigid.

"I thought so at the time. It was a mistake."

"Why?"

She twisted her napkin in her lap. "I thought you already knew what happened."

"Only what I read. I'd like to hear your version." He leaned forward in his chair, propped his elbows on the table and studied her. "You don't have to tell me if you don't want to."

"Maybe I should," she replied. "Then you'd understand why I think it's best to leave our relationship purely professional."

"Fair enough."

Stacey was so nervous her hands were sweating, She never liked discussing Jeff, and yet she felt compelled to have Nathan understand her. "Jeff and I decided to take Daniel camping one weekend. When we got to the campsite, I could tell that Daniel wasn't feeling well. He was whining and running a fever. I told Jeff that we should go back into town and have a doctor look him over, but Jeff was sure Daniel would shake it off. He'd come up to the mountains to fish and relax, and Daniel's illness was a bother. To make matters worse, at least in Jeff's opinion, I wouldn't leave the tent. So, Jeff began to drink while I stayed with Daniel. I was in the tent for hours, hoping for some sign that Daniel was getting better."

"But there wasn't any."

Stacey swallowed hard. "No," she whispered. "He was up all night, clinging to me. I held him, rocked him, gave him some acetaminophen, but nothing seemed to bring his fever down. I begged Jeff to drive us home, but by this time, he was pretty high. He refused. We got into a terrible argument…and well, it got pretty violent."

"Physical?"

"Yes," Stacey whispered, her fingers clenching at the horrible nightmare of a memory. "Jeff was angry and disappointed by that time, and he'd already had several drinks. I'd never seen him drunk before." Even now, while talking to Nathan, Stacey could envision Jeff's handsome face, the smooth features contorted in rage. It had been two years before, but it seemed like yesterday...

"THIS IS JUST an excuse," Jeff accused viciously as he poured more gin into a cup. "An excuse so that you won't have to sleep with me. Just like last time and the time before that! What's with you, Stace?"

Stacey was appalled. Jeff hadn't been the perfect father by any standard, but Stacey had felt that Jeff cared about Daniel and tried to do right by his son. Suddenly, all he could think about was her promise to spend the weekend with him. "Jeff, listen. I didn't plan this. You can see for yourself that Daniel's sick. He's running a fever, for God's sake!" She held the small boy to her breast, rocking him gently and trying to comfort him. "Surely you can see that he needs a doctor."

Jeff scoffed at her and laughed hollowly. Gin sloshed out of the cup onto the tent floor. "What I see is a frigid woman. We've been around this before, Stace. You're putting me off with the handiest excuse you can find."

"This is no excuse!"

"The hell it isn't" He finished his drink and reached for the pint of gin. When he discovered that the bottle was empty, he threw it to one side of the tent where it landed with a thud.

Daniel screamed.

"Get a hold of yourself," Stacey warned. "Daniel's sick, really sick. He needs to see a doctor."

"Isn't that what you are?"

"Of course not! I've got a degree in psychology. *That's all!* What Daniel needs is a medical doctor, maybe a hospital." She pressed her cool lips to Daniel's hot forehead. Whispering, she tried to console the child. "It's all right, sweetheart…"

Jeff ignored her pleas. "You're the one who needs a shrink, Stace. Put Dan down and come here." He grabbed at her arm and drew her next to him, the smell of gin heavy on his breath. "I'll show you how to relax and have a good time."

She held fast to Daniel, and the child shrieked in fear when Jeff pressed sloppy lips to Stacey's. Without thinking, she pulled free of Jeff's grasp and slapped his face. "Come on, Daniel. Let's go."

"You're not going anywhere," Jeff insisted. "Dan's fine—just fine! He's got a touch of flu or something."

"Maybe, but maybe not! And I'm not about to take a chance with his life. Now, I'm leaving this place and taking Daniel with me." Stacey's eyes blazed with authority. She shifted Daniel to a more comfortable position and started toward the flap of the tent.

"You're not leaving me!"

"Oh, Jeff, of course not. I'll drive, and you can sleep it off in the back seat. Come on, we don't have a lot of time." Daniel's face was flushed with the fever, his little brown eyes glazed.

"He's just tired."

When Daniel moaned in pain, Stacey couldn't stand it any longer. "We're leaving. You can come or you can stay." She reached for Daniel's coat. "Your choice."

"Come here, you goddamned, sanctimonious virgin! All you've done for the past two months is tease me and drive me out of my mind. There are names for women like you!"

Jeff attacked her then. Daniel slid to the floor of the tent as Jeff threw Stacey on the ground, and fell on top of her with his anxious body. The hard evidence of his desire pressed hotly against her as she tried to struggle free. "I'll show you my choice!" he yelled into her ear.

"Don't, please—" Stacey cried when she felt her blouse being ripped off her body and his rough hands on her naked breasts. "Jeff—please—don't. Oh, God… Daniel…oh, Daniel…"

When Daniel screamed, Jeff suddenly came to his senses. A flash of instant regret surfaced in his glazed eyes. "Oh God, Stace," he groaned, tears of self-disgust filling his eyes. "You…you make me so goddamned crazy, I can't stand it."

Cursing furiously, he rolled away giving her enough room to escape. She grabbed the child, rummaged in the pocket of Jeff's discarded jacket for the keys to his car and drove like a mad woman to the nearest town.

Less than a week later Daniel Brown, at the age of three, died from complications of influenza and pneumonia. Jeff blamed Stacey, naming her and the Edwards Institute in a lawsuit.

NATHAN WATCHED THE tortured play of emotions on Stacey's even features and silently cursed himself for bringing up Daniel Brown. "Stacey?"

She looked up and forced a smile, trying vainly to shrug off the vivid memory. "I'm sorry. It's not a very pleasant part of my life. Where was I?"

"You were talking about an argument."

Involuntarily, she shuddered. "The argument. Right. More like a war zone. After the fight, I drove Daniel to the nearest hospital, but it was too late."

"He died."

Her throat constricted and tears gathered in her eyes. "Yes."

"And Daniel's father blamed you?"

Nodding, she fought the urge to cry. "He even went so far as to sue the Edwards Institute for hiring me. It got pretty dirty." She reached for her glass with trembling hands and swallowed the cold wine, hoping it would somehow salve her pain.

"But you were proved innocent."

"Yes," she whispered. "Thanks to the testimony of the doctor in the emergency room who'd admitted Daniel and seen my bruises."

"Bruises!" Nathan experienced an unexpected explosion of fury. Fighting his anger, he ground his back teeth together. *"What* bruises?"

"I said we'd fought."

"To the point that you were hurt?" Nathan whispered in a quiet rage. "Just what the hell did that bastard do to you?" he demanded, his eyes becoming dark and deadly, the muscles in his shoulders bunching stiffly.

"It was only a few bruises."

"Only!"

"It could have been much worse." She still felt chilled at the thought of Jeff's hard body pressed against hers while his son had screamed in fear, but she forced herself to rise above the vile memory. "Anyway, it doesn't matter. The whole point is that Daniel died because I was foolish enough to get involved with his father. If I hadn't gone camping with Jeff, Daniel would be alive today."

"Maybe." Nathan finished his wine and rubbed the

underside of his jaw, trying to uncoil the hands that wanted to strangle Jeff Brown. "So that's when you came to Sanctity Island?"

"Margaret Woodward offered me a job—and a second chance," Stacey said, avoiding Nathan's hard gaze and staring into the night-darkened sea. "I was really a mess when I got here, but Margaret helped me and gave me more work than I could handle. I didn't have time to feel sorry for myself. It took a while, but at least I'm finally able to face what happened without an overburdening sense of guilt." She set her napkin on the table. "So that's why I don't become involved with my students or their guardians. After all the trust Margaret's put in me, I'd never do anything that would jeopardize her reputation or that of the school. I owe Margaret Woodward my life!"

"And you think that you could damage the reputation of the school by seeing me?"

"I don't know."

"And you're afraid to find out?" he challenged.

"I can't take the chance." *Besides, you may be involved with another woman.* She sighed and looked past him. "You haven't heard a word I've said."

Nathan smiled coldly. "Oh, yes, I have. Maybe more than you wanted me to hear. I already knew part of the story about Jeff Brown, though not all of it. Let me tell you, I'd better not run into that bum."

"It's over."

"It had better be!" Nathan said sharply before running his hands through his hair. "Look, what matters is that you're still the best teacher for Cindy." He stood and offered her his hand. "Trust me, Stacey. I won't hurt you."

And I won't give you the chance! But at the touch of his warm hand, she realized that she was treading in dangerous waters.

THE FOG STILL clung tenaciously to the beach when Stacey crawled out of bed on Sunday morning. She looked out the window, frowned at the dismal weather and then busied herself by cleaning the house until it shone, a job she usually saved until she had nothing better to do. She'd planned to rent a boat to take her to Hood Canal so she could look for octopuses this morning, but her trip had been thwarted by the fog.

It didn't help that she couldn't get Nathan off her mind.

"This fog will lift," she told herself, trying to concentrate on the weather rather than the man. "By noon it will be gone."

She hadn't heard from Nathan since Friday night, when he'd left her on her doorstep without so much as a good-night kiss. "So much for grand illusions of passion," she thought aloud as she tossed the dirty dust rag into the laundry bin.

Still feeling slightly guilty about spying on Nathan to see if he'd met the mysterious woman again, she felt herself blush.

He hadn't. The beach had remained deserted, as it had on the following night, and now, while pulling her wet suit and tanks from the closet, Stacey tried to convince herself that the man she'd seen passionately embracing the beautiful woman hadn't been Nathan at all. "As if it matters," she grumbled, angry with herself for caring.

"You're starting to look and sound like a jealous female, Monroe," she chastised aloud. "What he does or doesn't do on the beach with that gorgeous woman is none of your damned business!"

So why had she covertly watched the beach every night for the past three?

"Nancy Drew, I'm not," she said with a sigh as she noticed the fog beginning to lift.

Carrying her scuba diving equipment to the car, she heard the familiar rumble of Nathan's Jeep as it approached.

"Oh Lord, not today," she whispered, bracing herself as she turned toward Nathan's rig.

What now? she wondered desperately. She hadn't heard from him since Friday night and hadn't expected to see him again until he brought Cindy to school on Monday.

"Going somewhere?" he asked as he climbed out of the Jeep. Wearing cutoff jeans, an old paint-spattered gray sweatshirt and ragged tennis shoes, he looked windblown, rugged and carefree: a typical beach bum.

Stacey didn't buy it for a minute. "I hope so."

His smile was forced. "Alone?"

"Yes."

He relaxed a bit and glanced into her car, noticing the royal-blue scuba diving suit and air tanks. "Where?"

She wanted to tell him it wasn't any of his business, but didn't see what good provoking him would do. It wasn't his fault that her heartbeat quickened every time she was around him. "To Hood Canal. I'd like to find an octopus for the aquarium, and I haven't had much luck around here. I've heard you can catch them easily on the canal."

"Just what you need—more critters in that classroom."

Stacey responded to his gentle teasing with a grin. "I'm telling you, you can't argue with success."

"I wouldn't even want to try." He leaned the backs of his elbows against her car and stretched his long legs in front of him. The muscles in his thighs flexed slightly. "Care for some company?"

"You?"

"Don't look so shocked. I've dived before, but I don't think we need to go to that much trouble."

"So now you're an expert."

"I did a piece on octopuses for a science magazine."

"Anyone can go to the library," she said sarcastically.

He looked at her with his intriguing blue eyes. "Are you always so easy to get along with in the morning?"

"I guess I asked for that, didn't I?"

"Yep." His crooked smile touched Stacey's heart. "But then, I'm a glutton for punishment. Now, let's start again. How about some company?"

"I don't know…" *Don't do it, Stacey. Seeing him again will only spell trouble.*

"Please?"

"I don't think it would be a good idea…" She avoided his eyes and let out a long sigh.

"Because you're Cindy's teacher?"

"Yes! If I remember correctly, we've had this conversation several times already."

He crossed his arms over his chest, leaned his head against the roof of the car and stared up at the hazy sky. "I understand your feelings," he admitted with a frown. "I only wish to God I understood mine. I'm really not trying to intrude upon your life." When he looked back at her, he caught her disbelieving smile. "Okay, maybe I am. But you don't help things any."

"Me?"

"You. It would be a helluva lot easier if you were eighty years old and had a protective husband."

She laughed despite the tension in the air. "Maybe I should go dredge one up."

He lifted his head and his sad gaze touched hers. "I don't want to be attracted to you, but there it is!"

"There it can't be!"

"Sooner or later, you'll have to get to know me."

"Let's make it later!"

He grinned. "You're a frustrating woman, you know that?"

"I suppose," she admitted, weakening slightly. *Why was she listening to him?*

Glancing at her diving gear again, he said, "I could be a big help."

He looked damned charming with the wind catching his wavy hair and his honest blue eyes squinting against the sun. "I don't really think I need any help, and I know this is the dumbest thing I've done all week, but all right. I guess it never hurts to have a professional around," she demurred in mock respect, her full lips softening into a smile and her hazel eyes sparkling.

"Not a professional, just an expert. There's a difference."

"Oh, right. Remind me to have you explain it to me sometime."

"My pleasure." Through the fog, light from a pale morning sun shimmered against her honey-brown hair. Nathan noticed the few tiny freckles across the bridge of her nose and the delicate bones at the base of her throat.

"I think we'd better go," Stacey said, stepping away from him and hoping to break the sudden intimacy.

They drove into the small town of Serenity, down the single lane road to the docks, and parked the car in the lot near the moorage. Sail boats with fancy rigging and brightly colored sails, fishing vessels, and motorboats were berthed side by side, softly rocking in the tide.

When Stacey approached the attendant, Nathan took her by the arm. "Don't bother renting a boat," he said. "I've got a launch."

He carried her diving gear to his open boat and maneuvered the boat between the docks and into the Strait of Juan de Fuca. As the launch cut through the water, sending spray into Stacey's face, she gazed at the other islands in the San Juan chain. Mist surrounded the uppermost peaks of each island, partially hiding the abundant fir trees before slowly giving way to the pale sun.

Before reaching Puget Sound, Nathan turned the vessel into the long stretch of water known as Hood Canal. He passed by several resorts where fishermen and waterskiers shared the clear water of the canal before anchoring the boat near a private, somewhat rocky stretch of beach.

"How does this look?" he asked.

Stacey studied the rocky shore and thoughtfully pursed her lips. "You tell me—you're supposed to be the expert." She reached for her wet suit with the intention of putting it on. Nathan leaned back in the boat, his eyes narrowing to interested slits. "I don't think you'll need that, but don't let me discourage you."

"I won't." She lifted her sweater over her head to reveal her sky-blue one-piece swim suit.

He caught her satisfied grin and grimaced. "Spoil sport."

"Serves you right."

He smiled lazily. "Me? For what?"

"You know what I mean." Then, slightly self-conscious, she took off her shorts and placed them next to her sweater on a vacant seat in the boat.

His gaze caressed her curves and to avoid an embarrassed silence, Stacey decided to forget the wet suit and brave the cold water. Avoiding Nathan's interested stare, she grabbed her face mask, dived into the shallow sea and swam to the bottom of the canal. While holding her breath, she started searching the rocky bottom of the canal.

"Find anything?" Nathan asked when she surfaced and shook her wet hair out of her face. Lifting her mask and blinking against the water on her lashes and the harsh angle of the sun, she looked more intriguing than ever. He felt the unlikely surge of desire in his veins and gave himself a mental shake.

"Not yet."

"Maybe you need some help."

"Maybe—especially since you claim to be the expert."

Rising to her challenge, he pulled off his sweatshirt, unconsciously displaying the tanned muscles of his shoulders and chest. Stacey tried not to stare, but was fascinated by the way his muscles moved fluidly under his skin, rigidly cording across his chest and flattening over his abdomen. He removed his belt, and his cutoffs slid a little lower on his hips, displaying the white skin that was never exposed to the rays of the sun. He snapped on his mask, and with a deep breath, Nathan dived, his body gracefully entering the water near Stacey.

She breathed in deeply and followed him, her hair billowing away from her face as she swam along the bottom of the canal. They surfaced together and plunged to the bottom again before Nathan spied a shy baby octopus camouflaged between two rocks. Deftly, he pried it from its hiding spot, signaled to Stacey and returned to the surface.

"Wonderful," Stacey said, gasping for air as she took off her mask and examined the tentacled creature. "The kids will love him. I owe you an apology. You did seem to know what you were doing."

"And you doubted me." Nathan reached into the boat, found the bucket, filled it with water and placed the octopus into its new home. Then he put both masks into the boat.

"I guess I'm just a born skeptic," she said with a smile, and then became serious as she noticed the darkening of his gaze, the tightening of his jaw. She swallowed against the sudden constriction in her throat. "Thank you."

"Anytime." He swam nearer to her and searched her face. The gray of the water was reflected in the clear hazel depths of her eyes; saltwater flattened her hair to her head and beaded on her cheeks. He wrapped one arm around her while, with his other, he held onto the boat. Then he slowly lowered his head and captured her chilled lips with the heat of his.

His warmth spread through her in an eager rush. *Dear God,* Stacey thought, *this can't be happening.* But she couldn't pull away from him. A bittersweet torment began building within her, making her ache and long for more of the sensual touch of his lips against her skin. Holding on to Nathan, she closed her eyes. The feel of his lips on hers, the pressure of his chest against her breasts and the cold water swirling around them made her oblivious to anything but the man. His arm was strong as he wrapped it securely around her waist.

Remember Jeff, her mind insisted, but the memory faded with the passion of Nathan's kiss. Instinctively, she pressed closer to him, her skin sliding intimately against his in the water. His legs caught and tangled with hers to move seductively against her thighs.

When his tongue began to probe her parted lips, she forced herself to think rationally. With a jolt she remembered the night that Daniel became ill, the night that Jeff had attacked her. She became rigid in Nathan's arms.

"Please," she whispered, pushing away. "Don't."

He stared at her as if he could read her mind. "I won't hurt you."

"I just…can't."

He let out a long, weary sigh, silently cursing the hot desire flooding his veins. "I'm not Jeff Brown!"

She reacted as if he'd slapped her. Paling, she whispered, "I didn't say—"

"Oh, God, I know. I'm sorry."

Dear Lord, now he was apologizing! As if it were his fault alone. Hadn't she responded to him? "It's okay."

His eyes flashed when he looked at her. "It's *not* okay. Not by a long shot. What I feel for you…" He touched her tenderly on the cheek before flinging his arm over the side of the boat and staring into the launch. "Dear God, Stacey," he said with a sigh. Throwing back his head, he stared at the sky. "You're the damnedest woman I've run up against in a long time. I tell myself that I can't see you, and the next minute I'm on your doorstep. Then I tell myself that *you* don't want to get involved with me, and I find all kinds of arguments to break down your defenses."

His sudden intake of breath indicated that he'd noticed the hardening of her nipples and swollen breasts. Hot color spread up her neck and onto her cheeks.

"You're driving me out of my mind, you know."

"Believe me, it's not intentional," she whispered.

"That's the worst part of it," he muttered, flexing his arms and lifting himself into the boat. He slung a towel around his neck before offering his hand to her and helping her climb into the launch. Once she was inside the rocking vessel, he released her hand slowly and tossed her the towel. "I don't want to feel the way I do about you," he admitted and she believed him. "You complicate my life in more ways than you'll ever know."

Stacey remembered the woman he had met on the beach and tried to calm her racing heartbeat. All her instincts warned her to avoid Nathan Sloan, but she couldn't deny the attraction that was beginning to grow in her heart.

While she towel dried her hair, he started the motor and maneuvered the boat away from the shore. They returned to the island in silence, and Nathan drove her back to the cottage.

Once in the driveway, she reached for the door of the Jeep, but he captured her wrist. "Here, I found something for you."

"What?"

He lifted his hips from the seat and pushed his fingers into the front pocket of his cutoffs. "Something I found while looking for the octopus." He pulled a clear agate from his pocket and handed it to her.

She took the smooth stone, smiled and fought the urge to cry. Such a little gesture, but it said so much.

"I don't take gifts from strangers, you know."

"I know." Leaning forward he pressed a kiss against her forehead.

"Nathan, please. Don't." She looked up at him with tortured eyes.

"This won't work, you know," he said softly.

"What?"

"Pretending that we aren't interested in each other."

"We'll make it work," she said firmly, but her pulse had already begun to throb. "For Cindy."

He hesitated, and for a minute Stacey thought that he was going to confide in her.

I don't want to hear it, she thought wildly, clutching the small stone. *I don't want to know what kind of trouble you're in or how much you loved Jennifer, or if the woman on the beach is your lover....*

"For Cindy," he repeated and let go of her. Stacey climbed out of the Jeep on shaky legs and watched silently as Nathan backed the vehicle out of the driveway and turned down the road.

CHAPTER FOUR

AFTER NATHAN LEFT, Stacey took the small octopus to Oceancrest, plopped it into a tank and made sure that her room was ready for the first day of school.

It was dark by the time she got back to the cottage. Despite the heat, she built a small fire in the fireplace and sat on the hearth as she ate a bowl of canned chili and read the latest issue of a monthly psychology magazine. After restlessly tossing the magazine aside and placing her dishes in the sink, she wandered out to the porch. It was a warm, humid evening, and the sky was dark with the threat of rain. The floodlights on the edge of the cliff cast a ghostly illumination over the white strip of beach, jagged rocks and foaming tide.

Tapping her fingers on the smooth porch railing, she waited, but no one appeared on the sand. No Nathan and no raven-haired woman. "You probably imagined the entire scene," she told herself and began walking down the sandy path leading to the beach. The sound of the sea roared in her ears as she climbed down the bleached stairs.

Pausing on the bottom step, she kicked off her sandals, pushed her hands into her pockets and started walking north toward the staircase at the opposite end of the beach, the steps leading to Nathan's cabin. The bracing, salt-laden breeze cooled her skin and pushed her hair away from her face.

She'd walked about a hundred yards when she saw him. Dressed in a black leather pilot's jacket and equally dark pants, the man approached her with quickened strides, as if he'd been expecting to meet her.

"Barbara?" Nathan called, and then caught himself when he realized his mistake.

Stacey stood frozen to the spot. The sound of Nathan's voice jelled all of her cold suspicions. So he had been on the beach the other night, and the tall, dark-haired woman he'd embraced so passionately was named Barbara. A strange disappointment made her shiver unexpectedly.

"Stacey?" Nathan didn't miss a stride. He came toward her, his eyes glittering dangerously. "What the devil are you doing out here?"

"Taking a walk," she replied, telling herself that the anger and disappointment spreading through her like wildfire were totally unjustified.

"Alone?"

"It's not a crime."

Clenching his jaw, he looked away from her for a minute before scanning the ridge, trying to look past the floodlights.

"You shouldn't be out alone."

"Why not?"

He directed his gaze to her face and noticed the light of challenge in her eyes. "Because it could be dangerous."

"Dangerous!" she returned incredulously. "What're you talking about? I've been walking this beach alone for two years and nothing's ever happened. Besides, there's

not much crime on the island." Then she stopped herself. Babbling excuses like some teenager wouldn't solve anything or get to the root of the problem. "Dangerous to whom, Nathan. Me—or you?"

"Both of us."

Who was he kidding? "I don't know why you're being so melodramatic, and I really don't care." She pushed her hands into the pockets of her dress and shivered as the first drops of rain fell from the sky. "Who's Barbara?"

He looked angry, whether at her or himself, Stacey couldn't tell. Then he pushed his hair out of his face and frowned. "Barbara's a friend of mine," he said. "She's helping me—"

"Keep out of *danger*?"

"—with a story."

She almost believed him, but not quite. It showed in the set of her jaw. "How can the type of stories you write, tourist brochures and the like, be dangerous?" Nothing was making any sense, least of all Nathan's association with Barbara and all this mumbo jumbo about danger.

"Stacey…" He reached for her, but she drew away.

"And that's why Barbara met you the other night—because of this story?" she asked, the wind catching in her hair and pushing it away from her face.

He let out a disgusted sigh. "So you saw that, did you?"

"All of it."

"At least it explains the cold shoulder Friday morning," he muttered before grabbing her by the upper arms and forcing her to stare into his eyes. "Look, Stacey, you're going to have to trust me—for just a little while. I'm involved with something that I don't want you a part of."

"Don't tell me, what was it you said, a story on the ecology of the islands?"

"I'm serious," he said, exasperated.

"Because of some sort of peril?" she asked quietly. "Or because of Barbara?"

"That's a stupid question."

Stacey could see that his fear was real; his tense muscles and tight mouth indicated that something was wrong, very wrong. With a feeling of dread, she wondered what could be so dangerous and what it had to do with the black-haired woman. "What about Barbara? Is it dangerous for her, too?"

"Unfortunately, yes."

"This is all a little hard for me to swallow, you know," Stacey said, looking out to sea. "What you do with your personal life isn't any of my business, except where it concerns Cindy, but I wish you wouldn't try so hard to get me to like you if you're already involved with someone else!"

"It's not like that."

The rain had begun in earnest, showering them with heavy drops.

"Then tell me, what is it like?"

He hesitated a moment, and she thought he would confide in her. But a noise in the distance caught his ear. Squinting into the darkness, he tensed, every one of his finely toned muscles went rigid. "Damn!" Swearing under his breath, he propelled her backward. "You've got to get out of here."

"What! You can't just push me off the—" she stopped when she saw his face.

Impatience and fear gathered in his night-darkened eyes. Strain bracketed his mouth in deep grooves. "Look, you've got to go," he insisted, his eyes searching the darkness. "Please—Stacey—just...*trust me!*" He tugged on her arms, jerking her forcefully backward, toward the steps leading to her cottage.

"Let go—"

"Christ, woman! Don't argue!" The desperation in his voice convinced her. She stumbled over a large drift-wood log, let out a cry and tumbled to the sand. Before she could struggle to her feet, Nathan had pushed her behind a pile of driftwood and covered her body with his.

In the wet black night, with his body pressed over hers, Stacey could hear only the sound of her own heart and the thudding beat of his. Her face was pressed against the gritty wet sand that clung to her hair and stuck in the corners of her mouth. Rain pelted Nathan's jacket, slid down her neck and face and drenched the log. Muffled in the distance, the sound of the sea thundered against the beach.

Stacey strained to listen but could only hear Nathan's erratic breathing. He was heavy as he lay over her, holding her tightly, his prone body rigid and protective as it pressed her into the sand. His grip on her arms was punishing, but Stacey didn't try to move a muscle. She was afraid, and she knew instinctively not to make a sound. Dread made her mouth go dry. Whatever it was that Nathan was involved in, Stacey knew that he felt terror—genuine, heart-stopping, gut-wrenching terror.

They lay together for what seemed an eternity. After a time, she heard his breathing slow, and she felt him relax slightly before he rolled off her and, motioning her to keep silent, helped her to her feet. Without a word, his blue eyes darting from the beach to the cliffs and back again, he pulled her toward the stairs.

Following blind instinct, she mounted the weathered steps, her bare feet sliding on the rain-slickened wood, the fingers of her free hand gripping the railing.

When they reached to top of the bluff, Nathan broke into a run, dragging her with him. The wet grass beside the path scratched her legs, and she felt her dress tear as she stumbled once and cut her ankle on a sharp rock.

"Come on," he whispered harshly, jerking her to her feet.

She was breathless by the time they reached the house. Once inside, she turned on the lights, but Nathan quickly shut them off.

"What're you doing?" she demanded, trying to ignore the fear racing through her blood.

"Just being careful."

"You're acting like a lunatic!" she charged, but her eyes had rounded.

"I don't have time for this. Sit down and be quiet."

Frightened and angry, she sat on the edge of her favorite rocker, settled back in the chair, crossed her arms over her sandy dress and glared at him. She could feel the grit in her damp hair and the dull ache in her lower leg.

He glanced at her sharply, and then a smile tugged at the corners of his mouth. "You're probably right," he admitted, shaking his head, as if at his own foolishness. "I am acting like a lunatic." Impatiently, he flexed his fingers. "It's just that this whole mess is driving me out of my mind!"

"What mess?"

He looked at her and then glanced out the window, carefully drawing the shades. "It's too complicated."

"To explain?"

"For anyone to understand."

"Oh. So you won't tell me who or what we were running from."

"I'm not sure."

"Wonderful," she mumbled, running her hands over her face and brushing aside the lingering drops of rain. "That doesn't do much for my confidence, you know."

He sighed and leaned against the wall, letting his head fall back against the plaster.

"I know."

"So what about Barbara? Is she still on the beach, hiding from whatever we were."

"I wish I knew."

"Then she's involved?"

"Yes."

"In what?"

He glanced at her, and the dying light from the fire shadowed his face, making it appear harder than she remembered.

"You're a persistent thing, aren't you?"

"I think I have the right to know. Good Lord, you won't even let me turn on my lights, for crying out loud!"

"Dammit, Stacey, I can't tell you!"

"Look, Nathan," she said, standing and walking over to the fireplace to warm the backs of her legs. "You scared me. You scared the hell out of me!"

"I meant to."

"Why?"

"I can't tell you, dammit!" he said, swearing under his breath and pacing between the window and the fireplace.

"Why not?"

"I don't want you involved!"

"Since when?" she asked incredulously. "You were the one who arranged my meeting with Cindy. Remember?"

He winced and stared at the ceiling.

"And you were the one who insisted *I* get her enrolled.

Then, you practically twisted my arm to get me to go out with you and finally, just this morning, *you* came to my house and invited yourself on my boat trip. Now, if you didn't want me involved, you could have stopped coming around here over a week ago." She was shaking with confusion and anger by the time she was finished. In frustration she pushed her sandy hair away from her face and stared up at him. "I don't like playing games, Nathan, at least not the kind that terrorize me. I like my safe, peaceful existence here on the island, but now that it's been threatened, I think I should know why."

"I can't—"

"I know you can't tell me!" She held up one hand in resignation and let it drop when she felt it shake. "So don't bother with any of the lies. I don't want to hear any garbage about you being involved in some story with Barbara! Give me credit for a few more brains than that! I saw the way she ran up to you on the beach, the way you held her."

"I told you she's a friend."

Stacey's smile was brittle. "Some friend."

Balling one fist, he slammed it into the palm of his other hand. "I should never have come here."

"This is no time to feel sorry for yourself."

His head snapped up. "I don't."

"Then tell me what's going on, for God's sake. I think I'm a fairly sane person who can deal with just about anything. But I'm not cut out for any of these cloak-and-dagger, whodunit theatrics!"

"I should never have gotten you involved."

"Don't you mean you should never have gotten involved with me?" she asked softly.

He looked at her, and his dark brows drew together

over his intense blue eyes. "That would have been impossible, I'm afraid."

She swallowed back her fear. "Well, then, maybe you should understand something about me. I'm not a prude—at least I hope I'm not—but I can't deal with casual dates or being involved with a man who might have another lover—or wife. I can't handle that kind of relationship."

A muscle twitched at the edge of his jaw. "I wouldn't ask you to."

Her gaze caught in his. "Then why do I get the feeling that this Barbara person is special to you?"

"She is," he said, standing and pushing his hands into the back pockets of his jeans for lack of anything better to do. "At one time I thought I would marry her."

Stacey's heart lurched. "But you didn't."

"No."

"And she's still in love with you," she guessed.

"Maybe a little. I don't know. It doesn't matter."

"It does matter! It matters a lot!"

"Barbara and I aren't romantically involved, at least not any longer."

"But I saw—"

"You saw an *act*," he said, his voice harsh. "Barbara and I have to *look* like lovers in order to be convincing."

"Well, you did a bang-up job the other night."

"Good."

Dear Lord, what was he saying? "I think you owe me some honest answers," she said, walking into the bathroom and grabbing a towel to dry her hair. "Why all the secrecy? Why all the mystery?"

He hesitated and his expression softened. "Trust me, Stacey. I promise that I'll explain everything when I can."

"When it's safe?" she asked.

"Yes." Then he noticed the blood oozing from the cut over her ankle. "What happened?" He walked over to her, bent down and lifted her calf in his hands.

"It's just a little cut…when I fell."

His lips thinned, and he took the towel off her head to clean the wound. "It's deep."

"Not that bad."

With an impatient growl, he stood. "Where's your bathroom?"

"Right over there." She pointed toward the open door off the hall.

Nathan, his jaw thrust forward in anger with himself, strode down the hallway to the bathroom, rattled around in the medicine cabinet and came back into the living room carrying washcloths, bandages and antiseptic.

"It's just a little cut—"

"Hmph!" Ignoring his earlier warning, he snapped on the small lamp near the chair in which Stacey was sitting.

She tried to pull her leg away from him, but his fingers tightened over her calf. "Be still."

"You don't have to—"

His head snapped up and he glared at her. "Don't move, okay? I want to clean this and make sure there's no chance of infection."

"But—"

The look he shot her cut her to the bone. She didn't move, but watched as he cleaned the cut and the surrounding skin, applied antiseptic, which burned a little, and then placed a small bandage over her ankle. Satisfied with his work, he slowly released her leg and sat back on his heels. Stacey could still feel the imprint of his hand against her skin.

"I'm sorry this happened."

"Maybe if you hadn't been in such a big hurry it wouldn't have."

"Maybe." He flinched but didn't move. Instead, he stretched his legs in front of him, propped himself up with his hands and sat staring at her from the worn Persian rug in front of the fireplace. "I think you'll live."

"That's comforting," she remarked, still annoyed.

Slowly, he glanced up her body, and she felt the heat of his gaze as it traveled from her legs past her torn skirt and the swell of her breasts to settle on her eyes.

His leisurely regard of her was uncomfortable and slightly erotic. Stacey cleared her throat and looked away.

"So tell me, what were you doing on the beach tonight?" Nathan suggested.

"I already told you, I was taking a walk."

"Looking for me?"

"You, Mr. Sloan, have an incredible ego."

"So I've been told," he admitted wryly, his lips widening into an easy smile that gave his face a boyish charm. He touched the tip of her toe with one finger. "I didn't mean to come off—"

"Boorish?" she supplied. "Like Attila the Hun?"

He laughed. "It wasn't that bad."

"Close enough." If only he'd take his finger away from her toe. He was doing crazy things to her mind.

"You know, I can't figure you out," he admitted, staring at her sandy toe before lifting his gaze to her eyes.

Incredulous, she gasped, "*You* can't figure *me* out? Wait a minute. I think that was supposed to be my line."

He rested his head on one shoulder but continued to

stare at her as if she were a compelling and intriguing mystery. "You seem like a reasonable, attractive and intelligent woman."

"But—?"

"You have this temper that jumps up at me from nowhere! Calm one minute, defensive the next."

"Maybe that's because I don't know where I stand with you," she said, her hazel eyes filled with honesty. "It would be one thing if you were just Cindy's father and I dealt with you as the parent of one of my students. But nothing about you seems to connect and half the time I think I might be falling…"

"Go on," he prodded.

She took in a deep breath and twisted the torn edge of her skirt in her fingers. Admitting her feelings was difficult; she wasn't sure of them herself.

"Half the time I think I could fall for you. I don't want that kind of relationship."

He studied her for a moment and the thickening silence closed in on her. Her heart was pounding so loudly she could hear it over the ticking of the clock, the whisper of the wind and the pelting of the rain against the windows.

"Oh, lady, neither do I," he admitted with a sad smile as he pushed himself upright and brushed his hands on his jeans. "But I don't see that there's a damned thing I can do about it."

Leaning over her chair, he placed a hand on each of the arms and pushed his face close to hers. She could feel his warm breath, smell the rain-dampened scent of his hair. "I like you; I like you more than I should," he said. "And the worst part of it is that the feeling's more than physical. I can't afford that and neither can you."

"You're right," she whispered while gazing into the

ink-blue depths of his eyes, her body twisting inside with a hunger she didn't want to consider.

"But nonetheless, it's there." Slowly he moved forward until his lips brushed hers, gently at first, with a tenderness that made her quiver inside. Then he slid his arms around her waist and pulled her close to him, until she was hugging his body as he lay in the chair with her. His mouth covered hers, and his strong arms bound her against a flat, hard chest, muscular thighs and lean hips.

His warm hands tangled in her long, sandy hair, and he touched her gently on the crook of her exposed throat as his tongue dipped into her mouth. A warmth deep inside began to spread, and she wound her arms around his neck, enjoying the feel of his hard, male body pressed against hers.

"You're so beautiful," he whispered, damning himself for his attraction to her and knowing that if he didn't stop kissing her now, he would soon carry her up the stairs to her loft and make love to her until he was spent. And what then? What would happen when Robert Madison found out that Nathan was involved with Stacey? Would her life be in danger? It was a risk his conscience wouldn't allow him to take.

He pulled himself away from her. "I've got to go," he said, summoning all of his strength to look away from the hunger and disappointment in her beautiful silver-green eyes.

"To meet Barbara?"

"Yes."

Stacey felt cold inside, betrayed. Nathan was using her. Wasn't that much evident? "Why? Why do you have to meet her?"

"Shh…be patient," he whispered, bending over to kiss

her softly on the hair. "Believe me, if I had my choice in the matter, I wouldn't be going anywhere tonight."

Stacey blushed, but stared straight into his eyes and surprised herself by saying, "Don't go."

"I have to."

"Stay with me."

Groaning, Nathan hesitated but shook his head. "Dammit, don't you think I want to?"

"I don't know what to think."

"Don't do this to me," he said, trying to keep his mind clear. He stepped away from her but paused when he reached the door. "Stacey, you're the most attractive woman I've ever met. And there's only one thing I want more than to spend the night with you."

"What's that?"

"I have to make sure that it's safe. For all of us. You. Me. Cindy."

That again! "And Barbara?"

Nathan leaned his head against the door. "Yes, and Barbara."

Stacey's heart twisted painfully. She'd all but offered herself on a silver platter, and he'd chosen to leave her for Barbara. All because of some mumbo jumbo about danger and safety that didn't make a lick of sense. Or did it? His fear had been real. She'd felt it, smelled it in the air.

He saw the pain in her eyes and cursed himself for his weakness where she was concerned. "Trust me for a little while longer. And whatever you do, don't follow me. Okay?"

"I don't know."

"Stacey—"

"Tell me one thing," she said, trying to understand him. He stiffened and hunched his shoulders. "What?"

"Does whatever it is you're involved in have anything to do with Cindy?"

He stood rooted to the spot. "Why would you think that?"

"Because everything you do revolves around your daughter and the other day when you came into the classroom, you were pretty insistent that her files remain secret."

"I wouldn't want someone to use Cindy as a weapon to get to me," he said slowly. "She's been through more than her share of pain already."

"And she's barely four." Stacey shifted uncomfortably in the chair and tried to keep her fingers from trembling. Looking upward at Nathan, she attempted to still her racing pulse. "So what do you want me to do?"

"Trust me. For a few more hours."

"Will it be over then?"

"I don't know," he admitted, looking suddenly older than his years. "Probably not, but I hope to God it's all over soon."

He walked out the door and disappeared into the night. "So do I," she whispered fervently. "So do I."

THE BEACH WAS deserted when Nathan walked back through the driving rain. Barbara had probably left, convinced that he'd run into trouble. The last person he'd expected to come across on the beach had been Stacey, and the fact that she'd seen him with Barbara only made matters worse. He cursed quietly to himself and hunched his shoulders against the wetness sliding under his collar.

"Son of a bitch," he muttered, kicking a piece of seaweed from his path. He'd been a fool. A goddamned, grade A, idiotic fool for letting Stacey get under his skin. And kissing her had been the biggest mistake of all. He couldn't forget the feel of her or the taste of her. Now she was involved, maybe even in danger. All because he'd been careless and been seen with her. Even though he'd been careful by taking her to a secluded restaurant far up the beach, or swimming in the canal, someone could have seen him at her house. Or on the beach tonight. He swore again, more violently this time.

"About time you showed up!" Barbara's voice startled him. His eyes searched the darkness and he saw her—beautiful and carefree and walking slowly to him.

"I thought I'd missed you."

She wrapped her arms around his neck. "Don't you know that I'd wait forever?" she asked, and felt him stiffen as he held her. How long had it been since his arms had curved around her waist as if he really cared?

He kissed her lightly on the forehead.

"That's not very convincing," she whispered, twining her fingers in his hair and smiling up into his eyes.

"Do we have company?"

"I don't know. I couldn't tell, but I might have been followed."

"In that case…" He twirled her off her feet and kissed her with as much passion as he could muster. He was still filled with the scent and feel of Stacey, and he tried to transfer some of his earlier lust to the woman he was holding.

Though the embrace seemed genuine from outward appearances, Barbara could feel the restraint in his lips. Even when she molded her body against his, there was no response. All the old flames of desire she had once been able to ignite in Nathan had slowly died.

When he lifted his head, she laughed melodically, hoping that whoever was watching could hear.

Nathan held her tightly and they walked toward his cabin, his body stiff with the worry that his performance wasn't believable.

STACEY STARED DOWN at the beach in disbelief. From her darkened cabin, she'd watched as Nathan had walked toward his home. When the dark-haired woman had met him in the full light of the flood lamps, Stacey had had to lean against the railing for support. Nathan had grabbed Barbara and kissed her, lifting her off her feet and swinging her around him. The faint sound of laughter had caught in the air, and then they had leisurely walked arm in arm toward Nathan's cabin.

Stacey felt sick inside. *Trust me,* Nathan had said, over and over. *It's all just an act.* "And a very convincing one, too," Stacey whispered, wanting to believe him but finding it impossible.

She walked into the house and locked the door. Slowly, she strode over to the mantel and reached for the small agate that Nathan had given her earlier in the day. The smooth stone felt tiny and small.

Trust me.

"You're asking too much, Nathan Sloan," she said, staring at the rock in her hand. "Too damned much." Her fingers curled around the small stone, and she considered throwing it into the fire. "Now who's being melodramatic?" she asked, shaking her head and shoving the agate into the pocket of her sandy, torn dress.

CHAPTER FIVE

NATHAN PACED BETWEEN the window and the small table near the couch. His shoulders were tense, his black brows drawn over eyes that glowered angrily.

How could he have been such a fool?

He sat down at his desk, stared into the screen of the word processor and shut the damned thing off. He couldn't work, couldn't begin to think of anything but the night before and the mess he'd managed to make. And Stacey. God, if only he could forget her for just one second.

Damn, damn, damn.

Sweeping a hand over his face, he tried to erase the image of Stacey on the beach, her eyes wide with fear, her wet body trembling beneath his. Despite the danger, he'd reacted to her physically, the feel of her body enticing an unwanted reaction in his loins. Even now, alone in his cabin, he experienced the stirrings of desire firing his blood just as they had in her cottage. Seeing her in the lamplight—her hair a tangled mass of wild, honey-colored curls, her chin lifted in defiance, her wet dress sculpting her breasts—had make him lose his perspective. It couldn't happen again.

He laughed bitterly, took a sip of his cold coffee and grimaced at the black liquid in his mug. "You've made one helluva mess of it, Sloan," he muttered. He resumed his pacing and felt as trapped as a caged animal.

Glancing out the window, he noticed that the morning fog had begun to lift and the gray light of dawn was warming the beach. In a few hours, he'd have to take Cindy to Oceancrest and face Stacey for the first time since the fear and passion of the night before. No doubt she'd expect an explanation for his unpredictable behavior, and he didn't blame her. Hell, after being scared out of her wits, she deserved a better reason than some vague excuse about danger.

And what about your reaction to her?

"Son of a bitch," he muttered, trying to get the enticing woman off his mind. A woman, a beautiful woman, who was definitely a problem. The last complication he needed right now was another woman involved in his efforts to protect Cindy. Barbara was enough trouble as it was, and Jennifer, she'd started all the problems long before she died.

Walking to the sink, he tossed the last of his coffee down the drain. He eyed the phone but rejected the idea of calling Stacey. What could he say? Nothing that wouldn't make his predicament with Cindy more precarious.

His lips thinned into a hard smile when he considered what Stacey must be thinking of him. She'd probably decided that he was either a lunatic or a criminal—or maybe a little of both. The damned part of the whole matter was that she was right, and Nathan didn't like being reminded that he was walking a thin line with the law.

So, maybe she'd resist him next time, maybe she'd believe that he really was involved with Barbara. If he had any brains at all, he'd let her think the worst of him to protect her!

Don't go... Stay with me, she'd begged, and he'd spent the entire night savoring those words. Even now her pleas tugged at his soul, and he had to fight the urge to return to her cabin.

"You're a fool, Sloan," he muttered, "a goddamned bloody fool." Pushing his hands into the back pockets of his jeans, he strode angrily out of the house, letting the screen door bang behind him.

STACEY HAD MANAGED to hide the dark circles under her eyes and force a cheery, if false, smile onto her face as she approached the school. The night had been long, lonely and humiliating. How could she have begged Nathan Sloan, Cindy's father, to spend the night with her?

She had lain awake for hours, alternately condemning and fantasizing about Nathan Sloan, or whoever he was. The mystery surrounding the man was intriguing—as well as frightening.

"You're an idiot," she told herself as she walked into the classroom and placed her purse in one of her desk drawers. "The man is bad news. Stay away from him." But she couldn't convince herself. At the thought of his piercing eyes, or the sharp thrust of his jaw, she felt the traitorous urge to smile. "Get a hold of yourself," she reprimanded. "He's just a man, a man with another woman!"

She walked down the hallway, stopped at the teachers' lounge, poured two cups of black coffee, and squaring her shoulders, sauntered into Margaret's office.

"Morning," Margaret said, looking up from her

book and noticing the steaming cup of coffee Stacey
had placed on the corner of her desk. "You're an angel."

"Hardly." Stacey took a seat on the arm of the worn
couch facing Margaret. "But I try."

The elderly woman looked at Stacey and smiled. "Oh,
I get it, you want something."

Stacey, awed by Margaret's perception, took a sip
from her cup. "You always could read me like a book."

"So, out with it. What do you want?"

"All the information you have on Cindy Sloan."

Margaret swallowed a little of her coffee, frowned
and then pulled a couple of sugar cubes from her desk
drawer. After plopping them into her cup, she pulled her
lips together thoughtfully. "Now?"

"The sooner the better."

"Oh?" Margaret observed Stacey over the top of her
reading glasses. She closed the book she had been reading and placed it on the shelf behind her desk. "Why?"

Meeting the older woman's interested gaze, Stacey
replied, "It will help me deal with her today."

"You'll have a computer printout in a few days as
well as access to her files."

"I know, but I'd really like to get started today. It
can't be that hard to find all the information on Cindy
Sloan—she just registered last week."

"But this is the first day of school."

"And the kids won't be here for another—" a little
exasperated, Stacey glanced at the clock on the desk
"—forty-five minutes."

"Why are you so interested?" Margaret asked, leaning back in her chair and cradling the warm cup in her
hands.

"I look over all the reports on my students."

Margaret smiled and her kindly eyes gleamed behind her reading glasses. "But usually you wait until the information is in the computer. I don't think Andrea has had time to key anything in yet."

"You're smirking," Stacey accused, managing a grin as she read Margaret's thoughts.

"Maybe a little. You seem to have taken quite an interest in Miss Sloan. I thought it might have something to do with the girl's father. Didn't you say you had a date with him?"

"It wasn't a date. We just went out to discuss Cindy."

Margaret's gray brows arched.

"Look, all I want to see are the registration forms, personal history and medical history reports on Cindy Sloan. I'd like to know as much about her as possible because I think she's going to have a rough day."

"All right, all right," Margaret said, setting her cup on the corner of the desk and standing. "They must be here somewhere." Mumbling to herself, she walked into Andrea's office and looked through the overflowing basket on her secretary's desk. "If it's of any interest to you, I've written Cindy's psychologist in Fairbanks."

"Already?"

Margaret smothered a grin as she rifled through the untidy stack of papers. "I thought you might be interested. Guess I was right."

"Guess you were," Stacey admitted. "Let me know what he has to say."

"As soon as I get a response."

Andrea appeared in the doorway. "What's going on?" she asked as she hung her coat on the coatrack behind the door.

"Stacey wants to review the information on Cindy Sloan. Is it in the computer yet?"

"Are you kiddin'?" Andrea motioned toward the pile of paperwork in her basket.

Margaret cast Stacey an I-told-you-so glance over the top of her silver glasses.

Undaunted, Stacey asked, "What about the forms that Mr. Sloan brought in?"

"They're right here." Andrea walked around the desk and opened one of the drawers before pulling out a thick envelope.

"Do you mind if I look at them?"

"Be my guest." Andrea offered the envelope to Stacey. "Just bring it back before the kids get here. I'd like to get the information into the computer files as soon as I can. This is gonna be a long day."

"Will do," Stacey replied, waving to Andrea and Margaret as she headed back to her classroom.

Once in the preschool room, Stacey sat at her desk and looked quickly through the registration forms. She didn't know what she was looking for, but felt that something within the packet of information would give her some insight into the mystery that was Nathan Sloan.

"You should forget that man. He's still obviously in love with Barbara, despite what he told you." But her hazel eyes continued to scan the papers that had been completed in Nathan's bold handwriting. She looked through the registration form and found nothing.

"Where is Hercule Poirot when I need him?" she mumbled, studying the personal history form.

She stopped when she came to the information concerning Cindy's mother. "Jennifer Reaves," Stacey murmured. "I wonder why she never took Nathan's name?"

Several reasons came to mind. Maybe Jennifer had been a bra-burning feminist. Or perhaps she just preferred to keep her maiden name. Maybe she was a famous artist or something. Or maybe she and Nathan were divorced at the time of her death.

"So much for stumbling on clues. Even if I found one I wouldn't know what to do with it," she told herself crossly as she continued to read. The information on Cindy's mother was sketchy, practically nonexistent. Jennifer had died a little over two years before in an automobile accident. "Not much here to go on." Stacey pushed her hair out of her eyes and sighed.

Why had Nathan been so mysterious last night? And how was Barbara involved?

The door to the classroom opened and Stacey looked up sharply.

Nathan.

He walked into the room half dragging his daughter by the hand. His eyes were trained on Stacey, and her breath caught in her throat when she remembered the night before. His eyes, dark blue and brooding, reminded her of the passion that had exploded between them, turning her bones liquid and causing her to throw herself at him wantonly.

But other than the smoldering passion in his gaze, Nathan had changed. Gone was any trace of the jaded, dangerous man who had dragged her through the rain to her cabin, kissed her so violently that her entire world had turned around and then warned her of some vague danger before slipping back to a secret rendezvous with his lover.

This morning Nathan was dressed in cords and a sweater, his rich hair combed neatly, his jaw clean shaven. He looked very much like a concerned father bringing his child to Oceancrest for the first day of school.

Feeling as if she'd been caught spying, Stacey blushed, forced a smile on her face, shuffled the papers back into the envelope and shoved the small package into the top drawer of her desk. Then, hoping that she didn't look too guilty while avoiding Nathan's gaze, she approached father and child.

"Hi, Cindy," she said, bending on one knee and holding her hands out to the little girl.

Cindy, her blond hair braided neatly, her pink dress crisp and clean, a ratty-looking doll held in the crook of one elbow, held her arms up to her father. "I not stay here," she said anxiously, casting a nervous glance in Stacey's direction.

"Oh, sure, Cindy," Stacey replied before Nathan could say anything. "There will be more kids, and we're going to have lots of fun."

"No!"

"And—" as if conspiring with Cindy, Stacey winked at the child "—I'll let you name the octopus since you're the first one here."

Cindy shook her head, but her frown started to disappear.

"He's right over here." Stacey walked to the aquarium where the octopus was hiding. "As a matter of fact, we can thank your dad for finding him."

Cindy looked up to Nathan for reassurance. Nathan hauled Cindy into his arms and kissed her crown before setting her back on the floor. "Come on, pumpkin, let's take a look at him, okay?"

Slowly, Cindy inched over to the tank. The octopus

was hiding behind a rock, but Nathan pointed out the long tentacles to his daughter.

"Don't like him."

"He's shy, like you," Stacey pointed out. "This is his first day of school, too." Cindy's round blue eyes looked from the octopus to Stacey, all but accusing her of a lie. Stacey forged ahead. "And to tell you the truth, he's scared. He doesn't know what's going to happen today and it worries him."

Cindy didn't say anything, but continued to stare at the octopus.

"What would you like to call him?"

Cindy didn't respond, and Stacey noticed the storm brewing in Nathan's blue eyes. Knowing that he was about to give his daughter a lecture, Stacey placed a hand on his sleeve.

"It's okay. You can think about it for a few days, get to know him before you give him a name."

Two more students arrived, entering the room loudly, with lunch pails clanging and feet shuffling. Cindy looked worriedly at her father.

"It's all right," he said, with a brilliant smile aimed at his only child. The worry in Cindy's blue eyes cut him to the quick, but he'd caught the look in Stacey's eyes that silently asked him to leave.

"You take me home."

"Not now. But I'll be back later. I promise."

"Nooo! I hate it here!"

"I'll be back in a few hours. Right after lunch."

"Daddy!"

The muscles of his jaw worked, but Nathan walked to the door, Cindy following behind. "You be a good girl, okay?"

"No!" One little foot stomped and tears had gathered in her eyes. "You don't love me anymore!"

Nathan took the child into his arms, brushed her tears aside and kissed her forehead. "Oh, Cindy," he said with a sigh. "I love you more than you can guess, and I'll be back soon. You have a good time with Miss Monroe."

Then, his gut twisting violently, he placed his child on the carpet, glanced at Stacey and walked out the door just as another student was walking in.

Cindy hung by the door as if she could will her father to return, but soon all twelve preschoolers were in the room, making noise and playing with blocks, trucks or stuffed animals. Reluctantly, Cindy sat in a corner with the rag doll she'd brought from home.

During the songs and sharing time, Cindy was silent. Only when Stacey walked the children around the room, pointing out the new creatures in their various cages, did Cindy visibly brighten. When Stacey explained that Cindy's father had caught the octopus for the school, Cindy smiled shyly. A little later the little girl gave a halfhearted attempt at a painting, but throughout the rest of the morning she said nothing and looked longingly at the door for her father.

Andrea stopped by around ten-thirty and asked for the registration packet on Cindy Sloan. "I forgot all about it," Stacey apologized, handing the thick envelope to the secretary.

"Don't worry. The first day is always hectic."

That it is. Stacey thought to herself, but knew that she'd been distracted by Nathan's arrival. Just his presence in the room had caused her heart to beat irregularly and her palms to sweat. She tried to explain her reaction by the fact that she had almost been caught snooping into his life, even though she had every right to do so as Cindy's teacher. But her excuse didn't hold water. She'd forgotten about returning the information to Andrea because she couldn't get her mind off Nathan.

"I'll bring you a printout on Cindy as soon as I have one," Andrea said when she left the room.

Nathan came to pick up Cindy a few minutes late. Most of the other students were already gone and Cindy was fidgeting. When she saw her father, she threw herself into his arms and started to cry, as if she'd endured the worst morning of her life.

"Was it that bad?" Nathan asked, holding the wailing child close to him and looking over Cindy's shoulder to Stacey.

Stacey shook her head and ignored the fact that her pulse had begun to race. "This is a typical reaction."

"But the other kids—"

"Have been here before. They acted the same as Cindy on their first mornings. Very rarely do we get a child that falls in love with the place on the first day. Hang in there; by the end of the week she'll change."

"You're sure?"

"Reasonably. And though she'd probably like you to believe otherwise, Cindy didn't cry all morning. In fact she seemed to enjoy painting."

"Hated it!" Cindy corrected, casting a scathing look at Stacey and clinging more tightly to Nathan's neck. "I *not* come back here anymore!"

"Your friend here—" Stacey touched the sides of the aquarium where the octopus hid "—might get awfully lonely."

The little girl pursed her pouting lips and looked longingly at the glass cage. "He come home with us!"

"Afraid not, pumpkin," Nathan said, hugging the little girl. "He belongs to Miss Monroe." Nathan put his hand on the door just as another mother came to pick up her son. "I'll call you," he promised and walked out the door with the child. Stacey's spirits soared unreasonably.

"How did it go?" the young mother asked, once Nathan had gone. She was bending over her son and zipping his jacket.

Stacey dragged her eyes away from the door and smiled at the freckle-faced boy. "It went great, didn't it Tommy?"

"You bet," was the gruff reply.

"In fact, I wouldn't be surprised if Tommy will be ready for public kindergarten next year."

Tommy's mother straightened. "You mean it?"

"Margaret tested him today."

"Already?"

"You know our kindly doctor. She likes to get things done. She tested all of the children in my class who were here in the summer." Stacey walked over to her desk, retrieved the papers in question and handed them to the astounded mother. "If he continues to improve, I don't see why he couldn't start kindergarten next fall. He already knows most of his shapes, colors and letters. We have to work on numbers and a few social skills, but he's really made great strides. Right, Tommy?"

"Right." The boy beamed under the praise, and she winked back at him.

"That would be wonderful." Tears gathered in the corners of Grace Perkins's eyes. "I…we owe you a lot."

Stacey laughed and shook her head. "I think we'd better give credit where credit is due." Stacey looked down into Tommy's trusting brown eyes. "This guy—" she hooked her thumb in his direction "—did all the work, didn't you?"

Tommy smiled. "You bet."

"I don't know what to say except 'Thank you.'"

"You don't have to say anything. It's been fun, hasn't it, Tommy?"

In response, the once-shy child wrapped his arms around Stacey's legs and said. "I love you, Miss Monroe."

"I love you, too, Tommy." She felt her throat become thick and her eyes fill with tears. Blinking them back, she returned Grace Perkins's proud smile. "It's still early, of course. But, unless something unforeseen happens, I think Tommy will just have to graduate."

Grace Perkins and Tommy left, and Stacey felt incredibly alone. As much as she enjoyed watching the children become strong and whole, it was always difficult to let them go.

THE REST OF the week followed the same pattern as the first day. Although Nathan had promised to call, he hadn't. Nor had he come by. The only time she'd seen him was when he was bringing Cindy to school or picking her up, and during that time, the conversation always revolved around the little girl.

Stacey felt that Cindy was slowly improving, but by the end of the week, Cindy still kept pretty much to herself and only came out of her shell when painting or coloring. Several children had attempted to play with her, but Cindy had refused, preferring instead to sit in a corner with her favorite doll.

During the evenings, while Stacey was preparing art projects for the following day, she found herself hoping to hear from Nathan. When he didn't call or stop over, she decided that perhaps he had come to his senses and realized that a relationship with Cindy's teacher was out of the question.

Or maybe it was because of Barbara. That story about being in danger didn't wash—at least not now. That night, in the rain, Stacey had been inclined to believe it. But she'd been scared out of her wits at the time, and caught up in the romantic fantasy of the evening. She still trembled and blushed when she thought about her reaction to Nathan.

She'd watched the beach at night, but neither Nathan nor Barbara had met under the floodlights.

So maybe Nathan was telling the truth.

"Which is?" she asked herself for the thousandth time, and put away the scissors she had been using to cut out shapes of animals from construction paper. "It doesn't make any sense—none of it!" *And maybe Nathan and Barbara are meeting in another place, a secret rendezvous so you can't spy on them.*

The phone rang and her heart leaped. Her first thought was that Nathan had finally decided to call.

"Hello?"

"Stacey! I thought maybe you'd fallen off the face of the earth," her mother said.

"Not quite, Mom." Disappointment settled over her, but she tried to hide the fact from her mother.

"It's been a while since you called."

Guiltily, Stacey slid lower in the chair and rolled her eyes toward the ceiling. "I guess I've been busy. School started, you know."

"I realize you've got a lot to do," Mona said in her

usual moderate, perfectly controlled voice. "But you could pick up the phone once in a while."

"The lines run both ways, Mom."

"I know. *I* called. Remember?"

"Touché." Stacey began fingering the telephone cord and tried not to remember what it was like growing up with a mother and father who used her as the battle prize in a war zone. But it was odd for Mona to call. Something had to be wrong. "So tell me, how're you?" she asked.

"Fine, fine. Touch of the flu, but it's over, thank God. Charles didn't get it—impervious you know." Her mother chuckled and Stacey cringed at the mention of her stepfather who had been a pro golfer and whom her mother considered another Adonis. "Er, have you heard from your father?"

"Not in a few weeks."

"You might want to call him. He's...well, he's had a sort of financial reversal. Overseas investments that didn't turn out. Jacob would probably like to hear from you."

"I'll call him."

"Good. Good." Her mother seemed satisfied; the purpose of the call had been achieved. "So, tell me. How are you?"

"Just fine, Mom."

"Still living on that godforsaken island?"

Stacey smiled. "And loving every minute of it," she said, staring out the window at the calm Pacific. "Guess I'm a barbarian by nature."

Her mother laughed. "To each his own, I suppose. I just want to know that you're taking care of yourself."

"I am."

"And that Margaret person?"

"Dr. Woodward?"

"Yes, that's her name."

Stacey grinned and shook her head. Her mother had developed a sense of jealousy about Stacey's relationship with her employer. It was as if some latent maternal feelings or guilt had caused Mona some concern. "Don't worry, she sees to it that I'm busy."

"Not too busy, I hope. You need more than work and solitude, dear. You should be out socializing, kicking up your heels a little bit."

"I'll keep that in mind."

"You're patronizing me."

"Wouldn't dream of it," Stacey said with a sigh. "Say, when are you and Charles going to come and visit me?"

There was a pause while Mona collected her excuses. "I'm really not sure. Maybe in the spring. But I'll talk to Charles and see what his plans are."

"Mom?"

"Yes?"

Stacey held her breath for a second. "It would be nice to see you at Thanksgiving, or maybe Christmas."

"Why don't you come back to Boston for the holidays?" her mother asked and Stacey winced.

Boston. The Edwards Clinic. Daniel Brown. Mona's gala parties. Stacey's palms were suddenly sweating and her heartbeat had accelerated. "I'll think about it," she hedged.

"Oh, do! We could have a wonderful time!"

"I'll let you know once I've made my vacation plans."

"Good. Well, I'll talk to you later, Stacey, and don't forget to call your father."

"I won't, Mom. Goodbye." She heard the phone click

a continent away. Swallowing her pride, she dialed the phone and listened while a busy signal beeped in her ear. "Oh, Daddy," she murmured, biting on her lower lip. "What is it this time?"

Stacey was the only reason her parents had gotten married. Her mother had been pregnant when she'd married Jacob Monroe and never had there been two people less suited to live together. While Mona was an extroverted party goer, ready to climb any social ladder, Jacob was a homebody who wasn't interested in making a fortune or even providing for his small family. There had been bitter fights late into the night and Stacey had known that if it hadn't been for her, Mona Shipley would never have made the mistake of marrying so far beneath her social station.

"Damn it all anyway!" she said, tears blurring her vision. She wiped them angrily away with her fingers. With a sigh of disgust, she got up from the table and walked into the kitchen, shaking off her loathsome self-pity and intent on making a cup of tea.

When she looked out the window, she saw Nathan on the beach. It was still daylight and there was no one with him—not even Cindy. "It's time to have this thing out," she decided, turning off the kettle and sensing that she was about to make a big mistake. "Oh, well, one more won't make much difference."

She raced out of the back door, around to the front, down the sandy path, and hurried down the stairs. Nathan Sloan had a few questions to answer—questions that couldn't be asked when his daughter was around.

NATHAN'S MUSCLES TENSED when he saw Stacey running down the stairs, her golden-brown hair streaming behind her like a sun-gilded flag. Her hazel eyes were trained on him and a high color stained her cheeks as she kicked off her sandals and jogged toward him. Dressed in faded jeans and a loosely knit cotton sweater with its sleeves pushed over her forearms, she ran easily across the white sand.

"I'm glad I caught you," she said breathlessly, and then added, "alone."

He smiled, despite the fire in her gray-green eyes. "You've been looking for me?"

"I thought we should talk about Cindy when she isn't around. Where is she?"

"With Geneva." When Stacey didn't respond, he elaborated. "My neighbor, Mrs. McIver."

"Oh."

He tried not to notice that her breathing was labored or that her breasts were rising and falling beneath the loose weave of her white sweater. Instead he forced his gaze back to the sea. "What do you want to know?"

No time like the present, she told herself, but felt her stomach twist uncomfortably. "About her mother."

He didn't move. "Jennifer?"

"Right."

"Why do you want to know about her?" A deep furrow drew his eyebrows together as he turned and faced her again.

"It might help me," she replied. "With Cindy."

He shrugged, looked back to the sea and didn't say anything. Stacey stepped around to face him. "Look, you're the one who asked me to help your daughter. Remember?"

"How's she doing?"

Stacey frowned. "Not as well as I'd hoped, but better than I'd expected."

"What's that supposed to mean?"

"I'm not going to lie to you. Cindy's still withdrawn, and she shows no interest in interacting with the other children. At least not yet."

"Is that unusual?"

"No."

"Then?"

"Your daughter is tolerating Oceancrest, and I think that's a major victory."

Nathan let his guard slip a little and the brackets near the corners of his mouth softened. "I agree. After that first day, I never thought it would work."

"Neither did I," Stacey confided, smiling slyly.

"But you said—"

"I lied." She pushed her hands into her back pockets and stared at the horizon. "I knew that you were concerned, and I didn't want to upset you unless I was sure that Cindy wouldn't fit in."

"And has she?"

Stacey shook her head. "Not yet. But it's coming. She seems to have accepted me, at least a little, and I think that's a very big stumbling block for her to overcome."

Nathan raised a skeptical dark brow. "What do you mean? How has she accepted you?"

"As her teacher, the authority in the room."

"Has she ever shown you any signs of...affection?"

Stacey frowned a little. "No, but remember, she doesn't really know me. Not yet. Whenever I get too close to her, she withdraws and pulls the blank wall routine with me. There's no way I can get through to her then."

"What do you do?"

"Ignore her."

"Ignore her?" he repeated, his expression becoming hostile.

"Of course. I won't let her think that she's beaten me or it's all over."

"Like a game?"

"I don't like to think of it that way," Stacey replied, holding her hair off her neck and letting the breeze cool the small droplets of sweat that had collected at the base of her head. "It's not a game to Cindy, at least not one she knows she's playing. She's just reacting. I doubt she has any ulterior motives."

He gazed at her long and hard, as if fascinated by what he saw. Stacey stepped backward and let her hair fall down to her shoulders. "You're very trusting," he said.

"Of four-year-olds."

"Don't you think they try to manipulate you?"

"I suppose, but I won't let them. The same way I won't let adults maneuver me." She hesitated. "Well, with one exception."

"Meaning me, I suppose."

"Right. You've tried to manipulate me from the start by forcing a meeting between Cindy and me on the beach. Then we went out, enjoyed each other's company and the next thing I knew, you were involved with another woman, involved to the point that you couldn't be honest about it and kept hinting at some sort of danger." Nathan looked as if he were about to interrupt her, but she continued. "And then, to top if all off, you've been acting as if what happened on the beach the other night didn't exist."

"It didn't. At least, I don't want you to remember it."

She felt as if he'd slapped her. "Because of the danger?"

"Yes! Dammit woman, don't you see? I don't want you involved in this!"

"I was there! I've got the torn dress and a cut on my ankle to prove it! I am involved, whether you want me to be or not! You're the one who got me into this!"

He paled a little, but didn't move.

"Oh, what's the use?" she whispered, turning back to the cottage.

Nathan grabbed her arm and twisted her to face him. "I'm sorry."

"You should be! I'm only trying to help your daughter! That's what you wanted, wasn't it? That's why you had her find me on the beach, why you took me to dinner, why you came with me to find the octopus." She faced him head-on, daring him to argue.

A muscle worked in the corner of his jaw and he swallowed, his lips thinning with the angry throb that was beginning to pound at his temples. "That's part of it," he admitted, his ink-blue gaze delving into hers. God, she was beautiful. Anger made her tremble, gave her eyes a special silvery-green fire that ripped through all his pretenses.

"And what's the rest?"

"The rest is that I can't stay away from you," he admitted with a sigh.

The hands on her arms slid down to secure her wrists. The feel of his fingers against the inside of her arms made her skin prickle in anticipation. A seeping warmth trickled through her blood, spreading throughout her body. Looking into his eyes made her stomach quiver. And he had to be the one man she couldn't fall in love with!

"Is that why you came down here? Because you thought I might be here?"

"Yes." Gently, he reached forward and stroked her neck. "You're a beautiful woman, Anastasia," he whispered, fingers twining in her hair. "But there's more to you than good looks." He stared into her intelligent eyes as if attempting to solve an intricate, elusive puzzle.

Stacey's heart pounded. His intense gaze penetrated her defenses. "Thank you," she whispered before clearing her throat. "I'd like to think so." She glanced away from his magnetic gaze. *Don't forget the reason you came down here, so you could have things out with him!*

His warm fingers touched her cheek and caused her heart to beat erratically in response.

Nathan knew he was playing with fire. If he had a lick of sense he would distance himself from the allure of her silky skin and the promise in her wide eyes.

In the past two years he'd never wanted a woman so desperately as he did right now, in the thickening dusk on this lonely stretch of beach. The way he responded to Stacey was something he hadn't expected. Since Jennifer's death, he'd lost nearly all interest in women, or so he'd thought. Even Barbara hadn't been able to touch that corner of his soul that he'd kept hidden. Ever since the first moment he'd seen Stacey he'd been aching for her.

Overlooking the warnings, he let his gaze get lost in the silver-green entanglement of hers. Drawing her close enough that the tips of her breasts brushed his chest, he lowered his head and slanted his mouth over hers. His warm lips molded to hers, and he slipped his hands around her waist.

Stacey felt his tongue glide past her parted lips. It dipped and tasted of the sweetness of her mouth, touching and stroking her tongue that so willingly responded in kind.

Without thought, she wound her arms around Nathan's neck, burying her fingers in the thick hair that tickled his collar.

A groan that started in his loins passed by his lips, and his hands pressed feverishly against her sweater, urging her body into the cradle of his. Thighs pressed thighs, muscles ached to be joined, and Stacey felt the rock hard evidence of his desire press urgently into her abdomen.

"I've been out of my mind with wanting you," he groaned, burying his nose into her neck. She let her hair fall back, the loose sun-streaked strands brushing his arm.

His fingers moved upward to discover her breast. Small and firm, with a nipple pressed against her sweater, it strained to be touched by the sweet pressure of his hands.

"Stacey," he whispered urgently, feeling the dark bud beneath the rough fabric. He opened his eyes, and with a frustrated sigh, noticed they weren't alone on the beach. *Damn!* Another couple, and elderly man and woman, were strolling in their direction, calmly walking an arthritic terrier and doing their best to avoid looking at Nathan and Stacey's passionate embrace.

Nathan willed his hot blood to cool. The muscles in his body tensed as he stared at the beachcombers.

"Nathan?" Lifting her head, Stacey recognized her neighbors and blushed from the roots of her hair.

"Evenin' Stacey," Mr. Chambers said.

Stacey, extricating herself from Nathan's arms, smiled self-consciously and nodded in reply. "Mr. Chambers. Mrs. Chambers."

"Nice evening for a walk," Mrs. Chambers said with a smile as Rogan, their scruffy dog, sniffed the wet sand.

"You know them?" Nathan asked, steering her toward the staircase after the man and woman were out of earshot.

"Yes."

"How long?"

"Oh, I don't know. A year and a half, two years, I'd guess. They rent the cabin next to mine for the summer. Been doing so for years."

Nathan squinted into the twilight, searching the shadowed face of the cliff.

"Surely you weren't worried about the Chambers," she said, stifling the urge to smile as she thought about the sweet older couple.

"Never can be too cautious."

"About what?" Shaking her head, she finally laughed. "You are the most suspicious man I've ever met." She started up the stairs, still holding his hand. "If I didn't know better, I'd start to think you were some sort of secret agent, or international spy, or criminal wanted by the FBI."

The fingers around her hand tightened. She looked over her shoulder to find his face no longer animated. The trained calm had again masked his features, hiding any display of emotion, shadowing his eyes to make them unreadable.

Stacey's heart froze. Dear God, what had she said? Whatever it was, it was obviously close to the truth. Then it hit her. Nathan Sloan was running from the law.

CHAPTER SIX

"I THINK YOU'D better start leveling with me," Stacey said, once she and Nathan were inside the cabin.

"Leveling with you?"

"Right." She stood in front of him with her feet planted wide apart, her hands balled on her hips and her eyes looking straight into his. "No one in his right mind would be suspicious of Jim and Enid Chambers!" Nathan's lips thinned, but Stacey ignored the warning in his eyes. "Jim's a retired schoolteacher who likes to fish, and Enid spends her time doing needlework and making the best jam on the island! Every kid in town treats them like grandparents!"

"You've made your point," he said, running his fingers through his thick hair and trying to relax. He walked across the room to the window and, leaning his hip against the sill, he scanned the shoreline in all directions.

Stacey was so incensed, she couldn't bite her tongue. "Then maybe it was Rogan you were worried about!"

"Rogan?"

"Their fox terrier!"

Despite the tension, Nathan grinned crookedly, the furrows on his forehead softening. "Don't be ridiculous."

"That's like the pot calling the kettle black," she pointed out. "Honest to God, Nathan, Jim and Enid are two of the nicest people in Serenity, or on the whole island for that matter. They spend their summers here and sometimes their grandchildren come to visit. You couldn't have picked two more Norman Rockwell-family-type people if you tried!"

Nathan laughed, the rich sound seeming to echo off the exposed beams of the ceiling to settle in her heart. "I suppose you're right."

"Damned right I'm right," she said hotly, some of her anger slipping a little at his grin. "You're so suspicious, it's downright scary."

His blue eyes centered on her worried face and regret shadowed his gaze. "Believe me, the last thing I wanted to do was scare you."

"That's not what you said the other night."

He cocked his head and lifted one brow in an infuriating manner of arrogance.

"You remember," she prodded, "the night you dragged me back here and wouldn't let me turn on any of the lights? The night you were waiting for Barbara? You scared me out of my wits. And now you're jumping at shadows again!" She sighed loudly and tossed her hair over her shoulders to look at the ceiling. "Jim and Enid Chambers of all people!"

"Okay, okay, I made a mistake. It's not the first time."

"I'll bet not! I'm surprised you even trust me." When he started to say something, she raised her hands to wave off his protests. "I know, I'm different. You checked me out first! Well, maybe I was the one who should've done the checking. You know all about me, Mr. Sloan, but I don't know a damned thing about you, except of course that you don't trust anyone other than Barbara, whoever she is!"

The smile left his eyes. "I just like to be careful."

"To the point of paranoia!"

He walked back to her and pushed his face close to hers. "You should know; you're the expert! You think that all men are like Daniel Brown's father!"

Her eyes widened, and she stepped backward until her back was pressed against the door. Feeling cut to the bone, she found the smooth handle with her fingertips and gripped it tightly. "I think maybe you should go," she whispered.

Nathan saw the wounded look in her eyes and his anger dissipated. "You started this you know," he said softly, reaching toward her to stroke her face.

She turned away from his touch. "And you ended it." Swallowing back a thousand apologies, she jerked the door open.

Nathan pushed the door shut, trapping Stacey between the smooth wood and the strength of his body. "You've been spoiling for a fight."

"I'm just confused!"

He was so close she could smell him, see the hesitation in his midnight-blue eyes, watch as his jaw clenched and relaxed, as if he were caught on the horns of a weighty dilemma.

"I didn't want to feel like this," he admitted, one finger reaching upward to wind in the wild honey-colored strands of her hair. "I didn't want to even like you."

Her breath caught somewhere between her lungs and her throat, and Stacey couldn't breathe. Mesmerized by the seductive glint in his eyes, she waited, telling herself all the while that she was playing the part of the fool.

His finger slid along her jaw, down her throat, to the erratic pulse nestled between her collar bones. He drew lazy rings over the delicate bones while his eyes centered on the fluttering, sensitive circle.

"I can't let myself fall for you," he said, but his voice was throaty with desire. Nervously she licked her lips, the innocent but seductive action heating him further, urging release.

"And...and I can't fall for you," she replied, echoing his words as she tried to convince herself.

"Good." Lowering his head, he tasted her parted lips, felt the warm and trembling softness of her mouth. He groaned and pressed himself closer, feeling her smaller thighs molding to his, her warm breasts flatten against the weight of his chest.

Never had he wanted a woman more. Never had he needed the sexual release to take him for just a few minutes from the fear that gnawed at him like some hungry beast. Hot desire made his body hard against hers, stretched taut the bothersome fabric that kept her flesh from his.

Stacey felt the fire in his blood by the passion in his kiss. His tongue slipped through her lips to touch and taste the sweetness of her mouth. A warm, uncoiling heat radiated from the depths of her womanhood to every nerve ending in her body. Desire swept through her veins in heated waves, making her senses reel.

His hands slid to her waist and under the hem of her sweater. She felt the pads of his fingers against the soft muscles of her back. Warm and sensual, he moved his hands upward around her rib cage to touch the weight of her breasts.

He rubbed her nipples with his thumbs, circling gently against dark points until Stacey moaned and wrapped her arms around his neck. There was something wild and mysterious about Nathan Sloan, something vitally alive and masculine. Try as she would, Stacey couldn't fight the allure of his touch, the seduction in his eyes, the persuasion of his lips as they travelled down her neck to press against the pulse throbbing at her throat.

His lips skimmed above the neck of her sweater and she quivered. Warm hands encompassed her breasts, kneading the soft flesh and teasing the proud erect nipples that ached for his touch.

His tongue dipped into the small circle of bones at the base of her throat, laving the fluttering pulse until Stacey's knees grew weak and she slid to the hardwood floor. "Nathan," she whispered, her throat raw with emotion.

He lifted the sweater over her head and instinctively she covered her breasts with her hands. Inquiring blue eyes delved into hers before he pushed her hands aside and stared at the firm white mounds with the dark tips.

Lowering his head, he kissed one breast and it puckered sweetly between his lips.

Stacey's abdomen contracted and she tried to think of a reason, any reason, to push him away from her. Think of Daniel Brown and Jeff, she told herself, but couldn't find the strength to pull away from Nathan. She watched as he suckled at her breast, his beard-roughened chin dark against the white skin, his lips and tongue anxiously tasting her. Instinctively, she cradled his head in her arms.

Think about Barbara! Is this what he does to her? But instead of drawing away, she leaned over and kissed his thick, coffee-colored hair.

The delicious, swirling sensations argued against denying herself the pleasure of this mysterious man.

But he doesn't love you!

"Stacey," he whispered against her wetted breast. "Make love to me."

He slipped his hands beneath the waistband of her jeans, slowly tugging on the top button. She sucked in her abdomen as his fingers brushed across her sensitive skin. She felt as if she were melting deep inside.

"Love me," he said again, kissing her stomach and rimming her navel with his tongue. The seductive warmth of his breath against her abdomen made her writhe. His tongue dipped into her navel, sending waves of desire rippling through her.

"I... I can't."

The leisurely lapping in her navel stopped as he drew his head up and gazed at her flushed face. His slumberous blue eyes turned suddenly cold.

"Because of Jeff Brown?" he asked.

"Because I just can't!"

Lying across her, his sable-brown hair rumpled by her fingers, Nathan looked so ruggedly handsome and erotically male that she had trouble finding her voice. Saying no to him was the most difficult decision she'd ever made, and one that her body screamed to reverse.

"How many times do I have to tell you that I'm not Daniel Brown's father?" he demanded.

"It's not Jeff I'm thinking about," she said, searching for her sweater.

Nathan dived for her wrist and pinned it to the floor with his hand. The sweater was just out of reach. His gaze raked her naked, still wet nipples and soft breasts. If he wasn't careful, he could lose himself in Stacey Monroe. Lifting his gaze to her puzzled, embarrassed expression, he asked, "Who? Who were you thinking about?"

"Cindy, for one."

"Who else?"

Tilting her chin and narrowing her eyes, she jerked her hand from his hard grip and rubbed her wrist before retrieving her sweater and holding it over her breasts. "Jennifer Reaves, for one," she said. "Your wife, the woman who never bothered to take your name!"

Nathan blanched. "I don't see what she has to do with us."

"She was Cindy's mother, wasn't she?"

He nodded decisively, but his eyes remained tangled in her confused gaze.

"Then she has a lot to do with us."

"Who else?" he asked.

She tried to squelch the jealousy, but couldn't. "Barbara," Stacey admitted.

His shoulders slumped, and his lips pressed together in barely controlled anger. "I told you, she's helping me. With Cindy."

"Dammit, so am I! Because you wanted me to, remember? A few weeks ago getting Cindy into Oceancrest was all that mattered!"

"It still is."

"Then I need straight answers!"

"Stacey…" He reached for her, but she scooted away, still holding her sweater over her heaving breasts. "I'm doing the best I can," he rasped.

"At keeping me in the dark!"

"At trusting you."

"Trust is a two-way street."

"I know," he said, furious with himself, her, the whole damned world. He felt as if he were about to explode.

"And you don't trust me," he said, reaching forward and jerking the sweater away from her.

Blushing, she stared straight into his eyes, aware that her breasts were pointing proudly at him as they heaved with the strain of her labored breathing. "Would you?"

He sighed and looked away from the deliciously rising and falling mounds. Disgusted with himself, he handed her back her sweater. "I suppose not."

"All you have to do is level with me. Is that so hard?"

A shadowed pain flickered in his eyes and his face contorted. "You don't know what you're asking," he whispered, standing and staring through the window to the sea.

"Exactly my point!"

His gaze lowered to her breasts again, and he had to grind his back teeth together in restraint. It would be so easy to carry her upstairs, place her on the bed and cover her trembling body with his.

"Cover yourself," he said angrily, and then hearing how rough his voice sounded, he looked back to her and the hard planes of his face relaxed. "Please, put the sweater on. I can't think straight when you're...like that."

She jerked the sweater over her head and once her arms were in the sleeves, she pulled her thick hair through the neckline and shook it free.

Feeling awkward, she managed to stand and walk to the kitchen where she put on a pot of coffee. Her hands were shaking and the tightening in her abdomen was so fierce she had to hold onto the counter for support. What had she done? Once again, she had let her body rule her mind. Like a fool, she was still trembling with desire for a man she couldn't have. His being with her was a lie. The woman he cared about was waiting for him somewhere on the island, ready to meet him under the cover of darkness on the beach.

Nathan came into the kitchen, straddled one of the café chairs near the table and rested his arms across the caned back. Placing his chin on his arms, he looked up at her.

"I'm sorry," he said.

"Don't!" Stacey felt the sting of tears and her voice was shaking, clogged with emotion. "I don't want to get involved with you, and you claim you don't want to get involved with me. So it should be very easy to keep this relationship strictly professional."

"You don't believe that any more than I do." His calm voice convinced her that he had control of his emotions when she was falling apart at the seams, which only served to remind her that she had no business falling in love with him.

"I think we should only be concerned with what's best for Cindy, not our own selfish whims."

"I don't think what I feel for you could be classified as a whim."

She arched a disbelieving brow and then turned to face him, resting her hips on the counter as she thought about what life would be without him. "I don't want to hear it, Nathan," she whispered, pretending interest in the yellowed wax on the cracked linoleum. "We both got caught up in the moment."

"That's a lie and you know it!"

"What?" Her head snapped up, and she met the intensity of his gaze.

"You heard me." Hot with anger, he got out of the chair and retreated to the living room. Stacey followed him and found him scanning the dark horizon through the window.

She ached with the thought that he was looking for Barbara on the beach.

In frustration, Nathan shoved his hands into his pockets. Leaning a shoulder against the mantel, he turned narrowed, suspicious eyes in her direction. "So you want to know about Jennifer?"

Suddenly it didn't matter. Stacey didn't want to know about his relationship with his wife. He had convinced her that his private life was off-limits. "You don't have to—"

"But you were the one so hell-bent to understand. Right?"

"Only because of Cindy…"

His gaze told her he didn't believe her for a minute. "Well then, maybe you should know," he said, "but it's not something I like to talk about."

"I figured out that much." She dropped into a chair.

Nathan rubbed his chin and let out a long sigh. "Jennifer died when her car went off an embankment over Laurel Canyon. It was a beautiful day, no rain or ice on the road, not a cloud in the sky." His jaw tensed in anger. "There weren't even any skid marks; she never touched the brakes."

Stacey didn't move, except to study the weary lines on his face. "You mean you don't think it was an accident?"

"I mean I don't know." His countenance was grim, his blue eyes tortured. "There were a hundred reasons why she could have missed the curve. Maybe she was looking into the rearview mirror, maybe reaching for something on the floor…who knows?"

"Was Cindy with her?"

He blanched. "No, thank God. The car rolled down the hill and caught fire. No one inside could have survived."

"I'm sorry," Stacey whispered, feeling like an intruder into his personal pain. "I didn't realize…"

He ignored her, and as he leaned more heavily against the mantel he ran his fingers against the varnished pine. "Cindy immediately withdrew. At first I thought she'd get over it, but—" he shrugged "—it just never happened."

"Has she improved at all?"

"A little, but not entirely," he admitted, shifting uncomfortably from one foot to the other.

"And that's it?"

"Most of it. My relationship with Jennifer wasn't all that memorable."

She tapped her fingers on the threadbare arm of the overstuffed chair. *In for a penny; in for a pound,* she decided. "Why do I get the feeling that you're still not telling me all of the story?" she asked.

Lifting one shoulder, Nathan placed his foot on the hearth and grimaced. "I don't know what more you want to know."

"Maybe a little about your relationship with Cindy before your wife was killed."

"We weren't all that close," he admitted.

"Why not?"

He scowled and paced between the window and the fireplace. "Jennifer and I were separated at the time of the accident," he admitted. "We had been for some time."

"And then you were thrust back into Cindy's life, and

her mother was gone." No wonder the child was inse-
cure and withdrawn.

"Cindy and Jennifer were very close."

"And you?"

"I didn't really know my daughter."

Stacey's stomach knotted painfully. *Well,* she told
herself, *you asked for it!* "So you became a father when
you had to because your wife was killed?"

There was an awkward lag in the conversation. Nathan's jaw clenched, and he fought against the rush of
words that would clarify the situation. The less Stacey
understood about what had really happened in L.A., the
better for everyone concerned, especially his daughter.
He walked restlessly around the small room, alternately
glancing in Stacey's direction and then out the window.
"You have to understand that my job kept me busy."

"That's a cop-out and you know it."

His broad shoulders slumped. "Maybe. I hope not.
Anyway, I was gone a lot, following stories. News,
sports, whatever it was, wherever it was happening."

No wonder his wife had left him. A woman with a
baby needed more encouragement and support than a
vagabond writer was able to give. Still his story didn't
quite jibe. It was so evident that he cared very much for
his daughter, and Stacey had trouble seeing him as an
absentee parent.

"So that's why you separated?"

"What?" He stiffened.

"Because of your job?"

"Oh." He looked at her and then frowned. "Yes. Uh,
actually my relationship with Jennifer really hadn't
worked from the beginning."

"But there was a child involved, and neither one of

you could break it off," she said woodenly, knowing from her own experience how cold a relationship could become if the people involved only stayed together because of an unwanted conception.

"You act as if you understand."

"A little," she admitted with a frown, as she thought of her own childhood in Boston with parents whose only common link had been their one, strong-willed child. She shrugged off the old feelings of despair. "But what I can't figure out is this danger you keep talking about."

Nathan didn't move, but his muscles knotted until they ached.

Stacey, seeing that she'd hit a raw nerve, pressed blindly on. "All this talk about danger where Cindy is concerned—suspicion of everyone you meet including a sweet, elderly couple out for an evening stroll on the beach. It doesn't make a lot of sense to me. What are you afraid of, Nathan, and why can't you tell me about it?"

He gazed at her ruefully. "I guess I owe you that much," he said, going against his better judgment.

"I think so."

"There are some people—"

"Who?"

He hesitated. "Relatives of Jennifer's."

"What about them?"

"They don't think that I'm a model father."

"Considering what you told me, do you blame them?"

"Not really, no. But they want me to give up custody of Cindy."

Stacey fought the dull ache in her heart. Nathan so obviously loved his child. "How can they fight you? You're her father."

He winced slightly and tugged on his lower lip. "But

I wasn't a very good one, not until Jennifer died," he admitted with a frown. "Anyway, these relatives would like to take her from me, by force if necessary."

"And so you're hiding from them," she finished for him.

A sad smile touched his eyes. "Look, Stacey. We both know that Cindy has some emotional problems. Hell, maybe I'm partly to blame for them. But I think that if she's taken from me, she'll be worse than ever."

"I agree," Stacey said, thinking fondly of the chubby little girl with the wild blond curls. "She needs some security in her life right now; she needs you. I don't think any court would think otherwise."

"But I don't want to put her through the trauma of a legal battle. At least not yet."

Stacey couldn't argue with his logic even if she didn't agree with his methods. "I wouldn't either. But do you really think her relatives would come looking for you, clear up here?"

"I don't know." His jaw tightened, and he rubbed the aching muscles in his shoulders. "But they were in Fairbanks. At least one of them was, a man by the name of Robert Madison."

"Who is he?" Stacey asked.

Nathan hesitated and his eyes hardened. "Her uncle."

Madison not Reaves? "But Jennifer's name—"

Nathan's cold smile cut her off. "Madison was married to Jennifer's sister. His wife is dead."

"You don't like him much, do you?"

"Not much to like about him," Nathan said evasively.

"So why was this Madison in Fairbanks?" she asked as she got up from her chair, walked into the kitchen, poured them each a cup of coffee and returned to the living room.

Nathan had taken a seat in the antique rocker near the door and watched her approach.

"Black?" Stacey asked, holding out the cup to him.

"Yes. Thanks." He accepted the mug and took a long swallow of the hot liquid before closing his eyes and leaning back.

"Why would Cindy's relatives go to all the trouble?" she asked, looking into her cup and perching on the arm of the couch.

"Money."

"Money?"

"Money that was part of Jennifer's family fortune. Cindy stands to inherit a great deal of it when she turns eighteen. As far as the other members of the family can see, especially Madison, I shouldn't be allowed one red cent."

"But he's only an in-law—"

"And he considers me an outlaw," he said wryly.

"Madison has no right to Cindy's inheritance."

"Doesn't matter. He wants it and if the only way to get it is through Cindy, then he'll try to prove that I'm worthless as a father."

Stacey gripped her cup more tightly and walked to the stairs. "Do you want it? The money?"

"Hell, no. At least not for me. But I think Cindy should be able to claim it when she turns of age. The trouble is, the other relatives, Madison in particular, don't much like the idea."

"Have you talked to them?"

"They don't listen."

"Isn't there anyone in the family who trusts you?"

"No."

But there was one person on his side, Stacey thought, hating the jealousy that cut through her heart. She sat on the lowest step of the staircase leading to her loft and held her mug of coffee between her hands. Swallowing back a lump that had unexpectedly formed in her throat, she asked, "How does all this concern Barbara?"

"She's trying to help me."

"By pretending to be your lover?"

"Yes."

"How?"

Nathan drained his cup and stood. "Look, I've told you all I can," he said, running tense fingers through his hair. "Just trust me about Barbara."

"That's difficult," she admitted.

He walked over to the stairs and knelt beside her. "You're the only woman I care about, Stacey," he vowed, his eyes lovingly caressing her face. "Just believe that."

"I don't know if that's smart."

A crooked grin slashed across his face as he stared at her. With her wild, long hair and innocent hazel eyes, she could evoke more raw and tangled emotions than he had thought existed in his soul, emotions he'd thought were lost long ago. "I don't know if it is either," he said, his eyes caressing her face. Smiling, he noticed the bridge of her nose where a light dusting of freckles lingered from her youth.

She couldn't help but grin.

"Just hang in there with me," he suggested, kissing her crown. "Maybe we'll be able to muddle through this mess together."

"I'd like that," she conceded. "I'd like that very much." She smiled up at him and he kissed her softly on the mouth. "However, I still have some reservations about a personal relationship with one of my student's parents, y'know."

"I guess I'll have to convince you to change your

mind." He checked his watch. "But not right now; I've got to get back and relieve Mrs. McIver."

With a regretful smile, he was out of the house, and though Stacey wanted to watch his retreat to see if he met Barbara, she didn't. Instead she concentrated on finishing an art project for the following day and then called her father whose groggy voice reminded her that it was past eleven on the East Coast.

THE NEXT WEEK passed quietly. Too quietly. Nathan didn't even bother to bring Cindy to school. He sent his daughter with Mrs. McIver. The elderly woman also walked Cindy home after school.

Stacey began to wonder if her intimate conversation with him was all an act. His story about Cindy's inheritance and relatives was bizarre to begin with, and it could well have been a cover-up for his unpredictable behavior, especially where Barbara was concerned.

Stacey tried to concentrate on her work, but even her students couldn't rouse her out of the depression that lingered in her heart when she thought about Nathan and the fact that he was avoiding her. Maybe he'd rethought his position and decided that a relationship with Cindy's teacher wasn't what he wanted. But he hadn't lied about his desire for her; she'd felt it in his touch, seen it in his eyes.

Cindy was more difficult the next week than she had been the first, and she seemed to withdraw into her shell completely. When the week was over and Geneva McIver came to the school to pick her up, Stacey decided it was time to discuss Cindy's behavior.

"I need to talk to Cindy's father," Stacey said as Geneva was buttoning Cindy's sweater.

"I'll let him know when he gets back."

Gets back? From where? "I didn't know that he was out of town," Stacey remarked.

"Oh, yes. He left a few days ago. That's why I'm staying with our girl, here." She glanced affectionately at the blond child. "Nathan should be back by Monday."

"Good." Nathan's absence explained Cindy's behavior. The fact that he had left his child for several days would intensify the small child's fears of being left for good by the only parent she had left. Having already lost her mother, Cindy was obviously distraught that she had lost her father as well.

"I'll tell him you want to speak to him."

"That would be great."

The elderly lady took Cindy's hand and turned toward the door.

Stacey acted on impulse. "Mrs. McIver?"

"Yes?" Geneva looked over her shoulder.

"Would it be all right with you if I took Cindy to the park tomorrow? It looks like it will be another great day, and I'll pack a picnic lunch for the two of us."

"I don't know—"

Stacey cocked her head in Cindy's direction. "It might be just what she needs," Stacey said and caught Geneva McIver's understanding glance. Obviously Cindy had been a problem at home as well as at school.

"I guess it will be all right."

"Wonderful. I'll come by around ten-thirty."

Geneva smiled. "Good. I need to do a little shopping anyway and it's easier done alone." She patted the child affectionately on the head. "Come on, Cindy, we'd better be going."

Stacey watched the elderly woman and small child leave and wondered if she'd made another mistake.

CHAPTER SEVEN

SATURDAY DAWNED CRISP and clear. A salt-scented breeze from the north blew over the island, but by mid morning the sun had warmed the beach.

Stacey spent the morning shopping for picnic items and a kite. Then she packed a hearty lunch for herself and Cindy and walked along the beach to Nathan's home.

Geneva McIver was waiting for her and quickly opened the door when Stacey knocked. "We're just about ready," she said, scurrying around the small, weathered cabin. The structure itself was an odd blend of large windows, a steeply pitched roof and rough cedar walls. The ceilings were high and sloped, and the walls were covered with the crayon masterpieces of a four-year-old artist.

In one corner was Nathan's desk and word processor, a crowded bookcase and bulletin board covered with notes to himself.

"Come on, Cindy," Mrs. McIver insisted as she held Cindy's hand and directed her from a short hallway into the living room.

"Hi!" Stacey said when the child was in sight.

Cindy looked at her but didn't smile.

"We'd better hurry," Stacey encouraged, "or we'll miss the boats!"

"Boats?" Cindy said, squinching her little face.

"Sure, the fishing boats. The first ones return around noon. We'd better get a move on."

Intrigued, the child accepted Stacey's outstretched hand.

"I'll have her back by four," Stacey promised the older woman, who waved her off.

"Don't worry about it. I'll have dinner ready for her at the usual time, about six. So go on. Enjoy yourselves. Cindy, you mind Miss Monroe." Geneva McIver stood on the porch and watched Stacey and Cindy start toward town.

They walked together, hand in hand, down the dusty path near the side of the road leading to Serenity. Cindy stopped every once in a while and looked at an interesting flower, piece of litter, rock or insect. Stacey put up with the child's curiosity and couldn't help the feeling of contentment stealing over her.

The sun was warm, the sky a brilliant, cloudless blue, and all around them, the ever-present scent of the sea filled the crisp air. Sea gulls cried and slow moving cars passed by on the dusty road. It was a lazy, glorious Saturday.

They walked through the town, and Cindy paused to stare into the window of the pet store. She smiled at the rambunctious puppy that pressed its nose to the glass and yipped excitedly at the pedestrians on the sidewalk.

Cindy looked at the dog with pleading eyes and the fluff of a puppy wagged its tail, its two dark eyes sparkling.

"Your father would kill me," Stacey said, sensing Cindy's yearning for the little dog.

"I like puppies," Cindy volunteered and Stacey's heart nearly broke.

"Oh, I like puppies, too, but I can't get you one."

"This one." Cindy placed a chubby finger against the glass and the tan puppy responded by chasing his tail.

"He is beguiling," Stacey admitted, hovering on indecision. "Oh, I should be shot for this!" Ignoring her rational thought, Stacey took Cindy inside the pet store. The owner of the store obligingly let the child hold the puppy and Cindy giggled with glee when the little dog washed her face with his rough tongue.

Guilt stole over her, but Stacey couldn't refuse the expectant child. "I'll take him," she said, buying the dog, puppy food, a collar, dish and leash and wondering how she was going to break the news to Nathan that he was now a pet owner. With a sigh she decided that if Nathan were violently opposed to the dog, she'd keep the puppy at her house. After all, it was a rash decision and, for all she knew, Nathan or his child could be allergic to animals.

Delighted, Cindy held on to one end of the leash while the puppy tugged at the other. Led by the excited dog, they walked toward the piers, and Stacey lugged her parcel of dog paraphernalia under her arm, her free hand holding the picnic basket. By the time they reached the dock, she was exhausted.

"Hold it, Rover," she said to the dog and petted him before tying him to the railing of the pier. Once the dog was settled with a dish of fresh water, Stacey spread a small blanket over the rough wooden planks, dug into the picnic basket and retrieved the sandwiches, cookies and cans of juice for Cindy and herself.

While Stacey ate her sandwich and watched the bright sails of the boats near shore, Cindy happily fed her entire lunch, chocolate chip cookie and all, to the dog.

"You're gonna get hungry," Stacey warned with an understanding grin, but the child didn't seem to care. "Okay, have it your way. This is your day, Cindy."

Cindy smiled shyly as the puppy whined and strained at the short leash.

"I can see you're going to be a lot of fun," Stacey said wryly, patting the small dog's head. His curly tail wagged so furiously that it was little more than a streak. "Yep, Nathan's gonna strangle me when he finds out about you." The pup jumped up and licked Stacey's face, and she laughed.

A little later, they walked to the park, found a shady spot for the pup and then spent the afternoon playing on the equipment. Stacey slid down the slide with Cindy, climbed on the wooden jungle gym, pushed the child on the swing and sat beside her on the merry-go-round while the puppy slept, paws in the air, in the shade. The kite was a complete failure, and all Stacey accomplished by running up and down the length of the park was to exhaust herself and make her feel like a weakling. Her calves ached and her lungs burned with the failed effort.

"You'll have to get your dad to sail this," she finally said, sitting on a bench under the spreading branches of a spruce tree and folding the brightly colored Chinese dragon back into the basket.

"He'll make it fly," Cindy predicted.

"I hope so," Stacey panted. "I never have been able to get one of these things into the air."

It was an exhilarating afternoon and Stacey felt she'd made tremendous strides with Nathan's introverted child. For the first time since she'd known the girl, Cindy was laughing and bubbling over with chatter about the dog, the park and the beach. Stacey felt some of Cindy's reservations beginning to melt.

Smiling fondly at the curly headed child, Stacey read to her from a worn book she'd borrowed from the school library. They were sitting together on the bench, and Cindy's eyelids were drooping as she leaned against Stacey and listened to Rapunzel for the second time.

Stacey had just finished reading the story when she felt someone watching her. She looked over her shoulder and saw Nathan standing under a fir tree, his shoulder propped against the rough bark, his eyes taking in the entire scene. His face had softened with love for his daughter, and when Stacey's gaze met his, she saw that his feelings included her as well. A lingering desire smoldered in his eyes, but there was something else as well, and in that heart-stopping instant Stacey realized that Nathan cared for her, perhaps more than he wanted to admit.

In a flash, the kindness in his eyes disappeared, and he shoved his hands deep into his pockets as he approached Stacey and his daughter.

"What do you think you're doing?" he demanded.

"Daddy!" Cindy jumped off the bench and ran into her father's waiting arms. "Look what Miss Monroe got—see, a puppy!" She stretched out her hand and pointed a chubby finger at the dog, who yipped excitedly and tugged on his leash.

"You got a dog?"

"For Cindy."

"What!" Nathan looked as if he were about to explode. "You're not serious."

"Afraid so." Stacey went to the tree where the dog was tethered and untied him.

"I don't think we can keep him," Nathan said, glancing meaningfully at Stacey. "But maybe Miss Monroe has a place for him."

Cindy made a protesting sound, slithered out of her father's arms and ran to retrieve the leash from Stacey. "He's mine," she pouted, wrapping the leather leash around her hand.

Nathan's glare impaled Stacey, and an angry muscle worked in his jaw. He didn't say anything but was waiting for an explanation.

"Cindy spotted the dog in the window of a pet store. I couldn't resist. She's been positively animated since we got him, a changed little girl! Isn't that what you want?"

"But how long will it last?"

"I don't know, but I think loving an animal is one of the best cures in the world for her. She doesn't have a brother or sister, no friends to speak of. I thought she needed the dog, but if you can't keep it, I will. She can visit it at my house."

"I think I should be the one to decide if my child needs a pet."

"You weren't around!"

His eyes hardened. "Which brings me to the next point. What do you think you're doing parading her around town, taking her to the docks and then bringing her here for anyone to see?" He watched his daughter with angry, worried eyes.

"What I'm doing is showing your daughter a good time. We had a picnic, played in the park..." Her voice trailed off when she realized his anger wasn't caused by the dog. It ran much deeper than that, an anger born of fear.

"I told you that it might not be safe here!"

"Hogwash!" she snapped, her own temper flaring.

"Don't you remember anything I told you the other night?" he threw at her, his eyes still trailing his child and the frisky pup.

"All of it, except the holes you didn't bother to fill in," she replied, gathering up her books, parcel and basket.

"Such as?"

"The fact that you were leaving the island, leaving Cindy. She's had a rather hard week, you know, and I could have made it easier on her if only I'd known you were gone."

"Something came up."

"You could have called."

"Why?"

"Because I'm her teacher and I'm trying to help, dammit!"

Nathan's eyes grew hard and the cords in his neck bulged. "I was out of my mind with worry! I got home and no one was there. When Mrs. McIver returned and told me that you'd taken Cindy and had been gone for most of the day, I was worried sick!"

"Didn't she tell you where we were going?"

"Yes. And that's what concerned me. I don't like her out in public alone."

"I was with her!" She clutched the basket in one hand and her parcel of dog gear in the other. "And I would keep her safe. You know that!"

His rage faltered and his voice softened. "But I don't know that you would be responsible for your own safety."

"That's ridiculous! No one, especially not one of your ex-wife's relatives, wants to hurt me."

"You don't know Robert Madison," he said so coldly that despite the warm September sun, Stacey shivered.

Nathan took the parcel from her and called to his daughter. "Come on, pumpkin, we'd better go."

The puppy, Cindy in tow, headed out of the park. Nathan and Stacey had to run to catch up with them. Some of Nathan's hostility faded when he reached his daughter and saw the sparkle of excitement in her eyes.

"Maybe I owe you an apology," he said to Stacey.

"At least one," she replied, offering him a smile. "More like a thousand, I think."

He let out a long breath. "There are things I should tell you," he said, his eyes narrowing as they walked past the quaint shops of the town to the beach. The sun was low in the sky, hanging brilliantly over the ocean as the tide lapped the shore.

About time! "What kind of things?"

Nathan watched Cindy frolic with the small dog, laughing and tumbling on the sand with the frantic pup. "I was wrong," he admitted. He slung his arm around Stacey's shoulders and squeezed her affectionately. A warm, traitorous glow began to burn in her heart.

"About what?"

"The dog."

"Then you'll let her keep him?"

"I think I'd have mutiny on my hands if I didn't."

"Probably." Stacey laughed and Nathan smiled down at her, the rugged features of his face growing tender as he gazed into the sparkling gray-green depths of her eyes.

"You're the best thing that happened to Cindy."

"I didn't just happen," she reminded him with a teasing grin.

"No, I looked for you long and hard. Believe me, now that I've found you, I'm never going to let you go."

Stacey's smile grew, and the happiness stealing into her heart made her feel radiant. It seemed as if she'd waited forever to hear those words. If only she could trust him, believe that he cared for her.

"That's why I was so panicked this afternoon. When I thought that I'd lost Cindy and put you in some kind of danger..." His voice trailed off, and he pinched the bridge of his nose as if to ward off a headache.

"No one's going to hurt me."

"I hope you're right," he said, calling to Cindy as they climbed the stairs to his house. "I hope to God you're right."

STACEY PLACED THE last of the dried dishes into the pine cupboards while Nathan bathed Cindy. She could hear him laughing with his daughter, some childish squeals of delight, and then the quiet droning of his voice as he read Cindy a story before putting her in bed.

Folding the dish towel and draping it over the handle of the oven, Stacey leaned against the counter and smiled to herself. She'd just shared the most blissful day of her life. Other than the one argument with Nathan, the afternoon had been wonderful. A brilliant Indian summer day and the warm, homey feel of Nathan's rustic cabin combined to make Stacey's heart swell.

When they'd returned to the cabin from the park, Mrs. McIver had brought over a steaming kettle of clam chowder and a basket of warm sourdough biscuits. The homemade blackberry jelly she'd added had tasted suspiciously as if it had come from the kitchen of Enid Chambers.

After a cozy dinner and a wild game of hide-and-seek, Nathan had made popcorn, and Cindy, Nathan and Stacey had sat near the fire and eaten their fill of the buttery popped kernels. Then Nathan had whisked Cindy off to the bath and Stacey had finished washing the dishes.

Just like home, she thought, knowing that she was beginning to fall in love with Nathan as well as his child. How easy it would be to fit into a comfortable routine with him and Cindy, she mused, humming to herself.

And how dangerous! Not in the way Nathan imagined, but because she couldn't become romantically involved with the father of one of her students. She had only to remember Daniel Brown's horrid fate to realize that she couldn't let her feelings for Nathan deepen.

Sighing, she walked back into the living room and flopped down on the couch. Nathan was adjusting the logs in the fireplace with a poker. Bending from his waist and reaching forward, he prodded the blackened wood. His sweater climbed up his back, exposing his hard muscles and the ridge of his spine as he worked, and Stacey had trouble keeping her eyes off his tanned, tightly drawn skin.

"Cindy wants to say good-night to you," he said, without looking up from the glowing coals and the pitchy chunk of pine that hadn't yet ignited.

"I'll just be a minute."

Stacey walked down the short hallway to the small alcove that was Cindy's bedroom. Ruffled curtains surrounded the window and matched the pink quilt tossed over a snug pine bed that was pushed against one wall. Toys and books were heaped into an old cedar chest in the corner and scattered on the floor. The puppy was already nestled at the foot of Cindy's bed, and the girl was smiling when Stacey walked into the dimly lit room.

"I like Attila," Cindy said.

"Attila?"

Cindy pointed to the fluff of tan fur with the bright brown eyes. "Dad named him. Said you called him that."

Stacey smiled when she remembered calling Nathan a boorish Hun. She had to fight the tears that were suddenly building in her eyes. "I guess I did," she admitted, clearing her throat.

"Attila will stay here forever," the little girl announced, snuggling against the pillows and yawning. Her golden hair haloed her face in damp ringlets, and her thumb slipped into her mouth.

"Of course he will."

"Will you?" Cindy asked, trying to keep her eyes open.

Stacey's heart wrenched. "I hope so," she said, pushing a wet strand of hair off the child's face. "At least I'll be your teacher for as long as you need me."

"No, I mean, will you stay here with me and Daddy?"

"I wish I could," Stacey whispered, kissing the child softly on the forehead. "I wish I could." Cindy, too tired to continue the conversation, settled into the bed, and Stacey tucked the quilt under the girl's chin.

When she turned to leave the room, Stacey found Nathan lounging in the doorway. He was slumped against the frame, one arm resting above his head. He'd watched the entire scene between his daughter and Stacey and found for the first time in years that he wished he could ask a woman to marry him. Not just any woman; only Stacey Monroe.

If only there weren't so many secrets between them. Telling himself it was for her own good, he felt an inexplicable twinge of conscience.

Embarrassed, Stacey straightened and walked to the door. "She's absolutely adorable," she whispered, cocking her head in the direction of Cindy's bed. Her voice was rough from her losing battle with tears.

"Don't I know it," Nathan agreed with a tired sigh.

Once back in the living room, Nathan walked to a makeshift bar near the fireplace. "How about a drink?" he offered, eyeing his sparse selection of near-empty bottles.

"I don't think so."

He picked up an empty bottle of brandy, dusted it and glanced at Stacey, giving her a twisted smile. "Don't blame you. The bar's pretty meager."

"I'll live."

Smiling, he chuckled. "I'm counting on it." He lowered himself onto the hearth, his back to the orange flames.

Stacey sat on the seat of the large bay window and stared into the night. The sky was covered with the jewellike brilliance of the winking stars, and a silvery crescent moon cast a stream of light on the sea.

"Who takes care of Cindy when you go walking on the beach at night?" she asked.

"Geneva."

Stacey's brows drew together and she tried to sound casual, but her fingers nervously gripped the sill. "But when you come back here...with Barbara?"

"Mrs. McIver leaves, and she doesn't ask any questions," he said pointedly.

"Convenient," she murmured, her heart sinking, her dreams shattered. How easy it was to fantasize about Nathan, about living with him forever. But the fantasy would never be anything more than a pipe dream.

Nathan sensed her shift in mood. He stretched before walking to the window and placing his hands on her shoulders.

The soft pressure of his fingers was enticing, and when he leaned over to kiss her neck, Stacey didn't think about the fact that this was but a fleeting moment in time. She didn't care. She felt the warmth of his lips nuzzling her neck and she leaned backward, silently offering more of herself to him.

He groaned and murmured her name against her ear, sending thrilling little tremors down her spine as his tongue circled the sensitive skin and lingered for a minute.

Moaning in response, Stacey closed her eyes, letting his arms pull her gently backward along the window ledge until she was half-lying in his lap, looking into his night-darkened gaze.

She felt warm and safe and protected.

Gently, he pushed a clinging tendril of hair off her cheek and, as he stared into her eyes, she was lost to him. All thoughts of the future slipped from her mind as he kissed her softly at first and then with a quickening passion that stole the air from her lungs.

She wrapped her arms around his neck and felt his hands smooth the fabric over her breasts. They swelled beneath his touch and he tenderly kissed her skin. Stacey closed her eyes and gave into the ache deep inside her.

When he rolled off the ledge and lifted her into his arms, Stacey didn't protest. Her arms were wrapped around his neck, and her legs were draped over the crook in his elbow as he carried her to the bedroom. All the while his free hand was wrapped just under her breasts, softly tantalizing her with fingers that moved as he walked toward the bedroom.

Soft moonlight filtered through the windows and gave the room a silvery glow. Though it was dark, Stacey could make out the huge brass headboard, a dresser and a small night table. Nathan placed her on the bed, and the mattress creaked and sagged with their combined weight.

"I've wanted to be with you for a long time," he whispered against the waves of her golden hair that billowed over his pillow.

"So have I."

He kissed her neck and the sweater over her breasts until she felt she would go mad with desire.

Then she saw it—a small picture near the phone on the dressing table. At first she thought it was a portrait of Cindy, but as Stacey's eyes adjusted to the dim light, she realized that the picture was of a beautiful black-haired woman.

Barbara!

She didn't want to believe it; she wanted to go on making love to Nathan. But her arms fell limply to her sides.

He lifted his head. "Stacey?" Levering himself up on one elbow, he stared down at her. "Something's wrong."

It wasn't that she didn't want him or had any qualms about making love to him. Good Lord, she'd been fantasizing about him for weeks, but she couldn't share the bed in which he had probably slept with Barbara. Knowing that she was acting on irrational, raw emotion, she slid out of his arms and off the bed and felt the urge to vomit.

"I've got to go," she whispered, her voice trembling as she ran from the room.

He was after her in a second. "Stacey—wait!"

Grabbing her purse off the couch and avoiding the confused look in his eyes, she headed for the door and tried to hide her tears.

"What's this?" he asked as he walked into the room. "Are you paying me back for the last time I was with you?"

Her small, strangled sob cut Nathan to the quick. "I... I can't stand the thought of sleeping..."

"With me?"

"No!" she screamed, grabbing the handle of the door "In that bed. Barbara's bed!"

"Barbara's never been in there."

"Oh, God, Nathan, give me a break," she whispered. "I've seen you with her. You admitted that Mrs. McIver doesn't ask questions when Barbara comes over. And... and you've got her picture on the nightstand. You won't talk about her, and I've tried to believe your lies, but really, I'm not that stupid!" *Oh, God, I'm dying inside.*

"Damn!"

She had to get out of the room.

"Stacey, look at me." When she didn't, he said, "I think I'm beginning to fall in love with you." She glanced in his direction, saw his opened shirt, the strong chest beneath and the defeat in his eyes. Her heart yearned to believe him, to trust him, but she couldn't.

Her heart aching, she forced her chin up. "Goodbye, Nathan." Opening the door, she stumbled blindly into the black night.

Stacey flew down the steps, sobbing and crying uncontrollably. She had to get away from Nathan and his lies. Kicking off her tennis shoes once she hit the beach, she scooped them up, tucked them under her arm and started running as fast as she could.

She heard him call her name but didn't turn around. "I can't let this happen," she told herself fiercely. "I can't let myself fall in love with him! He's a liar and God only knows what else! Oh, God..."

The length of the white beach stretched out before her, and she didn't stop to think about why she was running.

She was nearly to the staircase at her end of the beach when she heard the running footsteps behind her. She knew instantly it was Nathan. Gasping for breath, she reached the bottom step and felt the splintery wood beneath her foot before she was wrenched away from the staircase and twisted to face Nathan, his dark hair falling over his eyes, his breathing as irregular as her own.

"Let go of me," she said, trying to pull free of the strong arms that wrapped possessively around her.

"Not yet."

"Nathan, please."

"I want to explain—"

"And I don't want to hear it, okay? Just let go of me and leave me alone. I don't need you and I don't want you!"

The firm line of his mouth twitched. "But I need you; I want you."

Liar! Without heed to her actions, she slapped him across the face as hard as she could. His head snapped backward, and his eyes glittered for a minute.

In that one angry instant, everything changed. Horrified at her own actions, she tried to apologize. "Oh, God, Nathan I'm sorry." She ran trembling, still smarting fingers through her wild hair before leaning her forehead against his chest. He didn't move, didn't bother to hold her close. "It's just that I'm tired of not knowing where I stand with you. I'm sick of all the half-truths and the lies. I've told you that I didn't want to be involved with you."

"And you lied," he said tonelessly.

"No—"

His anger exploded, and he clenched her wrists. He captured her lips with his, and the anger raging within him turned to passion, as hot and furious as the wrath he'd felt with the sting of her hand.

His tongue delved into her mouth and she couldn't stop him; nor could she still the fluttering of her heart, cool the heat in her blood.

She tried to think of anything that might discourage him. "Don't…don't you have to go back? Cindy's alone," she whispered, her voice thick with desire.

"I ran over to Mrs. McIver's house. She's with Cindy," he mumbled while kissing her ear, touching the sensitive skin with his tongue. Stacey trembled in his arms.

"But—"

"I told you, Geneva doesn't ask any questions." Impatiently he wound his fingers through her hair and pulled her head back, forcing her to look into his eyes.

"No questions?"

"None."

Unlike me, Stacey thought wildly, trying to keep her mind clear, trying to think of all the reasons she couldn't love Nathan, and not being able to remember a one.

"Nathan, I can't go on like this," she whispered.

"Neither can I."

"No, I mean—"

"Shh. Don't you know that I love you?"

If only I did! But all the fight was gone, and she surrendered to the beauty of the night and the passion of his kiss when his lips slanted possessively over hers. *It doesn't matter if I love him for one night or forever, I'll never forget him,* she told herself, wrapping her arms around his neck and feeling the fringe of his hair against her fingers.

She fit against him perfectly, her yielding body soft against the hard lines of his hips, thighs and chest. She kissed him back in anger and in love. Crazy and unwanted as the emotion was, she realized now that she was in love with Nathan Sloan. She probably had been since the first time she'd laid eyes on him. Despite his lies, despite the secrets surrounding him, despite his feelings for Barbara, Stacey was passionately in love with this one man, and now, at least for the moment, she didn't care about the future.

Without letting go, Nathan gently pushed her onto the sand, the weight of his body falling over hers as they collapsed on the cool ground beneath the staircase.

The hunger within him gnawed deep and hard. He kissed away the salty tracks of her tears before sliding her sweater over her head and staring down at her. Nearly naked and white, with her tangled hair billowed in moon-silvered waves surrounding her face, Stacey was impossible to resist. Groaning, Nathan gave into the demands of his body, hating himself for being so weak when it came to this woman.

Stacey couldn't stop herself. Her fingers wound in his hair and discovered the buttons of his shirt. She felt the cool night air against her bare skin, the warmth of his lips as he kissed her breast, the grains of sand against her back.

She slid his shirt off his shoulders and felt the tense, hard muscles of his back and upper arms. His hands were kneading her buttocks, and she let her fingers travel across his ribs and the thick dark hair matting his chest. He whispered her name and, with his hands, found the button on her jeans. His warm fingers brushed and teased her abdomen until Stacey could think of nothing but loving him. Her fingers strayed to the waistband of his pants, to the zipper that slid so easily downward.

"Stacey." Nathan took hold of her wrist. "Are you sure?"

She met his gaze with her silvery-green stare. "As sure as I am of anything right now," she replied, kissing his cheek.

"I don't want you to feel any regrets."

"No regrets," she promised with a smile that broke through his final defense.

He closed his eyes and tried to control himself as she slowly slid the jeans over his hips.

Within a few minutes they were naked. Lying together, legs and arms entangled in intimate embrace, there was no backing away from the inevitable union of their flesh as well as their souls.

While the moonlight filtered through the stairs, shadowing Nathan's face as he lay over her, Stacey looked into his midnight-blue eyes and knew that she would never love another man. She closed her eyes and a shudder of desire ran down her.

Watching her, Nathan moved slowly, parting her legs and gently filling the ache that welcomed him.

She gasped as he entered her, felt a quick, short pain before pleasure and need eased the discomfort. Then she was moving with him, to his rhythm, reveling in the delicious swirling sensations that propelled her upward, higher and higher, hotter and hotter until the bittersweet pressure that had been building within her exploded in an instant, and the entire world seemed to shatter into a thousand dizzying fragments of light.

Not knowing she cried his name, Stacey felt a deep shudder as he fell atop her, his perspiring and panting body holding her close, offering comfort to the tears that filled her eyes.

"Are you all right?" he asked, gently stroking her hair and brushing the tears from her eyes.

"I'm… I'm fine."

"Fine?"

She laughed and sniffed back the tears. "Okay, wonderful. Is that better?"

"Much." He nuzzled her neck and looked deep into her hazel eyes. "I meant it, you know. When I said that I'd never let you go—that was a promise."

"But…" She struggled with the strangled sound of her voice. "What about…"

"Barbara?" He let out a long sigh and rolled his eyes skyward, all the while holding Stacey tenderly. "Don't worry about her; she's just a friend."

"A good friend."

"A very good friend," he corrected with a dazzling smile that slashed across his rugged face as he lay back on the sand, one arm wrapped around Stacey's waist, the other cushioning his head as he stared up at her. "But not a lover. At least not for some time."

"How long?"

"Stacey—"

But she had to know. "How long?"

"A while ago. A long while," he admitted, sliding

his hand up from her waist to the back of her neck. "It's been over a year, Stacey. Long before I met you." His intense gaze held hers. "And even if I'd entertained any thoughts of becoming romantically involved with Barbara, once I'd met you, there wasn't a chance."

If only she could believe him. "How does she feel about it?"

He lifted a shoulder. "Like I said, we're very good friends."

"Good enough that you keep her picture near your bed?"

He grinned and touched her lightly on the nose. "Old habits are hard to break, I suppose. And I thought it would look more believable if someone broke into my house—"

"—and saw the picture, because of this 'act' you have with Barbara. Right?"

"Yes."

She reached for her clothes and silently pulled them on, trying to ignore the gritty sand that still clung to her hair and skin, trying to ignore the nagging doubts about Nathan's relationship with Barbara.

Nathan, knowing from experience that he couldn't say anything in his defense, fell silent. Stacey would make up her own mind. He took her cue and tugged on his own jeans.

Finally, Stacey tossed her hair away from her face and let out a long, tired sigh. "You know, I really do want to believe you."

"Then just—" He stopped midsentence and froze.

"What—"

He touched her on the arm and held up a hand, signaling her to be quiet. His ears strained for the unfamiliar sound that had caught his attention.

A new kind of fear tightened Stacey's throat. Her eyes sought Nathan's dark gaze. Slowly, he pulled her into the shadow of the staircase, against the jagged rock of the cliff.

There was a noise on the stairs overhead, a shuffling of feet. Stacey looked up but could see nothing in the darkness. Someone was there, slowly walking down the creaking stairs. But who?

There was a hissing sound, and a small light flared as a match was struck. The scent of smoke drifted downward. Nathan's arms drew Stacey tightly to him. She leaned against him for support and looked up and to see the glowing tip of a cigarette and the falling arc of the match as it was tossed from the staircase.

Hushed voices became more distinct over the roar of the sea as the footsteps paused on the landing directly above Nathan and Stacey. Her heart was pounding so loudly that she was sure the whole world could hear it.

"What you're telling me is that she meets him here every couple of weeks?" a deep voice asked.

"At least," was the reply. The voice sounded young, as if it belonged to a man barely out of his teens. "Maybe more often. Can't really say."

"But you're certain it's him."

"Hey, look. I told ya. I've seen 'em together."

Dear God, they're talking about Nathan and Barbara, Stacey realized. Nathan's muscles were rigid: she could feel his body bracing, coiling, ready to strike.

"Any pattern to their meetings?"

"What?" A pause. "Naw. Seems random to me."

"And they don't meet anywhere else?"

"No. I've been following him."

"Maybe she's just his girlfriend," the older voice suggested.

Stacey could visualize the leer that accompanied the words, and her stomach turned over.

"Maybe. Or maybe she's a fringe benefit." The younger voice laughed viciously, and the cigarette was flicked over the railing of the stairs to be extinguished in the sand not ten feet from where Stacey was standing. "I've seen him with another girl—the kid's teacher. They're pretty cozy, if ya catch my drift."

Nathan, still holding her close, stiffened. Stacey felt the color drain from her face, and she held her breath. *My God, they're talking about me! What's Nathan involved in?*

"I get it, but I don't buy it," the older voice objected. "Sloan wouldn't risk it. He'd have too many questions to answer if he got involved with the kid's teacher. And Madison checked her out. She had trouble a couple of years ago. Some kid in Boston died. She wouldn't risk seein' Sloan. Her reputation's on the line."

Stacey was crumbling inside.

"But I saw them together!"

"Yeah, probably talking about crayons and paintbrushes if ya ask me," the older, gravelly voice said with a disapproving snort.

Nathan had pulled her deeper into the shadows. They were half crouching beneath the steps, and Stacey was certain that the two men would discover them at any minute. She saw Nathan reach for a rock and hold it in his hand.

"Maybe we should just grab the kid and make a run for it," the younger voice suggested. There was an eager lilt to the sound that made Stacey's stomach turn. Nathan's already tense body coiled even tighter, and the look on his face was murderous.

"Are you out of your mind? Madison would kill us. Sloan might spot us. No, we'd better do it Madison's way. It's the same amount of cash one way or the other. So why should we risk our necks and get hung with a jail sentence? The way I see it, this is Madison's problem."

The two men descended the remaining steps and started down the beach. Nathan, his eyes glittering dangerously in the moonlight, watched their every move.

Stacey tried to see the men, hoped to place faces with the chilling voices, but all she could make out were dark silhouettes, another cigarette being lit, and then the men turned and walked back to the stairs. Because of the darkness, she couldn't distinguish their features although one—the taller one—had blond or silver-colored hair.

She and Nathan waited under the stairs until the men had climbed out of sight. Then, when Stacey tried to crawl out of the hiding spot, Nathan's hand tightened over her arm and he held her back. She got the unspoken message. It was a full fifteen minutes before he released her. When he finally did, he motioned her to stay put before he carefully climbed the stairs.

He was gone only a few seconds; it felt like an eternity. By the time that he got back, Stacey's knees were like jelly.

"Are you all right?" he asked.

"What was all that about?" she whispered, her eyes darting around the deserted beach. All of Nathan's remarks about danger came suddenly home.

"Cindy," he replied, barely controlling the rage coursing through his veins. His rough features hardened, and he thought that right now he would like nothing better than to kill the two bastards who had been on the staircase.

"Oh, God, Nathan, what's going on—what...what are you involved in?"

He tugged on his lower lip and continued to scan the ridge with worried eyes. His skin was stretched taut over his face, the furrow between his brows deep. "I'll tell you once I check on Cindy. Go back to your house and wait for me. I'll be there in about twenty minutes."

"And what if you're not?"

The corners of his mouth twisted upward in pleasure. "That probably means that our two friends have caught up with me. If they do, I'll kill them both."

She believed him. "Nathan—"

Without further explanation, he turned and ran down the beach, along the cliff, out of view from above, as fast as his legs would carry him. All of his thoughts were centered on Cindy.

"I'll be damned if I'll let you go alone," she said aloud, watching his retreating figure. She loved him and wasn't about to let him face his problems alone. With only a twinge of conscience, Stacey followed him, her heart hammering in her throat.

"Dear Lord," she prayed breathlessly as she stumbled over a sand-covered boulder, "let Cindy be all right."

CHAPTER EIGHT

STACEY WAS BREATHLESS, gasping for air. She pounded on the locked door of Nathan's cabin. "Nathan!" she screamed. "Nathan!"

The door swung inward and Nathan, balancing a sleeping Cindy in his arms, stared at Stacey in amazement. His eyes were cold, his chin thrust forward angrily. "I thought I told you to go home and wait for me! God, you probably woke up the whole damned neighborhood." He stepped out of the doorway and Stacey entered. Tension crackled in the air. "Don't you ever listen to anything I say?" he demanded.

Mrs. McIver was bringing a suitcase out of the bedroom. Pale and shaken, she clucked her tongue. "Oh, hush!" Geneva said to Nathan. Her brow knitted in worry as she closed the door behind Stacey. "This is no time to yell at each other." With quick, sure movements, she began to place Cindy's clothes in the case.

Stacey leaned against the door and tried to find her voice. "I wasn't going to leave you," she said, trying to remain calm. But she could feel his fury, see the fear in Geneva's eyes.

His face pinched in anger, Nathan placed Cindy on the couch. "You could have been followed."

"What about you?"

"It looks like I was," he suggested pointedly and then

relaxed a little. His anger melted into genuine concern. "Look, Stacey, I don't want you involved."

"Whether you like it or not, I am involved, up to my eyeballs! You're the one who saw to that the first day I met you!"

"What if someone followed you tonight?"

"Or you?"

"I was careful."

"So was I! You obviously didn't know you were being followed!" She ran trembling fingers through her hair and wondered why she was fighting with him. They should be working together instead of going for each other's throats.

"I've heard enough," Mrs. McIver said, her kind eyes shifting from Nathan's angry countenance to Stacey's flushed face and wrinkled, sandy clothing. "You two sort this out. And if you need me..." She glanced at the sleeping child before returning her worried gaze to Nathan.

"I'll call."

"Good." With a shrug and a shake of her graying head, Geneva McIver walked out the front door. Nathan stood on the porch and watched until the elderly woman was safely in her house. As previously arranged, the phone rang less than a minute later, and Mrs. McIver told Nathan that no one had been waiting for her, lurking in the shadows.

"Is all this necessary?" Stacey asked, her heart still racing.

"What do you think?"

She didn't need to answer. She trusted Nathan with her life. Whatever his secrets, they were for a good cause. Stacey looked at the sleeping child resting blissfully on the couch. Cindy slept, unaware of the danger surrounding her peaceful existence. Her unruly curls framed her cherubic face, and her lips moved in gentle little sucking motions that made Stacey's heart turn over.

"Don't you ever do what you're told?" Nathan asked with a cynical smile. Most of his anger had faded and whether he wanted to admit it or not, he was glad Stacey was with him.

"That depends."

"Oh? On what?"

"On who gives the orders, of course."

"Of course." His lips twisted into a wry smile. "Has anyone ever told you you're bullheaded?"

She laughed nervously. "I don't think you want to know the answer to that."

"I think I already do." He shook his head and walked over to his sleeping daughter. "Well, since you're here, why don't you help me get Cindy into the Jeep? I don't trust her here with Madison's two goons running loose."

Stacey agreed. Her skin crawled when she remembered the conversation she and Nathan had overheard.

"I'll take her to your place. Just for now. Come on."

While Nathan wrapped Cindy in a blanket and took her out to his Jeep, Stacey went to the child's room and retrieved her favorite stuffed animal, blanket and rag doll. The puppy, who had claimed a spot on Cindy's pillow, stretched and wagged his tail, thumping it against the pink coverlet.

Stacey couldn't help but smile. "Come on, Rover—er, Attila, or whatever your name is. I guess you'll have to come, too." She scooped the little dog off the bed and carried him along with the rest of Cindy's treasures outside to the Jeep. Nathan locked the door of his house, climbed behind the wheel, and slowly, so as not to attract unwelcome attention, drove through the back roads to Stacey's cabin. Once there, he checked her cottage and then dropped his precious cargo off and left again.

Stacey watched him leave, fear gathering as his taillights disappeared into the night. Her once cozy home seemed hostile. "You're imagining things," she chastised. Then, to keep her mind off Nathan, she double-checked to see that Cindy was sleeping comfortably on the trundle bed in the alcove off the living room. Once she assured herself that both child and dog were all right, she put on a pot of coffee and built a fire in the fireplace. While the coffee perked, she went upstairs, changed out of her dirty clothes and after a quick shower, she tugged on her nightgown and robe.

She glanced at the clock. Nathan had been gone half an hour. She turned on the TV and tried to watch the late movie, but couldn't keep her mind on the screen. With a sigh, she switched off the television and then paced restlessly waiting for Nathan's return. The minutes ticked by slowly and with each one, Stacey was certain Nathan had run into the two hoodlums.

"Quit borrowing trouble!" she told herself, as she looked in on Cindy for the fifth time and then went into the kitchen to pour herself a cup of coffee.

I'll kill them, he'd said, and Stacey believed that Nathan had meant it. If he ran into those two men again... Her heartbeat accelerated and her hands shook when she lifted the cup to her lips. What if Madison's thugs carried guns or knives? What if right now, just this minute, they were waiting for Nathan back at his cabin, ready to kill him?

"Don't do this to yourself, Stace," she cautioned, setting her mug on the counter and staring through the window over the sink. She could see the deserted beach and the ocean's white spray, stark against the black rolling sea. She turned out the lights and considered heading for bed.

The grandfather's clock chimed eleven times, and there was still no sign of him.

Nathan had been gone over an hour.

Stacey's heart thudded painfully. What if something had happened to him? What if he were lying dead on the beach? She glanced at the phone, considered calling the police and instead dropped onto the couch. The minutes ticked slowly by. Where was he?

NOT A SIGN of them. Not one bloody sign of the bastards! Nathan clenched his teeth together and cursed his luck. His blood chilled when he thought about overhearing their conversation and how casually they had talked about him, his daughter and Stacey.

He pounded an impotent fist against the steering wheel.

"Next time," he promised. If he hadn't been concerned for Stacey's safety, he might have confronted them. He was tired of running. But then his gut twisted when he remembered part of the conversation he'd overheard.

I've seen him with another girl—the kid's teacher. They're pretty cozy, if ya catch my drift...

Nathan parked the Jeep at his cabin and dropped his head against the steering wheel. He strained to listen for anything abnormal, but all he could hear were the wind and the sea, cars on the main road in the distance and the clicking noises of the Jeep's engine as it cooled.

"Damn, damn, damn," he muttered, leaning back against the seat. Unwittingly, he'd gotten Stacey involved in this fiasco with Robert Madison, and it was all about to blow up soon, very soon.

With dread climbing up his spine, he got out of the Jeep, locked it and started for the stairs.

He didn't hear them or see them until a blunt object connected with his skull and knocked him to the ground.

"Jesus Christ, man! What the hell did you do that for?" one man yelled to the other as Nathan stumbled forward, and his chin hit the hard ground.

In the bleary fog of his brain, Nathan looked up and felt a boot connect with his ribs, doubling him over. He lashed out with his foot, the effort causing fresh pain to sear through his body, but it was worth the effort. He managed to land a sharp blow to the young man's shins.

"Son of a bitch." The assailant lunged forward, but Nathan was ready and slammed a fist into the bearded jaw.

"Stop it!" the other goon roared.

The young man was jerked off him, and Nathan used that second to try and get to his feet. His head was swimming and he staggered a bit. Though the young hoodlum's arms were pinned backward, he managed to swing his foot and catch Nathan's jaw with his boot. Nathan reeled back, trying to retain consciousness.

"Where's the kid?" the young tough demanded.

"Damn it, man!" The gravelly voiced thug was furious with his younger counterpart. "I told you, he already put her off the island."

"No!"

"We checked the beach, the old lady's house and the

schoolteacher's place! He must've given the kid to the woman on the beach, the broad with the black hair!"

Nathan felt sick inside. He'd jeopardized everyone he cared about. His mouth was dry and he felt the urge to vomit, but when he wretched, nothing came up.

The younger man swore loudly, cursing Nathan, his bloody luck and the world in general. "He wouldn't send the kid away. I tell ya! He's a slimy bastard, and this is all just a trick."

"Sure he would; he'd get rid of the girl if he thought he could outfox Madison."

"So you're saying that the teacher and the old lady were just decoys?"

"Looks that way to me."

"Bah!"

The tall man with the uneven features had released the younger man, but the youth wasn't finished. He walked over to Nathan and kicked gravel in Nathan's face. Nathan sprang, lunging at the kid and forcing him to the ground. He got in two good punches before he felt an explosion at the back of his head and fell forward. The last thing he heard before losing consciousness was the young man swearing violently.

"If we've lost the kid, Madison will kill us."

The black hole of unconsciousness yawned and Nathan fell gratefully in.

HE AWOKE HOURS or minutes later, he couldn't tell which. He moved, stifled a groan of pain and slowly got to his knees. The world was spinning askew on its axis, but slowly Nathan was able to rise. His first instinct was to run to Stacey and see that Cindy was safe.

Instead, he stumbled up the two steps to his cabin,

fumbled with his keys and went inside. Once there, he turned on several lights, cleaned and bandaged his wounds and fought the urge to use the phone. He looked at the clock. Twelve-thirty. Stacey would be out of her mind with worry.

Hang in there, he thought and for the first time he was grateful for her plucky, independent attitude and fighting spirit, the same attitude that had attracted him to her in the first place.

He didn't bother to draw the shades, hoping that any eyes watching would size up the situation and think he was turning in for the night. If Madison's thugs thought he'd already gotten Cindy off the island, so much the better.

He sipped some tea in the kitchen, hoping that his anxiety wasn't evident on his face, then he snapped off the lights and went into the bedroom. Carefully drawing the shade he went through the motions of getting into bed. He lay there listening to the sounds of the night, not hearing a thing, his head and ribs throbbing in pain.

After nearly an hour of sweating in the darkness, he slid off the bed, grabbed his shoes and crawled into the kitchen pantry before stealthily climbing the shelves to the tiny window. It creaked a bit and when he slid through and jumped, he landed with a quiet thump on the sandy ground. The jolt sent fire racing through his wounds, and he had to lean against the side of the cabin to catch his breath.

Then, quietly, he slunk through the shadows to the staircase. A glowing cigarette and the smell of smoke told him that he wasn't alone. He slid backward, through the contorted pine trees and followed an overgrown path that the kids used to climb down the cliff. Although steep and unpredictable, hidden partially by berry vines, the path was unguarded. Nathan stole down the slick, muddy trail until he hit the beach, and then he retraced his footsteps along the overhang of the cliff, careful not to let even his shadow betray him in the blue light from the flood lamps perched high on the rocky face.

STACEY OPENED THE door the minute she heard his footsteps on the back porch. She threw herself into his arms. "Thank God," she cried, grateful that he was alive. "I was so afraid..." she took one look at his bruises and cuts and felt sick. "Oh, God...what happened?"

"Shh." He held her close and stroked her hair while offering words of comfort that sounded hollow and false. "It's all right."

"Is it?" she asked, pulling her head away from his chest and staring into his eyes. She touched the cut on his chin and the bandage over his ribs.

"I hope so. God, I hope so."

"But you're hurt."

Nathan smiled. "Pardon the cliché, but you should see the other guys."

So the danger that he had feared was real after all. Stacey realized that all too soon he would be gone. "What're you going to do?"

"Leave the island," he said flatly, while staring into her round, innocent eyes. "Where's Cindy?"

Stacey felt like dying. He was leaving. He'd never be back. It would be as if Nathan and Cindy hadn't been a part of her life. Her only memory would be the painful hole in her heart.

"She's asleep. In the back bedroom." Leading him down the short hallway off the living room, Stacey opened the door to the alcove. Cindy was sleeping peacefully, oblivious to all of her father's fears as she lay on the small daybed.

After Nathan was assured that his daughter was safe, he double-checked all the rooms to make sure that the doors and windows were locked and the shades were drawn.

"So it's not over," Stacey said, tracking his movements.

"Not yet."

Desperation began to claw at her. "When?"

"Soon, I hope," he said, as he returned to the living room and accepted the steaming cup of coffee Stacey offered him. He took a sip and felt the warm liquid slide down his throat. "What's this got in it?"

"Brandy."

"You thought I might need a drink?"

"No, I *knew* that *I* did. From the looks of it, you could use something stronger than coffee." She took a long swallow of the hot brew and hoped it would warm the cold empty feeling deep in the pit of her stomach. "I take it you found Madison's hoods."

"They found me. They were waiting at my cabin." His lips twisted into a deep frown. "Next time it'll be different."

"*Next time!* You're not seriously thinking of trying to catch up to them again?" Her worried eyes skimmed his body, taking in the blue bruises on his ribs and abdomen, the white swatch of gauze over his tanned skin and the deep cut on his chin.

"Not tonight."

"Never, I would hope!" She touched him lightly on

the shoulder. "I care about you, you know. I think I like you much better healthy than bruised and beaten."

"Not any more than I do, believe me."

She did. Staring into her cup, she let out a long sigh. "Maybe you'd better explain everything to me," she suggested, taking a seat in the corner of the couch and staring at the blood-red embers.

"Are you sure you want to know?"

"Yes." Her silver-green eyes didn't flinch. "Everything."

He slid his jaw to one side, contemplating the consequences of confiding in her. "You know that I have to leave the island," he said wearily, dropping to the hearth. "It's dangerous for Cindy here, and now they know about you."

"I guess that much is obvious," she said, cringing at the sight of his swollen jaw. "You should see a doctor."

"I will. Later. When I'm sure I've lost them."

There was no point in arguing with him. From the glint of determination in his eyes, it was obvious that his mind was made up. "Okay, so who are they?"

"Madison and his creeps." He scowled into his cup. "He won't give up until he finds Cindy. And he has, although I think the goons believe that Cindy is with Barbara. But that's only temporary."

As the thought struck him, he walked to the phone and dialed a long-distance number. *Barbara again.* Stacey tried to ignore the pang of jealousy that cut through her every time she thought about the raven-haired woman.

After a few seconds, Nathan got through. He told Barbara everything he'd told Stacey and concluded the conversation quickly, telling Barbara that he'd call her again in a few days, once he'd established himself elsewhere.

Stacey was numb with the thought of a future without him. When he hung up, she managed a forced smile. "You didn't tell her that you were in a fight," Stacey pointed out.

"She'd worry."

She eyed his recent injuries. "With good reason!" Looking away, she tried to hide her tears. "So you're really leaving," she whispered.

"Yes."

"Will you be back?" Her throat stuck on the words.

"I hope so."

Her teeth sunk into her lower lip. "How long do you think you can keep on running?"

"As long as it takes."

"Until?"

"Until Barbara can get enough evidence together to get Madison off my back. For good."

Stacey rimmed her cup with her finger. "What kind of evidence?"

He leaned back and rested his head against the bricks, looking upward at the rafters over the loft. "I know he's a crook; he swindles people out of their life's savings for investments he dreams up. Investments that never pan out."

"But he stays within the law."

"Technically—at least as far as we know. But I think he's into bigger things, smuggling for one. Maybe drugs."

"I don't understand. What would a criminal want with a four-year-old child?"

"I told you: her inheritance. But there's more to it

than that," he admitted, his dark brows drawing together. "Robert Madison thinks Cindy is his daughter."

"What?" Stacey nearly dropped her cup.

Nathan's blue eyes held hers. "There's a lot you don't know about me, Stacey," he said. "I thought that by keeping things from you, I could protect you, keep you safe."

"And in the dark."

Wearily, he lifted one shoulder. "Yes." He rubbed his hand over the tired muscles in his neck and then swiped at his beard-darkened jaw, wincing as his fingers came in contact with the jagged cut. "Cindy's mother—"

"Jennifer?"

His eyes narrowed and his lips thinned. "Jennifer," he repeated.

Seeing the hostility in his gaze, Stacey said, "I'm just trying to keep it all straight. It's a little confusing."

"I suppose it is," he agreed, drinking a swallow of his coffee and hoping that the brandy would help deaden the pain in his head and abdomen. "Anyway, when I knew Jennifer, she was a beautiful and wealthy young woman. We met at an art show and hit it off. We were very close, but we never married."

Stacey bit her lip. "You mean you had an affair with her?"

"A very brief, but passionate fling," he admitted.

Stacey's stomach knotted painfully. So Cindy was a "love child," just as Stacey had been. "And Jennifer got pregnant."

"I didn't know it at the time," Nathan said, his knuckles whitening around the cup. "She didn't tell me. She also didn't bother to mention that she was married. To Robert Madison."

"Oh, no..."

"When I found out that I'd been involved with a married woman, I confronted Jennifer and cut it off. That's when I took off. Until that time, I'd been living around L.A., but—" he shrugged his shoulders and sighed "—I had to leave. I went to the East Coast for a while, then the Caribbean Islands and Mexico." He ran his fingers in his hair and stared at her. "After a few years, I went back to L.A. She heard about it from a mutual friend. I wouldn't have anything to do with her, but she finally caught up with me. She told me that I had a daughter, that I'd fathered a child. I didn't believe her, of course."

"Of course," Stacey whispered, her throat dry. "So what changed your mind?"

"She did, eventually. She swore that Madison beat her and had even threatened Cindy." Nathan's eyes grew cold and distant. The cords in his neck protruded. "I still didn't want to believe her, but she showed me scars from a fractured rib and a broken wrist, bruises on her abdomen."

"Oh, dear God," Stacey murmured, feeling the bile rise in her throat.

"I wanted Jennifer to see a psychologist and a lawyer and get away from Madison."

"And she wouldn't?"

"She was scared stiff. Paranoid. She claimed that if she left him, he'd come after her and find her, hurt Cindy."

"But if Jennifer was a wealthy woman, certainly she could have gotten away from him. Didn't she have a family that would take her in?"

"I don't know. She said that her family wouldn't believe her, that she'd tried to tell her father what had happened and he'd told her she was imagining everything.

Jennifer had always been…whimsical, I guess you'd say. And her father thought that her marriage to Robert Madison was the best thing she'd ever done. Madison had social position and money—at least that's what Jennifer's father and the rest of L.A. believed."

"So you helped her."

"Yes." He found the liquor bottle himself and added more to his cup, not bothering with the coffee. "Even though I didn't believe that Cindy was my daughter, I felt that I owed Jennifer something. She was hysterical and adamant that the baby was mine. She even had proof of her husband's vasectomy, a bill from a doctor from five years earlier."

"And you didn't believe her?"

"I still had a lot of trouble believing that I was a father. We talked all night, and I finally convinced her to file a complaint against Madison. She promised that she would, if I would keep Cindy for a few days, just until she had managed to move out of Madison's house. She said she'd tell Madison that Cindy was spending the weekend with a friend."

"And you agreed?"

"I didn't want to take care of Cindy. It sounded like trouble—big legal trouble, the kind I didn't need complicating my life. But when I suggested she take her daughter to a friend, she claimed she didn't have any friends that wouldn't call Madison immediately. She was scared out of her mind. Robert Madison was a powerful businessman in L.A. According to Jennifer, he could buy any judge or policeman in the city."

Stacey listened in stony silence, silently sipping the remains of her coffee and feeling colder as he spoke.

"When I told her I wouldn't take Cindy, Jennifer

broke down and pleaded with me, begged for her child's life, claimed the girl would only be safe with me as her real father. It was only to be temporary, just until Jennifer could find a reputable attorney who would help her file for divorce and assure her of full custody."

Nathan felt his throat grow thick. In his mind's eye, he could still see Jennifer's round, brown eyes, reddened with tears, her makeup running in black rivulets down her skin. She had looked like hell. Her usually shiny and combed hair had been unkempt and dull. There had been blue circles under her eyes as she had begged Nathan to take care of his child. Shaking her image from his mind had always been difficult, but Stacey made it easier.

He cleared his throat with a long swallow of brandy. "I told her I wanted to confront Madison myself, but Jennifer fell to pieces. I was her only hope, she claimed, to get away from Madison. And I had to remain anonymous. Because of the vasectomy, Madison knew that Jennifer had been unfaithful and that her lover had fathered Cindy. But Jennifer swore that she'd never told him my name."

Stacey saw the anger clouding his eyes. "Certainly you didn't have it out with him!"

"No. Stupid as Jennifer's plan had been, I'd gone along with it because Jennifer had managed to convince me that Madison might hurt the child."

"So you kept Cindy."

"It was only to be temporary, and I'd already planned a personal vendetta against Madison."

"But you never got the chance."

Nathan's jaw hardened. "No. On the way back to Bel Air, Jennifer's car slid over an embankment. I never knew if she had confronted Madison or not. The death was ruled an accident."

Stacey shuddered. "Is that what you think?"

"I don't know. It was all too coincidental."

"You think someone killed Jennifer?" Horrified, she stared at him.

"Or she took her own life to save Cindy."

"And you wouldn't turn Cindy over to Madison."

His eyes darkened. "No. That's when I became a fugitive, so to speak. I did hire a lawyer to start paternity proceedings and Madison was informed. He insisted that Cindy be returned to him. He denied having a vasectomy and claimed that I was just after Cindy's inheritance."

"So why hasn't Madison contacted the police?"

Nathan smiled grimly. "Why indeed?"

Reading the message in his eyes, she shivered. "Because he doesn't have a leg to stand on?"

"I think he's afraid of all the bad press. I'm convinced that he's involved in some touchy business dealings, 'investments' in stolen gems, and he can't afford a scandal. He has friends on the police force, but even they would abandon him if it could be proven that he's as crooked as I think he is. And, he knows that if he goes to the press, I'll fight him tooth and nail."

"So it would be much neater for Madison to kidnap his own daughter."

"My daughter!" His shoulders hunched and then relaxed. "Yes, technically you're right, as Madison is her legal guardian. The easiest thing for him to do would be to take her from me. And there's nothing I can do."

Stacey cleared her throat and stared straight into his eyes. "And what if it can be proven that Cindy isn't your daughter, that Jennifer lied to you?"

His nostrils flared. "It doesn't matter."

"Except that you would be a kidnapper."

"Jennifer didn't lie about being abused," he said, clenching his jaw as he remembered Jennifer's scars. "I'll do anything to keep Madison away from the child."

"But there are social service agencies—"

"And I can't trust them. Not with Cindy's life." He glared at her for an uneasy moment. "Would you?"

She didn't hesitate. "Of course not. So that's why you stole your own daughter," Stacey said, shaking her head at the complexity of the problem.

"That's right. And I'd do it again. There isn't anything, *anything*, I wouldn't do to keep her safe."

"So that's where Barbara comes in," Stacey guessed.

"Barbara is a private investigator in L.A. She's working with the district attorney and trying to dig up the dirt on Madison. Dirt with conclusive evidence that Robert Madison is a smuggling, swindling wife beater who isn't fit to raise a child." He finished his brandy and set the cup on the mantel before turning to look at her. "That's why Barbara and I pretend to be lovers; it's her cover. She's really working very quietly with the D.A. so that none of Madison's informants on the force find out and report to Madison."

"But isn't he suspicious?"

He snorted. "The man was born that way. However, since Barbara and I...were...romantically involved several years ago, it doesn't look so much like a setup."

"I see," Stacey murmured, her heart still aching as she stared at the Persian rug lying over the hardwood floor.

"Stacey—"

"Yes?"

He walked across the short distance to the couch and sat next to her, his hands gently caressing her hair. "If you love me, you'll trust me and help me."

She swallowed and looked into the intensity of his indigo eyes. Honesty and pain were reflected in his gaze. "I do," she whispered. "But it scares me to death!"

"Me, too," he admitted, releasing a sigh and drawing her close. His lips pressed against her, and she had to close her eyes against the fires igniting deep within her. When he groaned and his arms tightened around her, she kissed him back with all the passion and desperation filling her soul. She didn't object when his lips lingered on hers before slowly moving down her cheek and neck to the hollow of her throat. She felt his fingers working with the knot of the tie securing her robe. When the knot was undone, her robe gaped open and Nathan kissed the white rise of her breast.

She tingled and held him against her, savoring the feel of his lips against her skin. She kissed his vital dark hair and cradled him close to her breast. The need to comfort and please him was as consuming as her love.

When he lifted her from the couch, she buried her head against his neck, drinking in the sight, smell and touch of him. Soon he would be gone, perhaps forever. She fought the tears of desperation that threatened to spill as he carried her up the stairs to her loft.

When he lay her on the bed, she lifted her arms to him. Tonight, whether it was the first of many nights, or their very last together, she would lose herself to him completely.

THE HOURS PASSED too quickly and the early light of dawn slipped through the curtains to color the room a pale shade of gray.

Stacey stretched, snuggled against the warm body lying next to hers, and then opened her eyes to stare into Nathan's blue gaze. Yawning, she stretched again and smiled. "How long have you been staring at me?"

"All night."

She laughed a little. "Be serious."

"I am." His mouth lifted at the corners, and white teeth flashed against his dark skin as he trailed a finger lazily down her neck to the swell of her breast.

Stacey felt the familiar desire begin to fill her blood and course through her body.

"In a minute you'll get to see just how serious I am."

"You're wicked," she teased, sobering a little when she saw the red, angry cut grazing his chin.

"Only with you, love. Only with you." Then his lips captured hers in a kiss that stole the breath from her lungs. She responded immediately, joyous in the feel of his hands against her breasts, her thighs and hips.

From the darkest corner of her mind came the unpleasant thought that she should protect herself from him and what he was doing to her, but Stacey didn't listen. Instead, she let her fingers slide down the lean muscles of Nathan's chest and abdomen, wondering at the pleasure touching him could bring. She paused when she encountered the stiff piece of gauze surrounding his bruised ribs. Starkly reminded of the danger he lived with, she wanted to throw her body over his and protect him.

You love him too much, the small voice nagged.

Never, she replied silently. *I can never love this one man too much.*

THE BACON WAS sizzling in the pan by the time that Cindy, her blond hair wild, one fist rubbing an eye, stumbled out of the alcove. "Daddy?" she called, a little frightened.

"Right here, pumpkin!"

Nathan scooped her up and planted a kiss on her cheek. The puppy jumped and whined against his leg. "About time you went out, isn't it?" Nathan said, looking through the window before opening the front door and doing a quick search of the yard. Aside from the threatening storm, nothing seemed out of the ordinary. It was still early. Not quite six. With any luck, Madison's men had a habit of sleeping late.

"Where are we?" Cindy asked, blinking her eyes.

"This is Stacey, er, Miss Monroe's house."

Cindy frowned. "I want to go home," she complained.

"Not until after breakfast," Stacey said with a smile. She was standing in the archway between the living room and the kitchen and invited father and daughter to the table. "I've spent the entire morning making pancakes." To prove her point, she held up the spatula for Cindy to see.

The child brightened a little. "Then we go home?" Questioning blue eyes looked up at her father.

"Soon," he replied vaguely. He placed her in a chair near a plate with a stack of three pancakes. "Now what do you want? Strawberry jam? Or peach? Or grape?"

"Syrup."

"Sorry," Stacey said with an apologetic grin. "Mrs. Chambers doesn't make syrup and I don't have any. So we'll have to rough it."

"I want cold cereal—"

"This'll be fine," Nathan insisted quietly, spreading the strawberry jam on the pancakes and shooting a quick glance at Stacey, begging her indulgence.

Cindy looked up at her father and really saw him for the first time. "What happened?" she asked, her blue eyes rounding at the sight of the scarred chin.

"Nothing much."

Cindy stared at Nathan's face. "Bad cut," she said.

"You probably could use a few stitches," Stacey agreed, but the look Nathan gave her made her keep silent.

"Eat up," Nathan instructed his daughter. "Today, we're going on a boat ride."

Stacey felt her insides wrench.

"Where?" Cindy asked.

"Someplace fun."

"Good. Is Miss Monroe coming, too?" Cindy asked.

"Not this time, sweetheart," Stacey heard herself saying while avoiding Nathan's probing gaze.

"Mrs. McIver will come with us," Nathan said.

"What about Attila?"

Nathan set aside his fork. "I think Stacey will take care of him for us. Okay?"

"No!" Cindy protested.

Stacey placed a platter of bacon on the table and took the seat next to Nathan's. It was all she could do to smile. "I'll take good care of him."

"You said I could keep him," Cindy said, looking from Nathan to Stacey and back again. "He's mine!"

"It's only for a few days," Nathan said, and Stacey stared at him, silently accusing him of the lie. "Come on, now, let's eat. Mrs. McIver is meeting us at the docks in less than half an hour."

Despite Cindy's protests, she dug into the pancakes, and the tension between Nathan and Stacey grew. The meal passed quietly and afterward, Stacey fed her uneaten breakfast to the hungry pup.

"You go get dressed," Nathan urged Cindy while following Stacey onto the back porch. Stacey sat on the railing and stared at the ocean, trying not to think of the fact that she'd probably never see Nathan again.

"You know that I can't let Cindy stay on the island any longer," he said at length, feeling the need to apologize and explain. "It's not safe."

"I know."

"It's best, Stacey." The wind pushed her hair out of her face as it blew in from the ocean. Storm clouds had gathered in the sky.

"Or easier."

"What's that supposed to mean?"

"Nothing. I know you have to go and take Cindy with you," she admitted, her voice faltering. "But I can't help being selfish and wanting you to stay. Now that Cindy's enrolled at Oceancrest and making incredible progress..." *And I love you both so dearly I can't let you go.*

The furrow between Nathan's brow deepened. "I don't want to leave, you know that. But I have to. To protect all of us."

"You can't run forever."

His eyes glittered defensively. "Believe me, I have no intention of running."

"But don't you see, that's exactly what you're doing. And how do you think it affects Cindy? She's a child, a small four-year-old child who's been through more than her share of emotional upheavals. She needs to stay."

"Not with Madison on our tails!"

"You don't have to get angry," she said, feeling defensive. "I think you should work through the legal system instead of against it. Life as a fugitive is no good for you or your daughter."

"I know that."

"Do you?"

"Of course."

"Then why did you bother to ask my opinion in the first place? You came here hell-bent that I get Cindy into Oceancrest, and I did. As a matter of fact, I've tried damned hard to help Cindy and she's done wonderfully. But all that time and effort will be for naught the minute you take her away, pull up her roots, run with her while looking constantly over your shoulder."

He began to pace along the porch. "I know you're right," he admitted reluctantly. "And, if it makes you feel any better, Barbara is already working with a lawyer to set the wheels of justice, rusty though they may be, in motion."

"That's a start."

"Barely." He pushed his hands into the back pockets of his jeans and then sighed as he stared out to sea. The circles under his eyes were deep, and the stubble along his chin seemed to emphasize how tired he really was. He slapped the railing and then approached Stacey. "I've got to go."

"Where?"

"I don't know yet."

"I'll come with you," she whispered, and Nathan felt as if his heart would break.

"I'd like that, Stacey," he whispered against her hair. "But it's safer for everyone concerned if you stay here on the island. Besides, you have your work with the children."

And nothing is important anymore if I don't have you.

"Act as if everything is normal." His fingers wrapped around her forearms, and he forced a smile through tight lips as he looked down at her.

She felt the tears, but refused to cry. Not yet. "I don't know if that's possible."

"We'll be back."

"When?" she whispered, tearing her eyes away from him to watch a lonely sea gull dip and swoop over the pewter-colored sea.

"I don't know."

"I'll miss you," she whispered and he pulled her close, embraced her as if he would never let go.

"And I'll miss you."

A premonition of doom slid down her spine and she shivered.

"Everything will work out," he said, kissing her crown and smelling the sweet scent of her windblown hair.

"Promise?" she choked, clearing her throat and sniffing as his breath whispered through her hair and his arms wrapped possessively around her.

"Promise."

Then the dam broke. All the tears that she had fought for days spilled from her eyes as she thought about the bleak days ahead. Knowing in her heart that she might never see him again, she sobbed against his shoulder until Cindy came onto the back porch and it was time for them to leave.

CHAPTER NINE

STACEY HAD BEEN brooding about Nathan and Cindy for nearly two weeks, ever since she'd left them on the docks and had waved frantically to the small boat as it had headed out to the open sea before rounding the tip of the island and turning inland.

Tears standing in her eyes, she'd stood on the dock while holding an umbrella against the buffeting wind and rain. With a wet and bedraggled puppy at her side, she'd waved to the disappearing boat until it was out of sight.

"I guess it's just you and me," she'd confided to the puppy, tugging on the leash and heading for her lonely, empty cabin.

Two weeks later, she was as morose as she had been on the day Nathan, Cindy and a worried Geneva McIver had sped away from Sanctity Island. All the vibrant colors in her life seemed to have faded, and her thoughts kept straying to the few short hours of happiness she'd shared with Nathan.

"Quit it," she told herself angrily on a Friday afternoon after the students had gone home for the weekend. She'd managed to make it through another lonely day, and she was in the process of cleaning up the last scraps of paper from the Halloween art projects when Margaret burst into the room. There were thunderclouds brewing behind Margaret's silver glasses, a stiff white piece of paper and a rolled newspaper clenched in her thin hands. There was a cynical turn to her lips and a glint of hostile determination in her eyes. Margaret Woodward looked positively ready to kill.

"Hi," Stacey said with a tentative smile. "Bad day?"

Margaret didn't bother with formalities. Her lips were pinched together to the point that all of her wrinkles bunched around them. "You're not going to want to hear this, Stacey, but I can't see any reason to hide it from you."

"Hide what?"

"This!" She handed a formal looking letter to Stacey, wrapped her arms and newspaper under her chest and stood waiting, tapping her foot while Stacey looked at the letter.

"What is it? Oh." Stacey's shoulders slumped a little.

The letter was from Dr. Lindstrom in Fairbanks. Included with a note of introduction was Lindstrom's case history of Cindy Sloan. Stacey had to sit back down in her chair to read Dr. Lindstrom's opinion that Cindy's mental condition was the direct result of psychological abuse from some member of her family, most likely the child's father.

"But not Nathan," she protested.

"That's not all," Margaret interrupted, brandishing the newspaper like a sword and offering Stacey a grim smile. She slapped a copy of the *L.A. Times* on the desk. It was opened to page eight. The article in the upper right-hand corner was devoted to a man's search for his kidnapped child. The man was Robert Madison. The child, Madison's daughter, Cindy. The man suspected of taking the little girl was Nathan Sloan.

"Dear God. Where did you get this?" Stacey asked, stunned.

"I used to live in L.A.; I still get the paper, even though it's usually a week late."

Stacey glanced at the date and confirmed Margaret's story. *Oh Nathan, where are you?* "I know about this," she said calmly. "I'm just surprised it's gone public —"

"You knew about it! And you didn't bother to tell me?" Margaret brushed her hands on her Pendleton skirt and leaned her hip against the desk. "Maybe you want to tell me about it now," she suggested. "Considering that the reputation of the school is at stake."

Just like before, with Daniel Brown! Stacey pinched the bridge of her nose and tried to think straight. "Yes, I think you'd better know. But it's complicated, and something must have happened for Madison to go to the newspapers."

"I've got all day," Margaret said softly.

"It's private; you can't go to the authorities."

Margaret frowned but nodded curtly. "I'm all ears." Folding her arms under her chest she observed Stacey and noted, not for the first time, the dark circles under her eyes and the pale color of her cheeks. Nathan Sloan had really done a number on her. Margaret's fury with the man was white-hot, though she did suffer a twinge of conscience when she remembered that she'd encouraged Stacey to go out with him.

"I knew something wasn't right from the beginning," Stacey admitted. "From the first day I met Nathan and Cindy on the beach, I sensed that there was some secret he was hiding from me. But he didn't confide in me until just before he left the island…"

It took over half an hour to tell Nathan's side of the

story. When she was finished, Stacey could read the doubtful glint in Margaret's wise eyes.

"I can't believe you actually bought a story like that," the older woman finally said with a sigh as she took off her glasses and wiped them on the hem of her jacket.

"It's the truth," Stacey said staunchly.

Margaret shook her graying head. "Too many holes to suit me. Why didn't he tell us the truth when he enrolled his daughter?"

"He couldn't. He was afraid Madison would find her, take her back. Nathan's working with the L.A. district attorney through a private investigator."

"He didn't have to worry about Oceancrest; we keep everything confidential here."

"He was afraid for Cindy's life—"

"Or afraid of getting caught? Even if Nathan Sloan's story were authentic, he should have known that Robert Madison wouldn't hurt the child. If Madison harmed Cindy, it would only make Sloan's story look more genuine."

"And then it would be too late. It wasn't a risk he could take," Stacey said defensively.

Margaret pursed her lips, but her kindly gaze softened as she looked at Stacey. "Look, Stace, you're taking a lot on face value, aren't you? How do you know that Sloan is Cindy's father? Because Madison had a vasectomy while he was married to Jennifer Reaves doesn't prove that he couldn't have fathered Cindy. For heaven's sake, you know as well as I do that it's possible to have a reverse vasectomy. Then there are the vasectomies that don't take or aren't reliable."

Stacey refused to waver. "Then why would Jennifer have come to Nathan?"

"Maybe she didn't. After all, you've only heard his side of the story."

"But the rest of it is true. Look, here," she pointed to a paragraph in the *Times*. It says that Jennifer Madison was killed in a single car accident in Laurel Canyon! Exactly what Nathan said."

"Except that he told you her name was Jennifer Reaves."

Stacey let out a sound of disgust.

"Stacey, listen. I'm sure that Sloan is clever enough to blend the truth with the lies."

"He's not lying!"

Margaret sighed. "I'm not condemning him, but the point is we both know that he deceived us. The question is, how much." When Stacey started to protest, Margaret lifted her hand and continued speaking. "Hear me out. It was obvious to me that he cared very much for Cindy. And, I, too, have trouble thinking that he was the brutal parent Dr. Lindstrom mentioned in his letter. But, really, what do we know about him? Only what he let us know."

"He loves Cindy," Stacey said staunchly.

"I'm not arguing with that. I'm not even arguing against the fact that he might be Cindy's biological father. God only knows that even if Robert Madison weren't the girl's father, any number of men might have been. That Jennifer Reaves, er, Jennifer Madison had an affair with Sloan or half a dozen men, any of whom might be Cindy's biological father, isn't the issue."

"Then what is?"

"The fact that he misrepresented himself to us," Margaret said. "Legally, Robert Madison is Cindy's father. He was married to Jennifer Reaves when she gave birth, right?"

"I think so."

"Then, according to the law, Cindy is his responsibility and Nathan Sloan is a kidnapper."

"But Madison was a wife beater! God only knows what he might do to Cindy!" Stacey was shaking with rage and impotence. Her hazel eyes gleamed in anger. "Can we sit back and let him hurt her?"

The color drained from Margaret's lined face. "Of course not! I'm only suggesting that Mr. Sloan should have stayed in L.A. and battled for Cindy through the courts. He should have gone to the police and the social services people!"

"He claims he wouldn't have a chance. Robert Madison is so powerful that he owns the police department."

"The Los Angeles police department? I find that hard to believe. Despite what you see in the movies, most police departments are honest."

"Nathan's trying to build a case against Madison, and he'll do it. He's already got the D.A., a private investigator and an attorney in L.A. on his side," Stacey said, though she felt defenseless. Margaret had quietly destroyed every argument. The fact that Stacey hadn't heard from Nathan since he'd left only reinforced Margaret's suspicions. Maybe he'd lied to her and then skipped out on her.

I don't believe it, she thought miserably, *I don't believe that Nathan would leave me high and dry without a word.*

"I know this is hard for you to accept," Margaret said quietly, taking Stacey's hand and dropping it before turning toward the door.

"I don't think I ever will."

Margaret sighed. "If it's any consolation, I hope

you're right about Sloan and wrong about Madison. For Cindy's sake, I hope the two men are battling for her because of love."

"One of them is," Stacey said.

"I just hope it all works out," Margaret murmured as she walked out of the room and closed the door softly behind her.

It will, Stacey swore to herself. *It has to!*

ANOTHER WEEK PASSED without a word from Nathan. Margaret went out of her way to be kind to Stacey, and she responded by trying to bury herself in her work and thinking about anything other than Nathan. It was an impossible task. Nathan's image was with her everywhere. She couldn't shake it off. She saw him on the beach, in her cabin, and at the school. When she wasn't thinking about Nathan, her mind would wander to Cindy. Where had Nathan taken the child? How was she doing? Had she withdrawn again?

It didn't help that Nathan, over Cindy's very loud protests, had left Attila with Stacey and the puppy whined all day while Stacey was at school.

"Come on, let's go for a walk," Stacey said as she went home a week after the confrontation with Margaret. "It's Friday and we both need a break. What do ya say?" The puppy wagged his fluffy tail, shaking his entire rear end as Stacey snapped on the leash. Eagerly, Attila led her out the door and down the stairs to the beach.

Once on the sand, Stacey removed the dog's leash and let the puppy run in crazy circles down to the water. She played tag with the dog, tried not to think about Cindy and ended up at the far staircase, climbing the weathered steps leading to Nathan's cabin. It looked just as he'd left it, and all of the doors were locked. The battered Jeep sat unattended in the drive. Nearly a week's worth of newspapers had piled up on the porch.

"Looks like he's gone for good," Stacey confided to the small dog. The numbing ache in her heart wouldn't subside. "Maybe Margaret was right."

She walked around back and noticed the fishing pole propped against the house and the pile of cut wood with a tarp spread haphazardly over it. "It's almost as if I imagined the whole thing," Stacey said to the dog as she snapped the leash onto the puppy's collar. "If it weren't for you, I'd almost believe that I'd never met Nathan and Cindy."

On impulse, Stacey walked next door to Geneva Mc-Iver's small house. She knocked loudly and was surprised when the door was opened almost immediately.

"Stacey!" the older woman said. "Come in, come in." She whisked Stacey, puppy and all, into the house. "I thought about calling you, but…" Feeling awkward, Geneva motioned to one of the velvet rockers near the bay window. "How about a cup of tea?"

"I'd love one," Stacey admitted, sitting on the edge of the chair. She was stunned to find the elderly woman at home. Stacey hadn't expected to see anyone connected with Nathan.

"Here you go," Geneva said, her already pink cheeks coloring slightly as she handed Stacey a cup of orange-spice tea.

"How long have you been back?" Stacey asked.

"About three days, and oh, how I wanted to call you." The bright blue eyes begged for Stacey to understand.

"But Nathan asked you not to?"

"He was adamant on the subject," Geneva admitted.

"All this business about his little girl; he's positively sick with worry about her."

Stacey's fingers shook. She had to set the fragile china cup on a nearby table. "Is Cindy okay?"

The older woman's lips pursed. "That depends on what you mean, I suppose. Oh, she's healthy all right." Mrs. McIver's mouth curved when she thought about the child. "Eats like a horse, you know. But…well, I guess you know she has some problems…"

"Emotional problems. She's withdrawn," Stacey urged.

"Yes. And she was getting so much better while she was here going to the school." The old shoulders lifted and sagged as Geneva took a sip of tea, "Now it's almost as if she had never made any progress at all."

Stacey's throat closed and she had trouble speaking. She took another sip of tea. "Where are they… Nathan and Cindy?" Stacey asked, holding her breath.

"I don't know."

Stacey's heart sank.

"We were on Whidbey island; that's where we met Barbara. Nathan, Barbara and Cindy were going on. I don't know where."

Dying a little inside, Stacey asked, "L.A.?"

"I don't think so." Geneva thought for a moment and scratched behind her right ear. "I'm sorry, I just don't know. And Mr. Sloan—well, he didn't want me talkin' to you, said you'd worry and be in some sort of danger from those toughs who beat him up."

"I don't think they'll bother me," Stacey said, pursing her lips. After two weeks of looking over her shoulder, expecting to run into Madison's goons, she was through with worrying about her own safety. "Did Nathan tell you when he'd be back?"

"That's hard to say." She looked straight at Stacey and shook her head. "I think he might not be coming back to the island, at least not permanently. He talked a little about selling the cabin."

The bottom dropped out of Stacey's world. "You're sure about that?"

"Yes. He asked me to check with several real estate agents in town, said he'd be calling one of them by the end of the week."

"I see," Stacey whispered, setting her cup on the mahogany table and rising. "Thank you for the tea."

Geneva stood as well and nervously rubbed her hands together. "Not that it's worth anything, but I'm going to give you my opinion on something."

Bracing herself for the worst, Stacey nodded and smiled at the anxious woman. "I'd... I'd like that."

"I've spent a good deal of time with Nathan Sloan and his daughter, and if you ask me, they're both pining away and miserable without you."

"I doubt that."

The old eyebrows raised. "I've seen a lot in my time, Stacey, and I recognize love when it stares me in the face. Nathan probably does, too. But he's afraid for your life."

"That's ridiculous."

"Told him that much myself," she admitted with a snort, "but then, he doesn't listen to too many people."

"I'd noticed," Stacey murmured.

"He's a good man, Stacey, but you might have to convince him that you're strong enough to be at his side, no matter what."

"I tried that," Stacey admitted, disgusted with herself for blushing when she thought of all the times she'd thrown herself at Nathan.

"Then you'll have to try a little harder, won't you? The man's stubborn, damned stubborn," she said, clenching a thin fist and realizing what she'd said. "Pardon my French."

Stacey grinned. "I know what you mean."

"Good. Then you'll have to let him know how you feel and get him to face his own feelings."

"If I get the chance."

"He'll be back," the older woman said smugly. "I don't know when. But you can't sell a house without the owner's signature, now, can you?"

Stacey visibly brightened. "I guess not." She turned to the door, but paused. "How did you know that I care about Nathan?"

"Simple." The older woman laughed. "You're suffering from the same symptoms he is."

THE NEXT FEW days were easier. Stacey kept replaying Geneva's encouraging words in her mind, and her heart soared on gilded wings. Her hope was short-lived, however. The next day she thought she recognized one of Robert Madison's hoodlums on the docks in the late afternoon. All of her hopes died. Nathan wouldn't return, he couldn't chance it. Cindy's safety was on the line.

From a telephone booth that she pretended to use, Stacey watched the young man standing on the dock near the moorage where Nathan had housed his boat. The man was short and lean with blond hair and a scraggly attempt at a beard. He paced restlessly on the dock, alternately drawing on a cigarette and staring through the drizzle at the open sea.

"You're getting paranoid," she told herself. After all, she'd never really seen Robert Madison's thugs. Not in the daylight. Because this twenty-year-old man was hard looking and smoked was no reason to convict him.

But he's hanging around the moorage, where Nathan's boat was docked. "Hardly a crime," she told herself, but as she watched, another man approached the thug. Stacey's heart stuck in her throat. The new arrival was a taller, older man with uneven features and a surly smile.

A prickle of fear raised the hairs on the back of her neck as the two men huddled against the rain and conversed quietly to each other. No longer did she have any doubt that they were Robert Madison's thugs.

Stacey hung up the receiver that had been beeping in her ear and hurried away from the phone booth. By the time she got home, she was shaking from head to foot, cold from the rain and her own fear.

For the next two days she was cautious, afraid that she might bump into the men when she least expected it. But so far she'd been lucky and the week had passed uneventfully.

Missing Nathan had become a part of her daily routine and when Margaret tried to comfort her on the day after Halloween, Stacey had forced a bright smile and said, cheerfully, that she was over him.

"You're a rotten liar," she'd accused herself hours later when she kicked off her boots and placed them at the end of her bed, the bed she had fleetingly shared with Nathan. "And both you and Margaret know it." She ran a finger along the small stitches on the quilt her grandmother had made for her when Stacey had been a child. At that moment she missed her grandmother terribly, though the woman had been dead for nearly twelve years. Her thoughts returned to the hours she'd spent at the school and her flippant declaration that she'd gotten Nathan out of her system. With a sigh, she told herself, "Margaret and the rest of the faculty know you're hung up on the guy."

Her loneliness was overwhelming. Trying to rise above her dejection, she went downstairs and poured herself a tall glass of Coke. "So here's to my lot in life: falling for the wrong men." She hoisted the glass in the air and smiled despite the teardrop that rolled lazily down her cheek.

Without really understanding her motives, she walked into the living room, curled up in the corner of the sofa and dialed her father. She heard the phone ring thousands of miles away. On the fourth ring, the call was answered by a tape of her father's voice. Stacey forced a cheery note into her own voice and told the recorder that she was just checking in and would call back in a couple of days.

"So much for turning to your family in your hour of need." She finished her drink and considered calling Margaret, but discarded the idea. Margaret was still convinced that Nathan Sloan had used Stacey and the school to his own advantage. Grudgingly, Stacey admitted that the older woman might be right.

"He should go to the police," Margaret had stated emphatically when Stacey had tried to defend Nathan. "That's what any law-abiding citizen would do." Since Margaret was echoing the sentiments that Stacey had voiced to Nathan earlier, she couldn't have disagreed.

"Damn the man anyway," she said as she returned to the kitchen, placed her glass in the sink and stared out the window at the black November night. Rain drizzled on the windows, and the wind howled through the rafters.

Beachcombing in the Indian summer sun and meeting a chubby curly-headed child and her blue-eyed father seemed to have happened centuries ago. "Oh, Nathan, where are you?" she wondered aloud.

Nearly an hour later, while half watching the television, Stacey noticed that Attila had perked up his ears. Soon he began to whine.

"Stop it," Stacey said, turning off the TV. "You're making me nervous." But the little dog jumped off the sofa and trotted into the kitchen, still whining and yapping. When Stacey heard the knock on the back door, she froze. Images of Robert Madison's two thugs leaped into her mind. "Get off it, Stace," she chided, walking into the kitchen. "You're imagining things." But she peered through the curtain before opening the door.

Nathan, shoulders huddled against the wind, stood on the back porch.

Stacey's heart skipped a beat, and she jerked open the door. Throwing herself into his open arms, she couldn't control the tears of relief that suddenly pooled in her eyes.

"I was afraid you weren't coming back," she whispered as he folded his arms around her and stepped into the kitchen.

"And miss out on a reception like this?" he asked, a weary grin slashing across his lean features. Still holding her, he kicked the door shut.

Stacey felt his arms tighten around her and tasted the rainwater on his skin. She'd forgotten how blue his eyes were, how they smoldered seductively when he gazed at her. "You didn't call or write or anything! I was out of my mind," she admitted, swiping at the tears and smiling through the drops that caught on her lashes.

"So was I."

"Oh, Nathan." She hugged him again and nearly sobbed with relief. "Where's Cindy?"

"With Barbara in Seattle."

"Seattle?"

"It's a long story."

"And I want to hear every word of it," she said, still clinging to him as if she were afraid he might disappear into thin air. "Oh, God, I've missed you!"

He was hugging her fiercely as he buried his face in her hair. "Thinking about you kept me going," he admitted, closing his eyes and lowering his head to taste her lips. They were as sweet and eager as he remembered, and he couldn't get enough of her. After three weeks of thinking about her, wondering about her, dreaming about her day and night, she was finally in his arms again.

His hands slid down her back to rest at the gentle curve of her waist as he pulled her against him. He had her buttocks pressed against the edge of the counter, his thighs fitting snugly to hers as his tongue slid past her parted lips to flick against the roof and sides of her mouth.

A radiating warmth uncoiled within her, leaving at its vortex an ache so violent she trembled with desire. His hands slid familiarly up her rib cage to capture the weight of her breast, and she sighed into his mouth.

Despite the weariness showing on his face, Nathan lifted her into his arms and carried her up the stairs to the loft. Once there, he tumbled with her onto the bed, moaning her name as his hands and mouth caressed her.

Honey-colored hair spilled onto the patchwork quilt to surround her face in a golden halo of shimmering silk. He looked down at her for several seconds while his fingers slowly released the buttons straining to hold her blouse together.

"I waited so long," she whispered, her voice quivering as the blouse parted and a ribbon of white skin contrasted against the blue fabric. He pushed the cloth aside, swallowing as he stared at the fullness of her breasts straining upward.

Bending forward, he kissed one nipple and watched as it puckered expectantly. "So have I," he whispered across the proud, dark point before claiming it with his lips. Then his hands unsnapped her pants and slowly pushed them over her hips.

She didn't hesitate to work on the buttons of his shirt before helping him remove his jeans. The warm, hard texture of his skin as it rubbed against her sent ripples of desire through her bloodstream. Her heartbeat accelerated, punctuated by her shallow breathing and Nathan's own moans of pleasure.

She gave herself to him completely, giving and taking of the intimate pleasure of his love. Unafraid, she moved with him, pressing her muscles against his, winding her fingers in his hair and shuddering in satisfaction when his explosion sent her rocketing to the heavens, shattering all thoughts of the past or future. Tonight, she was with the man she loved; they were safe and together. Nothing else mattered, she thought dreamily as she floated back to earth and held him close.

Moments later, while they still lay entwined, tears of happiness slid down her cheeks. She held onto him and placed her head over his chest, listening to the reassuring thud of his heart and feeling secure in his strong arms.

Nathan had returned to her as he'd promised, and Stacey smiled in contentment. She fell into a deep sleep knowing that he cared.

CHAPTER TEN

STACEY SMILED CONTENTEDLY as she watched Nathan sleep.

When he'd come into the cabin the night before, he'd looked as if he'd been to hell and back. His features had appeared leaner, more angular than she'd remembered. World weary, bone tired and filled with despair, he'd seemed ready to collapse.

But now, as he lay sleeping in her bed, his coffee-colored hair untidy against the pillow, the harsh planes of his face softened by slumber, he looked as innocent and carefree as a child.

"I do love you," she whispered, and was startled when he opened a striking blue eye and a smile crept from one side of his face to the other.

"I know." One of his arms settled comfortably over her waist, and his fingers played against the soft muscles of her lower back. "And I love you."

"You don't have to—"

He covered her protests with his mouth, and the kiss sent wave after wave of pleasure through her body.

"Wait a minute," she pleaded, gasping for air once he lifted his head from hers to gaze into her eyes.

"Why?"

"Why?" she repeated, trying to think beyond the fact

that his fingers were tracing erotic circles on her skin. "Because I want to find out about the past few weeks."

He grinned wickedly and his blue eyes gleamed. "Later," he promised, molding his mouth to hers and pulling her body to his. "Much later."

MUCH LATER CAME after a shower and breakfast. Nathan had spent nearly a half hour under the hot spray of the shower and then eaten as if he hadn't seen food for months. The sourdough biscuits, sausage, scrambled eggs and fresh grapefruit were devoured before he finally leaned back in his chair and cradled a cup of coffee in his hands.

"You're spoiling me," he accused.

"Wouldn't dream of it." Her hazel eyes sparkled merrily as she cleared the dishes from the table.

"Don't get me wrong, I'm not complaining."

She shot him an imperious look. "You wouldn't dare."

"I guess you're right." He sobered slightly and held her gaze as she returned to the table. "God, Stacey, it's good to be back. I just wish Cindy were here."

"So do I," she whispered.

"Did Geneva tell you that I planned to sell the house?"

Stacey had the desperate sensation that her world was slipping through her fingers. *How would she live without him and his precious child?* "She mentioned it."

He pushed aside his plate and placed his elbows on the table. "That doesn't necessarily mean I won't come back, you know," he said, noting the disappointment in her eyes.

"What, then, does it mean?"

"That I have to pull up stakes, at least as far as Robert Madison is concerned."

Stacey didn't argue, she couldn't, but she did ask the most important question on her mind. "You haven't really told me: how is Cindy?"

Nathan frowned. "Not much better, I'm afraid."

"*Any* better?" she asked and he shook his head.

Stacey bit her lower lip. "Worse?"

He twisted his coffee cup on the table. "No…yes… hell, I don't know! But she misses you and the school, and of course she can't get her mind off that blasted dog. I guess you were right; for the first time in her life she'd found a place where she thought she belonged."

Stacey felt her shoulders slump as she picked up her empty cup and set it in the sink. "So what are you going to do about it?"

The fire returned to his eyes. "Everything I have to. We went to Whidbey, but Madison's thugs followed us. That's why I sent Geneva back here and Barbara, Cindy and I went on to Seattle." His gaze grew distant as he looked through the window to the tide-battered rocks near the shore. "I thought it would be easier to get lost on the mainland."

"I see," Stacey said, feeling the familiar stab of pain she always did whenever he mentioned Barbara. Telling herself she was being a ninny—hadn't she spent the last twelve hours making love to Nathan?—she rose above the childish pang of jealousy.

He leaned back in his chair and gazed at her. With the sleeves of his sweater pushed over his forearms, his dark hair falling over his face and his intense blue eyes gazing at her, he looked positively male. The worst of it was he seemed right at home. The sight of him sitting in the kitchen and talking companionably as he sipped from a steaming cup of coffee made her ache for a simple family life with him and his charming little daughter.

Nathan, after taking a final swallow from his cup and setting it on the table said, "Barbara thinks she's uncovered enough dirt on Madison to put him in jail for life, but it will be tough. On the surface he's always kept his hands clean, had someone else who he paid in cash or stolen goods to do the dirty work. Proving his guilt will be tough."

For the first time Stacey was grateful to the dark-haired woman. "That's still good news."

"She uncovered a disillusioned employee who used to work for Madison, a pilot who helped him smuggle jewels and God-only-knows what else. The only cargo he'll admit to is emeralds. But, he's willing to bargain with the D.A. and help nail Madison. It's just gonna take a little time."

"But that's wonderful!" she said, grinning. "You and Cindy are home-free!"

"Not yet. It's not quite that simple. This pilot, who was once a friend of Madison's, seems to think that Madison had someone tamper with Jennifer's car the day that she swerved off the road and over the embankment in Laurel Canyon."

"What!"

"That's right. I thought Jennifer might have committed suicide, but it's beginning to look like murder."

"You thought that might be the case."

"But I never really believed it. Didn't want to, I guess."

Stacey was horrified and the blood drained out of her face. If what Nathan was saying were true, Robert Madison, Cindy's legal father, had killed the child's mother to gain the little girl's inheritance. Sick inside, Stacey leaned against the counter for support. "You always thought something like this was possible."

"Not really. I mean, I didn't think that Madison would stoop to murder, for God's sake!" Nathan's face hardened, and the grooves alongside his nose deepened in anger. "I'm going to nail him, Stacey. I'm gong to nail him to the wall before he gets a chance to hurt anyone else, especially my daughter."

Stacey twisted the dish towel nervously. "Is…is Madison still in L.A.?"

His head snapped up. "The last I heard. Why?"

She shrugged. "I don't know. It's nothing, I suppose. But I thought I saw those two men here the other day, you know, the ones we heard on the beach that night—"

"The guys who used me for a punching bag?"

She winced and nodded.

"You saw them?"

"I… I think so. Down at the docks, near the berth for your boat."

"They were back here?" he asked, slowly rising from his chair, his body aching for the chance to give them back theirs.

She nodded.

"Are you sure?"

"I don't know." She thought so hard she frowned. "I didn't get a good look at them that night, remember? It was pretty dark on the beach, and we were under the stairs. Besides which," she added ruefully, "I was scared to death."

Nathan had begun to pace. His eyes narrowed, and he rubbed the edge of his jaw where the scar from the cut on his chin was still visible. "Was anyone else with them?"

"No. But I got the feeling they were waiting for some-one. At the time I thought it was for you."

"And now?"

She let out a sigh. "It might have been Madison." Then she turned on the water in the sink, grabbed a dishcloth and started washing the dirty dishes. "Oh," she said angrily, "All this cloak-and-dagger business is getting to me. Maybe I'm imagining things! I just saw two men on the docks. One was smoking. He had a scraggly beard and was blond. The other man was older and looked as if his nose had been broken at least once. But that doesn't mean anything. They might not have even been the same two guys."

"I wouldn't bet on it." He placed his stocking foot on the seat of a chair and leaned over his knee. The fabric of his jeans was drawn taught over his thighs and buttocks. Stacey turned her attention back to the dishes but heard him mutter to himself. "I don't think Madison would risk coming here. If what Barbara says is true, the noose is tightening around his organization, and he can already feel it."

"Good," she whispered, her muscles relaxing slightly as she let go of the breath she hadn't realized she'd been holding. "So where does that leave you?"

"In L.A., the day after tomorrow."

Stacey felt her world crumble again. "So soon?" she whispered, her voice catching a little.

"I've decided you're right. It's time to face Madison with the truth. Now that Barbara's got the evidence against him, I've got to take my chances with the law."

She folded the dishcloth nervously. "And what then?"

He shrugged. "Depends, I guess on whether I win

or lose. Madison's gone public with the story that I kidnapped Cindy."

"I know. Margaret showed me a copy of the *Times*. But certainly no one would take Cindy away from you now."

"I hope not," he admitted his eyes becoming as cold as the Arctic sea. "I hope to God not."

THEY SPENT THE rest of the day together. After a walk along the beach and a drive into Serenity for lunch at Nathan's favorite delicatessen, they walked to the docks. Though Nathan's launch was anchored at its usual berth, there was no sign of either of Madison's thugs.

"I told you I probably imagined the whole thing," Stacey said, but Nathan's tight features didn't relax.

"Maybe they don't like the bad weather," he observed, noting the thick, dark clouds and pelting November rain.

"And maybe they were never here."

"Oh, they were here all right," Nathan said, rubbing the scar on his chin. "I just wonder if they came back here after following me to Seattle. In some respects that could be good, y'know."

"How?"

"If they came back here, it means they lost my trail in Seattle and that they don't know Cindy's in Seattle with Barbara."

"Let's pray that's what happened," she whispered as he took her hand in his.

BEFORE IT GOT DARK, they went to his cabin. Though the newspapers were still stacked on the porch, the interior of the rough house smelled of disinfectant and furniture polish. "I see that Geneva's waved her magic wand," Nathan observed, looking into the refrigerator and noting that it had been cleaned. Nothing had been left to spoil or eat.

Dust covers had been placed over the furniture, and all of the plants had been removed. "She obviously didn't think I'd come back."

"I think she took you at your word," Stacey commented.

"I guess so." He picked up the phone, found that it was dead and then walked to the door. "I should tell her I'm back," he said. "It'll only be a minute."

"I'll wait."

Nathan was gone for about ten minutes and while Stacey waited, she wandered around the rooms, remembering the last time she'd been in the cabin when she had been frightened out of her mind. It seemed like centuries ago.

"I'm back," Nathan announced, breaking into her thoughts. He locked the door behind him. His dark brows were drawn together, and his forehead was furrowed with deep, worried ridges.

"Something wrong?" she asked, her heartbeat accelerating. "What happened?"

"Geneva said there were a couple of men hanging around asking questions about my place and me. They claimed to be interested in buying the cabin for their parents, but Geneva didn't think they looked much like brothers, or even acted as if they were related. She said they both seemed nervous and—" his eyes cut straight into hers, "—they fit the descriptions of the two men who attacked me."

Stacey's knees wobbled. "So they did come back."

"Looks that way."

Stacey felt the old gnawing fear. Nathan saw her frightened eyes and walked over to her, placed his hands on her shoulders and kissed her on the forehead. "It's just about over," he promised.

"Thank God." Sagging against him, she listened to his breathing and the steady beat of his heart. His arms surrounded her. She held him tightly, thinking how empty her life would be without him.

"How...how was Mrs. McIver?" Stacey asked.

"Fine. She asked about you."

Stacey lifted her head. "Did she?"

"Um-hum. And she didn't seem to be too surprised to see me."

Stacey nodded, her cheek brushing against his rough, denim jacket. "She said you'd be back, if only to sell the place."

"I hate to do that," he said, frowning as he stared over the top of her head, his hands loosely joined behind her back. "This cabin is the first place I've called home in years." Sighing, he kissed the top of her head and breathed deeply of the scent of her hair. "But it might be necessary." He stared past her to gaze out the window for a minute. Finally releasing her, he forced a tight smile. "Maybe we'd better get to work before our friends show up again."

He walked into his bedroom, made a lot of noise and returned to the living room with a trunk and two suitcases. Then he began to gather a few necessities and toss them into open bags.

Stacey slowly sat down on the couch, aching inside.

"This place holds some great memories," he said, stacking his notes and tape recorder in a separate suitcase.

Stacey nodded, her throat too tight to speak.

"It's the first place that I felt that Cindy and I could call home together." He snorted in disgust. "You know, just the two of us, together, until you came along." His eyes lifted and held hers. "You and that damned dog. You made me want to change things, made me want things I hadn't wanted in years…"

"Such as?"

He lifted a dark brow. "Home and hearth, that sort of thing. A wife and a dozen kids. Even the blasted dog." He looked fondly at Attila who responded by cocking his head and lifting his ears. Sighing, Nathan shook his head. "Well, it was good while it lasted." He walked over to the window, ran his hand over his head and leaned against the wall while he stared at the fishing vessels returning to the island. "I'm going to miss it all."

"You could come back," she suggested, getting up to snap his trunk closed, then walked across the room to him, her heart pounding so loudly it seemed to echo in the small cabin.

"Maybe someday."

Stacey forced a brave smile that trembled and died. "I hope so."

He took her hand in his and squeezed it.

Tears gathered in the corners of her eyes. "I love you, Nathan," she admitted, swallowing her pride. "I can't bear the thought that you won't be back."

"Neither can I," he said, gazing into her eyes and drawing her close. Hesitating only an instant, he lifted her chin with one finger and kissed the tears from her eyes. "I love you, too, Anastasia Monroe. God knows I didn't want to and I fought it, but I couldn't help falling in love with you."

Stacey swallowed hard and smiled, though her gaze was blurred.

"Come to L.A. with me," he suggested, pulling her close and whispering into her ear. "Stand by me."

If only I could. "I want to," she whispered, wrapping her arms around his waist and holding him as if she were afraid to let go. "More than anything, I want to be with you and Cindy, help you fight Robert Madison."

"Then come to L.A."

"But my job—"

"There are other jobs."

That was true, but there was only one Nathan. She knew she couldn't do anything to risk losing him. Wondering if she were about to make the biggest mistake of her life, she threw caution to the wind. "Of course I'll be with you," she whispered. "But it may take a few days to arrange things at the school. I'll have to get a substitute teacher and pack and—" She was already planning her strategy when Nathan's lips claimed hers. Fire and possession burned in his kiss, and Stacey swayed against him. He pushed her gently to the floor, slowly unbuttoning her sweater and caressing the soft skin beneath the knit fabric.

She quivered in anticipation as his tongue played havoc with hers, and she could think of nothing save the warmth of his touch, the feel of his hands caressing her skin, the fever throbbing through her veins.

He kicked off his boots and gently tugged her sweater over her shoulders. Then he jerked off his shirt and jeans and threw them aside. His tanned torso, lean and sinuous and partially covered with a thick mat of hair, gleamed with sweat. Only a slight discoloration over his ribs reminded Stacey of the brutal beating he had taken from one of Madison's thugs.

She reached forward and touched the sensitive area. He drew in a ragged breath when her finger strayed to his flat nipples. "Stay with me forever," he begged, staring into her hazel eyes and noticing the leaping pulse at the base of her neck.

"I will," she vowed as he lowered his head and kissed the delicate ring of bones circling her throat.

Stacey quivered with desire and Nathan responded by slowly removing her slacks and lowering his lips.

"Make love to me, Stacey," he whispered against her vulnerable abdomen and she arched upward, letting his lips brush her skin. He looked down at her lying naked on the floor, her honey-brown hair splayed on the carpet, her softly rounded breasts straining upward. "Make love to me and never stop." He leaned forward, took a beckoning nipple between his lips and watched in satisfaction as Stacey's stomach muscles convulsed with desire. He planted one hand beneath her round buttock and rubbed against her, urging her to join with him.

In her wild, passionate state, it was all the invitation she needed, and she opened herself to him.

IF EVERYTHING IN life was timing, then Robert Madison had it all, Nathan thought angrily, and that included the men on his payroll. Nathan had just snapped the final suitcase shut when the pounding on the door thundered through the cabin. He knew in an instant that Madison's goons had caught up with him.

Damn! Motioning Stacey toward the bedrooms, Nathan walked to the door. Impassively, he looked to see who was standing on the porch, his eyes gleaming with satisfaction when his premonition was confirmed. Madison's henchmen were waiting for him.

"We know you're in there!" the younger man yelled.

Nathan took three strides to the fireplace, grabbed the poker, kept it at his side and opened the door. "What do you want?" he asked calmly, a thread of steel running through his words.

"You know," the older man said. "Same as always. Madison wants his kid back."

"Forget it."

"And he wants you to call off that detective woman."

"Sorry," Nathan said, his lip curling derisively.

"But he insists—"

"He can insist till hell freezes over!" Nathan growled. "Now you two back off!"

"I told you this wasn't gonna work," the younger, blond man insisted, his fists balling at his sides. "There's only one way to deal with him."

Nathan kicked the door completely open and walked out to the porch. "Any way you like, friend—"

"Nathan! No!" Stacey walked out of the hallway, and the thugs saw her for the first time.

"I told you he was hung up on the teacher," the younger man growled, his cold, hungry eyes skimming Stacey's figure, his fingers running through his thin beard.

"Leave her out of this," Nathan said, his tone deadly.

"I don't think we can," the older thug said. "Mr. Madison made it very clear that we were to use any means possible to persuade you to drop this custody suit as well as find a way to convince you that Barbara Jones had better quit snooping around where she's not wanted."

"Or else?" Nathan taunted.

"Nathan, don't!" Stacey whispered. *God, what if they decided to attack him again?* This time Nathan was ready and more than willing, but it was still two against one.

"Yeah, or else," the young man sneered, mustering his bravado again.

Tension sizzled in the air.

"You tell Madison that I'll see him burn in hell first."

The older man looked over Nathan's shoulder and smiled when he saw the fear in Stacey's eyes. "I'll give him the message."

"Good."

"You mean we're just gonna leave?" the bearded one whined.

"For now."

"But—" The young thug's evil looking eyes shifted from Nathan to Stacey and back again. All of his muscles were tense, and he looked as if he would very gladly tear Nathan limb from limb.

Nathan responded with a cold smile. "Try it."

The young man glanced at the poker wrapped in Nathan's fingers. "Just evening the odds," Nathan explained in a chilling voice that sent shivers down Stacey's spine and seemed to convince the thug that he was better off not challenging the furious blue-eyed man.

The two men left and Stacey collapsed against the wall. She tried to swallow, but her throat was so tight, she couldn't. Nathan stood at the door and watched until he was assured the men had gone. Then he locked the door and walked over to Stacey, folded her into his arms and held her until she stopped shaking.

"I think your options ran out," he whispered against her hair.

"What…what do you mean?"

"Before, I asked you to come to L.A. Now I'm going to insist on it. Those two hoods know that I care about you; before they weren't sure. Now your life is in danger."

"I don't think—"

He lifted his head and impaled her with his steely blue eyes. "No arguments. I'm not about to let what happened to Jennifer happen to you."

"But it won't."

"You're right, because I'm going to stick to you like glue. Got it?"

She smiled, despite the dread settling in her heart. "Got it!"

"Good. Now let's finish this and spend the night at your place. I think we'll be safer there."

"Why?"

"Because of the dog. If anyone tries to break into the house tonight, Attila will hear him, and," he added, his eyes narrowing, "I'll be waiting."

"You'd love it, wouldn't you?"

"What?"

"To teach those thugs a lesson."

He shook his head, but the gleam didn't leave his eyes. "It's Madison I want."

"Oh, Nathan," she worried aloud, but he took her into his arms.

"Just love me, Stacey," he whispered. "Love me and don't ever let go."

"Never," she vowed, wondering why the word seemed to ring with a premonition of doom.

CHAPTER ELEVEN

MARGARET'S OFFICE WAS as neat and tidy as always, and Margaret was sitting behind her desk, reading the latest copy of *Psychology Today.* She looked up quickly when Stacey hurried into the room. Margaret offered Stacey a smile that quickly died when she noticed Nathan. The older woman was worried as she watched Stacey take her usual spot on the arm of the couch.

Nathan lounged in the doorway, his body slack, his eyes cold as they darted around the outer offices.

Stacey watched as Margaret visibly angered. She'd asked Nathan to let her see Margaret alone, but he wouldn't hear of it. Ever since seeing Madison's henchmen the day before, Nathan had kept to his promise of sticking to her like glue. Until right now, it had been wonderful. Margaret was about to change all that. Stacey had predicted Dr. Woodward's reaction; Nathan hadn't cared.

"Mr. Sloan," Margaret said with a forced smile. "You're the last person I expected to see."

"Good morning, Dr. Woodward."

Margaret didn't have time for pleasantries. "You left the island rather suddenly, didn't you?"

Nathan glanced at Stacey and nodded. "Business," he replied. "I'm finishing it up tomorrow." He walked into the room and took a seat against the wall. "I know you've read about Robert Madison and his claims to my child."

Margaret pursed her lips together.

Undaunted, Nathan added, "There's a custody hearing on Thursday in Los Angeles. Hopefully everything will be straightened out then."

Softening a little, Margaret held his gaze. "I'm glad you decided to use the legal system our forefathers provided us," she said crisply.

"I always had planned to, but I wanted to make sure I had all the facts I needed."

"And you do now?"

"I hope so."

"That's why I dropped by," Stacey said nervously. "I'd like to go to L.A. with Nathan for the hearing. I was hoping you'd give me the next week off."

"You're going to L.A.?" Margaret asked, taking off her glasses to get a better look at Stacey.

"With Nathan."

"I see." She turned to Nathan. "Would you mind giving us a few minutes of privacy?"

His gaze swept the room and outer hallway. Then he lifted a shoulder. "I'll be out here," he told Stacey while cocking his head in the direction of Andrea's office.

"This will only take a minute," she replied tightly.

Nathan left the room and closed the door to Margaret's private office.

"Are you out of your mind?" Margaret asked, looking at the ceiling before staring at Stacey.

"I have to do this, Margaret."

The doctor, trying to get hold of herself, slid her hands down her face until they covered her chin. "Let me get this straight. You want time off from the school—"

"I've already contacted Sophie White. She'll substitute for me for the next week—"

"Okay, okay. So you've covered your bases here at the school, but what's all this nonsense about going to L.A.?"

"We told you, Nathan's involved in a custody hearing for Cindy. I want to be there."

"So he's actually trying to work within the law?" Margaret didn't bother to hide her skepticism.

"Yes."

"Thank God for small favors." Margaret sighed, reached into her purse for a packet of cigarettes, and then remembered she'd quit smoking a year before. She fidgeted with a pen on the desk. "Are you sure this is what you want?" she asked.

Stacey didn't falter. "Very much."

Margaret stood, stretched and walked over to the couch so that she could speak more quietly. "And what happens if Nathan doesn't get custody of Cindy?"

Stacey's heart twisted, but she lifted her chin bravely. "He will. He can prove that Robert Madison is a criminal, that he's cheated some people out of their savings and that he was involved in smuggling operations—jewels and possibly drugs."

"Not exactly citizen of the year," Margaret observed flatly, "but then, neither is our Mr. Sloan. Remember he, in effect, kidnapped that child!"

Stacey disagreed. "He did what he had to do. As for Robert Madison, it's worse than you know. Nathan thinks that there's a strong possibility that Madison planned his wife's death."

Margaret didn't speak for a few minutes. When she finally did, her voice was barely above a whisper. "Those are pretty rough charges," she said. "They could be considered slander."

"Does Nathan strike you as the type of man who would go around slandering someone?" Stacey asked.

"No…at least he didn't when I first met him. In fact, I have to admit that I was quite taken with him. He seemed so concerned about his daughter."

"There you go."

"But I can't forget that he lied to us, to the police, to everyone."

"Well, that's all over now," Stacey said, grinning engagingly.

Sliding her glasses back up her nose, Margaret observed Stacey with kindly old eyes. "You love him very much, don't you?"

Without batting an eye, Stacey replied, "Very much."

The older woman pursed her lips and smiled. "Then I hope it all works out for you and, yes, you can have a week off. Call me, and let me know how it all turns out."

"Oh, I will," Stacey said with a bright smile. "You'll be the first to know!" She walked out of Margaret's office on a cloud of optimism and beamed at Nathan. Soon, very soon, everything would be fine.

GENEVA MCIVER PROMISED to take care of Attila as well as watch both Stacey's and Nathan's houses. She had even driven them to the docks, and the puppy had gone along for the ride. He'd stood on the front seat, his front legs propped up on the dash, his nose pressed to the windshield.

"Of course I'll look after this guy," Geneva said as she drove into the gravel parking lot near the docks, and patted the puppy affectionately on his furry head. "We can't disappoint our Miss Cindy, now, can we?"

"Never," Nathan said from the back seat. He was sitting next to Stacey in Mrs. McIver's rumbling old Buick, and his arm was draped possessively over Stacey's shoulders.

Stacey and Nathan slid out of the car. Mrs. McIver rolled down the window as Nathan jerked the suitcases out of the trunk. Then he handed back the keys to Geneva. "Thanks."

"You give 'em hell," she told him as she started the car. With a roar, the engine caught and the wipers started slapping the rain aside. "Especially that Madison character. He'd better pray to Almighty God that I never meet up with him!"

"He's probably shaking in his boots," Nathan replied with a wry smile.

"He'd better be!" She put the car in gear and called through the open window. "So long." Waving as she rolled out of the gravel parking lot, Geneva drove away from the piers.

Stacey waved back and wondered why she felt a pang of remorse. *Probably the bleak day,* she told herself while following Nathan down to the slippery pier to his launch.

Once the baggage was secure inside the little boat, Nathan started the engine and headed the launch out to sea before turning south and then east. The small boat dipped and rolled on the uneasy sea.

"Not much longer," he said over the roar of the engine.

Stacey, huddled in a raincoat and boots, smiled despite the cold rain and gray skies. Secure in Nathan's love and knowing that soon he would be Cindy's legal guardian, Stacey managed to shake her feeling of doom and felt better than she had in weeks. *Like I'm coming home after a long and troublesome journey,* she thought distractedly as the small town of Serenity disappeared and they rounded the southern tip of the island to head inland, toward Seattle. Once there, she and Nathan would be reunited with Cindy. She could hardly wait! Smiling, she imagined how Cindy would react to the present she'd brought.

EVEN UNDER THE LEADEN, drizzling skies, Seattle was a bustling city. A blend of modern skyscrapers and turn-of-the-century brick buildings stood on the banks of Puget Sound. Traffic and pedestrians spilled onto the wet, hilly streets.

Nathan and Stacey took a cab to one of the smaller, but elegant, older hotels. Tea was being served in the dining room, and the smell of warm bread and the soft chatter of the patrons drifted through the open foyer of the elegant building.

Nathan didn't waste any time. He led Stacey to the elevator, rode to the third floor and strode down the hall to his suite.

"Daddy!" Cindy squealed when Nathan opened the door and walked inside. She ran to his open arms and flung herself at him with all the force and exuberance of her four short years. Clinging to Nathan's neck, the child stared over his shoulder and saw Stacey for the first time. A bright grin creased her cherubic face and she giggled happily.

Stacey was nervous, but Cindy positively beamed. The

child looked backward, over her shoulder and, pointing at Stacey said, "See. I told you. Stacey came, too."

"Yes, you certainly were right," a willowy, dark-haired woman said as she approached Nathan and Stacey. "Hi." She extended her hand, her dark eyes meeting Stacey's frozen gaze. "I'm Barbara Jones."

"Hello," Stacey managed to say. "Stacey Monroe."

"Oh, yes, I know. Cindy hasn't quit talking about you for a minute. You're her teacher—the woman who bought her this Atilla dog?" Barbara laughed softly, and her brown eyes twinkled in amusement.

Stacey's smile eased. "Yes."

"How'd you ever come up with a name like that?" Barbara asked, still chuckling.

"That's what Stacey calls Daddy," Cindy said.

Barbara smothered a smile. "Appropriate, I'd say."

"Nice Barbara, real nice," Nathan said, feeling the tension in his neck easing now that he was holding his daughter. "I guess I should have made introductions."

"Next time," Barbara said with a wink.

"Where is he?" the child demanded.

"Who?" Nathan asked, before grasping the meaning of her words. "Oh, the dog?"

"Uh-huh! Where is he? I want him!"

Nathan set Cindy on the carpet. "He couldn't come with us today. He's with Mrs. McIver. She'll take care of him until we go back home."

Barbara glanced up, obviously surprised. "I thought you were selling the cabin."

Nathan let out a sigh and frowned. "I will. But I'll have to move out of it first and when I do, I'll go back for the dog."

Stacey's heart lurched. She couldn't imagine life on

the island without Nathan. Shaking off the blues, she turned to Cindy. "I brought you something."

The child's blue eyes brightened. "Another puppy!"

"And risk being shot? No way. Besides, I thought Attila might get jealous." Laughing, she handed an ungainly bundle to the child.

"What is it?"

"Open it and see."

With no-holds-barred, Cindy ripped open the colorful package and squealed with childish mirth when she saw the stuffed octopus. "Just like at school!" she chimed.

Stacey lifted the child, octopus and all, onto her hip. "Not quite. This one has eyelashes."

"And it's pink!"

"*Very* pink," Stacey agreed with a smile.

The child wrapped one of the soft tentacles around her hand and laughed with glee.

"What do you say?" Nathan prodded.

"Thanks!" Cindy hugged her fiercely by wrapping a chubby arm around Stacey's neck.

"Oh, you're welcome, precious," she whispered, blinking back tears. She sat on the edge of the bed and talked to Cindy while the child played with her new toy.

"How did things go here?" Nathan asked, glancing from Cindy to Barbara.

"No trouble. I talked to your attorney as well as the district attorney in L.A. The case against Madison is coming along; it'll just take time."

"We don't have much," Nathan said angrily.

"I know, but Madison was very careful. It's hard to pin anything on him. Even the D.A. is nervous."

"Great."

"At least we've got the pilot to talk—I'm working on

a couple other of the men in his organization." Barbara gave Nathan an encouraging smile, and Stacey felt her stomach tighten. "So, how did it go on the island?" Her brown eyes swept from Nathan to Stacey and back again.

"Unfortunately, our friends managed to find us."

"That's not good," Barbara said, and Stacey considered her comment the understatement of the year. "Well, we'd better get a move on. The plane leaves in a little over an hour. Don't bother packing; I took care of it."

Nathan seemed relieved. "Thanks."

Stacey smiled tightly. She couldn't help but envy the easy way in which Nathan and Barbara worked together, smoothly and efficiently, taking each other for granted because they'd been together for years.

Though Nathan smiled and touched her arm as they left the hotel, Stacey felt like an intruder.

The flight to L.A. was uneventful. Stacey sat beside Nathan and spent most of the journey looking out the window. Nathan studied the notes and evidence that Barbara had prepared. He held Stacey's hand and she felt the tension in his fingers, saw the lines of strain on his face. For the first time in days, she began to wonder what would happen if he lost custody of his daughter.

Cindy sat alternately on Nathan's and Stacey's laps while playing with the stuffed octopus. The child was restless but never wandered off, and when any of the attendants on the flight tried to speak to her, Cindy would make a beeline for Nathan's lap and bury her head against his shoulder.

What would happen to Cindy, Stacey wondered, if the judge forced her to live with Robert Madison? She shuddered inwardly at the thought and understood why Nathan had "stolen" the child in the first place. *He didn't steal her,* she reminded herself. *The girl's mother left Cindy with him. There's a big difference!*

"Now, I've arranged for Cindy to stay with you tonight," Barbara said as they left Los Angeles International Airport and took a taxi to the hotel. A brilliant California sun streamed through the dusty windows of the cab.

"Of course she'll stay with me."

Barbara sighed and shook her head. "It wasn't that easy," she said. "It only worked because your lawyer knows someone from social services, and he vouched for you." Nathan looked as if he were about to interrupt, but Barbara wouldn't hear any of it. "You're not the most popular guy in town, you know. If it hadn't been for the pilot spilling what he knew about Madison to the police, you would have been arrested."

"Nice to know I'm held in such high esteem," he remarked. Nathan glanced out the window, and he tightened his arms around Cindy.

"As far as the police are concerned, except for the D.A., you're a suspect in a kidnapping."

"You don't have to remind me." He glanced at Stacey and his face softened slightly. She felt warm with the tenderness of his simple gesture of taking her hand in his. Soon everything would be perfect, and Nathan wouldn't have to spend the rest of his life looking over his shoulder.

"Okay, I wanted you to remember where you stood," Barbara said. "The police are very nervous about all this. Even the district attorney. Fortunately, you have a good lawyer. Conrad Billings is as honest as the day is long, and everyone in town knows it."

"Fortunately," Nathan commented wryly.

"Let's go over all of this again." And for what seemed the tenth time, Stacey heard Nathan's story as he would tell it to the judge. When the taxi pulled into the modern glass and concrete hotel on Wilshire Boulevard, Stacey was glad for the change in scenery. Stately palms and pomegranate trees gave some relief to the stark building.

"Would you watch Cindy while I talk to Billings?" Nathan asked once they'd checked into their adjoining rooms.

"Of course."

Stacey stayed with Cindy while Nathan, Conrad and Barbara were closeted in the next room. After changing from her raincoat and wool suit into a comfortable pair of slacks and a light sweater, Stacey pulled her hair away from her face and clipped it to the top of her head.

"How about you?" she asked Cindy. "Want to change?"

Cindy jerked a pair of shorts from her suitcase and held them up for Stacey's inspection.

Stacey grinned and shook her head. "Not today, sweetheart. Let's see…how about this?" Stacey took out a light blue dress with matching tights from the suitcase. "Just right for a November day in L.A., don't you think?"

Cindy couldn't have cared less. She let Stacey take off her corduroy overalls and sweater and tried to play with her doll when Stacey attempted to button the dress. "You're squirmier than a jar full of worms," Stacey said with a laugh.

"Ugh!"

"Ugh, indeed." Stacey grinned affectionately at the child, and Cindy responded with a small smile. "Come on, let's comb your hair and take a walk around the hotel. What do you say?"

In response, Cindy bolted for the door.

"So much for good grooming," Stacey thought aloud as she tried to keep up with the child.

They explored most of the main floor, stopping at the various shops on the ground level of the hotel. Stacey broke down and bought Cindy some jelly beans and window-shopped at the florist and imported dress shops before they wandered through an atrium near the back of the hotel. Golden sunlight streamed through the glass, and overhead the sky was a brilliant shade of Southern California blue.

In less than an hour, Cindy's short legs gave out. Stacey carried her back into the hotel room, and as soon as Stacey had closed the door behind her, Nathan burst into the room.

"Where have you been?" he demanded, his face white.

"Shopping." She saw the concern in his eyes. "Why?"

"Look what Stacey bought me," Cindy cried, her mouth smudged from the candy.

Nathan sat on the edge of the bed and wearily rubbed his eyes. "You can't leave the room," he said to Stacey. "At least not with Cindy. The social services woman, Lenore Parker, dropped by to see Cindy and," he lifted his shoulders, "I didn't know where you were."

Stacey was immediately contrite. "I didn't know."

"I realize that, but it didn't look too good."

"I'll bet not." She planted a kiss on his cheek. "You're on thin ice already. You don't need to look irresponsible. I'm sorry."

"It's okay." Nathan took her into his arms and sighed. "Just be more careful. Ms. Parker didn't buy my story that Cindy was with her teacher, or that you were a psychologist."

"Next time I'll let you know what we're going to do," she said with a humble smile. "I didn't want to disturb you."

"It's okay…"

"Is it?" she asked, noticing the worry in his eyes.

"Yes…it's just that I've got a bad feeling about all this." He shrugged. "It's hard to explain."

"It'll be over soon," she said, encouraging him with a smile. "And then you'll never have to worry about losing her again."

Nathan frowned and pinched his lower lip between his thumb and forefinger as he watched Cindy play with the jelly beans on a table near the window. The child carefully laid each piece of candy on the wood and then sorted out all the black beans.

"These are the best," she said proudly, holding up one tiny piece of black candy. "You want one, Daddy?"

"No, pumpkin, you keep them," he said, rubbing her head affectionately and smiling despite the worry in his eyes.

"Good!" Cindy popped the candy into her mouth and grinned up at Nathan. Her white teeth were stained black.

"You're a dentist's nightmare," he whispered. He picked Cindy up, touching her nose with his. "I love you, pumpkin," he whispered roughly. "You know that, don't you?"

"'Course I do." Cindy wiggled to the floor.

Stacey stood near the window and stared through the glass to the street below. White concrete, shadowed by a late afternoon sun, throngs of pedestrians and the clog of L.A. traffic were far below her.

Any other time, Stacey would have found the glamour and glitz of being in Los Angeles with Nathan romantic, but this afternoon she worried. Worried about Robert Madison. Worried about Nathan Sloan. And worried about Cindy. *And don't forget yourself,* she thought. *What happens when the hearing is over? Will you return to Serenity alone or with Nathan?*

She didn't have time to consider her options. Nathan came up behind her, placed his arms around her waist and kissed her lightly on the nape of the neck. A fresh tingle of desire skittered down her spine as there was a soft knock on the door, and Barbara walked in from the adjoining room.

Barbara saw the intimate embrace and a quick flash of regret showed in her eyes. Bravely, she forced a smile. "I'll see you tomorrow," she said, clearing her throat, "in the courtroom at ten. And Conrad would like to talk to you, Stacey."

"We'll be there," Nathan promised. Barbara walked out of the room, closing the door behind her. As the other woman left, Stacey had the cold premonition that something was about to go wrong.

Conrad Billings bustled into the room. A short man with piercing brown eyes and an all-business manner, he sat on the corner of the bed and spread his yellow legal pads around him. "Miss Monroe—"

"Stacey."

He lifted his gaze and smiled a bit. "Stacey, then. Do you think you could take the stand, be a character witness for Nathan?"

"If it will help," she agreed.

"Madison's attorney will try to block it, but we may as well try to put you on the stand. Then you can explain what you know about Cindy, as her teacher and psychologist, and what you know about Nathan."

"I don't think that will be a good idea," Nathan cut in.

"Oh?" The small lawyer looked at his client.

"Stacey's opinion is biased, and Madison knows as much."

"What do you mean?"

"Stacey and I are…more than friends," he said simply, and Stacey blushed a little. "Besides, there's a problem with her getting involved with the fathers of her students, a mix-up in Boston a few years ago."

The attorney's eyes narrowed. "Go on," he urged.

Stacey finished the story. "I was involved with Jeff Brown. His son, Daniel, was one of my students. I loved the boy very much." Her voice trembled a little. "We went camping and Daniel got sick…he died shortly thereafter. Jeff blamed me and the Edwards Clinic where I worked. There was a terrible scandal, and a lawsuit was brought against the clinic. Nothing came of it…" *Except that Daniel died!* She closed her eyes for a moment.

Conrad rubbed his temple. "Okay, scratch the testimony. It would only open a can of worms."

"It doesn't matter," Stacey said firmly. "If my testimony will help Nathan gain custody of Cindy, I don't care if the old scandal is brought up again."

"But I do. It sounds like trouble and it might sway the judge. Unfortunately, we didn't get lucky there. Judge Barclay isn't my favorite, and undoubtedly Madison's attorney knows all about you, Stacey. Pardon my expression, but he'd grind you into dog meat on the stand. We can't risk it."

"It would do more harm than good?" she asked.

"Exactly."

She met his dark gaze. "I'll do whatever I have to do."

"Good." He placed his notes inside his case and snapped it shut. "Then I'll see you tomorrow." The short attorney breezed out of the room, and Stacey's fingers clutched the lapels of Nathan's jacket. In a few short hours, Nathan's and Cindy's futures would be decided.

THE COURTROOM LOOKED as if it had been built sometime in the late fifties. The yellowed wood panels on the walls and the carved railing gleamed from years of use and coats of wax. Dirt had collected near the supports of the visitors' seats and huge glass lamps were suspended from a raised ceiling. One bank of windows, high overhead, let in the natural light through glass bricks.

Cindy sat with Stacey while Judge Barclay, a stern man with black hair and dark eyes, listened to each side of the story. His fingers tapped nervously as Nathan, dressed in a suit and tie, explained about his affair with Jennifer Madison, her resulting pregnancy and his agreement to care for Cindy until Jennifer was able to divorce Madison.

Robert Madison sat on his side of the courtroom and smirked. A large man with sandy hair and lifeless eyes, he watched as Nathan vehemently stated why he had kept Cindy Madison in hiding. As Nathan told his story, Madison's lower lip protruded, and he whispered occasionally to his lawyer. Stacey judged Madison to be a calm and deadly man by nature. Just looking at him made her palms moist. Poised and self-assured, he looked as if the entire courtroom scene were one big bore.

He knows something, Stacey realized, staring at the man. *He knows that Nathan will lose!* Dread took a stranglehold of her throat and involuntarily, she held Cindy more tightly.

Nathan, in direct contrast to Robert Madison, was passionate in his quest for his daughter. He had trouble keeping quiet when Madison spoke. He'd heard the lies before, and the fact that Madison would spread them during the hearing made him furious. He could feel the heat in his face, and his jaw ached from clenching it so tightly. A large vein throbbed in his throat, and his knuckles were white from clenching his fists.

Stacey could feel the tension in Cindy's small body when the girl first noticed Robert Madison. She stared at him a long moment and then refused to look away or stray from Stacey's lap. "It will be all right," Stacey promised, feeling her own sense of dread mounting with the tension crackling in the courtroom.

All of Barbara's evidence against Robert Madison was considered inadmissible by Madison's lawyer, and the judge concurred, throwing it out of court. Judge Barclay pointed out that to date, there had been no charges filed against Robert Madison.

Livid, Nathan rose to his feet, but Billings placed a calming hand on his arm.

With a sinking feeling, Stacey watched the judge and realized that the tide had turned against Nathan. Madison's attorney had painted Nathan as nothing better than a gold-digging gigolo who was only interested in gaining custody of Cindy because of her inheritance. The smooth lawyer insisted that Nathan had, indeed, kidnapped the girl and that Robert Madison was seriously considering pressing charges against Nathan Sloan.

"If that's the case, your honor," Conrad Billings said, "then maybe we should allow the child to speak. Let Cindy take the stand and tell the courtroom what she wants to do."

"Out of the question," Madison's attorney said as he jumped to his feet and objected. "Your honor, how could a four-year-old child possibly know what's best for her?"

They argued until the judge waived the arguments and ruled that a four-year-old couldn't be accountable for her actions.

Billings was outraged, Robert Madison pleased, and Nathan looked as if he'd turned to stone.

It seemed to Staccy that the entire scenario had been staged. She fought to maintain a level head and keep from trembling, although she felt her face drain of all color. Nathan was going to lose his child. If only there were something she could do! She listened to the rest of the testimony stoically, but her fingers curled possessively around Cindy's tiny hands.

Even though the evidence had proved that Nathan was a better guardian than Robert Madison, Judge Barclay awarded custody of Cindy to Robert Madison.

"No!" Stacey screamed holding the girl tightly, her heart thudding in fear. This couldn't be happening! Nathan and his daughter belonged together; they loved each other. Madison was the interloper, the one who didn't belong!

Nathan, shocked and furious, refused to leave the courtroom or his daughter. He took the child from Stacey's arms and held Cindy fiercely, his blue eyes blazing with fury as he stared at Robert Madison.

"You can't get away with this!" he shouted as Madison stepped forward.

Hearing the threat in Sloan's voice, Robert Madison paused, but only for a second. "I just did," he pointed out.

"Not for long." Nathan was still clutching Cindy.

"Mr. Sloan, please," the caseworker said, reaching for Cindy. "The court has awarded custody to Mr. Madison."

"But they had no right!"

"You had no right to abduct the child!" she said. "Now, I've given you every consideration, but you must allow Mr. Madison to have his daughter."

Nathan backed away. A grim-faced policeman approached him, and he finally, reluctantly, let the uniformed guard have his daughter.

The child cried and screamed. "Daddy! No! I not go! I not go!" Cindy turned her wild eyes on Stacey. "No," she yelled, kicking the policeman and trying to squirm out of his arms.

"Please...stop this," Stacey said, her heart wrenching. "Can't you see she belongs with her father?"

"She will be with her father," the caseworker interjected.

"No!" She touched the other woman's arm. "Believe me, this won't work. I've studied Cindy, observed her reactions. She has some deep emotional problems, and taking her away from Nathan will only make them worse."

"The judge made the decision," the social worker said.

"But—"

"It's over, Stacey," Conrad Billings said, gently pulling her aside. "At least for now."

Stacey couldn't believe what was happening. She believed in the justice system. How could the judge have been so blind?

Madison just smiled, his cold eyes unblinking. "Come along, Cindy," he said quietly, his eyes cold. "I'm sorry I had to put you through all of this, but that man stole you."

"No!" Cindy slithered away from the policeman and

started running, but before she reached Nathan, the officer managed to catch her.

"Come on, little lady," he said kindly, obviously confused by the proceedings.

"Daddy! Daddy!" Cindy wailed, tears streaming down her face, her arms stretched out to Nathan. "Don't let him take me—Daddy!"

Nathan's throat worked. "I'll get you back."

Madison sneered. "Don't count on it." But the deadly look in Nathan's eyes stopped him from saying anything else.

Cindy was no longer screaming; in fact, she became deathly still. She took one look at Robert Madison and slowly withdrew into her shell.

To Stacey, the quiet was worse than her cries. "Something has to be done!" Stacey said, starting after Madison.

"It will be," Nathan vowed, his eyes glinting angrily. "I won't let him abuse her! He can have the goddamned money. But if it's the last thing I do, I won't let him hurt her!"

"Nathan—"

And then, as if seeing Stacey for the first time, Nathan turned stone-cold eyes on Stacey and lashed out. "What're you doing here?" he demanded.

Stacey was struck speechless. She finally found a whisper of a voice. "Nathan?"

But all of his reason had vanished. He was raging. "You were the one who insisted that I work with the system," he whispered hoarsely, tears standing in his eyes, his chin thrust forward in anger. "If I hadn't listened to *you*, Cindy would still be safe with me. God only knows what will happen to her now that she's with that bastard!"

"Nathan, don't," Stacey whispered, but he couldn't even look at her. When she tried to reach him, he pushed her away.

"Why the hell don't you leave me alone?" he hissed, his throat working. "Cindy and I, we would have been better off if we'd never met you!"

"You don't mean—"

"I do. Get the hell out of my life, Stacey! Get the god-damned hell out of my life!"

Stacey slumped against the courtroom chairs. "Nathan…please," she whispered, tears of despair trickling down her cheeks.

"Get away from me!" Nathan looked around the room at the sea of worried faces. "All of you, leave me alone!"

Stacey reached forward, touched his arm, but he jerked away from her. He strode toward the doors, hate and anger radiating from his body with each vindictive stride. Shouldering open the courtroom doors, he was suddenly face-to-face with a loud bevy of reporters.

Barbara was at his side in a minute, guiding him through the throng.

Dying inside, Stacey knew that her knees were wobbling, and she had to sit down. Conrad Billings helped her to a chair, but she didn't notice the short, frustrated attorney.

"Are you all right?" he asked.

Never, she thought distractedly. I'll never be all right again. She waved off his anxiety and faced her worst fears. It was happening again! Just like before! Nathan had accused her and blamed her for Cindy's wretched future, as Jeff Brown had blamed her when Daniel died! With sobs strangling her throat, Stacey managed to get up and stumble out of the courtroom, weave through the crowded hallway and force open the door leading outside to the bright Southern California sunshine.

CHAPTER TWELVE

MARGARET, HER TEETH clenched in determination, walked into Stacey's classroom and forced a smile at Tommy and Grace Perkins as they walked through the door to the outer hallway. Fortunately, Margaret thought, the rest of the students had already gone for the day. Stacey was standing near the windows, cleaning the hamster's cage.

The younger woman looked up when she heard Margaret enter. Seeing her employer, Stacey offered a small, sad smile.

"Good afternoon."

Sensing the storm brewing in Margaret's eyes, Stacey tried to ward off the confrontation. "Oh, hi. What brings you down to this neck of the woods?"

"You," Margaret said, noting Stacey's pale color and the deep blue smudges beneath her eyes.

"What's up?"

"That's what I'd like to know." Margaret stood near the windows overlooking the playground, but kept her eyes fastened on Stacey. Leaning a hip on the sill, she said, "You look like walking death."

"Thanks a lot."

"I mean it, Stacey, I'm worried about you."

"Don't be. I'm made of strong stuff," Stacey said, finishing with the hamster and turning to face her friend.

"You're not doing any of us a whole lot of good, you

know. And when I'm talking about 'us,' I'm including your students."

"I'm trying, Margaret."

"I know. I know. And I'm not complaining, not really. Your work is fine, but not the same as it used to be. Ever since you got back from California, you're going through the motions. You seem to have lost your spark. We all miss it. Especially me."

Stacey flinched. She'd been back on the island for three weeks, and she still hadn't gotten over Nathan's rejection. "It's difficult," she whispered, her stomach tightening.

"Want to talk about it?" Margaret asked.

Stacey shook her head. "It's over."

The older woman sighed and clucked her tongue. "You and I both know you shouldn't keep your feelings all bottled up. Maybe I can help."

"I really don't think anyone can."

Grimacing, Margaret pushed herself upright and smoothed the pleats of her wool skirt. "Okay, okay, I tried. Now it's up to you. If you ever think you want to talk things out, you know where I am."

"Right."

Margaret walked to the door, but once there, paused. "Look, Stacey, if you don't have any plans for Thanksgiving, why don't you come to L.A. with me? I'm visiting my sister, and she'd love to have you."

Los Angeles. Not in a million years! Stacey managed a thin smile, but shook her head. "Thanks, but I really can't."

"It might do you a world of good. Think about it."

"Okay, I'll consider it," Stacey said, to placate her friend. The last place she wanted to be was California.

"Good." Margaret, still worried, walked out of the classroom, and Stacey felt her shoulders slump. She hadn't even been aware she'd been so tense.

She thought about Margaret's offer and frowned. Even though Los Angeles was a huge city, Stacey couldn't face returning to the place where Nathan had so violently rejected her only a few weeks before.

His rejection hadn't ended in the courtroom. Stupidly, Stacey had thought that Nathan, once his initial anger was over, would regret pushing her away. Hadn't he told her he loved her? Hadn't he wanted her with him in L.A.? She'd been certain that once the initial pain of losing Cindy had worn off, Nathan would forgive her and realize what a horrid mistake he'd made. But she'd been wrong. As wrong as wrong could be.

It had been late, after midnight, when she'd heard him stumble into his hotel room...

LYING STIFFLY ON the uncomfortable bed in her adjoining room, Stacey listened as Nathan's key went into the lock. She heard him open the door of the room next to hers. Without thinking about the consequences, she grabbed her robe, pushed her arms through the sleeves and opened the door connecting her room to Nathan's.

The only illumination in the room was from the neon lights outside, but Stacey's eyes were accustomed to the darkness. She could see clearly that Nathan had fallen against something and was lying on the floor, holding his shin, his face twisted in pain. His shirt was unbuttoned, his tie long gone and the smell of Scotch filled the air. A pint, nearly empty, lay on the nightstand. Some of the liquor had spilled onto the cabinet.

"Son of a bitch," he muttered, clutching his leg. "Son of a goddamned, bloody bitch!"

Stacey stopped dead in her tracks and looked down at him. He was dead drunk, writhing in pain and still suffering from the loss of his daughter.

He hadn't heard her enter the room. She walked over to him and put her hand on his arm, bending slightly so that her face was close to his. "Nathan?"

"What the..." He looked up and his glassy eyes focused on her. For a minute his angry features softened, and he swallowed hard. "Stacey..." he ground out, and he wrapped his fingers around her neck, a brief smile lighting his eyes, before all the events of the day pierced his dazed brain, and he dropped his hand. His head fell forward to his knees. "What are you doing here?"

She pushed the rumpled hair from his eyes, and he leaned back against the bed and groaned. "I want to help, Nathan."

"You can't."

"Please, let me," she whispered, placing a kiss on his cheek and sitting on the floor next to him. Her robe gaped open and the silky white nightgown shimmered against her body.

Trying to remain impassive, he closed his eyes, but his hands balled into fists. The skin over his cheekbones tensed, and a shudder ran through his body. "What are you trying to do to me?" he asked, his voice hoarse.

She kissed his eyelids tenderly. "I told you I want to help. Nathan, I'm so sorry," she murmured against his skin. "But we can't give up, we can't. We'll get her back..."

She was holding him now, cradling his head against her breast, whispering words of love. His shoulders heaved as he attempted to clear his head, remember clearly the events of the gut-wrenching day.

She continued to kiss him and when her lips touched his, the old fires flamed hot. He couldn't resist and all of his barriers slowly fell away. "Stacey," he whispered as he rolled over and began to control the lovemaking. His hands were warm and anxious as he parted the robe and touched her through the sheer lace of her nightgown.

As if to make up for his earlier reservations, he became feverish with passion. His fingers sculpted her breasts and traced her ribs to her waist, before slipping lower, to the hem of her nightgown, to the soft, silky feel of her inner thighs.

"Help me," he whispered desperately.

"Yes. Please, let me stay with you forever," she agreed, helping him out of his shirt and touching the hard, flexed muscles of his shoulders, the hidden nipples and the thick, dark hair covering his chest. He moaned her name as she removed his slacks, then fell against her once they were both naked. Stroking her lovingly, he entered her and with all the frustration and anger in his body, made hot, furious love to her, expelling himself in her in a shudder that rocked them both as they lay entwined in the sheets that had slipped from the bed.

She was still breathing shallowly, clutching his sweating body close to hers, when she heard the soft knock on the door.

He stiffened and rolled away from her. "Oh, God, what have I done?" he moaned, already reaching for his pants. Regret and disgust tainted his words.

Stacey knew in that instant who was on the other side of the door.

"Nathan?" Barbara called from the hallway. "Are you all right?"

"Fine," he bit out.

Humiliation washed over Stacey as she lay on the floor, the rumpled sheets clutched over her breasts. Nathan cast her a sorry look, scooped up her nightgown and tossed it to her before leaning against the door and wiping nervous, shaking hands over his sweating brow.

"Nathan?" Barbara called again, worry and concern audible in her voice.

Stacey wanted to fall through the floor. She flung the nightgown over her head and stood.

"Just a minute," Nathan called back to Barbara.

"Are you okay? You had a lot to drink. I was worried. Oh, Nathan, for God's sake, open this door so I don't look like an idiot!"

Like I do, Stacey thought angrily. She walked past Nathan and paused. He looked deep into her eyes, and Stacey thought she saw the flicker of regret before his mouth compressed and he said "I'm sorry. I should never have—"

"Don't apologize," she cut in. "It was my fault; it won't happen again."

Nathan's jaw clenched. "Stacey—" He reached for her arm, but she jerked away.

"Go to hell!"

He winced, but remained silent.

"I don't need this, Nathan. I came to help you, and you've treated me like dirt. It won't happen again. I won't let it!" She marched out of the room, closed the door behind her, locked it and slumped to the floor to cry quietly to herself. She heard the door to Nathan's room open and then close.

"Oh, baby," Barbara said and Stacey could imagine their tender embrace. "I was worried. Come on, you need to sleep it off."

Stacey never slept that night. She lay on her cold hotel room bed and stared at the ceiling, counting the seconds until she could get up, check out, grab a taxi and go to the airport. Though her flight wasn't for the following day, she planned to turn in her airline ticket and leave on the next available flight to Seattle. From there, she planned to take a boat back to the island.

She was up at the crack of dawn and spent twenty minutes under a hot shower before she put on traveling clothes and went downstairs to check out.

"The bill's already been paid," the clerk told her when she tried to settle her account. "Mr. Sloan took care of it."

Bastard! "Fine," she gritted through clenched teeth.

"I'll call the bell captain to help you with you things."

"I can manage," Stacey replied. "Only one bag." She turned toward the hotel doors and stood face-to-face with Barbara Jones. All of her confidence flagged at the sight of the beautiful, soft-spoken woman.

"Don't leave," Barbara said, her eyes clouded with worry.

"I have to get back—"

"Nathan needs you."

Stacey could have dropped through the floor. "For what? A whipping post?" she shot back and then instantly regretted her words. "I'm sorry, Barbara, but I've taken all I can from him."

Barbara placed her hand on Stacey's shoulder. "He didn't mean everything he said to you, you have to believe that. He's just suffered the most traumatic loss of his life."

So have I. "I know, Barbara, but I can't go to him. I've tried, more often than you know."

"Stacey, please. For his sake."

Stacey wavered, but only for an instant. "Does he know you're here?"

"No."

"Then I don't think it would be wise to go upstairs and throw myself at him. He's made it very clear how he feels about me." She started to step away.

"What about Cindy?"

Stacey froze and her entire body trembled. "I wish I could help him get custody of Cindy, but there's nothing I can do."

"You can stay here and support him!"

Stacey whirled and faced the dark-haired woman. "I told you that I tried and that it didn't work. He doesn't want me, Barbara. I don't really believe he ever did. I was just…convenient."

"You don't really think that!"

Stacey shrugged. "I don't know what to think," she admitted. "But I'm not about to throw myself at a man who doesn't want me, who blames me for the loss of his child." Her voice caught, and she had to square her shoulders.

"I know what you thought of me," Barbara said suddenly. "I want to tell you that once he met you, well, it was over between Nathan and me."

Stacey's heart twisted and she felt absolutely wretched. "Nathan knows where I live," she whispered kindly. "Goodbye, Barbara."

"You're making a big mistake,"

"You might be right, but it's certainly not the first, and probably a long shot from the last." With that, she turned and walked through the revolving glass doors to a waiting cab.

SHE HADN'T HEARD from Nathan since. She'd been back on Sanctity Island three weeks, and there had been no phone call, no letter, nothing. It was over, as simple as that.

If only she could convince herself that she didn't love him.

Walking home that afternoon in the cold November rain, she told herself that she would get over him. Somehow, she had managed to put Daniel Brown and his father behind her and she would find a way to forget Nathan Sloan and his blue-eyed daughter.

But how? And how long would it take?

Attila was whining to get out of the house. She opened the door, and the puppy ran in a few crazy circles before heading for the stairs to the beach.

"Not today," Stacey called. "Attila! Come here!" But the foolish pup kept right on running. Lankier now, but still full of pep, he bounded down the stairs with Stacey on his heels. "Cindy wouldn't recognize you," she said as the dog bounded and ran around her on the wet sand.

Without much enthusiasm, Staccy tossed a stick for him and he retrieved it, dragging it on the ground as he eagerly returned it to her.

"Don't you ever run out of energy?" she asked, hoisting the stick high in the air. It spun end over end and landed in the water. The dog reached it easily and loped back to her. "Ask a stupid question," she said as she realized the half-grown pup was tireless. "Come on, let's go inside where it's dry."

She looked down the beach and imagined she saw Nathan standing near the stairs to his cabin. For a moment her traitorous heart leaped, and then she realized that the person running toward her was another dark-haired man out for an afternoon jog on the beach. "Dreamer," she told herself bitterly as she climbed the stairs to her cabin.

Nathan's image wouldn't leave her alone. His ghost seemed to be everywhere on the island and the fleeting happy moments she'd shared with him lingered in her mind. Time after time, she told herself to shake it off and pull herself up by the bootstraps and, time after time, she failed.

"This is Thanksgiving vacation," she reminded herself, and the thought of four days away from her job made her miserable. Knowing that she was probably making a big mistake, she called her mother. Mona answered on the third ring.

"Stacey! Don't tell me, you're coming for the holidays."

"No, Mom. Just thought I'd call and check in."

"But we'd love to have you! The Schaeffers are coming in from Hartford and the Reeces, you remember Edward and Marie, they'll be flying in tomorrow. They'd all love to see you!"

Stacey cringed. "Maybe next year."

"I won't hear of it!" Mona reprimanded. "Charles and I are expecting you for Christmas, and I don't want to be disappointed."

"I'm not sure about that, Mom."

"Why not, for heaven's sake? If it's the money that's

bothering you, I'll send you the plane fare. Think of it; Christmas with the Reeces and the Schaeffers!"

Stacey thought about it and her stomach turned over. "I'll think about it," she promised, but her thoughts had already strayed to Nathan. What would he be doing for the holidays? And with whom?

"I want you to know that you're always welcome here."

Stacey's spirits rose a bit. "I know, Mom. Happy Thanksgiving."

"Same to you, dear."

"And say hello to Charles," Stacey said, almost as an afterthought.

"I will."

She hung up and for the first time in two years, she questioned her life-style on the island. She'd never return to Boston—that wasn't the issue. But maybe getting off the island, away from the memories of Nathan and Cindy would help. "And then you'd be running," she chastised herself, as she mounted the stairs to her loft. "You've got to stay here and work this thing out. This island is your home. The school is your life!" She kicked off her slippers and flopped on the bed, the bed she'd shared with Nathan.

Her thoughts were centered on him and his little girl. "I love you both," she whispered to the empty room, wondering if the ache in her heart would ever subside, before she finally drifted to sleep.

MONDAY MORNING CAME at last and Stacey was busy with her students. Wound up from the four-day weekend, the children were noisier and more restless than ever. Stacey loved the high level of activity. After a lonely four days, the children were what she needed to rejuvenate. She was even laughing when Tommy Perkins zipped his coat over his head and pretended to be the headless horseman of Sleepy Hollow.

"You're a little behind the times," she teased. "Ichabod Crane and Halloween are long past. Even Thanksgiving is over."

"And next comes Christmas!" Tommy said proudly as he poked his head through his coat.

"Right you are."

"Come on, Tommy," his mother admonished with a laugh. She grabbed his lunch pail and herded her small son to the door. "We had a wonderful Thanksgiving this year. A lot of the credit goes to you, Miss Monroe."

"I don't know about that." Stacey winked at Tommy. "Seems to me this guy's the big hero."

Tommy beamed as his mother led him down the hall.

"Looks like you've got yourself a fan," Margaret observed as she walked into the room.

"We all need at least one."

"That we do," Margaret agreed with a smile as she watched Tommy saunter confidently through the outside doors.

"So how was your vacation?"

"Wonderful," Margaret replied. "Except for the turkey. My sister doesn't believe that a turkey's done until it's dry as a bone."

"So why don't you get her a meat thermometer for Christmas?" Stacey asked with a smile.

"And offend her? No way. I just put up with it."

"And complain to me."

"Do you mind?"

"Wouldn't have it any other way."

"I thought not." Margaret smiled and then handed Stacey a clipping from a newspaper. "And I thought you might be interested in this. It's from the latest edition of the *Los Angeles Times*."

Stacey's heart missed a beat as she looked down at the front-page article. A large picture of Robert Madison accompanied the story. According to the article, Madison had been indicted on thirty counts of embezzlement and bribery. One of the judges on his payroll was Judge Raymond Barclay, the judge who had awarded custody of Cindy to Madison. The article indicated that there were further charges pending against Madison, including the possibility that he had something to do with his wife's death.

"Oh, God," Stacey whispered as she stared at the smaller photograph affixed to the report. It was a picture of Barbara Jones, Nathan and Cindy. Nathan looked wan and tired, but a smile creased his face as he held his daughter. One of his arms was draped lovingly over Barbara's shoulders.

Stacey's emotions ran the gauntlet from love to hate to white-hot jealousy. She was relieved and happy, of course, that Nathan was reunited with his daughter, but she couldn't fight the jealousy that stabbed her heart as she stared down to the black-and-white picture of Barbara's glowing face.

"So it seems you were right after all," Margaret said softly.

Trying not to cry, Stacey agreed. "I guess so."

"I thought you'd like to see it, and I wanted to apologize for being such an old fool about Mr. Sloan."

"It's all right," Stacey said, her voice giving away her emotions. "You're not the only one who misjudged him."

Margaret sighed and sat on the corner of Stacey's desk. "You know, I usually don't make it my business to pry." At the disbelieving rise of Stacey's brow, she quickly amended her statement. "Well, I *try* not to. But in this case, I think I'll make an exception."

"Oh?"

"Have you thought about going back to L.A. and looking him up?"

Only a million times. "It wouldn't work."

"You're sure?"

"Yes."

"But you've been miserable without him."

"I'll get over it," Stacey insisted. "It takes time."

"If you're sure—"

"I'm not sure of anything right now," Stacey admitted. "But I know that throwing myself at Nathan would be the worst thing I could do."

"You're certain?"

Stacey stared straight into Margaret's eyes. "Yes."

Margaret thought for a moment and then shrugged. "It's your life," she said, going to the door. "But if you ever need someone to talk to—"

"You'd be the first on my list."

"Good." With that, Dr. Woodward left the room.

DECEMBER WAS COLDER than had been predicted, and the ice around Stacey's heart refused to thaw. She should have thrown away the article Margaret had given her and cut her losses, but she couldn't. That newspaper clipping was her final link to Nathan and Cindy. Calling herself a masochist of the worst order, Stacey read the article over and over and cried until she had no more tears to weep.

IT SNOWED FOR Christmas vacation, and the children in Stacey's class were out of their minds with ecstasy. On the final day of school, when the last child had gone home, toting his surprise gifts for his parents, Stacey locked the doors of the classroom, promised Margaret she would visit her on Christmas morning and took the long way home, along the beach. She was carrying the hamster cage under one arm and a bag of presents from her students under the other.

Noting with regret that Nathan's cabin seemed occupied, she sighed and hunched her shoulders against the falling snowflakes that clung to her hair and melted against her cheeks. The sky was slate-gray, the sea an opaque green.

Nathan must have sold the cabin as he'd planned, and Stacey felt the familiar ache in her heart when she realized that he must have been on the island and hadn't bothered to stop by to see her.

"Well, what did you expect?" she asked herself as she watched the smoke billowing from his chimney and remembered how cruel he'd been. "Life goes on. With or without Nathan Sloan. In your case, Miss Monroe, without."

So what were her options? she wondered as she gripped the hamster cage more tightly. Maybe she should have taken her mother up on her offer and gone to Boston for the holidays. At least then, she wouldn't have to spend Christmas Eve alone.

Looking up the beach, she stopped dead in her tracks. Nathan and Cindy were running toward her, in an obvious race. "It's your mind playing tricks on you again," she warned herself, but even as she spoke, she knew that she wasn't imagining things. Trembling, she waited, bracing herself for the onslaught against her raw emotions.

Nathan, dark hair ruffling in the wind, skin tight over his angular features, approached. He looked heart-stoppingly masculine in worn jeans, a faded shirt and thick jacket. Striding easily toward her, he stared into her eyes with that deep blue gaze she'd always found so erotic.

Cindy was with him, running as fast as her short legs would carry her.

Her eyes filling with tears of relief, Stacey bent on one knee, set the hamster down with a jolt and opened her arms wide for the careering child.

"I told you she would be here!" Cindy said to her father as she threw herself at her teacher, and Stacey, overcome with emotion, wrapped her arms around the precious child. Try as she might, she couldn't stem the flow of tears from her eyes or swallow the huge lump in her throat. "Where's Attila?" Cindy demanded precociously.

"At the house, and will he be glad to see you!" Stacey choked out, sniffing and lifting questioning eyes to Nathan.

"Me, too?" Nathan asked, stopping just short of her.

"Probably…"

"And what about you?" he asked gently, his expression tight. "Are you glad to see me?" Snowflakes clung to his wind-rumpled hair and his blue eyes were warm and kind.

Stacey's heart twisted painfully. "I… I don't know."

He helped her to her feet and stared deep into her eyes. Stacey's arms involuntarily wrapped more tightly around Cindy and she balanced the child on her hip. "I'm not sure how to apologize for being such a jerk," he said. "I've thought about it a long time, and there's nothing I can say that won't sound wrong."

"You're probably right," she agreed.

He smiled sadly. "I'm trying my best to be humble, you know. It's not really my nature."

"I know."

He sighed. "Look, Stacey... I'm not much good at apologizing."

"Is that why you're here? To apologize?"

"For starters, if you'll tell me how." His blue, blue eyes pierced into her soul.

She swallowed hard. "How about a thousand years of penance?"

He lifted his dark brows, and his mouth quirked at the corners. "Would that be enough?"

"Probably not, but it's a beginning."

His gaze swept to the sea before returning to her face. "Okay. How about if I told you I loved you and couldn't get you out of my mind, no matter how hard I tried?"

Stacey smiled a little. "That would help your cause considerably," she said, unable to remain angry. It was so good to be with him again. And Cindy. God, it felt good to hold her.

"And if I asked you to marry me?"

Stacey froze, her arms wrapped tightly around Nathan's child as she tried to think sensibly. The wintry air caught in her lungs at the unexpected question. "I don't know," she heard herself say. "So much has happened..."

"I see." He picked up the hamster cage and the bag of gifts, and he began walking to her cabin.

She held Cindy tightly, but her thoughts were spinning crazily, and her sturdy legs felt suddenly weak.

Marry Nathan? Impossible. But her heart leaped at the thought. It was too good to be true, and she felt like pinching herself to make sure she wasn't dreaming.

Once back in her cabin, with Cindy occupied by a frantic, ecstatic puppy, Nathan drew Stacey into the circle of his arms. Strong and tanned, they folded easily around her waist. She felt warm and safe and protected. The love in her heart grew with each second she was near him, and she knew that she loved him as passionately as she ever had.

"I'm serious, Stacey," he whispered into her hair. "Marry me."

"It's not that easy."

"It's as easy as you make it," he murmured, kissing her softly on the lips before the dormant passion in his blood burst to life. "I need you."

The kiss deepened and Stacey was lost to him. She wound her arms around his neck and sighed against him. "I never could deny you anything," she conceded.

"Then you'll marry me?"

"Wouldn't have it any other way," she admitted with a thoughtful smile.

Hours later, they had tucked a tired but happy Cindy into her own bed in Nathan's cabin. Attila had reclaimed his spot in Cindy's room, and Nathan and Stacey were finally alone.

They sat together on the couch near the fire. Their stockinged feet were propped on the coffee table, and Stacey's head was resting comfortably on Nathan's shoulder as he explained about the past few weeks and that the torment of Robert Madison was finally over.

"There's only one more thing to make my life complete," he said, kissing the hair on her crown.

"Oh? And what's that?"

"For you to forgive me—"

"I do."

"And marry me." Reaching deep in his pocket, he withdrew a gold ring with a single, sparkling diamond. The bright jewel winked in the firelight. "Cindy needs you, and so do I."

"And I need you," she admitted, watching in fascination as he placed the ring on her finger. Everything was perfect, she thought as she snuggled contentedly against him, as long as she had this one man's love. The snow on the windowpanes, a brightly lit Christmas tree in the room and a rosy future with Nathan and Cindy. Nothing would make her happier.

"I want to get married tomorrow," Nathan said.

"But tomorrow's Christmas—"

"Okay, how about the day after," Nathan said, pulling her closer to him.

"Perfect," she agreed, snuggling into his arms. "Couldn't be better."

Two days later, Stacey Monroe proudly became Mrs. Nathan Sloan.

* * * * *

MYSTIC

PROLOGUE

Beaumont Breeding Farm—Summer

SAVANNAH SLOWED THE mare to a walk and patted Mattie's sweating neck. Her breath was as short as that of the mare; the sprint through the open pastures had been exhilarating. A soft breeze rustled through the branches of trees along the fence and made the July afternoon tolerable as it cooled the trickle of sweat running down her back. She pushed her black hair away from her face and squinted against the hot sun in the northern California sky.

"I guess it's time to go back home," she said reluctantly as she reined the mare toward the gate at the far end of the field. Mattie flicked her ears forward expectantly.

Looking east, Savannah noticed a tall broad-shouldered figure near the gate. She squinted as she approached and tried to place the man repairing the sagging fence. *Must be a new hired hand,* she thought idly, fascinated nonetheless.

She pulled Mattie up short, several yards away from the man, and waited in the dappled shade of an old apple tree. Unable to get through the gate until he was finished with his work, she leaned back in the saddle and observed him.

He was wearing only dusty jeans and boots. His shirt had been tossed over a post, and his deeply muscled back, tanned and glistening with sweat, was straining as he stretched the heavy wire around a new wooden fence post.

I wonder where Dad found him, Savannah mused, admiring the play of rippling muscles and straining tendons of his shoulders and back as he worked. His hair was dark with sweat, and the worn fabric of his jeans stretched taut over lean hips and muscular thighs.

"That should do it," he said, rubbing the small of his back as he straightened and admired his work. His voice was strangely familiar.

Then he dusted his hands together and turned, as if he'd felt her staring at him. Shielding his eyes against the lowering sun, he looked in her direction and every muscle in his body went rigid. "Savannah?"

The sight of Travis's eyes fixed on her made her stomach jump unexpectedly. Savannah urged her horse forward and stopped the mare only a few feet from him. "I… I didn't know you were back on the farm," she replied, blushing slightly at being caught staring at him. *It was Travis for God's sake. Just Travis!*

His amused smile stretched over the angular features of his face. Wiping the sweat from his forehead, he stretched his aching back muscles. "The prodigal son has returned, so to speak."

"So to speak," she whispered, her throat uncomfortably tight as she stared into his steel-gray eyes. The same gray eyes she'd seen most of her life. Only now, they seemed incredibly erotic, and the corded muscles of his chest and shoulders added to his intense masculinity—a sensual virility she'd never noticed before. He'd always just been Travis, almost a brother. "I thought you had a job in L.A."

"I do." He leaned insolently against the post and the hard line of his mouth turned cynical. "But I thought I'd spend the rest of the summer on the farm before I get stuck in the rut of three-piece suits and three-martini lunches."

"So you're staying?" *Why was her heart pounding so wildly?*

"Until September." He glanced around the farm, taking in the whitewashed buildings, the rolling acres of pastureland, and the dusky hills in the distance. "I'm gonna miss this place, though," he admitted, his gaze darkening a bit as it rested on the scampering, long-legged foals in the next field.

"And we'll all miss you," Savannah replied, wondering at the unusual huskiness in her voice.

Travis's head jerked up and he stared at her for a moment. His brows drew together in concentration before he cleared his throat. "Not much to miss, really," he argued. "I haven't been around much."

"That's what happens when you go to school to become a politician."

"Lawyer," he corrected.

Savannah shrugged. "That's not the way I heard it. Dad is already planning a future for you in politics." She cocked her head to the side and smiled. "You know, I wouldn't be surprised if someday you become a senator or something."

"Not on your life, lady!" Travis let out a hollow laugh, but his gray eyes turned stone cold. "Your old man is always scheming, Savannah. But this time he's gone too far." He reached to the ground and picked up a bottle of beer that had been hidden in the dry grass.

"But your father—"

"Was a senator from Colorado, and now according to the press, the old man might not have been as lily-white as the voters thought." Travis scowled, swore under his breath and kicked at the fence post with the toe of his boot. "But then you already knew that." Eyeing her over the top of the bottle, he lifted his chin and took a long swallow of beer, then tossed the empty bottle to the ground. With a sound of disgust, he wiped the back of his hand over his mouth and then raked tense fingers through his hair in frustration. "It seems to be the popular thing to do these days, digging up the dirt on dead politicians."

Savannah didn't know what to say, so she looked away and tried not to notice the way the afternoon sun played in Travis's rich, chestnut-colored hair. Tried not to notice the ripple of his shoulder muscles as he shoveled a last scoop of dirt around the post, or the fact that the curling hairs over his chest were dark with sweat and accentuated the flat contour of his abdomen.

"I can't worry about it, anyway. What's done is done. Right?"

"Right."

He looked up at her again and she couldn't help but stare at his mouth. Thin lips curved slightly downward in vexation as he noticed the intensity of her gaze.

He pretended interest in his work and avoided her eyes. "Still going with that boy… David what's-his-name?" he asked.

"Crandall. And no."

"Why not?"

She lifted one shoulder and shifted uncomfortably in the saddle. For the first time since she could remember, she didn't like Travis poking his nose into her private life. "I don't know. It just didn't work out."

His jaw tightened a bit. "Want to talk about it?"

"No, uh, I don't think so."

"You used to tell me whatever was on your mind."

"Yeah, but I was just a kid then."

"And now?" He slid a glance up her body.

"And now I'm seventeen." She tossed her black hair away from her face and sat up straight in the saddle, shoulders pinned back, unconsciously thrusting her breasts forward.

Travis sucked in his breath and frowned. "Oh, I see; all grown up."

"Just like you were when you were seventeen." She arched a disdainful eyebrow, hoping to appear more sophisticated than she felt sitting astride Mattie. Her T-shirt and cutoff jeans, wild black hair and freshly scrubbed face didn't help the image. She probably looked the same as she did when she was a skinny kid of nine.

"Seventeen. That was so long ago, I can't even remember."

"I do. That's how old you were when you moved in with us."

"You remember that far back?"

"Give me a break, Travis. I was nine, and I've got a great memory. I thought you were so… I think the word they use today is 'awesome.'"

Travis shook his head. "I was a rebellious brat."

"And I was impressed by your total disrespect for anything."

Travis winced. "Reginald wasn't."

"Dad is and always has been the ultimate authoritarian. That's why I thought you were so...brave." She laughed and some of the growing tension between them dissolved. "And now you're an old man of twenty-five."

"Yeah, I guess so." He leaned against the wooden post and crossed his arms over his chest as his smile faded. "And it's time to quit sponging off your dad and try and make a living on my own."

"You've never sponged off Dad!" Indignation colored Savannah's cheeks. "Maybe some people don't know it, but I do."

"He took me in—"

"And you worked. Hard. On this farm. For nothing. Just like you're doing now! As for your education, you had a trust fund. You didn't exactly come here as a pauper, you know!"

"Whoa!" He laughed deep in his throat. "I didn't know I had such a bulldog in my corner."

"Just stating the facts, counselor." She smiled and blushed a little under his unyielding stare. The warm familiarity that had existed between them just seconds before suddenly vanished.

"You never cease to amaze me, Savvy," Travis said, using the nickname he had given her all those years before. His voice was barely above a whisper as his flinty gaze locked intimately with hers. Savannah's heart began to pound in the thickening silence, and Travis's eyes narrowed.

A stallion whistled in the distance, and Mattie snorted, breaking the silence. Travis gave his head a quick shake, as if to dislodge an unwanted thought. "Remind me to hire you when I'm having trouble getting the jury to see my client's side of the story," he joked, picking up his shirt, empty bottle and shovel and carrying them to a Jeep parked on the other side of the gate.

"I doubt that my testimony would make an impact."

"I don't know," he said, rubbing his square, beard-shadowed chin thoughtfully. His gaze inched up her bare, suntanned legs before lingering slightly on her waist and breasts and then finally reaching her eyes. She felt as if she'd just been stripped bare, and her cheeks burned under his assessing stare. "I just don't know."

Somehow she understood that he wasn't referring to his fictitious courtroom scenario, and her heart fluttered. To save herself from further embarrassment, she kicked Mattie and the game little mare broke into a gallop. Savannah leaned forward in the saddle and raced away from Travis and the odd feelings he'd unwittingly inspired.

THE NEXT FIVE weeks were torture. Savannah saw Travis every night at dinner. Every night, that is, that he wasn't with Melinda, his fiancée. Why his engagement to Melinda Reaves bothered Savannah now eluded her. Melinda was a nice enough girl—make that woman, she corrected herself—and Travis had dated her for years. It was only natural that someday Travis and Melinda would marry. Right? Then why did she feel sick inside every time she thought about Travis and Melinda together?

During the days, Savannah ran into Travis working around the farm. In the stables, in the tack room, at the lake, in the stallion barn, everywhere. There didn't seem to be a place she could hide without experiencing the sensation that he was watching her. She had even caught him staring openly at her more than once, though he'd always looked quickly away when she caught his gaze. Though Savannah had tried to be discreet, she was fascinated by him. She'd watch him work and her mind would create deliciously wanton fantasies about him.

"Don't do this," she warned herself on more than one occasion when she found herself dressing with more care than was her custom. "This is Travis you're thinking about. Travis!" But the pain in her middle wouldn't go away, nor could she keep her eyes from straying to his face, his hands, his lips, his thighs. Oftentimes she found herself wondering just what it would feel like to have Travis touch her with those large, work-roughened hands, what it would taste like to have his sensual lips brush against hers…how it would feel to become his lover. Just the thought of his hard, male physique pressed hungrily against her body made her break into a nervous sweat and her heart beat savagely.

"You're out of your ever-lovin' mind," she told herself.

"WHAT'S WRONG WITH YOU, Savannah?" David asked as they were driving back to the farm.

The date with David had been a disaster from the start, and she knew now that she never should have agreed to it.

Though she'd tried not to think about Travis, she hadn't even tasted the gourmet food or paid any attention to the movie that David had taken her to.

"Nothing's wrong with me." *Except that I took this date out of spite, because Travis is with Melinda again.* She felt uneasy, and some of the uncomfortable feeling was from guilt. She'd used David to lash back at Travis.

Not fair. David was a friend, a good friend. And Travis hadn't even noticed.

"Give me a break. You've been brooding all night. Why?"

"I'm not brooding."

"Look, just tell me, was it something I did?"

Savannah smiled and shook her head. "No, of course not."

David sighed in relief and parked the car behind her house, near the back porch. He cut the engine and switched off the headlights. The breeze that filtered through the open windows of the car was little relief from the stifling night. Savannah felt hot and sticky as she reached for the handle of the door.

"Wait." David's hand touched her on the shoulder and she stopped. His brown eyes searched hers. "There's someone else, isn't there?"

"No," she lied. Her feelings for Travis were just school-girl fantasies and she recognized them as such.

"Then, what, Savannah? Don't you know I love you?"

It was the last thing she wanted to hear. "David, you're a good friend and I like you very much—"

"And I sense a big 'but' coming here," he complained.

"Can't we just be friends?"

"Friends?" he repeated. "Friends. Savannah, for cris-sake, didn't you hear me?" He placed a finger under her chin and forced her to look into his intense gaze. "I *love* you."

"David—"

But she couldn't stop him as his arms tightened around her and he kissed her with more passion than she'd ever thought possible. When he lifted his head, her lips were throbbing painfully. "David, please, don't," she whispered, trying to pull away from him.

"You used to like me to kiss you," he rasped in disbelief.

"I told you… I just want to be friends."

"Like hell." He pulled her close to him again and this time when he kissed her she felt his tongue press against her teeth and his sweaty hands reach below the hem of her sweater to touch her naked abdomen and inch upward to her breasts.

I can't! she thought desperately. *I just can't let him touch me!* Gathering all her strength, she wrenched one arm free and slapped him across the cheek. It had the effect of a bucket of cold water. He drew back his head and his eyes glittered frightfully. "Don't push me, Savannah," he ground out.

"And don't push *me!*"

He released her then and his face slackened. "I just don't understand. Why did you go out with me?"

"Because I like you. I thought you were my friend."

"There's that word again," he said, rubbing his cheek. "I never thought I would hate being called a friend, but I do." He placed his hands over the steering wheel and let his head fall forward. "There is someone else, isn't there?" She understood his despair. Wasn't she in the same position herself?

"I don't know, David," she said, tenderness softening her voice. "I…do care for someone else…" He flinched. "But believe me, he doesn't know I'm alive… I'd… I'd better go."

"I'll walk you to the door."

"No! It's okay. Really. I can make it."

This time she got the door open.

"Savannah—"

"Yeah?"

"I'm sorry."

Tears stood in her eyes. "I know, David." She didn't wait for any further confessions from him. All she knew was that she'd probably lost a very good friend and she'd humiliated him in the bargain. She got out of the car and slammed the door shut.

"I can't seem to do anything right," she thought aloud as she climbed the two steps to the porch. She heard David's car start and listened as he drove away. "Thank God," she whispered and realized that she'd started to cry.

Reaching into her purse for her keys, she heard a sound: the heel of a boot scraping against the flagstones. She nearly jumped out of her skin. Swallowing back a small lump of fear she turned and faced Travis, who was sitting in the shadows of the porch in a rocking chair. *Oh, God...*

"You should be more careful about who you go out with," he said, his voice cold.

"And you should be more careful about sitting in the dark. You nearly scared me to death."

"I thought you weren't dating David."

"I'm not."

Silence. Savannah could hear her own heart pounding.

"You're leading him on," he accused.

Savannah heard the irritation in his voice, though she could barely see his face. "You should mind your own business."

"Then maybe next time, you'll have the decency to roll the windows up." With a sinking sensation, Savan-

nah realized that Travis had heard all of her conversation
with David. She was mortified and kept rummaging in
her purse. *Where was the damned key?*

"Maybe next time *you'll* have the decency to mind
your own business and not eavesdrop."

"I wasn't eavesdropping."

"Than what're you doing out here all alone? Where's
Melinda?"

"At home." His voice sounded dead.

"Oh."

Her fingers found the key ring, but it was too late.
Travis was on his feet and walking toward her. As the
gap between them closed, her pulse began to race wildly.
He stopped only inches from her, close enough that she
could feel the heat radiating from his body, see the pain
and concern etched over his harsh features. "I'm serious, Savannah. You shouldn't lead that boy on. And that
advice goes for any other man as well."

"I told you, I wasn't leading him on."

"He cares about you, and when a boy, a young man,
cares about a woman, sometimes he gets carried away.
He can't help himself. He stops using his brain and starts
thinking with his— Oh, hell, I'm making a bloody mess
of this!"

"You sound as if you're speaking from experience."

His muscles became rigid. "Maybe I am."

Savannah thought of Melinda and felt like crying all
over again. Travis leaned a shoulder against the wall and
she felt his eyes staring at her mussed hair and flushed
face.

"Just be careful, Savannah," he said tenderly, touching the edge of her jaw. "Don't get yourself into a situ-

ation that you can't get out of. I won't always be here to take care of you."

The feel of his fingers on her skin made her pulse jump. The heat of his touch seemed to scorch a path to her heart. "A lot of good it did having you here."

"I didn't want to butt in. It really wasn't any of my business. But, believe me, if David hadn't come to his senses when you slapped him, I would have jerked open that car door and beat the living hell out of him."

"David wouldn't hurt me."

"I didn't know that."

The thought of Travis willing to fight to protect her virtue was pleasant and she couldn't help but smile.

"This is serious business, Savannah."

The finger at her jaw moved slowly to her throat and Savannah felt herself melting inside. A warm ache stretched deep inside her and it was hard to keep her mind on anything but Travis's warm finger and his dark, searing gaze. It took her breath away.

"I… I know."

"Just don't make the same mistake Charmaine did."

Savannah felt herself color. Her sister, Charmaine, had gotten pregnant the year before and was now married to Wade Benson, the father of her little boy. "I don't need a lesson in sex education," she tossed back.

"Good." He let his hand drop and even in the hot night she shivered. "'Cause I'm sure as hell not the one who should be giving you one."

"What's that supposed to mean?"

He closed his eyes. "Oh, Savannah, you just don't have any idea what you do to a man, do you?" Opening his eyes, he looked at her lovingly for a fleeting moment. "Just don't underestimate your effect on men or overestimate a man's self-control."

Her throat was dry, but she had to ask the question. "All men?"

"All men."

"Does that include you?" she whispered.

"All men," he repeated and opened the door to the kitchen. "Now go upstairs to bed and get some sleep before I forget the fact that I'm supposed to be a brother to you, that I should be looking out for your best interests."

"I don't need a keeper, Travis," she said, placing her fingers on his arm.

His eyes were cold and assessing as he measured the innocence in her gaze. "Well, maybe *I* do." He took hold of her wrist and his face became expressionless as he forced her hand away from him. "You've heard the old expression, 'Don't play with fire unless you're ready to get burned'?" he said, his jaw tight. "Think about it."

And then he strode away, into the dark night.

For five days Savannah didn't see Travis, and she discovered that it was more difficult to work on the farm when he was absent than when he was there. Just how much of the conversation with David had he heard, and how much had he pieced together? Had he realized that he was the man she cared for? Savannah wondered.

That she loved Travis McCord came as an unwelcome and painful realization. The fact that he loved another woman made the situation all the more intolerable.

JUST TWO MORE WEEKS, Savannah thought as she lay on the top of her bed, staring at the ceiling, wondering where Travis was at one in the morning. *Just two more weeks and then he'll be gone.*

At the thought of his leaving and marrying Melinda Reaves, Savannah's heart wrenched painfully. She rolled over and looked at the clock, just as she had every two minutes for the past half hour. "This is crazy," she told herself.

For nearly as long as she could remember, Travis had been a part of Beaumont Breeding Farm. When his parents had been killed in a plane crash, her father and mother had taken him in as if he were their own. Savannah had always looked up to the rebellious young man as the older brother she'd never had. Never in her wildest dreams had she imagined that she would fall in love with him. Well, not "in love" exactly. She loved him. He still thought of her as a kid sister and it was probably best that way. If she could just make it through the next two weeks without letting him know how she felt about him, everything would work out. Travis would marry Melinda, and Savannah would go to college. *If she didn't die first!* Her small fist curled and pounded the unused pillow on her bed.

Her restlessness finally got the better of her and she threw off the covers, grabbed her robe, slipped on a pair of thongs and sneaked down the hallway. The only sounds in the house were the soft ticking of the hall clock and the hum of the refrigerator. One of the steps squeaked as she hurried down the staircase. She froze, but no one in the house stirred. Taking a deep breath, Savannah quietly hurried down the rest of the stairs, softly opened the front door, slipped outside and closed the door behind her.

The night was illuminated by a lazy half moon and a sprinkling of stars that peeked through the wispy, dark clouds. The smell of honeysuckle and lilacs filled the air and the soft croaking of frogs was interrupted by the occasional whinny of a mare calling to her foal. Other than those few noises, the night was still.

Savannah walked down the worn path to the lake almost by instinct. She climbed over the gates rather than risking the noise of unlatching them. When the scrub oak and pine trees gave way to a clearing and the small irregular-shaped lake, Savannah smiled, slipped out of her thongs, tossed her robe to the ground and waded into the water. It felt cool against her skin and she dived to the bottom before surfacing.

She had been swimming about fifteen minutes when she realized that she wasn't alone. Her heart nearly stopped beating and she braced herself for one of her father's stern lectures.

"Dad?" she called unsteadily at the figure of a man leaning against the sturdy trunk of an oak tree. "Dad, is that you?"

For the first time in years, Travis had consumed more alcohol than he could handle, and he intended to clear his head with a long walk. The argument he'd had earlier in the evening with Melinda was still ringing in his mind. She'd accused him of being aloof, disinterested in her, and maybe she was right. Because for the past few damning weeks, he'd been thinking solely of Savannah Beaumont. *Reginald's daughter, for God's sake!* And the thoughts he'd had about her were far from brotherly.

From the first time he'd seen her, half-dressed, her firm breasts straining against a T-shirt, her supple legs wrapped around that bay mare, he'd been out of his mind with lust. The burning desire had tortured him with wildly erotic fantasies that took away his sleep.

He'd even had to leave the farm for a couple of days to get his head back on straight. The last thing he needed was to get involved with a seventeen-year-old girl, the daughter of the man who'd raised him. But it was confusing. Confusing as hell. And he didn't blame Melinda for being angry. Since he'd seen Savannah again, he hadn't been able to concentrate on Melinda at all—to the point that his interest in making love to her had all but disappeared.

He let his shirt gape open, hoping that the cool air would help clear his head. Leaning against an oak tree, he heard the splashing in the lake. His head was spinning crazily, but even in the darkness he recognized Savannah and the fact that she was swimming nude in the inky water. His fingers dug into the rough bark of the oak tree for support. *Oh, God,* he thought, trying to think straight. *Give me strength.*

Then she called to him. "Dad?" Silence. Travis's heart thundered in his chest. "Dad, is that you?"

"What the devil are you doing here?" Travis asked, barely trusting his voice.

Not Travis! Savannah's heartbeat accelerated when she recognized his voice. *Not here!* "Minding my own business," she managed to choke out.

Silvery light from a iridescent moon rippled on the water, alternately shadowing and highlighting the firm white swell of her breasts and the dark tips of her nipples. Her black hair was slicked away from her face and her chin was thrust forward defiantly. Drops of water clung to her lashes and slid down her cheeks and a traitorous ache began to throb in Travis's loins.

"You shouldn't be here," he said, his throat uncomfortably tight. "Someone might see you."

"*Someone* has."

"You know what I mean." Travis fought to clear his head and he battled against the fire radiating from his loins. Shifting against the tree, he willed the natural re-action of his body to subside. And failed. *Leave right now,* he told himself, *before you say or do something foolish.*

"Where's Melinda?" Savannah asked, swimming nearer to him.

He heard the tremor in her voice, saw the quiet suf-fering in her eyes. *Go away, Savannah, don't look at me like that.* "I don't know." He closed his eyes and tried not to watch the gentle water caress the satin-white skin of her body. "I don't think we'll see each other again."

"But you're engaged."

"Not anymore." He fished in the pocket of his jeans and retrieved the diamond ring. Holding it up to the moonlight, it winked mockingly at him. His fingers curled around the cold metal and stones before he cursed and hurled the ring into the water. It settled into the lake with barely a splash.

"You shouldn't have done that," Savannah repri-manded, edging closer to the bank, but she couldn't hide the pleasure in her voice.

"I should have done it a long time ago."

"You're drunk."

"Not drunk enough."

"Oh, Travis," she said with a shake of her head. "If you're not careful, you'll self-destruct."

The comfort in her voice touched a primitive part of him and he knew the battle he was alternately fighting and surrendering to was about to be lost.

He saw her robe near the bank and he pushed himself

upright to retrieve it. As he stood, he swayed slightly. Righting himself, he walked over to the bank. "You'd better get out of there," he said. "It's the middle of the night, for crying out loud."

She laughed and dipped back into the water. Knowing that he wasn't tied to Melinda made her feel as if a tremendous weight had been lifted from her shoulders.

"Savannah—"

"Don't worry about me," she said, resurfacing and shaking the hair out of her face.

"Does anyone know you're out here?"

"Just you."

"Great," he muttered, his eyes riveted to the fascinating hollow of her throat and the pulse throbbing there. The reaction that Melinda hadn't been able to stir began just at the sight of Savannah's wet body.

"Oh, all right." She swam to where her feet touched the soft silt at the bottom of the lake and began to walk out of the water. Travis, knowing that his duty was done and that he should walk away, stood fascinated as she slowly emerged from the water.

Savannah knew there was no way she could hide her body. The best thing to do was get to the robe and cover up as quickly as possible, but she could feel Travis's eyes upon her, two gray orbs sizzling into her flesh.

Travis sucked in his breath as he watched her. Her white skin contrasted to the black night and droplets of water slid seductively down her throat to her breasts. He watched the gentle sway of her breasts as she walked toward him. Her waist was small and her navel a provocative dimple in her abdomen.

Travis's breath was tight in his lungs as her hips and thighs emerged. He tossed the robe to her.

"Put it on before you catch cold." He was forcing himself to walk away and had taken the first step when Savannah, intent on putting on the robe as quickly as possible, tripped against the root of a tree and fell to the ground.

"Savannah!"

In two steps he was beside her. "I'm okay," she said, holding on to the shin she had banged when she hit the ground.

"Are you sure?"

"Yes, yes." She shook her head and covered herself with the robe. "Aside from being mortified, that is."

His hands were on her upper arms, his fingers lingering against the silky texture of her wet skin. He felt her tremble at his touch and when he kissed her comfortingly on her temple she sighed and didn't draw away.

"I don't know what came over me," she said, thinking back to her wanton behavior and trying to ignore his tender kiss. She'd just walked out of the lake, stark naked, straight at Travis. She hadn't even had the decency to ask him to look the other way. She felt like a complete idiot.

Travis wanted to comfort her…hold her…never stop making love to her. *Push me away,* he thought as his physical needs overcame common sense. She looked at him with wide innocent eyes and the moonlight caught in her dazzling gaze. Travis felt his resolve waver as he tried to keep the robe from falling off her shoulders. Though she tried to knot the belt, her fingers fumbled and the neckline continued to gap despite her efforts to cover herself.

"What—" He cleared his throat and tried not to concentrate on the dusky hollow between the two silken mounds. "What were you doing out here?"

"I couldn't sleep."

"Why not?"

She shook her head and the droplets of water in her hair caught in the moonlight and sparkled like fine diamonds. "I don't know." He was so damned close to her. She could smell the scent of brandy on his breath, read the smoky desire in his eyes. Her heart throbbed with the thought that he wanted her and her skin quivered from the warmth of his breath on the back of her neck.

"I'm having trouble sleeping these nights myself."

"Because of…the problems with Melinda?"

He shook his head. "Because of the problems with you."

"Oh."

His fingers traced the pout on her lips. "I haven't been able to think of much besides you lately. And it's driving me out of my mind." His eyes caressed her face and watched as she swallowed when he touched her throat, his fingers inching lazily up and down the soft white column.

"Travis—"

"Tell me to leave you alone, Savannah."

"I… I can't."

"Tell me to take my hands off you," he suggested, but she shook her head.

"Then do something, anything, slap me the way you did that kid who attacked you the other night."

"I can't, Travis," she moaned as his fingers slid lower to trace the lapels of her robe.

His face inched closer to hers and the weight of his body leaned against hers as he kissed her, tenderly at first and then with such savagery that it tore through her body.

Her lips were chilled from the water but responded when his mouth settled over hers in a kiss that questioned as much as it claimed. He was asking and taking all at once and she leaned closer to him, her fingers touching the muscles at the base of his neck.

The fires that had started as a dull ache in Travis's loins burned through his bloodstream and destroyed all of his rational thought. When she parted her lips, his kiss became fierce and hungry, his tongue eager as it discovered its waiting mate.

He lifted his head and saw her swollen lips, the seduction in her eyes. "This is crazy," he groaned. "Haven't you had enough?"

"I don't know if I could ever have enough of you," she admitted.

"Don't do this to me, Savannah, I'm not made of stone, for crying out loud! I was just trying to shock some sense into you!" But the painful ache between his legs told him he was lying.

Savannah's arms wrapped around his neck, her fingers touched the sensitive skin over his shoulders and he groaned before lowering himself next to her and kissing her with all the passion that was dominating his mind and body.

She responded in kind. When he rolled atop her, one hand pressing the small of her back upward against him, she felt the hard evidence of his passion. He rubbed anxiously against her and one of his hands slid beneath the lapel of her robe to discover the creamy softness of her breast.

Her body arched up from the ground, molding her flesh to his, fitting against him perfectly.

Stop. Stop me, Savannah, he thought, but he slid lower on her body, his lips kissing and caressing her skin, finding the pulse at her throat, lingering seductively before his hands and mouth parted the robe, inched down her ribs and found the dark, waiting peak of her breast. He rimmed the nipple with his tongue and Savannah moaned his name into the night. Then slowly, with the delicate strokes of a dedicated lover, he licked and suckled at the straining breast until he felt her fingernails digging into his back.

"Oh, God, I should be shot for this," he muttered, attempting to grasp onto some shred of his common sense, But even as he did, he slid his belt through the buckle and kicked off his jeans.

"Just love me," she begged, trembling beneath him.

"I do. Oh, God, Savannah. I do."

He was naked then, his lean body glistening with sweat as he lay upon her. She welcomed the burden of his weight and when he entered her, she felt a sharp jab of pain before she was lost in the brilliant and beautiful bursts of their union. She stroked the hard muscles of his back with her fingers and kissed at his face and chest and heard herself scream as the increasing tempo of his strokes pushed her upward to a precipice and then over the edge in a dazzling climax that sent aftershocks rolling through her body for several minutes. As she fell slowly back to earth, she sighed in a contentment heretofore unknown to her.

With Travis's arms wrapped securely around her, Savannah listened to the sounds of the night—Travis's irregular breathing, the clamoring of her heart, the sound of a fish jumping lazily in the water and, farther away, the sound of a twig snapping.

Travis's body stiffened. He kissed her softly on the forehead and drew the robe around her. "Go back to the house," he whispered against her ear and cut off her questions by pressing a finger to her lips.

"But—"

"Shh." He squinted into the darkness. "I heard something. I don't think we're alone. I'll come to you—soon," he promised.

Then soundlessly, Travis was jerking on his clothes. Savannah didn't argue, but followed his instructions to the letter. Holding her robe closed with one hand, her thongs in the other, she ran barefoot along the path, feeling the sharp stones and twigs that cut into her feet.

Breathlessly she sneaked back into the dark house, hurried up the back staircase to her room and waited in the bed, her heart clamoring, her ears straining for any sound of Travis's arrival. She was sure that he would be true to his word and come to her. It was only a matter of time.

WHEN THE FIRST gray light of dawn streaked through the room, she realized that Travis had probably been held up by whomever it was who had come to the lake. It didn't matter. She'd meet him later in the day.

Facing her father—or whoever it was who had stumbled upon Travis and her—wouldn't be a picnic, but Savannah was convinced she could handle it. She drifted off to a heavy sleep and woke up much later—sometime after ten. She showered, dressed and went downstairs to discover her father sitting at the kitchen table, stirring a cup of coffee, and reading the morning paper.

"Good morning," Savannah said, eyeing him. Everything looked normal. Obviously, Reginald had been out to the stables at the crack of dawn as was his usual custom. He was clean shaven, his boots were by the door to the porch, and he'd already finished breakfast. His plate still held a few crumbs of toast, though it had been pushed to the side of the table.

Reginald looked up sharply, frowned and put down his paper. "Morning."

"Good morning, dear," her mother, Virgina, said, when she came breezing through the door to the kitchen from the dining room. Her dark hair was perfectly combed, her makeup looking as if she'd just applied it. "You overslept this morning. It's too bad, too. You weren't here to say goodbye to Travis."

"Goodbye?" Savannah repeated, stunned.

"Yes." Virginia poured herself a cup of coffee and then sat down at the table across from Reginald. "Seems he and Melinda decided to get married as soon as possible—and high time, I say. They've been dating forever. The wedding will probably be next week, so he went to Los Angeles to see if he could rent his apartment earlier than he'd originally planned."

Savannah sagged against the counter, her cup of coffee nearly spilling from her shaking hands.

"I guess he got tired of working here at the farm," Reginald said. "Don't blame him a bit. Since he passed the bar exam, there's no reason for him to be hanging around here, when he could be out chasing ambulances."

"Reginald!" Virginia admonished, but Reginald chuckled to himself and Virginia's blue eyes sparkled at the prospect of a wedding.

Savannah felt the tears burn at the back of her eyes.

"I'm surprised no one woke me up so that I could say goodbye," she said.

"No reason to," Reginald said with a shrug. "Travis will be back. Bad penny syndrome, you know. They always have a habit of showing up again."

"Father! Listen to you," Virginia said, but smiled.

"Didn't Travis want to—talk to me?"

"I don't think so. He never mentioned it. Did he, hon?"

"Not to me." Virginia saw the hurt in Savannah's eyes and sent her a kindly smile. "But then he's pretty busy, what with the wedding plans and all. You'll see him then."

Savannah felt a traitorous burn in her heart, but she told herself not to believe anyone—not until she heard from Travis.

The problem was, he never called or came back to the farm. And he married Melinda Reaves two weeks after having made love to Savannah by the lake.

"I'll never speak to him again," Savannah told herself angrily on the morning of the wedding. To her mother's disappointment, she refused to attend the marriage ceremony.

"I can't, Mom," she said when Virginia pressed her for a reason. "I just can't."

"Why not?" Virginia asked, sitting on the edge of the bed and surveying her youngest daughter with concern as Savannah stood at the window of her room and pretended interest in the view.

"Travis… Travis and I had a disagreement."

"All brothers and sisters—"

"He's *not* my brother!"

Virginia arched a knowing brow. "Oh, I see."

"I don't know how you possibly could," Savannah said, feeling wretched inside. No one could possibly understand, least of all her mother. So why didn't they all just leave her alone in her misery?

"How involved with Travis were you?" Virginia asked gently.

"I'm not—" Savannah's voice caught. "Oh, Mom," she whispered, her fingers winding in the soft fabric of the curtains.

"It's all right, honey," Virginia consoled, walking over to her daughter and placing a comforting arm around Savannah's shoulders.

The tears that had been threatening for two weeks ran down Savannah's face. *It wasn't all right. Never would be.* She turned and sobbed against her mother's shoulder for a few minutes.

"Loving the wrong man is never easy," Virginia said thoughtfully.

"But how could you know?"

"Oh, I know, all right," Virginia said with a sad smile, as if she wanted to confide in her daughter. "I was young once myself. I've…well, I've made a few mistakes."

"With Dad?" Savannah sniffed, eyeing her mother.

Virginia avoided Savannah's eyes. "Yes, honey. With your father." There was something cryptic in Virginia's voice, but Savannah couldn't think about it, or anything else for that matter. Melinda Reaves was going to be Travis McCord's wife! Savannah felt as if her entire world were crumbling at her feet.

"But I love him so much," she admitted.

"And he'll soon be a married man. There's nothing you can do about it. Not now."

"Oh, yes, there is," Savannah said, the tears still

streaming down a suddenly thrusting chin. "I'm going to forget about him. I'm never going to speak to him again. And...and I'll never let myself fall for any man again."

Virginia was smiling through her own tears. "Don't be so rash, there's still a few good men out there. David Crandall cares for you."

"Oh, Mom—" Savannah said, rolling her eyes to the ceiling. "David's just a boy...a friend."

"And Travis was more?"

"Yes."

"So it was that way, was it?" Virginia asked quietly. "Are...are you all right?"

"Do I look all right?"

"I mean—"

"I know what you mean," Savannah said softly, reading the worry in her mother's eyes. "You won't be shamed by me."

Virginia sighed. "And you still love him?"

"Not anymore," Savannah vowed, her fist clenching in determination. "Not anymore and *never again*." Whatever it took, she would throw off the shackles of her love for Travis. He would soon be Melinda's husband and Melinda's problem. As far as Savannah was concerned, she didn't care if Travis McCord lived or died.

She had no idea that nine years later she'd still be trying to convince herself that she despised him.

CHAPTER ONE

Beaumont Breeding Farm—Winter, Nine Years Later

SAVANNAH DIDN'T REGRET moving back to the farm. The gently rolling countryside northeast of San Francisco had been a welcome sight to her when she'd returned. She hadn't realized how much she'd missed the hazy purple hills surrounding the farm and the fields of lush green grass and grazing horses.

The bustle of the city had been exciting while she was a college student and for a few years when she worked in San Francisco in an investment firm. But she was glad to be back at the breeding farm even if it meant putting up with her brother-in-law, Wade Benson.

In the past few years Wade had given up most of his accounting practice to manage the farm, and he was being groomed to step into Reginald's boots, whenever her father decided to retire. That might be sooner than he had planned, Savannah thought sadly, considering her mother's poor health.

It was just too bad that Travis hadn't stayed at the farm and followed in Dad's footsteps, she thought idly and then mentally chastised herself. Though it had been nine years since he had left the farm to marry Melinda, Savannah had never really forgiven him—she'd even managed to avoid him most of the time. Now there were rumors that he would run in the next election for governor of the State of California. Hard to believe.

"Hey, Aunt Savvy, want to go riding?" Joshua, Charmaine and Wade's only child, called as he ran up to her.

Savannah smiled as she looked into the nine-year-old's earnest brown eyes. His cheeks were flushed, his brown hair in sad need of a trim. "I'd love to," she said, and the boy broke into a grin.

"Can I ride Mystic?"

Savannah laughed. "Not on your life, buddy! He's Grandpa's prize colt!"

"But he likes me."

"The way I understand it, Mystic doesn't like anyone."

"Hogwash!" The boy kicked the toe of his sneaker at an acorn on the ground in frustration. "I know I can ride him," Josh boasted proudly, his eyes twinkling mischievously.

"Oh you can, can you?" She smiled at the determination in Josh's proud chin. "Well, maybe someday, if Grandpa and Lester think it's okay, but not today." Savannah eyed the graying sky. "Tell ya what, I'll saddle Mattie and Jones, and we'll take a couple of turns around the field before it starts to rain."

"But they're old nags. They're not even Thoroughbreds!"

"Shame on you. Even old non-Thoroughbred-type horses need exercise. Just like obstinate little boys! Come on—" she gave Joshua a good-natured pat between the shoulders "—I'll race ya."

"Okay!" Joshua was off across the wet grass in a flash and Savannah let him win the race. "You're old, too," he said with a laugh once she had crossed the imaginary finish line at the stable gate.

"And you're precocious."

"What's that mean?"

Savannah's eyes gleamed with love for the little boy. "That no one but an aunt could love you."

He immediately sobered and Savannah realized she'd said the wrong thing. "Well, no one but Grandma and Grandpa and your mom and dad and—"

"Dad doesn't love me."

"Of course he does," Savannah said, seeing the sadness in the little boy's eyes and silently cursing her brother-in-law.

"He never does anything with me."

"Your father's very busy—" *Damn, but she hated to make excuses for Wade.*

"He's always busy," Joshua corrected, and Savannah rumpled her nephew's floppy brown hair.

"Managing this farm is a big responsibility."

"But you have time to play with me."

"That's because I'm totally irresponsible." Savannah laughed. "Now, quit feeling sorry for yourself and find the saddle blankets."

Joshua, appeased for the moment, found the required blankets as Savannah bridled the two horses and silently told herself to have it out with her brother-in-law. No father should be so indifferent to his only son.

"Stay here a minute," she told Joshua after tightening the cinch around Jones's girth. "I'll see if there's anything to drink in the office. Wouldn't you like a Coke while we ride?"

"Sure!"

"I'll be right back."

She walked through the stable door, down the cement walk running parallel to the clapboard building, and up the stairs to the office located directly over that part of the stables used as a foaling shed. The door of the office was partially open, and she heard voices within. Her father and Wade were involved in a heated discussion.

"I just don't think you can count on him," Wade was saying. Savannah took a step forward, intent on telling her brother-in-law to pay some attention to his child, but Wade's next words made her hesitate. "McCord's just about over the deep end, and Willis is damned worried about him."

Travis? What was wrong with him? Savannah's heart began to pound with fear.

"Willis Henderson worries about anything that comes along," her father replied calmly.

"Maybe there's a reason for that. He's McCord's law partner, for God's sake. He works with McCord every day."

"And he thinks Travis is—"

"Cracking up."

Savannah stifled a gasp. "Nonsense," Reginald said. "That boy is tough."

"Willis says McCord hasn't been the same since his wife's death."

Reginald sighed. "Look, Wade, I'm telling you that Willis Henderson is jumping at shadows! Lawyers tend to do that. Travis McCord will end up the next governor of this state, just you wait and see."

"I don't know. I certainly don't want to bet on it."

"Of course not," Reginald said with audible disgust. "God, you accountants are all so damned conservative."

"There's nothing wrong with that. If you had been

a little more conservative in the last five years, we wouldn't be in this mess."

"It's not a mess!" Reginald roared.

"I call zero cash flow a mess."

"You're as bad as Willis Henderson; always borrowing trouble," Reginald muttered. "Lawyers and accountants cut from the same cloth."

Savannah, feeling guilty about eavesdropping, and yet overcome with worry for Travis, walked into the room. Reginald and Wade, both seated at the table, looked up from their cups of coffee. "What kind of trouble are you talking about?" she asked her father.

Reginald scowled into his cup before sending a warning glance to Wade. "Oh, nothing. Wade's a little concerned about cash flow."

"Is it bad?" Her eyes moved to her brother-in-law.

"Yes," Wade answered, his gaze shifting uncomfortably under her straightforward stare. He tugged nervously at the hairs of his blond moustache.

"No." Reginald shook his graying head and adjusted his plaid cap. "Wade's just being…cautious."

"That's my job," Wade pointed out.

Savannah didn't listen. "What were you saying about Travis?" she asked, walking over to the refrigerator and trying not to look overly interested though she felt a nervous sheen of sweat break out on her palms.

Reginald's jaw worked. "Oh, nothing serious. That partner of his, Henderson, is worried about him. Thinks Travis is…depressed. Probably just let down from that last case he won. Got lots of publicity with that Eldridge decision and we all know how tough it is to get back into the regular office routine after all that hoopla. It's

just a letdown. The same way we felt after Mystic won
the Preakness."

"So you think he'll still run for governor?"

Reginald smiled. "*I'd* be willing to bet on it," he said,
casting Wade a knowing glance.

Savannah grabbed a couple cans of Coke from the
refrigerator and closed the door. "Did Willis Henderson call you? Is that how you found out about Travis's
'depression'?"

"No." Her father avoided her eyes.

"I ran into him at the track," Wade said hurriedly.
"Just yesterday at Hollywood Park."

Savannah raised a eyebrow skeptically; she could
feel that Wade and her father were deliberately hiding
something from her, but she couldn't delve into it. Not
right now. Joshua was waiting for her in the stables and
she wasn't about to disappoint him.

"Since you got back to the farm," she said, looking pointedly at Wade, "have you bothered to talk to
Joshua?"

"Huh? Well, no. I just got in last night, and then he
got up and went to school this morning. Not much time."
Wade squirmed uncomfortably in his chair.

"Maybe he needs a little fatherly attention."

"I'll… I'll talk to him tonight, when I'm not so busy."

"I think it would be a good idea," Savannah said,
striding out of the room and feeling an uncomfortable
tightening in her stomach. She'd known there were
money problems at the farm, of course; there always
had been, but she didn't like the sound of the conversation between her father and Wade, especially the part
about Travis.

"What's the matter, Aunt Savvy?" Joshua asked when

she returned. She led the horses outside and tried to concentrate on anything other than Travis.

"What? Oh, nothing, Josh," she said, mounting Mattie and remembering that she had encountered Travis all those summers ago while riding the very same mare. "Let's take the horses over by the lake today."

"But you never like to go to the lake," the boy pointed out after climbing onto Jones's broad back.

Savannah smiled sadly. "I know. But today is different. Come on." She urged Mattie into a trot, and Joshua followed behind her on the gelding. The path between the trees was overgrown from lack of use, and the lake, usually calm, had taken on the leaden hue of the winter sky.

"Why'd you want to come here?" Joshua asked, sipping his Coke, oblivious to the cold weather that suddenly cut through Savannah's jacket like a knife.

"I don't know," she admitted, staring at the lake, her thoughts lingering on Travis as raindrops began to pelt from the sky and dimple the dark water. "It used to be a place I liked very much."

Joshua looked at the barren trees, exposed rocks and muddy banks surrounding the lake. "If you ask me, it's kinda creepy."

"Yeah, maybe it is," she whispered, shivering from a sudden chill. "Let's go back to the paddocks." *Maybe then I won't think about Travis and wonder what's happening to him...*

IT HAD ALL started again a little over a month ago, Travis reflected dourly, when he'd seen Reginald Beaumont and Wade Benson at the racetrack. That in itself wasn't so unusual. After all, Reginald's prize three-year-old colt,

Mystic, had been running, and Wade was now, under Reginald's guidance, managing the farm. What had been odd was the fact that Reginald was at the racetrack with Willis Henderson, Travis's law partner. Henderson had never mentioned the fact that he was interested in the races and Reginald had no reason to know Willis Henderson, except through Travis. When Travis had questioned his partner, Willis hadn't wanted to discuss his day at the track.

Later, learning that Savannah was now back at the farm with her father and Wade, Travis had begun to think about her.

And now it seemed as if he could think of nothing else.

She just wouldn't leave him alone, even after nine long years. At the most inopportune moments, her image would come vividly to Travis's mind and he would be teased by the memory of her wide, sky-blue eyes, gleaming ebony hair and seductive smile. In the nine years that had passed since he'd found her swimming in the lake, her image still lingered.

"Mr. McCord!" The sharp voice of Eleanor Phillips brought Travis back to the present, and the image of Savannah faded quickly. Travis's eyes focused again on the stylish but overdressed woman sitting on the other side of the desk. "You haven't heard a word I've said!"

Travis offered a slightly apologetic smile and stared directly into her eyes. "Oh, yes, I have." He couldn't hide the cynicism in his voice. "You were talking about the woman your husband met in Mazatlan."

"The girl, you mean. She was barely twenty!" Eleanor Phillips said with self-righteous disgust. "You know she was only interested in Robert for his money—my money."

Travis listened impatiently while Mrs. Phillips continued to rant about her husband's indiscriminate affairs. The way his wife told it, Mr. Phillips had the sexual appetite of a man half his age.

As she went on about Robert Phillips's indiscretions, Travis glanced out the window of his office, noticed that it was getting dark and checked his watch. Five-thirty. So where was Henderson, his partner? And why wasn't he handling Eleanor Phillips? Too many things had been happening in the law firm that didn't add up, and Travis wanted it out with Henderson.

"So you see, Mr. McCord, this divorce is imperative," Mrs. Phillips said in her high-pitched voice. "I want you to work with the best private investigator in Los Angeles and—"

"I don't handle divorces, Mrs. Phillips. I tried to tell you that on the phone, and when you first came into the office today. You deliberately lied to me—said that you wanted to see me about a take-over bid by a competitor."

She colored slightly and Travis knew he had offended her. The trouble was, he really didn't give a damn about Eleanor Phillips, her husband's sex life or Phillips Industries. As Henderson had so often accused, Travis was suffering from a serious case of "bad attitude." Thinking about Savannah only made it worse.

"But I've been with your firm forever. You've handled all my legal work," Eleanor complained, fingering the elegant string of pearls at her throat.

"On corporate matters." Travis tried to remain calm. The woman only wanted a divorce from her philandering husband and that in itself wasn't a crime. In fact,

Travis didn't blame her for wanting out of an unhappy marriage, but there was something in her superior attitude that rankled him, and he wondered if Mr. Phillips was as bad as his wife had insisted, or if her cold, money-is-everything way of looking at life had driven him from her bed.

"Oh, I see," Eleanor Phillips said primly, reaching for her purse and looking around the well-appointed office in disgust. "Since that Eldridge decision, you're too big to take on something as simple as my divorce."

"That has nothing to do with it—"

"Hmph."

"I'm sure one of the associates, or perhaps Mr. Henderson himself, can help you." *If I ever find the bastard.* "I'll speak to him."

"I want you, Mr. McCord! And I think you owe it to me to handle this yourself...after all, I need complete discretion. And you have a reputation that's spotless."

Travis winced at the ridiculous compliment and instead of feeling flattered, he suffered from a twinge of conscience. "I don't handle divorce."

"But you will for me." She smiled knowingly and Travis experienced the unlikely urge to shake some sense into her cash register of a head. *Wealthy women,* he thought cynically, *he'd met enough to last him a lifetime!* He jerked at the knot of his tie. Once again the suite of modern offices seemed confining.

"I've already contributed to your campaign," Eleanor pointed out, raising her brows.

"What!"

"My contribution."

"What the devil are you talking about?" Travis's jaw hardened and his eyes glittered dangerously.

For the first time that afternoon, Eleanor Phillips had gained the advantage in the conversation and she was pleased. "It was a very healthy contribution," she rattled on. Travis's eyes narrowed, but the expensively clad woman only smiled to herself. "Mr. Henderson took care of it and promised me that you would handle this divorce personally. He also said that you would be able to assure me that my husband won't get a dime of my money—and not much of his."

Travis's jaw tightened and his lips curved into a grim smile. "When did you talk to Mr. Henderson?"

"Just last week…no, it was two weeks ago, when I called to make the appointment with you."

Two weeks ago. Just about the time Travis had noticed some discrepancies in the books.

Eleanor Phillips rose to her full five feet two inches and focused her frigid eyes on Travis. "I'll be frank, Mr. McCord. I want to divorce my husband as quickly as possible, and I expect you to take him to the cleaners." The smile she offered was as chilly as a cold November night.

"Mrs. Phillips," Travis said slowly, as if to a child, as he stood and leaned threateningly over the desk. "I don't handle divorce and I'm not sure what Mr. Henderson told you, but I haven't decided to run for governor."

"Well, I know it's not official—"

"And I haven't seen your…contribution. I wouldn't have taken it if I had." His gray eyes glinted with determination. "But I can assure you of one thing: Willis Henderson will return it to you." *If I have to persuade him by breaking every bone in his feeble little body.*

"Then perhaps you'd better speak with Mr. Henderson. I assure you I gave him a check for five thousand dollars. Good luck, Governor."

Eleanor Phillips walked out of the room, and Travis punched the extension for Henderson's office. There was no answer. "You slimy son of a bitch," Travis muttered, slamming down the receiver, grabbing his coat and thrusting his arms into the sleeves, "what the hell kind of game are you playing?"

Before leaving the room he looked around the office and scowled at the expensive music box on the shelf collecting dust; a gift from Melinda. The desk was polished wood, and leather-bound law books adorned the shelves of a walnut bookcase. The liquor cabinet housed only the finest labels. The carpet had been found in Italy by Henderson's interior decorator. And Travis hated every bloody thing that had to do with L.A. and his partnership with Willis Henderson.

"Today, ol' buddy, you've just gone one step too far," Travis said, shaking his head. "It's over. Done. *Finis!*"

He marched into the reception area. "Where is Henderson?" he demanded of the blond secretary.

"I really don't know." She quickly scanned her calendar. "He had an appointment out of the building today."

"With whom?"

"I don't know," the girl said again, obviously embarrassed. "He didn't say."

"Did you ask him?"

"Oh, yes."

"And?"

The secretary shrugged. "He said it was personal."

"Great." The muscles in the back of Travis's neck began to ache with tension. "Great. Just great." He rubbed at the knotted muscles in his back. "Do you have *any* idea where he might be?"

"I'm sorry—" A negative sweep of the short blond curls.

Where the hell was Henderson, and why did he take Eleanor Phillips's money? "I know it's late, and you're about to leave, but if he comes back here before you go, tell him to call me."

"I will."

"And I want to speak to our accountant. Call Jack and see if he can come into the office later this week."

"Jack Conrad?" The girl looked confused.

Travis held on to the rags of his thin patience. "Yes, the accountant for the firm."

"But he doesn't handle the books any longer."

Travis had been heading for the door, but he stopped dead in his tracks. The day had just gone from bad to worse. "What do you mean?"

"I, uh, I thought you knew. Wade Benson is handling the books."

"Benson!" Travis felt his fingers curl into tight fists.

"Didn't Mr. Henderson tell you?"

"You're sure about this?"

"Yes." She looked oddly at Travis before reaching into a file drawer. "Here's a copy of the letter from Mr. Benson and the response from Mr. Henderson. Mr. Benson's accounting fees are much lower than Mr. Conrad's were."

"But Mr. Benson doesn't take on any clients. He's working for Reginald Beaumont now, as the manager of the Beaumont Breeding Farm." *With Savannah.* Travis smiled twistedly. Hadn't he been looking for an excuse to see Savannah again? It looked like Willis Henderson had just handed it to him on a silver platter.

The young blonde shrugged. "Maybe he decided to do it as a favor to you. You've known Mr. Benson all your life, haven't you?"

"Most of it," Travis acknowledged. *So why hasn't Henderson told me any of this?*

Travis pushed open the glass doors with the gold lettering and strode into the hall, down three flights of stairs and through the lobby of the building. As he walked to his car, a crisp Southern California breeze rustled through the palms and rumpled his hair, but he didn't notice.

His thoughts were centered on his partner. *Some partner.* Right now Travis would like to wring Willis Henderson's short, Ivy League neck! Accepting a contribution, legal or otherwise, from Eleanor Phillips wasn't the first of Henderson's none-too-subtle attempts to force a decision from Travis, but it was damned well going to be the last! And this business of switching accountants...

Wade Benson, for God's sake! Travis didn't trust the man an inch. It was bad enough that Benson had married Reginald's eldest daughter, Charmaine, Savannah's sister, and become manager of Beaumont Breeding Farm, but now he was encroaching on Travis's domain. *But not for long!* Travis didn't want anything more to do with Wade, Reginald Beaumont or his raven-haired daughter.

Savannah again. Would he ever be able to get her out of his system?

He smiled grimly to himself. "Your own fault," he reminded himself before concentrating on the problem at hand. Travis had already decided what he was going to do with the rest of his life, and it was a far cry from running for governor of California. And if Willis Henderson, Eleanor Phillips and all the other people who were willing to contribute to his campaign for personal favors didn't like it, they could bloody well stuff it!

Henderson's condominium was across town in Malibu Beach. It would take nearly an hour to get there, but Travis didn't hesitate. If Willis wasn't at home, Travis would wait.

Why did Willis want him to run for governor? Prestige for the firm of Henderson and McCord? Maybe. But Travis couldn't help but feel there was something more to it. It was that tiny suspicion that gnawed at him until he made his way through the snarl of L.A. traffic and reached Willis's home.

Willis was outside, in the driveway, with someone. Travis parked on the street and observed his partner. It was too dark to see clearly, but when the visitor stepped into the light from the street, Travis recognized him. An uncanny premonition of dread slithered up his spine as he stared at Wade Benson.

Swearing softly under his breath, Travis watched the two men. Because his first reaction was to corner Henderson and Benson and have it out with them, he reached for the handle of the door. But there was something slightly sinister in the clandestine meeting, and he stayed in the car. "You're losing it, McCord," he whispered to himself, but couldn't take his eyes off the two men in the driveway.

It was bad enough that Wade had suckered Reginald Beaumont into his confidence, but Henderson as well?

The whole setup seemed out of place. Wade was the manager of Beaumont Farm, but the legal work for the farm was handled by Travis, not Henderson. Or was it?

Quietly, Travis rolled down the window, but his car was parked too far away from the condominium to hear any of the conversation.

Wade lit a cigarette and laughed at some comment uttered by Henderson. *Just like old fraternity brothers,* Travis thought unkindly. The anger in Travis's blood was replaced by cold suspicion. He watched as Wade walked back to his car and tossed his glowing cigarette butt onto the ground before stamping on it and opening the car door.

So Wade was involved with Willis. What about Reginald, Savannah's father? Did he know about this meeting? Probably. Travis had seen Reginald and Wade at Alexander Park with Willis Henderson when Reginald's colt, Mystic, the favorite, had run and lost. What the hell was going on?

Everything he had seen and heard could just be an unlikely set of circumstances. Henderson had the right to fire an accountant and he certainly could go to the races any time he damned well pleased.

But Willis couldn't take a campaign contribution for a campaign that didn't exist!

Unless, of course, Eleanor Phillips had been lying. Travis wouldn't put it past her.

An ache settled in the pit of Travis's stomach as he thought about Reginald Beaumont's Thoroughbred farm and the fact that Savannah was still there, working with Wade.

"Dammit all to hell," he whispered, watching Wade's car glide out of the driveway.

Pensively rubbing his jaw, he watched as Willis Henderson walked back into his condo and shut out the lights. Then, Travis slowly got out of the car, stretched and walked up the concrete walk to Willis Henderson's front door.

SAVANNAH WAS SEATED at her father's desk in his study, sifting through the mail, when the phone rang. "No one's here," she said to the ringing instrument and eyed the stack of unpaid bills on the corner of the desk. If the caller was another creditor...

"Beaumont Breeding Farm," she answered automatically.

"I'd like to speak with Wade Benson. This is Willis Henderson," an imperious voice requested.

Savannah straightened in the chair. Willis Henderson was Travis's law partner, the man who had talked to Wade at the racetrack. Her fingers curled more tightly around the receiver and she gave her full attention to Travis's partner.

Maybe something had happened to Travis—an accident. She felt a surge of panic wash over her, but managed to keep her voice calm. "I'm sorry, Mr. Benson is out of town."

A pause. "Then maybe I could talk to Reginald."

"He's also gone for the week. Is there something I can do for you, Mr. Henderson?" Savannah could sense the man's hesitancy to confide in her, so she gave him an out. "Or should I have Wade return the call when he gets back next week?" She eyed the calendar. "Wade should be back by the twenty-third." Two days before Christmas.

"Let me talk to...whoever is in charge."

Savannah bristled a bit, but she smiled wryly. "You're speaking to her. I'm overseeing things while Dad and Wade are away."

"Dad?" Henderson repeated. "Oh, you mean Reginald?"

"Yes. I'm Savannah Beaumont." Savannah settled

back in the chair, took off her reading glasses and braced herself for the worst. "Now, what can I do for you?"

Only a slight hesitation. "Ah, well, this has to do with Travis McCord."

Savannah felt her spine stiffen slightly. "What about him?"

"There's been a little trouble."

Her pulse jumped and nervous sweat dotted her forehead. *Trouble.* The second time she'd heard that word in connection with Travis. "What kind of 'trouble'?"

Henderson hedged. "Well, that's why I wanted to talk to Wade."

Savannah frowned at the mention of her brother-in-law. Travis and Wade had never been close. But then, Henderson had bumped into Wade at Hollywood Park... "As I said, Mr. Benson isn't here and he won't be back until next week—just before Christmas. Now, if Travis is in trouble, I'd like to know about it."

"Look, Miss Beaumont—"

"Savannah."

"Yes, well, Savannah then. I don't want to worry you, but Travis... Travis, he's, well, in a bad way."

Savannah's heart nearly stopped beating and a few dots of perspiration broke out on her back. "What do you mean? Has he been in some kind of accident?"

"No—"

Thank God! Her tense muscles relaxed a little and she fell back into the soft leather cushions of the chair.

"—But he's...well, to put it frankly, Miss Beaumont, Travis has checked out. He's lost all interest in the business, doesn't come into the office, refuses to see me. And all that talk about him running for governor in a couple of years; that's gone, too. He's just not interested. In anything." Once the dam was broken, Henderson talked freely, his words spilling out in a gush. "You probably know that he hasn't been the same since his wife died, but I thought he would pull himself out of it. When Melinda passed away he threw himself into his work, especially the Eldridge case, and now that that's over, he seems to have lost his will to live, I guess you'd say." He stopped abruptly, as if having second thoughts about discussing his partner's personal problems to Savannah. "Well, to put it bluntly, Miss Beaumont, I think he's gone over the deep end."

Savannah tried to think clearly, but her worried thoughts were centered on Travis—a man she should hate. "I don't understand, Melinda's been dead for over six months."

"I know. God, don't I know." He let out a long sigh. "At first he seemed to snap out of it, you know. But it was all just an act. He had the Eldridge case, you see. And once he won that decision and got all the publicity, well, there was talk, a lot of talk, about him running for governor, but I think he's about to chuck it all. It's gotten to the point where he doesn't bother to show up at the office at all. So far I've been able to cover for him, but I don't know how long I can. And what with all this talk about him running for the governorship... I just don't think we can hide what's going on."

"We?" she repeated.

"Wade and I."

Wade again. "What's Wade got to do with it?"

"Wade and your father are pushing Travis toward governorship—you knew that?"

"I'd heard," Savannah admitted sarcastically.

"Well, that's why I'm calling. Travis came by to see

me the other night, told me to dissolve the partnership, that he would sell his half to me, and that he was leaving on the noon flight to San Francisco today. I thought he was joking, but when he didn't show up at the office or answer his phone the last couple of days, well, I had to assume that he was serious!"

"Did he say why he wanted out?"

"No...not really, he just said that he was going up to Reginald Beaumont's Breeding Farm. He intended to talk to Wade and Reginald. He asked if I'd have Wade pick him up at the airport."

Savannah glanced at the grandfather clock in the foyer. It was after eleven. "What time will he be in?"

"I think he said one-thirty. Yes. Flight number sixty-seven on United. Will you see that someone goes to meet him?"

"Of course."

"And you'll get in touch with Wade?"

"I'll tell my sister, Charmaine. She's Wade's wife. He should be calling tonight and Charmaine will give him the message that you need to speak with him."

There was a sigh on the other end of the phone. "Thank you, Miss Beaumont," Henderson said before hanging up.

Savannah replaced the receiver and thought for a moment. Several of the hands weren't on the farm, and with Reginald and Wade gone, the farm was being run by a skeleton crew. She couldn't afford to let anyone off to drive to the airport.

"It would serve him right if he had to walk here," she muttered, some of the old bitterness she'd felt toward Travis rising to the surface.

"I guess I get to do the honors," she decided before

she grabbed her purse, walked out of the den, across the tiled foyer, and pulled her jacket off the coat rack. *So Travis was finally coming home. But why and for how long? And how much of Willis Henderson's story was true?*

She walked out of the two-storied plantation-style house, turned her collar against the chill December rain, and half ran down the brick path to the garage. Taking the steps two at a time, she climbed upward to the loft that her sister, Charmaine, had converted into a studio and ignored her tight stomach.

It was pouring and Savannah shivered as she rapped on the door and then pushed it open to find Charmaine wrist deep in potting clay. Charmaine looked up from her work and slowed the foot treadle. The revolving, undulating and as yet indistinguishable objet d'art folded in upon itself into a lump of sloppy gray clay.

"Sorry about that," Savannah apologized, nervously gesturing to Charmaine's work. She hated being in the loft.

"It's okay. Wasn't turning out anyway. Good Lord, you're soaked!" Charmaine observed.

"Just a little." Savannah wiped the drops of rain from her face and tried to forget that this loft had once been Travis's.

"No such thing as 'just a little' soaked."

"Look, I'm going to the airport," Savannah said.

"Like that?" Charmaine asked, eyeing her sister's casual jeans and sweater in disapproval.

"Like this. Can you keep an eye on Mom?"

Charmaine grimaced slightly at her work. "I suppose." She wiped her hands on her cotton smock and stood up from the potter's wheel. "I've got to stick around and wait for Josh's bus anyway. What's up?"

"Travis is coming home."

Charmaine started visibly. "Here?"

"I guess. Anyway, that's what his partner, Henderson, said on the phone just now. The flight arrives in San Francisco at one-thirty, so I've got to run. If Wade happens to call, tell him to phone Henderson or, better yet, have him call back tonight once Travis gets here."

Charmaine scrutinized her sister thoughtfully. "Why is Travis coming back to the farm? Why now?"

"I don't know. But I think I should tell him about Mom, so warn her. He'll be furious when he finds out that she's been ill."

Charmaine agreed. "Good luck. You're going to need it." She pursed her lips. "Do you think that he heard about Mother and that's why he's coming back?"

Savannah was in too much of a hurry to sit around and conjecture, and thinking about Travis always brought out a lot of feelings she didn't want to examine. Though her hostility had lessened in the past nine years, it was always there, just under the surface, and she hated to admit it. "Beats me. Henderson said something about Travis needing a rest. He's had a rough year."

As for Henderson's story, it bothered her, but she wanted to make sure it was true before she passed it along to Charmaine or anyone else. Besides, Savannah had never trusted Wade, and Charmaine was his wife. Nervously she shoved her chilled hands into the pockets of her jacket.

Charmaine studied her sister suspiciously. "And that's all?"

"That's all that I know," Savannah lied.

"Hmph." After casting Savannah an I-know-you-better-than-that type of glance, Charmaine capitulated. "Well, I suppose you're right. Melinda's death was a blow to Travis. He loved her very much."

Savannah only nodded but her fingers tightened around the keys in her pocket.

"And now all this talk about him running for governor, right on the heels of that Eldridge decision. He probably does need a rest, but I don't think he'll get much of one here." Still slightly disturbed, Charmaine settled back on her stool and began working the clay. "Sure, I'll look in on Mother."

"Thanks." Savannah left the studio and climbed down the steps quickly. She raced into the garage and hopped into her father's car. As she left the farm her thoughts were centered on Travis. She couldn't remember a time in her life when she hadn't loved him, first as a brother, then as a woman loves a man. Wholly, completely.

Then he'd used and betrayed her.

"Well, that was then," Savannah said with determination. "And I was a fool. A stupid, little girl of a fool. But I'm not about to make the same mistake twice, Travis McCord. You taught me too well. I don't care what's bothering you, I'd rather hate you than fall in love with you ever again."

CHAPTER TWO

TRAFFIC WAS THICK near the airport and it took Savannah nearly twenty minutes to park and get into the terminal building. Pushing her cold hands into the pockets of her jacket and telling herself that she had made a big mistake in coming to get Travis, she threaded her way through the crowd until she reached the concourse where Travis's plane was to unload. The seats near the reservation desk were filled with people waiting for their flights. Carry-on luggage, overcoats and brightly wrapped gifts occupied the vacant seats while tired travelers sat reading, smoking or pacing between the rows of uncomfortable chairs. Above the din of the crowd, faint strains of piped-in Christmas music filtered through the terminal.

Peace on earth, good will to men, Savannah thought as she stood at the gate, but she couldn't help feel a premonition of dread. Inside her pockets, her cold hands began to sweat. She tried to relax and forget that Travis had left her without so much as an explanation, that he had married another woman and walked out of her life without bothering to say goodbye, that he had used her because he was angry with himself and Melinda. But the old bitterness still reared its ugly head.

"It's over and done with; you're a grown woman now," she chastised herself. But this was the first time in nine long years that she would be with Travis alone.

Whenever she had seen him in the past, there had always been plenty of people around him, and Melinda had been at his side. The crowds had been convenient, and now Savannah wondered if facing him alone was such a good idea.

She looked through the window and watched as the plane pulled into its berth. *Get a grip on yourself, girl.*

Travis was one of the first people off the plane. To her disgust, Savannah's heart pounded traitorously at the sight of him.

He looked older than his thirty-four years; more cynical. Deep lines bracketed the corners of his hard mouth, and smaller lines formed webs at the outside corners of his eyes. His shirt was rumpled, his tie askew, his chin already darkened with five o'clock shadow, though it was early in the day. A black garment bag was slung over one of his shoulders, and he carried a briefcase in his free hand.

It has been two years since Savannah had seen him, but he seemed to have aged ten. Probably due to the loss of Melinda, she told herself. They had been inseparable. No doubt the fatal boating accident that had taken Melinda's life had destroyed a part of Travis as well.

Savannah forced a smile to her face and walked toward him. He stopped dead in his tracks and the look on his face could have turned flesh to stone.

"Hi," she greeted, tilting her face upward and meeting his cold gaze.

"You're the last person I expected to see," he muttered, unable to disguise his surprise.

"Yeah, well, I'm glad to see you, too."

Something flickered in his gray eyes. "You always were quick to rise to the bait."

"Maybe too quick. Willis Henderson called the farm this afternoon. He was looking for Wade or Dad."

Beneath his shirt, Travis's broad shoulders stiffened. His gaze hardened. "Go on."

"They're both gone this week. So—" she eyed him with the same cynicism she saw in his gaze "—whether you like it or not, you're stuck with me."

"Great." The brackets around his mouth tightened.

Refusing to "rise to the bait" again, she nodded toward the long concourse. "The car's in the lot. Do you have any other bags?"

"No." He shifted his garment bag. "Let's go."

Without further conversation, they walked with the flow of people through the main terminal and outside to the parking lot. Sliding a glance in Travis's direction, Savannah found it difficult to believe that the man beside her could have been the man she had fallen in love with so desperately all those years before.

A winter-cold wind sliced through her jacket and blew her hair away from her face, chilling her cheeks. She huddled her shoulders together and wondered if she was shivering from the wind or the ice in Travis's eyes.

Henderson was partially right, Savannah thought uneasily. Travis looked tired and beaten; world-weary. But there was still a spark of life in his gray gaze, a flicker of interest that argued with Henderson's theory that Travis was "ready to chuck it all." Travis seemed bitter and cynical, but far from suicidal. *Thank God for small favors.*

Once they had made it to the silver sports car, Travis took one look at the BMW and frowned. "Is this yours?"

"Dad's."

"Figures." He tossed his garment bag into the back seat and slid into the passenger side of the car. Once there he pushed the seat back as far as it would go, lowered the backrest so that he could recline, jerked at his tie and let it dangle unknotted at his throat and then unbuttoned the top two buttons of his shirt. Savannah pretended interest in starting the car, but found herself fascinated, as always, with him. She saw the tufts of dark hair visible now that the throat of his shirt gaped and noticed the angry thrust of his jaw as he raked his fingers through his thick hair.

As Savannah started the engine and drove out of the parking lot, Travis leaned his head against the headrest and closed his eyes. His breathing became regular, so Savannah decided not to disturb him. *Let him sleep,* she told herself angrily. *Maybe he'll be in a better mood when he wakes up.*

It started to rain again and she flicked on the wipers. When she glanced at Travis, she found him staring at her. His gaze was thoughtful as it moved lazily over the soft planes of her face. "Why did you come to the airport?"

"To get you; Willis Henderson said—"

"I don't care what he said. Why didn't you send one of the hands?"

"We're shorthanded."

He let out a sound of disgust and looked out the window. "Not exactly flattering."

She felt her temper begin to ignite. "What's that supposed to mean?"

"I thought maybe you wanted to see me again."

After nine years! The arrogant, self-centered bastard! "Sorry to disappoint you."

"I doubt that you ever could," he muttered. "It just

seems strange that after nine years of avoiding me, you came to the airport. Alone."

"I haven't avoided you."

He turned his knowing gray eyes back to her face, silently accusing her of the lie.

"Every time you were at the house…" Her voice trailed off and her fingers clenched around the steering wheel. "There were a lot of people around."

"The way you wanted it. You wouldn't let me near you."

"You were married."

A satisfied smile curved his thin lips and Savannah's anger burned again. "I just wanted to talk to you."

"A little too late, don't you think?" she pointed out, gritting her teeth and trying to concentrate on the road ahead. "Look, Travis, let's not argue."

"I'm not."

"No, you're just being damned infuriating."

"I just thought that since we're alone, I should explain a few things."

"I'm not really interested in any excuses, or apologies," she said "No reason to rehash the past."

His gaze darkened angrily and he shook his head. "Fine—if that's the way you want it. I just thought you should know that I never intended to leave you."

"Oh, sure. But it just couldn't be avoided? Right?" She shook her head and her fingers tightened around the steering wheel in a death grip. The pickup in front of her swerved and the driver slammed on his brakes. Savannah stood on hers. The BMW fish-tailed, but stopped before colliding with the red pickup. "Oh, God," Savannah whispered, her heart thudding in her chest from the tense conversation as well as the close call on the road.

"Want me to drive?" he asked, once the cars started to move.

"No!"

"All right. Then, let me explain what happened at the lake."

Savannah's nerves were shattered. She glanced from Travis to the traffic and back again. "Look, I'd rather not discuss this, not now. Too much time has passed."

"Okay, not now. When?"

"Never would be okay with me."

He cocked a disdainful dark brow and frowned. "I'm too tired to argue. So, have it your way…for now. But we are going to talk this out. I'm tired of being manipulated and forced to live a lie."

"I never—" She started to protest and then snapped her mouth shut. She wasn't ready for a conversation about the past, not yet. She needed time to reassess her feelings for Travis before she let herself get trapped in the pain of that summer. It seemed like eons ago. "So that's the reason you're coming back to the farm."

"One reason," he admitted, staring through the rain-spattered windows to the concrete ribbon of freeway and the clog of traffic. An endless line of red taillights flashed ahead of them and blurred through the wet windshield. "I think it's time to set a few things straight with you—" Savannah's breath caught in her throat "—and the rest of the family. Speaking of which, where is Wade?"

"With Dad in Florida. They're considering stabling some of the two-year-olds there in the spring. When Mystic won the Preakness, Dad thought it might be time to move some of the stronger colts to the East Coast."

"And you disagree?"

"The Preakness was only one race—one moment of glory. After winning at Pimlico, Dad was on cloud nine and he really expected Mystic to go on to win the Belmont." She shook her head sadly. "And the result was that Supreme Court, the winner of the Derby, walked away from the field at Belmont. Mystic finished sixth. He hasn't won since. He's back on the farm now and Dad's trying to decide whether to run him next year, sell him or put him out to stud."

Travis didn't comment. Instead he slid a glance up her body, taking in her scruffy boots, faded jeans, blue cowl-necked sweater and suede jacket. His cold gray eyes seemed to strip her bare. "That still doesn't tell me why you came to the airport."

"When Henderson called, there wasn't much time."

The corners of his mouth turned downward at the thought of his partner. "Good." He leaned back against the headrest again. "Maybe it's better if I don't see your brother-in-law for a while. And, as for you—" he placed a hand on her shoulder, but she didn't flinch; his fingers were strong and gentle, just as they'd always been "—you may as well get used to the idea that we're going to talk about what happened, whether you want to or not."

"I don't."

"And so you came to the airport all alone." He let out an amused laugh before dropping his hand. "You're lying, Savannah, and you never were much good at it."

"I thought you were coming to the farm to talk to Wade," she said.

Travis scowled. "Him, too. But he's not gonna like what I've got to say."

"And what's that?"

Travis slid her a knowing look and there was just the trace of bitterness in his eyes. "I think I'd better tell Wade myself."

She frowned as she turned off the freeway and onto the country road that cut through the hills surrounding the farm. Wet leaves piled against fence posts and rising water ran wildly in the ditches near the road. "Do you honestly think I'd worm something out of you and then call Wade?" The idea was so absurd that she almost laughed.

"Don't you like your brother-in-law?"

She pursed her lips, but shook her head. "It's no secret and the feeling's mutual but there's nothing much I can do. He's Charmaine's husband."

"And your dad's right-hand man."

"Looks that way," she said wryly, considering her sister's husband. A first-class bastard, in Savannah's opinion. Unfortunately no one at the farm agreed with her, except maybe her mother, and Virginia wouldn't say anything against Wade.

"So what about you?" he asked quietly.

"What about me?"

"I thought you were going to marry that Donald character—"

"David," she corrected.

"Right. What happened?"

Her shoulders stiffened. "I had second thoughts."

"And cold feet."

For a moment, she felt her temper start to flare, but when she looked at Travis, she saw a glimmer of amusement in his eyes. The old Travis. The man she had loved. "Yeah, cold feet," she agreed. "David wasn't keen on a wife who liked to work with horses. He said he didn't like the smell of them and always had a sneezing attack whenever he was near the stables."

Travis grinned. "Then what the hell was he doing with you?"

"He thought he could change me," she said.

"I remember," Travis replied, thinking back to the night that he'd wanted to kill David Crandall when the kid had pushed himself onto Savannah in the car, all those years ago. Travis's mood shifted again and he felt tense. "Crandall didn't know you very well, did he?"

Savannah could feel his gaze on her face, but she kept her eyes steady on the road. "I guess not."

"Do you still see him?"

"Occasionally. He's married now. Has a wife and two kids." She smiled to herself. "A proper, respectable wife who gave up her career as a chamber musician to be his bride."

"Ouch."

Still grinning, Savannah shook her head, and her ebony hair brushed across the shoulders of her jacket. "It didn't really hurt. Well, maybe my pride was wounded a bit. He married Brenda just three months after we broke up, but it all worked out for the best."

"You're sure?" Travis eyed her speculatively.

"Yep. Can you imagine me living in San Francisco as the wife of an architect?"

"No."

Neither could she. "Well, there you go."

"So you came back to the farm."

After four years of college and three years of working in an investment firm in San Francisco, she'd longed to return to her family and the breeding farm. "I got tired of the city."

Savannah turned off the main road and drove down the long lane leading to Beaumont Breeding Farm. Barren cottonwoods and oaks lined the asphalt drive leading to the main house and garage.

Once Savannah had parked the car in its reserved spot in the garage, Travis gathered his bags, slid out of the BMW and stared at the house. "Some things don't change much," he observed.

Thinking of Virginia, Savannah was forced to disagree. She touched him lightly on the arm. "Maybe more than you know."

He looked at her and his eyes narrowed suspiciously. "Meaning?"

She cleared her throat. "I think you should know that Mom's...not well." He continued to stare at her and the only evidence that he had heard her at all was the whitening of his lips as his jaw clenched. "She's suffered from a series of heart attacks...small ones, but still, she's not well."

"Heart attacks!" Travis looked as if he didn't believe Savannah, but the gravity of her features convinced him. "Why wasn't I told?" he demanded.

"Because that's the way Mom wanted it."

"Why?" His angry glare burned through her.

"Mom didn't want to bother you. You've had your share of problems, y'know." When he didn't seem convinced, she spelled it out for him. "The first attack happened about a week after Melinda was killed in the boating accident. Mom didn't want to worry you."

"That was over six months ago," he said sharply, his voice edged in steel.

"And the next attacks... A series of small ones happened when you were in the middle of that Eldridge case."

"Someone should have told me. *You* should have told me."

"*Me?* I couldn't!"

He leaned against the car. "Just why the hell not, Savannah?"

"Mother insisted on it and Dad—"

"Your father wanted me kept in the dark?"

Savannah shook her head. "He knew how important that case was for your career, he knew that you had been shattered by Melinda's death. He was just looking out for your best interests."

"Like hell!" he roared, grabbing her shoulders in frustration. "I'm a thirty-four-year old man, Savannah. I don't need protection. Especially from your father!"

"But Mom—"

"Where is she?"

"In the house…probably her room."

He released her and controlled his rage. "So level with me—how bad is it?"

Savannah gritted her teeth and decided that despite her mother's request, she couldn't lie to Travis. "It's not good, Travis. Lots of days Mom doesn't come downstairs."

The skin tightened over his face. "Why isn't she in the hospital?"

"Because they can't do anything for her. A private nurse visits the house every day."

"Great," he said with a sigh. "Just great. And no one bothered to tell me." He rubbed the back of his neck in frustration. "I'm going to see her, y'know."

"She'd kill you if you didn't." Savannah offered him

an encouraging smile as they entered the house. He took off his jacket and headed up the stairs, his jaw clenched in determination.

Savannah started to follow him, but paused. Virginia would need time alone with Travis. She'd been a second mother to him and Savannah didn't want to interfere in the private conversation. She went back down the stairs and into her father's study, but couldn't concentrate on the stack of bills she'd been sorting earlier in the day. All of her thoughts returned to Travis and memories of that summer long ago filled her mind. "You're a fool," she muttered to herself and tossed the large pile of invoices back on the desk in exasperation.

After pacing in the den for a few minutes, Savannah decided to walk out to the barns and see that the stable hands were taking care of the horses. With the intention of speaking with Lester Adams, the trainer of the farm, she walked outside and turned her collar against the cold December wind.

Dealing directly with Lester was usually her father's job, but since Reginald was in Florida, Savannah worked with the grizzled old trainer and listened to his complaints about the horses as well as his praise.

"REGINALD SHOULD HAVE sold this one," Lester said for the second time as he leaned over the fence and watched the colt's workout. "He looks good, but he's hell to work with."

"So was Mystic." Savannah smiled and watched Vagabond run with the fluid grace of a champion. He was a beautiful bay colt with dark eyes that glimmered menacingly and a long stride that seemed effortless.

"He's different."

"Same temperament, I'd say. Besides, I thought you were the one who said you liked a colt with fire."

"Fire, yes. An inferno, no!" Lester shook his head and his gray eyebrows drew together in frustration. "This one, he's got a mean streak the likes of which the devil himself has never seen."

"He could be a winner."

"If he doesn't self-destruct." The old man put his boot onto the bottom rail of the fence as he studied Vagabond's long strides. "He's got the speed, all right. And the stamina."

"And the heart."

Lester laughed and shook his head. "Heart, you call it." He chuckled softly. "Geez, that's kind. I call it blasted stubbornness. Nothing else."

"You'll find a way to turn him into a winner," Savannah predicted as the horse slowed. "Just like Mystic."

The trainer avoided her eyes. "It'll be a challenge."

"Just what you like."

"Hmph." The old man cracked a wise smile. "That's enough, Jake," he called as the exercise boy slowed Vagabond to a canter.

"Good." The small rider slid down from the saddle, and patted Vagabond's muscular shoulder. Sweat and mud covered the colt's sleek coat. "I'll go clean him up now."

Lester nodded his agreement, pushed his fedora down over his eyes and reached into his breast pocket for a crumpled pack of cigarettes.

"So Travis came back today," he said as he lit up and inhaled deeply. Leaning against the fence, he watched Savannah through a cloud of blue smoke.

"He's at the house now."

"Will he be staying long?"

"I don't know, but I doubt it. He only had one bag with him." She looked past the workout track, over the fields surrounding the farm, and studied the craggy mountains in the distance. Snow was visible on the higher slopes, above the timberline. "He wants to talk to Wade."

"About runnin' for governor?"

"I don't know," she admitted. "I never got around to asking."

"I can't figure it out," Lester said.

"What?"

"It just seems strange, that's all. Travis, he always did well with the horses. And I know he liked working with them, it was obvious from the start. I had a feelin' about that boy, that he'd…well, that he'd stay on here at the farm. But I was wrong. Instead he goes off to college and becomes a lawyer—hardly ever sets foot on the place again. It just never made much sense, not to me."

He flicked his cigarette onto the wet ground and ground it out with the sole of his boot.

"To top things off," Lester continued, "that sister of yours marries Wade Benson…well, I guess she had her reasons. But Benson, for God's sake, a man I swear couldn't tell a mustang from a Thoroughbred, gives up his accounting practice to work with the horses. It just don't seem right."

"Wade still does the books for the farm," Savannah said, and then wondered why she was defending the man when she, like Lester, had doubted Wade's motives from time to time.

"Yep, but that ain't all. He's managing the place most of the time."

"I know. Dad's been thinking about retiring, because of Mom's condition."

"A shame about your mother," Lester said quietly. His black eyes darkened with an inner sadness.

"Yes."

"A damned shame," Lester muttered before slapping the top rail of the fence and clearing his throat. "I guess I'd better go check on the boys—make sure they're earning their keep and watching over the yearlings." He started off toward the broodmare barn, and Savannah, her thoughts once again centered on Travis, turned back to the house.

A few minutes later Savannah took off her boots on the back porch, stopped to scratch Archimedes, her father's large Australian sheepdog, behind the ears and went into the house through the kitchen.

Sadie Stinson, who served as housekeeper and cook, was busy slicing vegetables, and the room was filled with the tantalizing scent of roast pork.

"That smells wonderful," Savannah said, peering into the oven and warming her hands against the glass door. "I missed lunch."

Sadie Stinson clucked her tongue. "Shame on you."

"Oh, I don't know. From the looks of this, it was worth the wait."

"Flattery will get you nowhere," the cook said, but beamed under the praise. She eyed Savannah's red face, stockinged feet, and damp hair. "Now, you go and get cleaned up. I'll have this on the table in half an hour."

"Can't wait," Savannah admitted, her stomach rumbling in agreement.

"You'll have to."

"Spoilsport," she teased and Sadie chuckled. "By the way, have you seen Travis?"

Sadie's mood changed and the smile fell from her face. "That I have. He's in your father's study, pouring himself into a bottle, it looks like." She began slicing the zucchini with a vengeance. "Probably won't even appreciate all the work I've gone to."

"I doubt that," Savannah lied and walked out of the kitchen and down the short hallway to the den. Travis was inside, sitting on the broad ledge of the bay window, his legs braced against the floor, his eyes trained on the gathering darkness. He'd changed out of his suit and into worn cords and a flannel shirt that he hadn't bothered to button. His eyes were narrowed against the encroaching night and he held a half-filled glass in his hand. A fire was crackling in the stone fireplace.

Travis glanced over his shoulder and noticed Savannah in the doorway. Her black hair framed her face in wild curls and her intense blue eyes were focused on him. At her studious stare he experienced a tightening in his gut. He'd forgotten how really beautiful she was. "Come in, join me," he invited with a grimace as he lifted his glass.

"I don't think so."

Shrugging indifferently, he turned toward the window and leaned insolently against the frame. "Suit yourself."

"I will." She walked into the room and closed the door before kneeling at the fireplace and warming her hands near the flames. "Did you see Mom?"

The broad shoulders bunched. "Yes." He took a long swallow from his glass and, once it was empty, walked over to the bar near the fireplace and poured himself another three fingers of Scotch. "You should have told me."

"I couldn't."

"Like hell!"

"Mom thought—"

"She's dying, dammit." He accused her with cold gray eyes. "I thought that I could trust you, Savannah."

"Me?" she repeated, incredulously. "You thought you could trust me?" *What about the trust I put in you nine years ago? The trust you threw away with the morning light?*

"You know what I mean. When we were kids, we had secrets, but we were always straight with each other."

Except once, she thought angrily. *Except for the one night that you told me you loved me and I believed it with all of my heart.*

"We're not kids any longer and Mom asked me not to say anything," she said. "I keep my word, and besides, Mom said that Dad would tell you when the time was right."

"And when was that?"

"How am I supposed to know?" She shot him an angry glare and then started for the door. "I've got to get cleaned up for dinner. If you don't drink yourself into oblivion, I'll see you then."

"Savannah—"

Her hand was on the brass handle of the door, but she turned to look over her shoulder and for a fleeting second she saw honest regret in his eyes before his expression turned hard. "I'll be at dinner," he said.

"Good." With her final remark, she walked out of the room.

DINNER WAS TOLERABLE, but just. Virginia was tired and had her meal in her room, Charmaine was brooding over the fact that Wade hadn't called and Travis showed no interest in the spectacular feast that Sadie Stinson had prepared.

Wonderful, Savannah thought sarcastically. *This is just great!*

The only person who genuinely enjoyed himself was Josh, and Savannah was grateful for the little boy's company and constant chatter. "So how long are you stayin'?" Josh asked Travis.

"I don't know."

"I heard Dad say that you were going to be president or something!"

"Governor, Josh," Charmaine corrected, and Travis winced before leaning back in his chair and smiling at Josh.

It was the first time Travis had really smiled since he'd gotten off the plane, and it had a disastrous effect upon Savannah.

"Is that what he said?" Travis asked.

"Yep." Josh pushed his plate aside and leaned forward eagerly. "Dad thinks that's where you belong, at the... wherever the governor is."

"Sacramento."

"Yeah, he says that it's best if you're anywhere besides here on the farm."

"Is that right?" Travis drawled, his grin widening and pleasure gleaming in his eyes.

"Joshua!" Charmaine said, coloring slightly. "If you're done with your meal go upstairs and do your homework!"

"Am I in trouble?"

"Of course not, Josh," Savannah cut in, giving Travis a warning glance and pushing aside her chair. "Come on, I'll get you started."

"It's math," Josh warned.

Savannah pulled a face. "Not my forte, but I'll give it a shot anyway. Let's go." She waited for the boy and together they climbed the stairs. Once on the landing, she hesitated. "You go and get started," she suggested, "and I'll check on Grandma. Okay?"

"Sure," Josh replied and ran down the hall.

After knocking softly on the door, Savannah entered her mother's bedroom. Virginia smiled. "I wondered when you'd show up," she chided.

"Couldn't stay away." Savannah walked over to the bed and took the tray off the bed.

"And how are you getting along with Travis?"

Savannah let out a sound of disgust and leaned against one of the tall posts of the bed. "As well as can be expected considering the fact that he's got a chip on his shoulder the size of the Rock of Gibraltar."

"He's had a rough year," Virginia said, her brow puckering slightly.

"Maybe you're right," Savannah said, deciding it best not to worry her mother unnecessarily. Travis's problems were of his own making and they didn't concern Virginia.

"Then give him a chance, for Pete's sake."

"A chance?"

"To heal his wounds."

"Did he tell you why he came here?"

Virginia's head moved side to side on the pillow. "As a matter of fact, he was rather vague about it. I got the impression that he had some business to conclude with

Reginald and that he was taking a rest. It does him good to be here, you know. He always enjoyed working on the farm, with the horses. He can even have the loft again, for an apartment..." Her voice faded slightly.

"Look, I'll take this tray downstairs and see you later," Savannah said. "Right now I promised Josh I'd help him with his math."

Virginia chuckled. "The blind leading the blind..." Savannah laughed aloud. "No faith in your own daughter. Won't you be surprised when Josh aces his next test?"

"With you tutoring him? That I will be," Virginia said as Savannah carried the dinner tray to the door.

"I'll see ya later," Savannah said before walking down the long hall to Josh's room and finding the boy on the floor, Transformers and Gobots spread out on the carpet in a mock battle.

"Who's winning?" Savannah said with a smile.

"The Decepticons!"

"I thought you were supposed to be working on math."

"Aunt Savvy..." Josh pleaded, turning his bright eyes up at her.

"Right now, mister." She gathered up some of the toys and set them on Josh's already overloaded dresser.

"You could play with me," he suggested.

Savannah sat on the edge of the bed and shook her head. "Maybe later. Right now we've got math to master." She kicked off her shoes and crossed her legs. "Hop to it."

"I hate math," the boy grumbled.

"So do I, but, though I loathe to admit it, arithmetic,

geometry, algebra, etcetera are very important. Someday you'll find out."

"Not in a million years." Josh grabbed his book and
put it on the desk. Then he took a seat and hunched his
shoulders over his homework.

Savannah concentrated on the problems. "This'll be
a breeze," she predicted. "Simple multiplication."

A few minutes and several problems later, a soft
cough caught her attention and she looked over her
shoulder to find Travis lounging in the doorway. One
of his shoulders was propped against the frame and his
hands were pushed into the pockets of his jeans. How
long he had been there, watching her with his slate-
colored eyes, she could only guess. "How's it going?"

"It's not," Savannah admitted.

"Horrible!" Josh said.

"Need some help?"

"Yeah!" Josh was more than eager to have Travis
help him. Savannah's heart went out to the boy. All Josh
wanted was a little positive fatherly attention and he got
very little from his own dad.

"Sure. Why not?" Savannah said. "I've got to take
this tray down to the kitchen anyway." She stood up
and reached for the tray she had set on the nightstand.

"Don't let me scare you away," Travis said, saunter-
ing into the room, his gaze locking with hers.

"You're not."

"And you're lying again," he accused. "Bad habit,
Savannah. You'd better break it."

"I guess you just bring out the worst in me," she whispered through clenched teeth, hoping that Travis would
take the hint and drop the subject.

"Or the best." His eyes roved down her rigid body to rest on the thrust of her breasts against her sweater.

Under his stripping gaze, anger heated her blood and colored her cheeks, but she kept her tongue still because Josh had turned his head to study her.

"Is something wrong, Aunt Savvy?"

"Nothing," she replied tightly. "I just have a couple of things to do. I'll… I'll see you later." Controlling her anger with Travis took an effort, but she managed to give Josh a genuine smile before leaving the room and telling herself that she would only have to suffer Travis's indignities a few more days, only until Wade and Reginald returned to the farm.

And what would happen then? Savannah grimaced to herself when she realized that she was looking forward to the reunion with both anticipation and dread.

CHAPTER THREE

WADE DIDN'T CALL that night, and Savannah didn't know whether to be thankful or worried.

The next day Savannah tried to avoid Travis, finding it easier to keep out of his way than risk another confrontation with him. It wasn't difficult. Travis spent his time locked in the study, on the phone, or in the loft, which Charmaine had partially cleared out of. Savannah went grocery shopping, then made it a point to work with Lester and the horses during the day, before going up to her room in the evening to shower and change for dinner. She dressed in black slacks and a red sweater and tried to tell herself she wasn't primping as she brushed her hair.

Savannah walked into the dining room and was surprised to see that her mother was already at the table. Seated at the head of the long table and dressed in a rose-colored caftan, Virginia looked healthier than she had in weeks.

Travis sat to the left of Virginia with Charmaine on his other side. His eyes followed Savannah as she walked into the room and took the empty seat across the table from him. Wearing an open-necked shirt and leaning on one elbow, he sipped a glass of wine and appeared relaxed as he talked with Virginia. *Like a vagabond son returning home,* Savannah thought, meeting his interested gaze. Only when she entered the room, did he show any sign of tension.

"Glad you could make it down, Mom," Savannah said, bristling slightly as Travis poured her a glass of wine.

"It's not every day that Travis comes home," Virginia remarked with a pleased smile. "I'm just sorry he didn't tell us he intended to be here earlier so that we could welcome him properly yesterday."

Properly must have meant with silver, linen napkins, a floral centerpiece, flickering candles and shining crystal, Savannah thought, eyeing the table. The chandelier had been appropriately dimmed, the silver polished until it gleamed. Virginia always had liked to put on a show.

"Not necessary," Travis said, his gray eyes moving from Virginia to Savannah and lingering on the proud lift of her chin.

"Of course it is." Virginia laughed. "You haven't been home for nearly two years!"

Small talk carried Savannah through the meal, though she could feel the weight of Travis's gaze as she ate. He leaned back in his chair and observed her with amused, but cynical eyes that seemed to look into the darkest corners of her mind.

Joshua was seated beside Savannah and he appeared preoccupied. His small brow was creased with worry and he barely touched his food. Any attempt to draw the boy into the conversation met with monosyllabic responses.

Despite the formal decorations and the mouth-watering meal, Savannah felt the undercurrents of tension in the room. *Just like the calm before the storm,* she thought uneasily as she shifted her gaze from Josh's brooding expression to Travis's intense gaze.

"Wade called this afternoon," Charmaine announced, setting her fork on her plate after dessert.

The strain in the room exploded.

"What!" Travis's head jerked toward Charmaine, and he pinned her with his angry glare. "Why didn't you tell me?"

Charmaine met his gaze and lifted her chin. "You were in the stables with Lester. I didn't want to bother you. Mother was resting and Savannah was in Sacramento doing the grocery shopping. So I took the call and told him you were here and anxious to speak with him."

Travis scowled, his impatience mounting. "Maybe I should phone him."

"No. He said he'd be home tomorrow. The plane lands about six, and he and father should be here by seven-thirty at the latest." She placed her napkin on the table and pushed her chair back, but didn't stand. "If it's any consolation, he was as anxious to talk to you as you are to speak with him."

"I'll bet," Travis mocked.

Charmaine overlooked his remark and turned to Josh. Her voice was still tight, but she attempted to appear calm. "So Daddy will be here in plenty of time for Christmas. Isn't that great?"

The boy had been pushing the remains of his apple pie around in his plate. He stopped, looked past his mother and shrugged.

"Joshua?"

"I don't want him to come home," Josh mumbled, glancing at Savannah before pretending interest in his plate.

Charmaine, obviously embarrassed, cleared her throat. "Joshua. Surely you don't mean—"

"I do mean it, Mom." Tears had gathered in his eyes, though he was bravely trying to swallow them back. "Daddy hates me."

Virginia gasped. "Oh, dear," she whispered, trying to think of something to cut short the uncomfortable scene.

Stiffening slightly, Charmaine blushed. "You know that's not true, Josh."

"It is, too. And I finally figured it out," Josh blurted. "Some of the kids were talking at school today…"

"About what?" Charmaine asked, dread tightening the corners of her mouth.

"I know the only reason you married Dad is because of me!" he said miserably, guilt weighing heavily on his small shoulders.

To her credit, Charmaine didn't flinch. "I married your father because I loved him."

"Because you *had* to!" Joshua said brokenly, partially standing, but managing to hold his mother's gaze. "That's what the kids at school said."

"Josh," Savannah cut in, but Charmaine held up her hand.

"This is my problem, Savannah." Then, looking back at her son, she said, "No one *had* to marry anyone."

"Would you have married Dad if you weren't pregnant with me?" He blinked against the tears in his eyes.

Virginia went pale and picked up her water glass with trembling fingers.

"Of course—" Charmaine whispered tenderly.

"No!" Josh screamed, his face red and tear-stained.

Charmaine braced her shoulders. "Joshua, I think

you should go up to your room and I'll come talk to you there," she said in measured tones, her voice shaking.

Savannah tried to touch Josh on the shoulder, but he jerked away and Savannah's stomach knotted in pain. "Josh—"

"I don't want to talk," the boy said angrily, his fists balled at his sides. "It's true—it's all true and I don't want Dad to come home! I wish—I wish that I didn't have a father!"

Travis looked from Savannah to the boy and back again, his jaw tight, his eyes filled with understanding for the rebellious youth.

"You don't mean that," Charmaine insisted.

"I do! I do mean it!"

Joshua's chair slid back from the table, scraping the floor. He ran out of the room and clomped noisily up the stairs.

"No," Charmaine murmured, closing her eyes to steady herself.

"I'm sorry," Savannah whispered, knowing there was no way to console her older sister.

"No reason to be," Charmaine said tightly. "This has been coming for a long time. Wade and Josh have never gotten along. Sooner or later Josh was bound to figure out that his dad resents him. I just…never wanted to face it, I guess."

"I'll go," Savannah offered, fighting her own tears.

"No. This is my problem, a mistake I made ten years ago. I'll handle it." With new conviction Charmaine got out of her chair and hurried out of the dining room. "Joshua," Charmaine called and Savannah had to close her eyes to fight her own tears. "Joshua, don't you lock that door!"

When she opened her eyes again, Savannah found Travis staring at her intently. His jaw was rigid, his gray eyes cold. He finished the wine in his glass and rubbed an impatient hand over his jaw.

"I suppose it had to come to this," Virginia said, breaking the silence and throwing her napkin on her plate in disgust. "I just hoped I wouldn't see the day." She stood shakily from her chair and Travis got up to help her. Virginia, though pale, anticipated his move and waved him away. "I'm all right. I just want to go upstairs for a while. I can make it on my own."

"Are you sure?" Savannah asked.

"I've been climbing those stairs for over thirty years," she said with a worried smile. "No reason to stop now."

With a proud set to her shoulders, Virginia walked out of the room and slowly mounted the stairs.

"When I get my hands on Wade Benson," Travis warned, his voice low, his angry eyes focused on Savannah, "he'll wish he'd had the common sense to stay in Florida or wherever the hell he is." Setting his half-empty wineglass on the table, he stood up and walked out of the room. A few seconds later the front door slammed shut.

Still concerned about Joshua, Savannah helped Sadie clear the table and straighten the kitchen to get her mind off Josh as well as Travis. Then, telling herself that she wasn't looking for Travis, Savannah went outside to the stables, checked on the horses and filed some reports in the office over the foaling shed. Travis wasn't in the yard or the office and Savannah felt a twinge of disappointment when she decided to go back to the house.

"You're a fool," she told herself with a frown. "Stay as far away from him as possible." She stretched before locking the door to the office, then climbed down the stairs. The night was bitterly cold and starless. Huddling against the frigid air, she raced across the parking lot and through the back door of the darkened house.

Archimedes stirred on the back porch and thumped his tail loudly as she kicked off her boots and slipped into the kitchen. The only sound disturbing the silence of the house was the hum of the refrigerator and the ticking of the grandfather clock in the hall.

"God, I'm tired," she whispered, opening the refrigerator. She poured a large glass of milk and slowly drank it while staring out the window to the darkened stable-yard. Thoughts of Travis wouldn't leave her alone and she wondered again where he was and why he had come back to the farm.

After putting the empty glass in the sink, she rubbed a hand over her eyes and walked toward the study to put away the mail.

The den was dark, illuminated only by the light of the dying fire. When Savannah entered the room, she found Travis lounging on the hearth, his fingers clasped around a glass, his back to the blood-red embers, his long legs stretched in front of him.

"What're you doing here?" she asked.

"Waiting."

"For?"

"You." He looked up at her, his intense gaze causing her heart to flutter.

"Okay," she whispered. "I'm here." She planted herself in front of him by leaning against the desk and balancing her hips against the smooth, polished wood. She reached for the lamp.

"Leave it off."

"Why?"

"The room seems quieter that way…less hostile."

Savannah let out a soft laugh. "You should know. Lately I think you wrote the book on hostility."

"Not with you," he said, taking a sip from his glass. "Why'd you interfere with Josh?" he asked slowly.

"I didn't."

A crooked grin sliced across his face. "Call it whatever you want, but it's the second time you've done it."

She lifted a shoulder and frowned, her dark brows drawing together as her thoughts returned to her nephew. "I don't think I'm interfering," she argued. "Sometimes I feel that he doesn't get enough attention or credit around here. Everyone points out his faults, but no one ever seems to pat him on the back."

"Except for you?"

"And his grandfather. Despite what you feel about him, Reginald's been a damned good grandfather, just like the kind of stepfather he's been to you. Just in case you've forgotten."

Travis's square jaw hardened. "What about Charmaine? How does she get along with her son?"

"Josh is a difficult child and Charmaine nearly raises him by herself. Obviously Wade doesn't have much time for the boy."

"Obviously," Travis commented dryly.

"As for Charmaine; she tries. But sometimes she has trouble understanding Josh. You know, she expects perfection and won't let him just be a kid."

"So that's when you step in."

"Only when I think Josh needs a little extra support. It's not easy being the only nine-year-old in a house full of grownups, y'know." She crossed her arms under her chest, unconsciously sculpting her sweater over breasts.

"You love him very much."

"Who wouldn't?" she asked, smiling to herself.

"Maybe Wade?"

Savannah's jaw tightened and she couldn't hide the impotent rage she felt every time she thought about Wade's treatment of his son. "I don't know if Wade is capable of loving anyone, even himself," she muttered. "And Josh is right about one thing: Wade should never have become a father." Then, thinking better of confiding in Travis, she tried to let go of her anger and changed the subject. "Do you know that Josh fantasizes about riding Mystic?"

"And what do you fantasize about?" he asked, his gray eyes focused on the proud lift of her chin, the flush in her cheeks and the elegant column of her throat. Her tousled black curls gleamed against her white skin and brushed the soft red sweater.

"I don't," she replied, slightly unnerved.

He looked as if he didn't believe her. "No dreams, Savvy?" he asked, and his voice caressed the familiar nickname he had given her when he had first come to the farm and she'd been just a skinny kid of nine.

"Not anymore."

He dragged his eyes away from her and stared into his drink. "Because of what happened between us."

"That's part of it," she conceded, feeling the old bittersweet pain in her chest.

He took a long swallow of his Scotch before lifting his eyes to her face. "So tell me, if you're so fond of Josh, why didn't you have any children of your own?"

"Simple. No husband."

"That's always puzzled me."

She shifted her gaze to the fire before returning it to him. His chestnut hair glinted with red highlights in the firelight and his tanned face looked more angular from the shadows. "I thought I explained that. David and I—"

"There were other men. Had to have been. You went to college at Berkeley, worked in San Francisco. You can't expect me to believe that you lived the life of a nun."

She bristled, thinking how close he had come to the truth. "Not quite. But I guess I never found a man that I thought would be right."

"That was probably my fault, too."

"Don't flatter yourself."

Ignoring her bitterness, he crossed his legs before him and finished his drink. "For what it's worth, you would have been one helluva mother."

"I suppose I should take that as a compliment."

"It was intended as one."

She felt an uncomfortable lump in her throat and tried to use the feeling of intimacy that was stealing into the room to her advantage. "A little while ago you said that we used to share secrets."

"We did."

"So why don't you tell me why you're here. Why now? And why is Henderson, your partner, so upset?"

"I'll tell you when—"

"I know. When Wade and Dad get back. Tomorrow. A good thing, too," she added mockingly.

A muscle in the corner of his jaw began to work. "Why? Are you getting tired of me?"

"No, but you couldn't last here, counselor. At the rate you're going, we'll be out of Scotch in two days."

He cocked his head to the side and a laconic smile sliced across his face. "You think I'm a lush."

"You're doing a damned good impersonation." Standing up and stretching her tired muscles, she kept her eyes fixed on Travis. "Why don't you just tell me why you came back? I already know that you're planning to dissolve your partnership with Henderson and I know that you're probably going to give up on the idea of running for governor, despite the current rumors or any grassroots ground swell."

"Henderson talks too much."

"He didn't want to."

"But with your powers of persuasion, you convinced a respected member of the bar, a man who had held his tongue in a courtroom when it was to his client's advantage, to bare his soul," he prodded, the corners of his mouth pinching.

She ignored his blatant sarcasm. "Something like that."

"Like I said, he talks too much." His eyes slid slowly up her body, lingering at the swell of her breasts. "And you're too inquisitive for your own good. Always have been." His gaze continued upward, hesitating a moment at the corner of her mouth before reaching her eyes.

Savannah's throat worked reflexively. There was something inherently male about Travis that reached her on a very sensual level. There always had been.

"Why did you come back?" she asked, hoping to break the thickening tension in the room.

"I don't want to discuss it."

"Why not?"

He grimaced into the remains of his drink. "Because I want to talk to Reginald first. Something's not right."

"With what?"

He rubbed the bridge of his nose and closed his eyes. "Oh, Savvy, with everything—the law practice, the campaign. There're a few things that don't add up and—" He stopped himself, realizing that he was confiding in her. "Just trust me on this one, okay? Once I talk to Wade I'll be able to sort everything out."

"What does Wade have to do with anything?" she asked.

"I think he's involved."

"In what?"

A muscle in the corner of Travis's jaw tightened. "I haven't put it all together," he admitted in disgust. "But frankly, I'm not sure that I want to."

"You're afraid."

Travis smiled grimly and shook his head. "I just don't know if it's worth all the trouble."

"Something's eating at you."

"I don't like to be a pawn. That's all." He got up and paced around the room. "Have you ever wondered *why* it's so damned important to your father that I run for election?"

"I guess I really hadn't thought about it."

"Well, he's pushing, Savannah. He's pushing very hard. And the only reason I could see that it would matter to him at all is for personal gain—his personal gain."

"You really have become a cynic, haven't you?" she tossed back, but the seriousness of his expression made her heart miss a beat.

"Think about it. Why would he care? What's it to him—unless he were expecting something from me."

"Like what?"

"I don't know…" He lifted his hand and then dropped it again. "Maybe you can tell me."

"I don't have an inkling of what you're talking about."

"Don't you? I wonder." He slid a suspicious glance in her direction before staring at the fire. "You could be in on it."

"You're crazy!" she said angrily.

He laughed a little, leaned an elbow on the mantel and raked his fingers through his hair. "Far from it, I'm afraid."

"You can't just come back here, to the man who all but raised you as his son, and start accusing him of God only knows what. You, of all people, should know that, counselor!" Savannah's temper got the better of her and she looked at him with self-righteous eyes.

"I haven't accused anyone of anything."

"Yet!"

Travis leaned back and smiled sarcastically. "Okay, let's use logic. The governor has a lot of responsibilities. Surely you agree."

"So?"

"For example: the governor of California is the supreme power behind the California Horse Racing Board. The Governor appoints members to the board and may remove a board member if it can be proved that he's incompetent or negligent. And that doesn't begin to touch what the governor is responsible for in the case of land use, corporations…you name it. The governor has a lot of power—the kind of power that some people might like to abuse."

"Like Dad?"

"For one. Wade and Willis Henderson wouldn't be standing very far behind him."

Savannah's eyes widened. Travis really believed what he was saying. "Be careful, Travis. You're talking about my father. My father! A man who has only done what he's thought best for you."

"Maybe not always."

"This is all idle speculation—half-baked theories!"

"I don't think so. Four of the board members' terms are up during the next term of governor. Four. Out of seven."

"And you think Dad cares?" Savannah was seething.

"Of course he cares! Everyone who owns a race horse in California cares!" He came up and stood before her. "For all I know, Reginald might want to be on the board himself or try to convince me to appoint the right people, friends of his who could be easily swayed to his point of view."

"But why?"

"Power, Savannah."

"That's crazy—"

"Power and money. The two biggest motives mankind has known."

"Don't forget revenge," she reminded him.

"Oh, I haven't." A ruthless smile curved his lips. "I visited my partner, Henderson, the other night."

"The night that you told him you wanted out of the partnership?"

"Right. The same night that he met with Wade."

Savannah froze. "I don't understand…"

"Wade and Willis Henderson seem to be working together on several schemes."

"Such as?" she asked, breathless.

He considered her a moment and then decided it didn't really matter what she knew. "Such as the fact

that Wade Benson is doing the books for the law firm—
without my knowledge."

Savannah couldn't hide her surprise. As far as she
knew Wade only did the books for the farm. "So what
does that have to do with anything?" she asked.

"In itself, not much. But the fact that Henderson admitted that he and Wade have already been taking contributions for my campaign…" Travis shook his head
and the thrust of his jaw became more prominent. "That
I saw as a problem. Henderson claims that your father
was in on it."

"But you haven't announced your candidacy."

Travis's lips twisted cynically. "And won't." He finished his drink. "You can see my point."

"If what you're saying is true…"

Travis squinted into the fire. "Why would I lie?"

"I don't know," she said, "because I don't know you
any more."

"Sure you do." His voice was gentle, as gentle as it
had been years ago before the bitterness and pain had
settled in his eyes.

"You've changed."

He offered a humble smile. "Not for the better, I assume."

"What made you so callous?" she asked. "Melinda's
death?"

"I wish it were as simple as all that," he muttered, finishing his drink. "She wouldn't have liked this, y'know.
She expected me to run for some political office and she
was behind my ambitions…she and your father." He
frowned into his empty glass. "And then there was the
Eldridge decision," he said bitterly.

"But I thought you won," Savannah said, reflecting

on the newsworthy decision. Travis was the lawyer who had successfully brought a major drug company to trial for the family of Eric Eldridge, who had died from taking a contaminated anti-inflammatory drug.

"So did I."

"What changed your mind?" she asked, knowing that he was carrying an unnecessary burden of guilt.

"Everything," he muttered disgustedly as he strode over to the bar and splashed three fingers of Scotch into his glass. "The law firm made money; the Eldridges got an award so large that they sent me a magnum of champagne and bought themselves two new cars and a yacht."

"What they did with the money doesn't matter."

He took a long drink. "But it didn't bring their son back, did it?" he asked, shaking his head and closing his eyes. "Grace Eldridge got up on the stand and wept for her lost son," he said, as if to himself. "A month later she came into the office wearing a new fur coat and a Bermuda tan and asked if I thought there was any way to file another lawsuit against the drug company." He studied the amber liquid in his glass. "It left a bad taste in my mouth."

He walked back to her and placed his glass on the desk. "That's what I meant when I said all that matters is power and money."

"And revenge," she reminded him.

He was standing in front of her again, his eyes, luminous in the darkened room, drilling into hers. "Right. Revenge." When his hands came up to take hold of her shoulders she didn't move.

The warmth from his fingers permeated her sweater to spread down her arms. She trembled inside, as much from his touch as from the realization that he was, indeed, suspicious of her father's motives. "So that's what you came here to find out," Savannah whispered. "How my father is involved in your 'campaign' or lack thereof."

"Partly," he admitted, his voice husky.

"What else?" Savannah's heart was pounding betrayingly from the feel of his hands on her arms.

"Just this." He lowered his head and gently brushed his lips across hers, tantalizing her with the feel of his mouth against her skin.

"Don't do this to me," she whispered. "Not again." Jerking free, she took an unsteady step backward and stared into his eyes. "Tell me…tell me what you think Dad's up to," she said, not wanting to think about the passion behind his kiss or her immediate reaction.

"I'm not sure; I'll need your help to find out."

"No, Travis," she whispered. "You really can't expect me to go against my own father."

"I haven't asked that."

He was so close, so damned close, and all she could think about was the power of his body over hers. "But you're trying to—"

"Find out the truth. That's all."

"Then talk to Dad!" she said desperately.

"I will. When he gets back. Until then, I may need your cooperation."

"I can't help you, Travis!"

"If it makes you feel any better, I hope that this is all a big misunderstanding. I would like to think that Reginald's motives are as pure as you seem to think."

"But you won't."

"I'm too realistic."

"Jaded," she corrected.

"Prove it," he dared, his eyes glinting in the firelight.

"I don't know—" She cleared her throat and tried to stop the hammering of her heart.

"Prove me wrong, dammit! You were the one who pushed me, lady. I didn't want to tell you any of this, but you insisted."

"But you're asking me to prove to you that my father, a respected horse breeder, is…what? Trying to get you elected so that he can defraud the racing public? Is that what you're suggesting?"

"Maybe you can verify your opinion."

"Of course I can! If Dad's so hell-bent to abuse your powers as governor, if and when you're elected, it would only affect him here, in California. Then why would he bother with stabling the horses in Florida? Tell me that! There wouldn't be much of a point, not when he knew that here, in the Golden State, he could manipulate the racing board at will!"

"You're being sarcastic."

"And you're talking nonsense!" she nearly shouted, angry with herself for even listening to him.

"Prove it," he suggested.

Savannah's blue eyes sparked at the challenge. "I will."

"Good." His grin was filled with ruthless satisfaction as he leaned against the mantel, his narrowed eyes lingering on her lips. "I don't suppose your father ever told you who was at the lake that night nine years ago." He touched her softly on the underside of her chin.

Savannah jerked her head to the side. "He knew?"

"Of course he knew."

"I don't believe it! He would have said something…"

"Why?"

"He wouldn't just forget about it."

"I don't think your father forgets anything."

She took in a steadying breath. "How did he know?"

Travis's smoldering eyes delved into hers. "Because Melinda told him."

"And how did Melinda know? Did you confess?" Savannah asked, hardly daring to breathe as she relived that night so long ago.

"She saw us."

"Oh, God." The memory came back with crystal clarity: a twig snapping, Travis going to investigate. *Melinda had been the intruder at the lake!* Embarrassment poured over Savannah and she started for the door, but Travis reached for her. His hand was incredibly gentle on her arm. "I don't want to hear this," she whispered, refusing to be dragged back to the pain of the past. "It's over—"

"Is it?" In the dim light from the fire, with only the sound of the crackling flames and the wind against the rafters, his gaze scorched through her icy facade and into her heart. "I never stopped wanting you," Travis admitted, self-disgust twisting his mouth cynically.

"There's no reason to lie."

His fingers curled over her arm and he gave her a shake. Raw emotion twisted his face. "Dammit, Savannah. I'm not lying. I hate like hell to admit it, but not one solitary day has gone by that I haven't thought of you...wished to God that I'd never left you that night."

"You could have come back," she whispered, her pulse racing.

"I was married! And you were Reginald's daughter!"

Savannah didn't want to hear the excuses or think about the lies of the past nine years. "There's no reason to discuss this, Travis," she murmured, trying to break free of his embrace, but his fingers tightened painfully.

"I never wanted to love you," he said, his voice rough, his eyes glittering in the fire glow. "In fact, I tried to lie to myself, convince myself that you were nothing to me, but it just didn't work. All the time I was married to another woman, I couldn't forget you. That night at the lake was burned into my mind and my soul like no other memory in my life." He took in a long, ragged breath. "And at night...at night I would lie awake and remember the feel of you and I couldn't stop wanting you, dammit. Melinda was right there, in the bed with me, and all I could think of was you!"

"What's the point of all this?" she asked, her breath tight in her throat and tears threatening her eyes. The words of love she'd longed to hear sounded out of place and disjointed with nine years standing between them.

"The point is that I got used to living a lie. But there's no reason to live it anymore."

Savannah's throat ached, but she lifted her head high and shook her hair out of her face. "Because Melinda is dead?"

"Yes."

She squeezed her eyes against the tears and lifted her chin. "I don't like being second-best, Travis. I never have."

"Don't you even want to know why I married her?"

"No! It really doesn't matter. Not anymore..." Her voice cracked with the lie.

The fingers around her arms gripped into her flesh and he pushed his head down to hers. He was so close that she could feel the angry heat radiating from his body, smell the Scotch on his breath, see the rage in his eyes. "It *does* matter. It all matters. Don't you understand? I've come here to break away from the lies of the past...all of them. Including the lie of marrying the wrong woman." His gray eyes delved into hers, scraping past the indifference she pretended to feel. "I *loved* you, Savannah and damned myself for it. You were the daughter of the man that raised me—and until that summer I'd always thought of you as a kid sister."

In the thick silence that followed, Savannah stared into his flinty eyes and saw the smoldering passion in his gaze. Her heart throbbed with the thought that once, long ago, he had loved her, and that he still wanted her. The fingers around her arms were a gentle manacle, but when she tried to tear away from his grasp, his hands tightened to the strength of steel.

"And you loved me," he finally whispered.

Tears burned her eyes, but she refused to break down. "The man I loved would never have left me," she said, her voice breaking before she took in a long, steadying breath. "He would never have left me without so much as a word of goodbye or an explanation."

Travis's nostrils flared and his eyes narrowed. "I've made more than my share of mistakes, lady. God knows I'm no saint and I should have demanded to see you before I agreed to marry Melinda, but everyone, including your father, thought it would be better if I just left."

Savannah shuddered. "How did Dad find out about us?"

His jaw was tense, the muscles of his body taut. "Melinda went to Reginald with the story that she was pregnant. Or else they worked out the story together."

"I don't understand." Savannah felt her knees grow

weak, but the grip on her arms held her upright and Travis's features became harsh.

"She claimed that the only reason she and I had argued earlier in the night was because she was frightened. Afraid that I would leave her and the child. Then, she had second thoughts and tracked me down."

Savannah couldn't believe him. "How did she know you were at the lake?" she asked angrily.

"Just a lucky guess. My car was in the garage, but I wasn't sleeping in the loft, or in the office. Melinda knew that I went to the lake whenever I wanted to think things out, so—"

"She found us," Savannah whispered, her blue eyes flashing with embarrassment and fury.

"Yes."

She felt tears touch the back of her eyelids but refused to release them. "So you married her because she was pregnant."

"Because she *told* me she was pregnant."

"And the baby?" she murmured.

"Probably never existed."

"What!"

A twisted smile contorted the rugged features of his face. "Oh, yes, Melinda claimed to be pregnant. I didn't question her and that was probably a mistake." His steely eyes inched down her face to her breasts before returning to her gaze. "Obviously not my first."

Savannah tried to pull away from him but was no match for his strength.

"Melinda claimed to miscarry about three weeks after the wedding. I didn't doubt her until much later, when I thought that we should have a child in an attempt to save the marriage." He read the protests in Savannah's eyes. "I know it's a lousy excuse to have a kid, but I was desperate. I wanted to make things right between us because all the time that we were married, she knew that I'd never forgotten you. Do you have any idea what kind of hell she must have put herself through?"

"Or the kind of hell she put you through, because of your guilt," Savannah thought aloud.

"She was my wife, whether I loved her or not. Anyway, Melinda wasn't interested in a baby then and I doubt if she ever was. I think Melinda lied to me, Savannah, to force the marriage." His eyes darkened to the color of slate. "And your father was all for it."

Savannah digested his words slowly. "That doesn't make sense."

"Sure it does. Especially if he believed she was carrying my child."

"I don't see that what happened in the past changes anything. You could have come to me and explained."

"And how would you have felt?" he demanded.

She felt the color explode on her cheeks. "Maybe a little less...used."

He closed his eyes and dropped his forehead until it rested against hers. "Oh, lady, I never wanted you to feel that I used you."

"How was I supposed to feel?" she demanded, her wounded pride resurfacing. "Did you think that one night with you was all I wanted?"

"Of course not! But I thought the less people that knew about what happened between us, the better."

Anger, nine years old and searing, shot through her. She wanted to strike him, lash out against all the pain she had borne, but she couldn't because he was still gripping her arms. "And what would have happened if *I'd* been the one to turn up pregnant?"

"I thought about that. Long and hard."

"And?"

"I would have divorced Melinda."

"And expected me to fall into your arms?" She shook her head and felt every muscle in her body tense. "I would never have married you, Travis," she said through clenched teeth. "Because it would have been a trap, for you and me and the child and in the end we'd end up with a child caught between us, just like Josh is caught between Charmaine and Wade!"

"You don't believe that any more than I do."

"I do," she insisted, stamping a foot to add emphasis to her words. But her gaze was trapped in his magnetic stare. "I would never—"

His head lowered and he smothered her protest by capturing her lips with his. The force of the kiss was undeniable, the passion surging. Savannah wanted to push him away, to walk out of the room with her head held high, but she couldn't resist the sweet pressure on her mouth.

"No," she whispered, but he only drew her closer, crushing her body to his hard, muscular frame. The taste of him lingered on her lips and when his tongue pressed against her teeth, she willingly parted her lips.

The pressure on her arms became gentle and he pulled her body to his. Her breasts crushed against the rock-hard wall of his chest and began to ache for his touch. She felt a warmth invade her body, stealing from the deepest part of her and flowing through her blood.

Travis moaned and the kiss deepened, his moist tongue touching and mating with hers until Savannah felt her knees go weak and her fingers clutch his shoulders. Blood pulsed through her veins in throbbing bursts that warmed her from the inside out.

She trembled when his mouth left hers to explore the white skin of her throat and the lobe of her ear. Unconsciously she let her hair fall away from her face and quivered when his tongue slid along her jaw.

"Travis," she whispered, her breathing more labored with each breath as his hands slipped beneath the hem of her sweater and his fingers found the soft flesh between her ribs. She sucked in her abdomen and felt the tips of his fingers slide beneath the waistband of her jeans before climbing upward to mold around the straining tip of a breast. She moaned when his fingers captured the warm mound.

Fire burned within her body and soul as he toyed with the erect nipple and pressed his anxious lips to her mouth.

Vague thoughts that she should stop what was happening flitted through her mind, but she couldn't concentrate on anything other than the power of his touch. He leaned against the fireplace, his muscled legs spread and pulled her to him, forcing her against the hard evidence of desire in his loins, making her all too aware of the burning lust spreading through him like wildfire.

"Tell me again that you don't want me," he whispered against her hair.

Savannah was drugged with passion. When Travis cupped her buttocks and pulled her close she could hear the hard thudding of his heart. "I don't... I can't..." The raw ache within her burned traitorously and her thoughts centered on making love to this one very special man.

"Tell me that you never loved me."

"Travis…please," she gasped, trying to make some sense of what was happening. She couldn't fall under Travis's spell again, *wouldn't* love him again, and yet her body refused to push him away.

The arms around her tightened, and he raised his head to stare into the mystery of her eyes. Gone was any trace of passion in his gaze. If their bodies hadn't been entwined so intimately, Savannah would have sworn that she had imagined the entire seduction. "Don't ever be ashamed of anything that's happened between us. Whether you believe the truth or not, the fact is that I loved you more than a sane man would let himself love a woman."

"But it wasn't enough."

"We were caught in a web of lies, Savannah. Lies spun by the people we trusted. Otherwise things would have been different. I swear that to you, and I hope to God you believe me." His face was drawn, his eyes gleaming with the truth as he saw it.

"It doesn't matter," she said, feeling bereft when he released her.

"Oh, but it does," he argued, pushing his hands into the back pockets of his jeans and trying to compose himself. "It matters one helluva lot!" Striding across the room he stopped at the bar and poured himself another stiff shot. "Because I'm back now and things are going to change in a big way. No one—not you, not Henderson, your father or your brother-in-law, is going to manipulate my life any longer. That's over. When I have it out with Reginald, I'm leaving."

"Running away," she accused.

He lifted a shoulder and smiled at a secret irony. "Just the opposite, lady," he said, the muscles in his face tightening in determination. "For the first time in my life I'm doing things exactly as I please. I'm not running *away* from anything, I'm just burying the past and all my mistakes with it."

"Mistakes like me? Well, bully for you," she hurled back at him, stung by his remark. "And just for the record, *I've* never done anything to manipulate you."

He winced. "Not intentionally, I suppose," he acquiesced. "But you sure have a way of turning me inside out!" With a look that cut her to the bone, he walked out of the room, through the foyer, out the front door and into the night. Savannah stood in the den with her arms crossed, hugging herself. *Oh, Travis,* she thought angrily, *why did you even bother coming back? Why didn't you just run away and leave me out of it!*

CHAPTER FOUR

SLEEP WAS NEARLY impossible that night. Savannah tossed and turned, knowing that Travis was only a short walk away. She thought about everything he'd said about his reasons for leaving her all those years ago and wanted desperately to believe that he was, as she, a victim of fate.

"That's just wishing for the stars," she told herself angrily. "If he'd really wanted you, he'd have come back and at least explained, worked things out with Melinda…" *But how?* He'd really believed that Melinda had been pregnant. Or so he'd claimed.

And what about her father? Travis seemed to be on some vendetta to prove that Reginald was a scheming, conniving, power-hungry old man hell-bent on ruining Travis's life.

Savannah closed her eyes and tried to sleep, but was awake when the first pale streaks of dawn pierced through the windows of her bedroom.

Realizing that she wouldn't accomplish anything by tossing and turning in bed, she threw back the covers, got up, took a hot shower and dressed in warm work clothes. She didn't bother with makeup and tied her hair way from her face with a leather thong.

The morning was wet and cold with the promise of still more frigid air to come. The sky, darkened by gray clouds, seemed foreboding, and Savannah shuddered as she walked across the parking lot, past Lester's pickup and up the stairs to the office over the foaling shed.

Pulling off her gloves, she shouldered her way into the office. The smell of perking coffee mingled with the faint odors of saddle soap and horses when she walked into the small room.

Lester was already inside, sipping a cup of coffee and reading the paper at a small table near the corner window. From his vantage point, he could watch a series of paddocks near the stables.

"Mornin'," he said, rubbing a hand over his chin and looking up at her with worried eyes.

"Is it?" she asked. "You look like something's wrong." She poured a cup of coffee and sat at the table across from the small man. His tanned crowlike features were tight with strain.

"Probably nothin'."

Cradling her cup in her hands, Savannah blew across the hot liquid and arched her black brows inquisitively. "But something's bothering you."

"Yep." The trainer leaned back in his chair and scowled into his cup before glancing up at her. "Just a feeling I've got. Everything was fine when I left here last night."

"I know. I checked the horses after you left."

He brightened. "Did you, now?" Pushing his chair back, he walked over to the wall housing the security alarm. "Then you know about this?"

"What?"

Lester was fingering a loose wire to the control panel. "This must've broken last night."

Savannah felt cold dread slide down her spine and

her muscles went rigid. She set her cup on the table and walked over to the alarm system controls. "I didn't touch it last night," she said, studying the broken wire. "I used my key to get into the barns and then I came up here with some files."

"Was the wire broken then?"

"I don't know, I didn't notice." She saw the worry in Lester's eyes and read his thoughts. "You think it might have been cut?"

"Nope."

Savannah relaxed, but her relief was short-lived.

"Pulled maybe, but not cut. The break isn't clean." He rubbed his jaw thoughtfully. "It could've just worn out or it could've been yanked on purpose."

"But why?" She thought about the horses; they were valuable, but it would be difficult to steal any of them. The same was true of the equipment. There was no cash in the office, nor any to speak of on the grounds. And the broken wire wasn't enough damage for vandals. "Have you checked the horses?"

"All safe and accounted for."

"No other damage?"

"None that I've found, and I've looked."

"Then it must have just snapped on its own."

Lester frowned, his lower lip protruding thoughtfully. "But it seems strange it should happen when Reginald is out of town, and just a couple of days after Travis shows up."

Savannah's stomach knotted at the implication. "You think Travis had something to do with this?"

"No." The old man shook his head and scowled. "That boy's straight as an arrow. But there's a lot of people interested in his campaign...or lack thereof."

"I can't believe that a broken wire has anything to do with political intrigue," she said, taking a calming swallow of coffee. Lester came back to the table and stared through the window at the gloomy morning.

"I hope not, missy," he thought aloud. "I sure hope not." His shoulders bowed as he leaned over his lukewarm coffee.

Savannah glanced at the dangling wire. "Maybe it just wore out," she said again, as if to convince herself. "The system's pretty old."

"Maybe." Lester didn't seem to believe a word of it.

"I'll call the people who installed it and see what they come up with."

"Good idea," he muttered, rubbing his scalp.

"Is something else wrong?" Savannah asked.

"Probably nothing, but I just have this feelin'." He laughed at himself. "Maybe I'm just gettin' old. But when I walked into the stallion barn this morning, I sensed, you know, felt that someone was there."

"But no one was?"

"No." He shifted uneasily in his chair. "The stallions, well, they seemed different, like they'd already seen someone and then I thought I heard a noise, up in the loft. So I checked." He shrugged his narrow shoulders. "Didn't find anything."

"Maybe a mouse?"

"And maybe it was nothin'. I don't hear as well as I used to, y'know."

"Well, just to be on the safe side, have one of the hands search the building for mice, squirrels, rats…and whatever else you can think of. I don't want them eating all the grain."

"Already done," he muttered. "I'll sure be glad when Reginald gets back."

"He'll be home this evening."

"Good."

Lester, who was facing the door, frowned slightly as Travis entered the room. Savannah felt her back go rigid and the argument of the night before echoed in her mind.

"Good morning," Travis drawled, pouring himself a cup of coffee and leaning on a windowsill. He stretched his long legs in front of him and watched Savannah as he took an experimental sip of the hot coffee.

"Mornin', yourself," Lester replied, checking his watch. "I've scheduled Vagabond for a workout in about forty-five minutes. Want to come along?"

"Sure," Travis replied, a leisurely smile stealing across his angular face.

"Savannah?" Lester asked.

She set her empty cup on the table and felt the challenge of Travis's glare. He was watching her every move, expecting her to find a way to avoid being with him.

"Love to," she agreed as pleasantly as possible, meeting his gaze. "Let's see if he's improved any from the last time I saw him run."

"Getting that one to pay attention to the jockey is like trying to tell a rooster to crow at midnight," Lester grumbled. He pushed his fedora onto his head and walked out of the office, leaving Travis and Savannah alone.

Savannah lifted her eyes and stared straight into Travis's amused eyes. He was leaning forward on his elbows, a small smile tugging at the corners of his mouth. "Is something funny?" she demanded.

"I was just wondering if you were still mad?" Travis asked.

"I wasn't mad."

He laughed aloud, surprising Savannah. "And a grizzly bear doesn't have claws."

Ignoring his remark, she stood and walked to the door. It was too early in the morning to be unnerved by Travis's taunting gaze, and Savannah wasn't up to playing word games with him. "I'll see you at the workout track. I'm going to check on the stallions before I watch Vagabond run."

"Any particular reason?"

"I just want to make sure that everything's okay. Lester discovered this." She walked to the alarm control and held up the broken wire and Travis followed. "I just want to double-check on the horses and make sure that the system fell apart on its own and that it wasn't helped along by someone."

He examined the wire carefully. "Do you think it was?"

"No. But I believe in the 'better safe than sorry' theory, especially since Lester thinks he might have heard a noise in the stallion barn this morning." Savannah explained the conversation with Lester to Travis, who listened quietly while he finished his coffee.

The laughter in his eyes faded slightly. "I'll come with you," Travis decided.

"Don't you have anything better to do?"

"Nothing," he said with a lazy grin that cut across his face in a beguiling manner and softened the hard angles, making him seem less distant and allowing a hint of country-boy charm to permeate his tough, touch-me-not exterior. No wonder everyone was anxious to have him run for governor, Savannah thought. If the campaign were decided on looks, virility and charm alone, Travis would win hands down.

"Then let's go," she said a little sharply, angry with herself for the traitorous turn of her thoughts.

"You *are* still mad."

"Just busy." She brushed past him and hurried down the steps to the brick path leading to the stallion barn.

Before she'd gone five steps, Travis had caught up with her and placed a possessive arm around her shoulders. "Lighten up, Savannah," he suggested.

"You should talk."

"At least I don't hold a grudge."

She slid a glance in his direction and found him grinning at her with a smile that melted the ice around her heart. Shivering against the cold air, she tried not to huddle against him. "What're you trying to do?"

"Just prove my undying affection, lady," he quipped, kissing her lightly on the hair.

Just like all the pain of the past nine years didn't exist. Savannah clenched her teeth and walked faster. "So what happened to the outraged, self-righteous lawyer I saw last night?"

"Oh, he's still here," Travis reassured her, "but he's had a good night's sleep and a hot cup of coffee with a beautiful woman."

"I swear, Travis, you could sweet-talk the birds out of the trees one minute, and cook them for dinner the next!"

Travis's laughter rumbled through the early dawn and he hugged her close to his body.

JOSH, HIS SHOULDERS hunched against the rain, was standing at the door of the stallion barn. He'd started toward the house, but stopped when he noticed Savannah and Travis approaching.

"What're you doing here?" Savannah asked when she was close enough for the boy to hear her. "And where's your coat? It's freezing!"

Guilt clouded Josh's young face and Savannah was immediately contrite. Obviously the boy was still brooding about the night before and the last thing he needed was a lecture from her.

"I... I just wanted to see Mystic before I went to school."

"Next time put on a jacket, okay?"

"Okay."

Travis patted Josh firmly between the shoulders. "You like Mystic, don't you?"

"He's great!" Josh said, his dark eyes shining.

"Well, Grandpa would agree with you, and I guess I'd have to, too." Savannah said. "Now, tell me, have you eaten breakfast yet?"

"No."

"I didn't think so. You'd better hurry back to the house and eat something so that you don't miss the bus."

"I don't need breakfast," Josh complained.

Savannah smothered a fond smile for her nephew, forced her features into a hard line and pointed her finger at the house. "Scoot, Josh. You don't want to end up in any more trouble, do ya?"

"I guess not," the boy conceded.

Travis cocked his head toward the house. "Do as your aunt says, and when you get home from school, we'll go cut down a Christmas tree."

Josh, unable to believe his good fortune, looked from Travis to Savannah and back again. "For real?"

"For real," Travis said with a laugh.

"Awesome!" Josh said with a brilliant grin before taking off toward the house at a dead run.

"You won't disappoint him, will you?" Savannah asked, once Josh was out of earshot.

"You know me better than that." Travis hesitated a minute. "Or do you?"

"It's just that I don't want to see Josh disappointed. He's had more than his share of false promises."

"Scout's honor," Travis said, his gray eyes twinkling in the dim morning light. "I intend to take him looking for a tree this afternoon. You can come along if you like." He pulled her into the circle of his arms and kissed her chilled lips.

Savannah wanted to back away, but couldn't resist the sparkle in his eyes. "I would like. Very much."

"Good, now, why don't you tell me about Josh's fascination with Mystic," Travis suggested, holding the door to the barn open for her.

The scent of warm horses and hay filled the air. The stallions stirred, shifting the straw in their stalls and jingling their halters. Disgusted snorts and a soft nicker filled the long barn as the inquisitive Thoroughbreds poked their heads over the stall doors.

"Maybe it's because Wade wouldn't let him get a dog or a horse of his own. A few years ago, I bought Josh a puppy for his birthday and Wade made him give it away. He called the gift inappropriate for a six-year-old with no sense of responsibility."

Savannah frowned at the memory. "And then, Josh happened to be in the foaling shed when Mystic was born. From that point on, he's had a special feeling for the horse, though it scares Charmaine to death."

Travis closed the door and looked around the barn. Nothing seemed out of place. Graceful horses, shining water buckets, fresh hay and grain stored in barrels filled the long, hall-like room.

"Why is Charmaine afraid of him?"

"Mystic's got what's known as a 'bad rep.'"

"Not the most friendly guy at the track?"

"See for yourself." Savannah was walking to the end of the double row of stalls and Mystic's box. As she walked, she scrutinized the interior of the barn and looked at each of the stallions, talking softly to each one.

The black colt stretched his head over the top rail and snorted at the intrusion. His pointed ears flattened to his head and he nervously paced in his stall. Rippling muscles moved fluidly under a shining black coat.

"I can see why Josh thinks he's special," Travis said, leaning over the rail and looking at the perfect contours of the big ebony colt. Barrel chested, with strong, straight legs and powerful hindquarters, Mystic was a beautifully built Thoroughbred. His dark eyes were sparked by a keen intelligence, his large nostrils flared at the unfamiliar scent. Mystic looked at Travis and shook his head menacingly.

Savannah patted the black nose and Mystic stamped a hoof impatiently. "When Mystic was running, Joshua read the papers every day, out loud, to me. And when Mystic lost to Supreme Court in the Belmont, Josh really took it to heart." Savannah smiled to herself. "To hear Josh tell it, Mystic lost because Supreme Court boxed him in on purpose."

"Is that the truth?"

"My opinion?"

"Yep. And it won't go any further than these—"

Travis looked around at the whitewashed barn "—four walls."

"Okay." Savannah folded her arms over the stall door and studied the big colt. "Mystic could have won the race, I think, if the jockey had given him a better ride. However, whether Supreme Court's jockey intentionally boxed Mystic in is neither here nor there. He didn't do anything illegal. Maybe it was strategy, maybe just luck of the draw. The point is, Supreme Court won and Mystic didn't. End of story. Except that everyone expected Mystic to win at Belmont."

Travis slid a glance in Savannah's direction. "Maybe everyone expected too much. Winning the races he had as a two-year-old and topping it off with the Preakness when he was three was no small feat." Travis patted the horse and Mystic backed away. "Sometimes people expect too damned much."

"Are you talking about the horse or yourself?"

He smiled crookedly. "I never could lie to you."

"Only once," she said.

Travis pushed his fingers through his thick hair and shook his head in disgust. "And that was the biggest mistake of my life. I've been paying for it ever since."

Savannah felt her throat become tight. If only she could believe him—just a little. "We can't go back," she said, but Travis turned to face her. His hand reached forward and slid beneath her ponytail to caress her neck.

"Maybe we can, Savannah." His voice was low and intimate and it made her pulse leap. "Maybe we can go back, if we try."

The fingers against her neck were warm and comforting and if she let herself, Savannah could easily remember how desperately she had loved him.

She pulled away from him. "I think it would be best if we forgot what happened between us," she said.

"Do you honestly think that's possible?"

"I don't know." She stared up at him, her gaze entwining in the enigmatic gray of his, before she looked away.

"Why do you keep lying to yourself, Savannah?"

"Do I? Maybe it's easier."

His hand reached forward and twined in the thick rope of her black hair. "You're afraid of me," he accused. He pulled her head back, forcing her to meet the intensity of his gaze.

"Not of you," she whispered. "Of us. The way we feel about each other doesn't make any sense."

"And everything in life has to be rational?"

"Yes."

"Tell me," he said, eyes narrowed, gaze centered on her lips. "How *do* you feel about me?"

"I think I should walk away from you."

Slowly, gently, his fingers caressed her skin. "Okay, that's what you think. Now, answer my question, how do you feel?"

Her breath was shaky, and the feel of his hands against her neck made thinking nearly impossible. "I should hate you," she whispered through clenched teeth.

"But you don't."

"You lied to me! Used me! Left me! And now you're back." He was toying with the edge of her jacket, his fingers grazing the soft skin at the base of her throat. She tried to jerk away, but his fingers took hold of the lapels of her coat. "I should hate you for what you did to me and what you're insinuating about Dad!"

"I don't think you're capable of hate."

"Then you don't know me very well."

"Oh, I know you, Savannah," he said, his face only inches from hers. "I know you better than you do yourself."

And then he kissed her, long and hard. A kiss so filled with passion that it killed all the protests in her mind and held at bay her doubts. The sweet pressure of his lips crushing against hers helped the years and the pain slip away. The hand on her nape explored the neckline of her jacket and her pulse began to throb expectantly.

She felt his tongue slide between her teeth and she welcomed the sweet taste of him. He drew her close and her own hands were fumbling with the buttons of his suede jacket. She touched the soft flannel shirt that covered the corded muscles of his chest. An ache, deep and powerful, began to burn deep within her.

"I've always loved you, Savannah," he whispered against her midnight-black hair. "God help me, I've always loved you," he confessed, "even when I was married to Melinda."

"Don't—"

His lips cut off any further protest as he kissed her with the surging passion of nine lost years. His fingers twined in her hair, pulling her head backward and exposing the gentle curve of her neck. "Being near you is driving me out of my mind," he whispered. "Do you know, can you imagine, how much self-control it took not to follow you into your bedroom last night?"

Easily, she thought, falling against him and returning the fever of his kiss. "This...this can't, it won't work."

"Savannah, listen to me!" His gray eyes were filled with conviction. "Just trust me. For once in your life, trust me."

"I already tried that, nine years ago!"

"And I won't hurt you again." The honesty in his gaze touched the darkest corners of her soul.

Trust him, dear Lord.

Without any further questions, Travis lifted her into his arms and carried her to an empty stall at the end of the barn. He tossed his jacket down on the clean hay, and gently lay her upon it. Slowly, he untied the thong restraining her hair. The black curls tumbled free.

The zipper of her jacket slid easily open and he helped her out of it as he kissed her face and neck.

"Travis, I don't think—"

"Good!" Kissing her hungrily, he molded her body to his, her soft contours fitting against the harder lines of his frame. His breathing was erratic, his heartbeat as wild as her own.

She pressed against him, unaware of anything but the sweet taste of his tongue sliding over her teeth and the warmth of his hands as they pulled the wide neck of her sweater down her shoulder to expose the white skin of her breast.

He kissed her feverishly and she returned his passion, her fingers working on the buttons of his jacket and sliding it down the length of his muscular arms. He tossed it aside and jerked the sweater over her head to gaze at the rounded swell of her breasts peeking over the lacy fabric of her camisole.

Dark points protruded upward against the lace, inviting the warmth of his mouth. He took one soft mound into his mouth, moistening the sheer fabric and caressing the nipple with his tongue. Savannah writhed beneath him, the sweet torment he was applying to her breast a welcome relief. She curled her fingers into his thick hair, holding on to his head as if to life itself.

"I've missed you," he whispered hoarsely, his breath fanning the wet fabric and the throbbing peak beneath.

And I've missed you.

He slid one of the straps of the camisole over her shoulder, baring the firm breast to him, and he gazed upon the swollen mound hungrily before caressing it with his lips.

Savannah shuddered as he lowered the other strap over her shoulder. She was lying half-naked on the straw, her dark hair billowing away from her face, her blue eyes dusky with passion.

Slowly he unbuttoned his shirt.

Savannah stared upward to watch the ripple of his muscles as he tossed the unwanted garment aside. "This time I'll make it right," he vowed, lowering himself over her and watching as her fingers reached upward to caress the dark hairs on his chest.

"And this time I won't expect more than you can give," she whispered, trembling as his lips found hers and his weight fell across her. The hard muscles of his chest rubbed against her breasts, the soft hair teasing her nipples as his hands splayed against the small of her back, pulling her so close that she could hear the erratic beat of his heart. Fingertips brushed past the waistband of her jeans, tantalizing the skin above her buttocks.

Liquid fire began to spread through her body as he touched and caressed her.

"I love you, Savannah," he vowed, his breath fanning the hollow of her throat.

When she didn't respond, he stared into the blue intensity of her eyes. "I love you," he repeated.

"But...but I don't want to fall in love with you," she said, her throat tight. "Not again."

"You're afraid to trust me." It wasn't a question, just a simple, but distasteful, statement of fact. Travis pulled away from her, rubbed his hand behind his neck and muttered a rather unkind oath at himself.

Savannah was left lying on the straw, feeling very naked and vulnerable. "Can't we just leave love out of it?"

He looked disdainfully over his shoulder. "Is that the way you want it? Just sex? No emotion?"

Blushing slightly, Savannah looked away and reached for her sweater.

Travis laughed bitterly and glanced at the rafters. "I didn't think so." He curled his fist and slammed it into the side of the stall next to Mystic. The colt snorted nervously. "Dear God, woman, what am I going to do with you?"

"As if you have any say in my life."

"I sure as hell do," he said. His gray eyes gleamed possessively.

With unsteady fingers, she tugged the sweater over her head, squared her shoulders, jutted her chin and faced him again. "I think it's time to go watch Vagabond. *If* you're still interested."

"Wouldn't miss it for the world," he said, sliding a bemused glance up her body.

Anger surged through her at the insolence of his stare. Plunging her arms through the sleeves of her jacket, she began to stand, but Travis reached for her wrist and restrained her. "I just hope that someday soon you'll get over your bull-headed pride and realize that you still love me."

"Dreamer."

"Am I?" His gaze slid down her neck, to the pulse

jumping at her throat. "I don't think so." The confident smile that crossed his face was nearly a smirk. "Let me know when you change your mind."

"I won't."

He lifted a dubious dark brow. "Then I'll just have to convince you, won't I?" He pulled on her wrist, drawing her closer, but she jerked away and raised her hand to slap him, then thought better of it when she recognized the glittering challenge in his eyes.

"You're an impossible, insufferable, arrogant bastard. You know that, don't you?" she accused, walking toward the door.

"And you've got the cutest behind I've ever seen."

She twirled and faced him, her face suffused with rage. "That's exactly what I mean. What kind of infantile, chauvinistic male remark was that?"

"The kind that gets your attention," he said, sobering as he stood. He picked up his shirt and held it in his hands, his naked chest a silent invitation. The lean muscles of his abdomen and chest, the curling dark hair arrowing below the waistband of his low-slung jeans and the tight muscles of his thighs and hips, hidden only by the worn fabric of his jeans, all worked together to form a bold male image in the harsh lights of the barn. "I'm just waiting for you to realize that I'm not about to make the same mistake I did nine years ago."

Her blue eyes sparked. "Neither am I!" she said over her shoulder, her small fists balling and her heart slamming wildly in her chest. "Neither am I."

VAGABOND WAS ALREADY on the track by the time Savannah met Lester at the railing. It had just begun to rain and Lester was leaning over the top rail of the fence studying a stopwatch as Vagabond raced passed, his graceful strides carrying him effortlessly over the ground. Lester flicked the watch with his thumb and smiled to himself.

"That was a helluva time," he muttered, his gray brows quirking upward in appreciation as his eyes followed the galloping bay. "He's got it in him. Faster than Mystic, he is."

"I thought you were all for selling him," Savannah teased, stuffing her hands into her pockets and hunching her shoulders against the cold drizzle. She knew that Travis had joined them, but refused to look at him or acknowledge his presence. "Or have you changed your mind in the last couple of days?"

"It's controlling him that worries me," Lester remarked.

"Makes your job interesting," Travis observed.

Lester laughed and watched as the colt took one final turn around the track at a slow gallop. "That it does," he agreed, his black eyes never leaving the horse. "That it does." He waved to the rider and called, "Go ahead and take him inside. That's enough for today."

Lester rubbed his hands together and turned toward the stables before hazarding a glance at Travis. "I always wondered why you didn't stick it out, here on the farm."

"Funny," Travis replied, his gaze shifting to Savannah, "lately I've been wondering the same thing myself."

"We could still use you, y'know. Always need a man who knows horses." He walked toward the stables and Savannah felt Travis's eyes on her back.

"Do you think I should take his advice and stay?" he asked.

Savannah's heart nearly stopped beating. "I think it

would be the worst mistake of your life," she lied before turning toward the house and walking away from him.

JOSHUA WAS RELEASED from school early for the holidays. He raced into the house at one-thirty and threw his books on the kitchen table.

"What's the rush?" Savannah asked. She was sitting at the table, trying to balance her checkbook. Deciding that a five-dollar discrepancy with the bank wasn't a life-or-death situation, she stuffed the statement and checks back into the envelope and focused all of her attention on her nephew.

"Don't you remember?" Josh asked. "Travis said we could all go out and cut a Christmas tree today!"

"He said what?" Charmaine asked, walking into the room and frowning at the untidy pile of books on the table.

"That we could go cut a Christmas tree today," Josh repeated, grabbing an apple from a basket on the kitchen counter and biting into the crisp fruit.

"But Grandpa usually buys one in Sacramento," Charmaine said, looking from Savannah to Josh and back again.

"I know," Savannah said. "But Travis did promise."

"When?"

"This morning. Before breakfast at the stallion barn."

"Were you out there again?" Charmaine asked, paling as she turned to the boy.

Josh froze.

"How many times do I have to tell you not to go out there unless you're with Daddy or Grandpa? Those stallions are dangerous!" Charmaine warned.

Travis walked in from the back porch and heard the

tail end of the conversation. "It was all right, Charmaine. Savannah and I were out there."

"I don't like it," Charmaine replied. "Mystic almost killed Lester last year, did you know that? And another time he kicked one of his grooms and nearly broke the man's leg."

"He wouldn't kick me, Mom."

"How do you know that? He's an animal, Joshua, and he can't be trusted. Now you don't go out to that barn again without Grandpa. Got it?"

"Got it," Josh mumbled, his eyes downcast and his small jaw firm with rebellion.

"Hey, sport. Come on, let's go get that tree," Travis said, patting the boy on the shoulders. "Want to come?" he asked Charmaine.

Charmaine hesitated, but shook her head. "I'd better not. Someone has to stay with Mother and I've got something I've got to get done in the studio, if you don't mind me up there, Travis."

"No, that's fine," he replied.

"That's okay, I'll go," Savannah said, hoping to ease some of Josh's disappointment.

Charmaine sighed in relief.

A few minutes later, Travis, Savannah, Josh and Archimedes were piled into a pickup and driving along the rutted lane through the back pastures leading to the hills. Snow mixed with rain began to collect on the windshield.

"Maybe it'll snow for Christmas," Josh said excitedly, looking out the window as the wet flakes drifted to the ground and melted.

"I wouldn't count on it," Savannah said.

"Spoilsport," Travis accused, but laughed. "Now, tell

me, what's all this nonsense about Mystic nearly kill-
ing Lester."

"He didn't!" Josh said. "No way!"

"Lester slipped when he was in Mystic's stall and
the horse stepped on him. It was an accident and not
very serious."

"You're sure?"

"Lester is and everyone else agrees except Charmaine," Savannah said.

"Mom's just freaked out by Mystic, that's all."

As Travis drove up the lower slopes of the hills, the
snow was definitely sticking, and Josh's spirits soared.

The boy continued to search the forested hills for the
perfect Christmas tree. "There's one," he said for the fif-
tieth time as he pointed to a small fir tree.

"Not big enough," Travis thought aloud, but parked
the truck to the side of the road near a clearing.

While Travis pulled the hatchet out of the back of the
truck, Josh and Savannah, with Archimedes on their
heels, scoured the woods. The snow was clinging to the
branches of the trees, dusting the evergreens with a fine
mantle of white and clinging to the blackened branches
of the leafless maples and oaks.

Josh hurried ahead with Archimedes. Travis caught
up with Savannah and placed an arm comfortably over
her shoulders. "This is how it should be, y'know," he
said, watching Archimedes scare a winter bird from
the brush. "You, me, a kid or two, a lop-eared dog and
Christmas."

Savannah smiled and shook her head. Snowflakes
clung to her hair and melted on her face. "The way it
should have been, you mean."

"It still could be, Savannah."

Her heart nearly stopped beating. "You're very persuasive, counselor," she said, refusing to argue with him in the wintry afternoon. Snow continued to fall and cling to the branches of the trees. The mountains seemed to disappear in the clouds.

"Along with self-righteous, insufferable, impossible and arrogant?"

Savannah smiled. "All of the above."

"I hope so, lady," he whispered against the melting drops of snow in her ebony hair. "I hope to God that I'm as persuasive as you seem to think."

"Over here!" Josh shouted, and they followed his voice until they came upon him almost dancing around a twelve-foot fir. "It's perfect!"

"I thought the word was 'awesome,'" Savannah said with a smile, and Travis laughed, giving her a hug.

While Travis trimmed off the lower branches and cut the tree, Josh ran through the forest and tossed snowballs at an unsuspecting Archimedes. The spotted sheepdog barked and bounded through the brush.

When Josh's back was turned, Savannah hurled a snowball at him, and it landed on his shoulder. Josh whirled and began throwing snowballs at Savannah so rapidly that she had to dodge behind a tree for protection. When she was brave enough to peek around the protective trunk of the oversize maple, two snowballs whizzed past her nose. Travis had gotten into the game and was quickly packing another frozen missile.

"No fair!" she called. "Two against one."

"You've got Archimedes, remember?" Josh taunted with a grin.

"Four-footed allies don't count. Oh!" A snowball landed in the middle of her back and she turned to face

Travis, who had sneaked around the maple tree. "Enough already. I give!"

"Don't I wish," Travis murmured, a smile lurking on his lips before he wrapped his arms around her and kissed her feverishly. Josh continued the assault, and Travis had to let go of Savannah. He switched alliances and began hurling snowballs at the boy until Josh squealed and laughed his surrender.

"Okay, let's call it quits and get the tree into the truck!" Travis suggested, dusting the snow from his jacket as he looked at the sky. "It looks like this storm isn't going to let up, so we'd better get back to the farm while we still can."

Josh's brown eyes were shining with merriment, his grin stretching from one ear to the other, as Travis and Savannah loaded the tree into the back of the pickup for the drive back to the farm.

The rutted lane was slippery, and the truck lurched, pushing Savannah closer to Travis. She tried to keep to her side of the seat, but the warmth of his thigh pressing against her was irresistible. It even felt natural when Travis's fingers grazed her knee as he shifted gears.

With a sinking sensation, she realized that despite her vows to herself, she was falling in love with him all over again.

CHAPTER FIVE

THE LIVING ROOM smelled of fir boughs, scented candles, burning wood and hot chocolate. Savannah was still helping Josh trim the tree, although Charmaine had already taken Virginia upstairs. The night was peaceful and still, with snow collecting in the corners of the windowpanes and the lights from the tree reflecting on the glass. A fire was glowing warmly in the fireplace. It crackled against the pitchy fir log in the grate.

Savannah set her empty mug on the mantel before stepping on the ladder and trying to straighten the star on the top of the tree.

"I wish Travis would come help us," Josh complained, placing a bright ornament on the bough closest to him.

Savannah slanted the boy an affectionate grin. "He will."

"When?"

She shrugged. "Whenever he's finished."

"What's taking him so long?"

"I haven't the foggiest," Savannah replied truthfully. "He said he had some paperwork to finish." Sighing when the star refused to remain upright on the tree, she climbed down the ladder.

"So why is he locked in Grandpa's study?"

"Good question," she admitted, sneaking a glance

through the archway, across the foyer to the locked door of the study. "I guess he needs privacy...to concentrate."

"On what?"

"Look, Josh, I really don't know," she admitted.

"Grandpa doesn't like anyone in his study," Josh said.

"I know, but it's all right for Travis to be in there; he's the attorney for the farm."

"Well, I wish he'd get done."

"So do I." Savannah picked up the empty mugs. "What about another cup of cocoa?"

"Sure!"

"You finish with the tree and I'll be back in a flash," she said with a smile as she walked out of the living room and paused at the door of the study. Travis had locked himself inside nearly two hours before. When she'd asked him to stay and trim the tree after he'd placed it in the stand, he'd shaken his head and told her he had something he needed to do before Reginald and Wade returned. His eyes had darkened mysteriously and Savannah had experienced a feathering of dread climb up her spine.

She knocked softly on the door. Travis opened it almost immediately and she couldn't help but smile at him. A rebellious lock of his chestnut-colored hair had fallen over his forehead and the sleeves of his sweater were pushed over his forearms.

"You're a sight for sore eyes," he said, his voice low.

"So why lock yourself away?" She looked past him to the interior of the room. It was obvious that Travis had been working at her father's desk. An untidy stack of papers littered the desktop and the checkbook for the farm was lying open on a nearby chair.

"Business." The lines between his eyebrows deepened and he frowned slightly.

"Can't you even take time out to see the tree? Josh is dying to show it to you."

"In a minute."

She angled her chin up at him and sighed loudly. "Okay, you win. Go ahead and be mysterious. How about a cup of coffee or some hot chocolate?"

He smiled at her, but shook his head. "I'm just about done in here, then I'll join the rest of the family. Okay?"

"Scrooge," she murmured and he kissed her softly on the nose.

"Be sure to put up the mistletoe," he commanded with a suggestive smile teasing his lips. Then he turned back to the study, entered and closed the door behind him.

"Merry Christmas to you, too," Savannah remarked.

Puzzled by Travis's behavior, she walked into the kitchen and refilled the mugs. Why was Travis looking through the books of the farm? An uneasy feeling stole over her, but she tried to forget about it. The day with Travis and Josh had been too wonderful to spoil with unfounded worries or fears. Travis certainly wasn't hurting anything. Besides, Wade and Reginald were due home any minute. Their arrival was enough of a problem for her to deal with.

Carrying the steaming cups back into the living room, she found Josh returning tissue paper into the packing boxes that had housed the ornaments for the past year.

"It's the best tree ever!" Josh exclaimed proudly as he stood and took a cup from Savannah's outstretched hand.

"I think you're right." Savannah laughed.

"We should go get Travis and Mom."

"In a minute, sport. First let's finish and clean up this

mess." She gestured to the empty boxes stacked haphazardly around the tree. "You've done a good job, but we've got a lot of work ahead of us."

The sound of a car's engine caught Savannah's attention, and she felt her pulse jump nervously.

"Looks like Grandpa and your dad finally made it," she said to Josh, who was carrying a load of empty boxes out of the living room to the closet under the stairs in the foyer. "And only three hours late."

"About time," Josh mumbled.

"They couldn't help the fact that the airport's a mess because of the snow. Even the weathermen weren't prepared for a storm like this," she said cautiously when Josh returned. "Come on, let's not borrow trouble, huh?"

"Okay."

Just then the front door opened and Reginald strode into the living room.

"Well, what do we have here?" Reginald asked, eyeing the tree while pulling off his gloves. He unwrapped the scarf from around his neck and tossed both it and the gloves onto the couch.

"You know, Grandpa! It's the tree!" Josh exclaimed with excitement. "Aunt Savvy and Travis and I went to get it today, up in the hills! We even had a snowball fight!"

"Did you now?" Reginald took off his coat and tossed it over the back of one of the wing chairs before patting the boy on the head and admiring the tree. "Who won?"

"Travis and me!"

Reginald glanced at Savannah. "Two on one?"

"Archimedes was on my team," she said wryly. "He wasn't too much help."

"I'll bet not," Reginald said with a hearty laugh.

"So what do ya think of the tree?" Josh asked.

Walking around the Christmas tree, Reginald surveyed it with a practiced eye. "You picked a winner, my boy."

"I found it all by myself, but Travis had to cut it down."

Reginald winked fondly at his grandchild. "Next year you'll probably be able to handle it all by yourself."

"Maybe," Josh agreed.

"So where is everyone?" Reginald asked, facing Savannah.

"Charmaine took Mom upstairs about forty-five minutes ago."

A thoughtful frown pinched the features of Reginald's tanned face and he glanced up the stairs. "Tell me, how's your mother been?"

"Actually, Mom's been a little better since Travis came back to the farm. Having him here seems to have lifted her spirits a bit. She's had dinner downstairs twice and she helped trim the tree until just a little while ago."

"That's good," the older man said with obvious relief. "Maybe I'd better run up and check on her."

"You'd never hear the end of it if you didn't."

As Reginald left the room, Wade entered the house. His leather shoes clicked loudly against the tiled floor of the foyer as he approached the living room. His even-featured face was tight with tension, his taffy-colored hair slightly mussed.

Josh visibly stiffened at the sight of his father.

"Hi, Dad," the boy said. "See the tree? Travis and I cut it down."

At the mention of Travis's name, Wade frowned and tugged on his mustache. "Oh, ah, it looks good," Wade said without much enthusiasm and glanced at the clock. "What're you doing up so late?"

"Josh helped me decorate the tree," Savannah cut in, trying to avoid the argument she felt brewing in the air. "He's done a terrific job, hasn't he?"

"Terrific," Wade repeated without a smile.

"We're just about finished," Savannah explained.

"Good. It's a school night, isn't it?"

Josh shook his head and grinned. "School's out for vacation."

Wade scowled. "Doesn't matter. It's late."

"But Aunt Savvy said—"

"No 'buts' about it, son!" Wade snapped, his short temper flaring. "I'm home now and you'll do as I say." Then, feeling slightly embarrassed, Wade gestured toward the boxes still lying on the floor. "You finish up here right away and go upstairs. I've got business to discuss privately with your grandfather."

Josh wanted to argue, but Savannah wouldn't let him. "We'll be done in no time, right, sport?"

"Right," Josh mumbled, bending over to pick up the loose boxes.

Once Wade was convinced that Josh was going to obey him, he took Savannah's arm and pulled her away from the tree, close to the windows. "Where's McCord?" he demanded.

"In the study. He said he'd be here in a minute."

Wade paled a bit and his eyes hardened. "What the hell's he doing in the study? Dammit, he comes back here one day and just takes the hell over! Why is he in Reginald's den?"

"I don't know. You'll have to ask him." She looked over Wade's shoulder and saw Travis striding across the hall, his hands thrust into the back pockets of his cords, his sleeves still pushed over his forearms. His mouth was pinched into a tight, angry line that softened slightly as he met Savannah's worried gaze.

"What do you think?" Joshua asked, stepping away from the brightly lit tree.

"Best tree I've ever seen," Travis said with a brilliant smile for the boy. "Maybe you should go into the business!"

"And maybe he should go upstairs to bed," Wade grumbled, raising his eyebrows at his son. Then, as if dismissing the child ended that particular conversation, Wade turned all of his attention to Travis. "Now, McCord, what the hell's going on? What's all this nonsense about you not running for governor?"

"It's not nonsense," Travis replied, helping Josh with a stack of boxes. "Just the facts." He carried them out of the room and stacked them in the closet under the stairs.

"Great!" Wade muttered, swearing under his breath. He pushed himself out of the chair, walked over to the bar at the end of the room and poured himself a stiff drink.

"Dad," Josh interrupted, sensing the growing tension in the air and trying to find some way of easing it. "Travis cut this tree down all by himself."

Wade looked at his son as if seeing him for the first time. In an obvious attempt to control his irritation with the boy, he gripped his glass so tightly his knuckles whitened. "I think you already said that, son, and I told you I liked it."

"Aunt Savvy says it's awesome."

"Well, she's right, isn't she?" Reginald said, walking back into the room, picking up Josh and hugging the boy to his broad chest. "The important thing is that I think Santa Claus will be able to find it."

"There is no Santa Claus," Josh replied, wearing his most grown-up expression.

"No!" Reginald expressed mock horror and both Josh and Savannah laughed. "I'm going into the kitchen to look for a snack—why don't you come, too?" he asked the boy.

Josh smiled but shook his head. "Not until I finish the tree," he said.

"Have it your way," the old man said, beaming at his grandson before heading into the kitchen.

Charmaine came down the stairs and entered the living room. "You did a wonderful job on the tree," she said to her son before noticing the hard line of Wade's jaw and the glittering challenge in Travis's eye. "Come on, Josh, I think it's time you went to bed," she suggested.

"Not yet."

"You heard your mother," Wade said, irritably waving the boy off. "Go upstairs."

Josh mutinously stood his ground. "But I'm not done fixin' the tree."

Wade tensed and his eyes turned cold. "It'll wait."

"Please?"

Oh, Josh, don't push it, Savannah thought, searching for a way to avoid the fight that was in the air.

"No, son! You heard me! Get your butt upstairs right now!"

"But, Dad—"

"Don't argue with me!" Wade snapped, color flooding his face, rage exploding in his eyes.

"It's just one night," Savannah protested, instinctively

standing closer to Josh, as if to protect the boy. "We're almost finished, aren't we, Josh?"

Wade's eyes were as frigid as ice. "This is none of your business, Savannah. Josh needs his sleep and I want to talk to Reginald and McCord alone." His stern gaze rested on the boy. "Now go upstairs and don't push it, Josh, or there just might not be a Christmas this year."

"Wade!" Charmaine whispered sharply, but held her tongue when her husband's eyes flashed angrily in her direction.

"There's always a Christmas," Josh said, holding his ground.

"Not if you're bad," Wade warned the boy.

"I'm *not* bad."

"We know that," Travis cut in. "You're a good kid, Josh. Don't let anyone tell you differently." He turned deadly eyes in Wade's direction, slicing through the blond man's angry veneer. "I'm sure you dad didn't quite mean it the way it came out."

Wade glanced around the room, obviously embarrassed, and then finished his drink in a quick swallow before quickly pouring another stiff shot. Though he attempted to control his anger, his seething temper was visible in the muscle working in his jaw. "Sure," he said unsteadily, smoothing his hair with quaking fingers. "You're a good kid, that's why you'll behave and go upstairs."

"Come on, Josh," Savannah said, offering a hand to lead him out of the room.

"Just butt out, Savannah," Wade exploded. His entire body was beginning to shake with the anger he could no longer contain. "Just butt the hell out of my son's life!"

Travis became rigid. "Benson—"

"This is between my son and me!" Wade growled, turning his furious gaze on Josh and spilling some of his drink. The sloshed alcohol infuriated him further. "Now march yourself up those stairs right now, young man!"

"No!"

"I mean it!" Wade's face was red with fury as he set his drink on a table and advanced toward the boy.

"Leave him alone," Travis warned, reaching forward. He caught hold of the back of Wade's jacket, but the incensed man wriggled free of Travis's grip.

"Wade, don't!" Charmain pleaded, hurrying forward, but she was too late.

"I hate you," Josh said, standing proudly before Wade's wrath.

"You need to learn to respect your father," Wade returned. "And I'll teach you!" Quick as a snake striking, Wade raised his hand and slapped the boy across the cheek. The blow had enough force to send Josh reeling into the Christmas tree.

Savannah gasped. Tinsel and glass ornaments clinked on the wobbling tree.

Travis was in time to stop the second blow from landing. He grabbed Wade by the back of the neck and spun him around. Every muscle in Travis's body was bunched, ready to strike, and the fire in his eyes burned with rage. "You dumb bastard," he growled, looking as if he wanted to kill Wade. His hands tightened powerfully over Wade's shoulders. "Leave the boy alone."

"This has nothing to do with you, McCord."

"It does as long as I'm here. Now leave him alone or I'll give you a little of your own."

"He's not your kid," Wade replied, whirling on his heel, fists clenched as he faced Josh again.

"I wish I was!" Josh shouted, his eyes filled with tears, one hand rubbing the bright red mark on his face. "I know you hate me and I wish I wasn't your son."

"You little—"

"Stop it!" Savannah warned, grabbing Josh and pulling him close to her. "Stop it, all of you!" She felt the warmth of the boy's tears against her blouse. "Josh, oh, Josh," she murmured, kissing his hair. "Don't you ever so much as come near him again," she said, her cold eyes clashing with Wade's.

"You've got no say in it. Josh is my son."

Josh held his cheek and glared upward at his father with open hatred in his young, tear-filled eyes. "You never wanted me," he said between sobs. "But that's okay, because I don't want you either!"

"Josh, no," Charmaine whispered, ignoring her husband and walking to the boy. When Wade took a step toward the child again, Charmaine whirled toward her husband. "Don't you touch him," she threatened. "I mean it, Wade, don't you ever lay one finger on my child!" She straightened and took Josh's small hand in hers. Though she was pale, she managed to square her shoulders and lift her chin proudly. "Come on, Josh. Let's go upstairs." Her lips were white when she added, "Daddy's just tired from his long flight!"

Josh looked at Savannah, and she offered him an encouraging smile. "I'll be up in a few minutes to read you a story...or maybe you can read one to me. Okay?"

"Okay," he whispered, his voice breaking.

Once Josh and Charmaine were out of the room, Savannah, her hands shaking with rage, advanced upon her brother-in-law. All of the worry and anger that had been building over the past few months erupted. "If you ever strike that child again, I'll call the police and have you brought up on charges," she warned, pointing a finger at her brother-in-law and wishing she could strangle him.

"Don't go off the deep end, Savannah," Wade said nervously. He finished his drink, walked to the far end of the room, behind the couch to the bar and poured himself a glass of brandy.

"I'll back her up," Travis said.

"The boy was out of line," Wade pointed out.

"He's just a child!" Savannah said. "A very confused child who feels unwanted and unloved!"

"A lot you know about it," Wade threw back at her.

"I know your boy better than you do," she said in a low voice, accusations forming in her eyes. "And I have enough common sense not to humiliate him in front of his family!"

"He was asking for it." Wade tossed back his drink, but some of his determination seemed to dissolve under Savannah's attack. When he lifted his glass to his lips his hands shook.

"You touch that kid again and I'll personally beat the hell out of you," Travis said calmly, walking over to the bar and pouring himself a drink. He leaned close to Wade, grabbed one of the lapels of Wade's suit and tightened his fingers around the polished fabric before smiling with wicked satisfaction. "And don't think I wouldn't enjoy every minute of it."

Wade had trouble swallowing his drink.

Reginald had walked back into the room and heard the last part of the conversation. "He will, you know," he said, nodding his agreement. "When Travis was about eighteen, I saw him beat the tar out of a kid a couple of years older and forty pounds heavier than he was. I'd listen to his threats if I were you."

"Now wait just a minute," Wade admonished, jerking at the knot of his tie and trying to repair some of his bruised dignity. "Don't tell me you're on his—" he hooked a thumb in Travis's direction "—side!"

"We're talking about my only grandson, Wade," Reginald pointed out as he sat uncomfortably on the corner of the stiff velvet couch. "I know Josh has a mouth on him, but you'd better find a way of dealing with it."

"I am."

"Poorly," Travis said, sipping his drink and smiling to himself.

"I didn't fly two thousand miles to hear about how I raise my kid," Wade said, straightening his vest.

"Then you shouldn't have made a public spectacle of yourself," Travis muttered.

Wade shifted his gaze around the room and cleared his throat. "I think it's time we got down to business."

"Not yet." Travis finished his drink and set it on the bar. "First I think I'll check on *your* kid."

With this pointed remark, he walked across the room to Savannah, took her hand and led her up the stairs.

"Bastard," Travis whispered, his jaw thrust forward and his gray eyes dark with anger.

"You'll get no argument from me," Savannah agreed. When they reached the top of the stairs, Savannah could hear Joshua sobbing in his room. "Oh, no," she said with a sigh. She hesitated before knocking softly on his door. "Josh?"

"Yeah?"

"Are you okay?"

Charmaine opened the door and though she was pale

and her eyes were red, she managed a thin smile. "We're okay," she said.

"You're sure?" Savannah looked from her sister to Josh, who looked small and vulnerable beneath the covers of his bed.

"Yes."

"Yeah," Josh agreed, sniffing back his tears.

Savannah's heart went out to the brave boy. "You still want me to read you a story?"

Josh shrugged, but seemed to brighten. "Sure."

"Good. Just give me a few minutes, okay?"

"Okay."

Charmaine had come into the hall and Travis touched her lightly on the shoulder. "Will you be all right?"

She swallowed back her tears. "I think so."

"You don't have to take that kind of treatment, you know."

Rolling her eyes to the ceiling she visibly fought the urge to break down. "Are you speaking as a divorce lawyer?"

Travis shook his head and his shoulders slumped a little. "As a friend. There's just no reason to put up with any kind of abuse—mental or physical."

"It won't happen again," Charmaine insisted, though she couldn't meet Travis's concerned gaze. "Just let me have a little time with Josh alone. And... I'll be able to handle Wade."

"You're sure?" Savannah asked.

"Of course." Charmaine wiped away her tears and forced a trembling grin. "I've got that man wrapped around my little finger."

"Oh, Charmaine—"

"Shh. You go on. Maybe you two can find out what's eating at him."

I wish, Savannah thought hopelessly. She left Josh's room with the feeling of impending doom.

"Has it always been this bad?" Travis asked, placing a comforting arm around her.

"Never," she whispered. "I've never seen Wade hit Josh." She shuddered at the memory. "I didn't think it would come to a physical battle."

"You think it was the first time?"

"It better have been," she said, her anger resurfacing and her blue eyes sparking, "and it had damn well better be the last!"

When they entered the living room again, Wade was standing by the fireplace, one arm poised on the Italian marble of the mantel, his other holding a drink. He seemed somewhat calmer as he looked from Travis to Savannah and frowned.

"Okay, McCord," he said, glancing at Reginald before studying the amber liquid in his glass. "I guess I got out of line. I admit it." Shifting from one foot to the other, he sighed and shook his head. "I'm sorry."

"You're apologizing to the wrong person," Travis said coldly.

"Yes. Well, I'll take care of that. Later. Now, why aren't you running for governor?"

"I'm just not interested."

"You can't be serious."

"I am. I told you that before."

Wade pushed the hair from his eyes and looked to Reginald, who was seated in his favorite chair near the window.

"Why do you care?" Travis asked, leaning against the bar.

Savannah took a seat on the couch, not really wanting to be a part of the conversation, but not knowing how to avoid it.

"Because a lot of time, effort, and money has already been spent toward your candidacy."

"Maybe someone should have cleared all that with me."

"You were too busy—or don't you remember?—playing hero with that Eldridge decision. You were thinking about running. Anyway, that's what you told Reginald."

"And you just assumed that I would follow through."

"A natural assumption, I'd say."

"So you already started collecting campaign contributions, working with my partner on the books of the company and God only knows what else." Travis's jaw had hardened and his eyes glittered angrily.

"Reginald was counting on you."

"Were you?" Travis demanded, sliding a glance in the older man's direction.

"Seems a shame to throw away an opportunity like this," Reginald said. "And yes, I'd say I was counting on the fact that you'd run," he admitted, reaching into the pocket of his vest and withdrawing a pipe.

There was a tense silence in the room as Reginald lit the pipe.

"Even if I did run," Travis thought aloud, "there's a damned good chance that I wouldn't win in the primary, much less take the general election! Why's it so damned important?"

"Reginald has plans," Wade said.

"Well, maybe he should have let me in on them!" Travis walked over and stood in front of Reginald. "Ever since I was a seventeen-year-old kid, I've tried to please you, to the point that sometimes what I wanted got tangled up in what you wanted from me. Well, that just doesn't work anymore."

Reginald ran his fingers around the bowl of his pipe, glanced at Wade and scowled at the brightly lit tree.

Travis sighed loudly and rubbed the tired muscles at the base of his neck. "So, I think we should do something about all those contributions Willis Henderson and the rest of you took in my name. I expect them returned to the people who gave you the money. I want it all over by the end of the year. And I'll pay interest on any of the contributions."

"You don't understand—" Wade said.

"And I don't want to." Travis held Reginald's gaze. "I'm out of it. I don't like the feel of politics any better than I like the feel of corporate fighting, divorces, child-custody hearings or any of the rest of the bullshit that goes with being a lawyer."

"You liked the glory from the Eldridge case," Reginald remarked, puffing quietly on his pipe. The smell of the rich smoke wafted through the room.

"Even that went sour," Travis said, finishing his drink.

"But you can't just drop out," Reginald said, lifting a hand.

"I already have. Talk to Henderson. He knows that I'm serious." Travis stretched and set his glass on the mantel before leaning over the back of a velvet sofa and staring at the Christmas tree. "I don't know exactly why it was so damned important that I run for governor of this state, but I'm really not interested."

"I've worked a long time to see that day when you'd take office," Reginald whispered, as if to himself. Disillusion weighed heavily on the old man's face.

Savannah could almost feel her father's disappointment.

Travis smiled cynically. "I'd like to say that I'm sorry if I interrupted any of your plans, but I'm not. I don't like the way all of you have been doing things behind my back, and I've got to assume that even *if* I had managed to get elected, you'd still be calling the shots. I think it's time the people of the state got the kind of a governor they deserve, one that wants to serve them."

"That's horseshit and you know it," Wade said. "Idealistic words don't work in the real world."

Travis looked at Savannah. "And you thought I was cynical?" He laughed bitterly and shook his head. "That's all I have to say about it."

With those final words, he walked out of the room and into the foyer, where he took his coat off the hall tree. Savannah followed him.

"Come on, let's take a walk," Travis muttered. "I need the fresh air."

"I promised Josh that I'd read him a story." Reluctantly she started up the stairs, but stopped on the second step when he called to her.

"Savannah?"

Turning to face him, she read the passion smoldering in his steely gaze. He was standing at the base of the stairs, close enough to touch. Tense lines radiated from the corners of his mouth and eyes, sharpening his angular features.

The burning stare he gave her seared through her clothes and started her heartbeat racing uncontrollably. The thought flashed through her mind that now that Travis had told Reginald he was dropping out of the campaign, there was no reason for him to stay on the farm. Tonight might be their last together. The realization that he would soon be out of her life again settled heavily on Savannah's shoulders.

"I'll be down in a minute," she said, touching him lightly on the shoulder. "Will you wait for me?"

His mocking grin stretched over his face, softening his ruggedly handsome features. "I've waited nine years, lady, I can't see that a few more minutes will hurt." Then he placed his hand around her neck and drew her head to his, the warmth of his lips pressing urgently to hers in a kiss filled with such passion that she was left breathless, her lips throbbing with desire, her senses unbalanced.

I'm lost, she thought, closing her eyes and wrapping her arms around his neck. *I've never stopped loving him and I never will.*

His arms tightened around her, pulling her body against the taut muscles of his. She fit perfectly in his embrace, her softer contours yielding to the hard lines of his body. "Don't be long," he whispered against her ear.

"I won't," she promised. When she opened her eyes she was looking over Travis's shoulder toward the living room, and Reginald was standing in the doorway, watching her eager embrace with a frown creasing his ruddy features. "I'll be right down."

Travis smiled and then walked out of the house, leaving Savannah on the second step, holding on to the rail to support her unsteady legs.

"That's a mistake, y'know," Reginald commented,

drawing deeply on his pipe and walking into the foyer. "Gettin' involved with him again will only hurt you, Savannah."

So Reginald did know! Travis had been telling the truth! The knowledge left her exhilarated and disappointed all at once. Though Travis had been honest, her father had been lying to her for nine long years.

"I'm not a seventeen-year-old child any longer," she said, her fingers digging into the wood of the banister. From her position she could see Wade. He was lying on the couch, staring at the fire, his back to the foyer and apparently lost in his own drunken thoughts.

"Maybe not, but you're still my daughter." His bushy gray eyebrows arched. "And Travis McCord is not the man for you."

"Why not?"

"He's always loved Melinda."

Savannah paled and fought the urge to scream and shout that it didn't matter. Instead she said quietly, "But Melinda's gone."

"Maybe to you and me, but never to Travis. She was his first love, Savannah. You'd better face that."

"Why didn't you tell me that you knew I was involved with Travis?" she asked. "You've known for a long time."

Reginald smiled sadly and studied the bowl of his pipe. "Because it was over. He'd hurt you, but it was over."

"And now?"

Sighing, Reginald offered her a fatherly smile. "You're not right for each other. You want to live on the farm, work with the horses, get married and raise a family. But Travis, well, he's…different, cut out of another piece of cloth. He needs the glamour of the courtroom, the glitter of politics—"

"Didn't you hear a word he said?" she asked, incredulous that her father still saw Travis as a politician.

"He's just disillusioned right now. He's tired. Melinda's death and the Eldridge case, they took a lot out of him." Reginald's faded eyes glimmered. "That'll change. You'll see."

"I don't think so."

"Ah, but you have a habit of misreading him, don't you? You thought he and Melinda had broken up nine years ago."

Savannah came down the two steps to the foyer so that she could stand level with her father. "Travis thought she was pregnant," Savannah said. "You backed her up."

"I believed her."

"It was a lie."

Reginald frowned. "I don't know about that—is that what he told you? Well, yes, I suppose he would." The older man sighed loudly. "You have to remember, Savannah, that nobody put a gun to his head and told him he had to marry Melinda, baby or no. He married her of his own volition and they managed to stay married for nearly nine years. Nine years! This day and age that's quite a record.

"Oh, I'll grant you that he was attracted to you. Always has been. But it's just a physical thing—the difference between lust and love, a mistress and a wife." He patted her gently on the arm when he read the stricken look in her eyes. "I'm only looking out for your best interests, y'know."

"Are you, Dad?" she said, barely controlling her

anger. "I wonder. The least you could have done is tell me that you knew about Travis and me."

Reginald shrugged. "Why? What would have been the point? Your affair with him was over and he was married. If you're smart, you'll let well enough alone."

"When are you going to understand that you can't manipulate my life any more than you can force him into running for governor?" she said.

Reginald looked suddenly weary. "I'm not trying to manipulate you, Savannah. I'm just trying to help you make the right decisions."

"And the right one would be to forget about Travis?"

"I just don't want to see you hurt again," he whispered, brushing her cheek with his lips. "Isn't one rocky marriage in this family enough?"

"But you and Wade—"

"Are good business partners, don't get me wrong," Reginald said, looking into the living room where Wade was still draped over the couch. "But he should never have married Charmaine and he's a lousy father to his son." He offered her a tight smile. "Just use your head, Savannah. You've got a good brain, don't let it get all confused by your heart."

Reginald turned and went into his study, and Savannah tried to ignore his advice as she climbed the stairs and walked down the short hallway to Josh's room.

CHAPTER SIX

THE SECURITY LIGHTS cast an ethereal blue sheen on the white ground and surrounding buildings.

Travis was waiting by the stables. His tall, dark figure stood out against the stark white walls and snow-covered roof of the barns and snow-laden trees.

Savannah pushed her father's warnings out of her mind and approached him, shivering a little from the cold.

"So how was Josh?" he asked once she was in earshot.

"All right, I guess."

"You're not sure?"

She shook her head, disturbing the snowflakes resting in her ebony hair. "How would you feel if your father had humiliated you in front of the rest of the family?"

"Not so great."

"You got it," she said with a sigh. "Josh is definitely feeling 'not so great.'"

Travis took her hand, wrapped his fingers around hers, and pushed their entwined hands into the pocket of his jacket. "You can't solve all the problems of the world, you know."

"Is that what they taught you in law school?"

"No." Shaking his head, he led her around the building to the overgrown path leading to the lake. "Believe it or not, I learned a lot of things on my own."

"And I don't want to solve the problems of the world, just those of one little boy."

"He's not your son."

"I know," she whispered. "That's the problem."

"One of them," Travis agreed.

Frosty branches leaned across the trail, brushing her face and clothes with their brittle, icy leaves as she walked. Both pairs of boots crunched in the new-fallen snow.

The mud at the bank of the lake was covered with ice, and the naked trees surrounding the black body of water looked like twisted sentinels guarding a private sanctuary—a sanctuary where a feeble love had flickered to life nine years before.

Travis stopped near the old oak where he had been sitting so long ago. "It's been a long time," he said, staring at the inky water.

The pain of the past embraced her. "Too long to go back."

"You were the most beautiful woman I'd ever seen," he said. "And it scared me. It scared the hell out of me." He shook his head in wonder at the vivid memory. "I'd just spent two days trying to convince myself that you were off limits, barely seventeen, Reginald's youngest daughter, for God's sake! And then you walked out of the lake, without a stitch of clothes on, your eyes filled with challenge." He leaned one shoulder against the oak. "It did me in. All of my resolve went right out the window."

"You were drunk," she reminded him.

"I honestly don't think it would have mattered." He wrapped his free arm around her and traced the curve of her jaw with his finger. His hand was cold but inviting, and she shivered.

His gray eyes delved into hers, noticing the way the snow clung to her thick, curling lashes. "I was hooked, Savannah. I didn't want to be. God knows, I fought it, but I was hooked." He smiled cynically and added, "I still am."

When his chilled lips touched hers she heard a thousand warnings in her mind, but ignored them all. The feel of his body pressed against hers was as drugging as it had been nine years before, in the summer, in that very spot.

Strong arms held her, moist lips claimed hers and she could smell and taste the man she had never quit loving. She felt pangs of regret as well as happiness build inside.

Lifting his head, he gazed into her eyes. "I want you to stay with me tonight," he whispered, his warm breath caressing her face. "You don't have to promise me the future; just spend one night with me and we'll take it from there."

The difference between lust and love, a mistress and a wife.

"Travis—"

"Just say yes."

Delving into his kind eyes, she swallowed and blinked back her tears. "Yes."

Travis took her hand again and led her back down the path toward the buildings of the farm. He was staying in the loft over the garage, and Savannah didn't argue when he helped her climb the stairs to Charmaine's studio.

After shutting the door behind them, Travis rubbed his hands together and blew on them for warmth. The temperature in the dark room was barely above freezing; Savannah could see her breath misting in the half-light.

Savannah stared at her sister's private domain. Pale

light from the reflection of the security lamps on the snow filtered through the windows. Charmaine's draped artwork was scattered around the room, looking like lifeless ghosts propped in the corners of the studio.

"It's changed a little in nine years," Travis observed, not bothering to switch on the lights.

Originally the second story over the garage had been one large apartment, and Travis had lived in the three sloped-ceilinged rooms whenever he was on the farm. A few years before, Charmaine had converted what had been his living room and kitchen into an artist's studio.

The bedroom was still in the back. Travis had been using it since he arrived at the farm and now, in the darkness of the frigid night, he tugged on Savannah's hand and pulled her down the short hallway to what was left of his quarters.

Savannah hadn't been in the room in years. It held too many memories of Travis, too much pain. She leaned against the tall post of the bed and felt the old, angry deception stir in her heart. Looking into his night-darkened eyes she wanted to trust him, but his betrayal was as fresh as it had been on the night he'd left her all those years ago.

"Try to forget the past," he said, as if reading her mind. His hand reached forward and he cupped her chin. "Trust me again."

Savannah's breath caught in her throat when she felt his arms surround her and tasted the warmth of his lips against hers. She told herself to push him away, pay attention to her father's advice, but she couldn't. Instead, her pulse quickened and her blood heated with desire.

He groaned when she responded. "We don't have any more excuses, Savannah," he whispered against her hair. "Tonight there's nothing and no one to stand in our way."

And we're running out of time, she added silently to herself. *Tomorrow you'll probably leave.* Desperation gripped her heart and she wound her arms around his neck, returning the passion of his kiss with the fierce need of a woman who'd been held away from the man she'd loved for far too long.

She felt the warmth of his mouth against her lips, her eyes, her cheeks. His tongue slipped through her parted lips to search and dance with its anxious mate.

His hard body, covered by straining, bothersome clothing, pushed against hers, and she felt the volatile tension of taut tendons, corded muscles and unbridled desire pressing against her flesh. His lips caressed her, his fingers explored and stroked her neck and face.

"I've waited a long time for you," he said, anxiously unbuttoning her coat and pushing it off her shoulders to fall to the floor.

"And I for you," she agreed, her voice low, her fingers working at his clothes.

Slowly the cloth barriers slid to the floor, until finally there was nothing to separate their bodies but the pain of nine lost years.

He stood before her, a naked man silhouetted in the night. His hand reached upward and his fingers shook a little as he touched one dark-tipped breast.

Savannah quivered beneath his touch. The gentle probe was light at first, a sensual stroking of the breast that made her knees weaken and the warmth within her turn liquid. "Travis," she whispered.

"Shh." His fingers continued to work their magic and Savannah leaned backward against the cold polished wood of the four-poster. Travis pressed harder against her, the warmth of his body contrasting to the smooth, cool post at her back.

His mouth was hungry, his tongue plundering as he tasted the soft skin at the base of her throat, and one of his strong hands reached downward to fit over her buttocks and pull her against his thighs. Hot, tense muscles fitted against her softer flesh, melting away the memory of betrayal.

His hands molded her body as lovingly as those of a sculptor shaping clay, and Savannah's doubts escaped into the night. "I've never wanted a woman the way I want you," he admitted, kneeling and kissing first one ripened breast and then the other. The wet impression left on her nipples made the dark points stand erect, as he stroked them with his thumbs. "God, you're beautiful," he whispered, his breath fanning her navel.

Involuntarily her abdomen tightened, and when he rimmed her navel with his tongue, she moaned and her knees sagged. She would have slid to the floor, but he caught her, forcing her back to the bedpost as he kissed the soft skin of her abdomen and hips. Her fingers twined in his thick hair, and dampness broke out upon her skin. The ache deep within her became more intense. She was twisting and writhing with an emptiness that only he could fill.

"Please," she whispered somewhere between pain and ecstasy. "Travis…please…"

"What do you want?" he asked, his tongue and teeth tantalizing her skin.

"Everything."

When he picked her up, letting her knees drape over one arm while cradling her head with the other, she couldn't resist—wouldn't, even if she had the strength.

Black hair spilled over his arm as he gently placed her on the bed. The patchwork quilt was ice-cold against her back and goose bumps rose on her flesh, but the fire in her eyes burned brightly.

"I'm glad you decided to stay with me tonight," he admitted, looking into her blue gaze and tracing the pout on her lips with one finger.

Trembling with anticipation, Savannah's fingers wrapped around the back of his neck and she pulled his head to hers. Her eager, open lips fused to his.

The weight of his body fell over her, flattening her breasts with the hard muscles of his chest. His dark, swirling hair rubbed erotically against her nipples. A soft sheen of sweat oiled the corded muscles of his back and chest.

Savannah moaned as Travis's legs entwined with hers. She felt the exquisite torment of his tongue and teeth playing with her nipples before his lips once again claimed hers and he positioned his body above her.

"I love you, Savannah," he admitted, closing his eyes against the truth. "I always have."

Moving below him, she stared into the steely depths of his eyes as he slowly pressed her knees apart and entered her. She felt the heat of his body begin to fill her as his strokes, slow at first, increased in tempo until she was forced to move with him, join him in the ancient dance of love.

She clung to him, tasted his sweat, stared into his fathomless gray eyes as he rocked them both with the fever of his passion until at last the shimmering lights in her mind exploded into a thousand tiny fragments of that very same light and she nearly screamed his name.

A moment later he stiffened and fell upon her, cradling her shoulders and resting his head on her breasts.

"God, I love you," he said, still fondling her breast before falling asleep in her arms.

Do. Oh, please, Travis do love me, let me believe you, she silently prayed as tears burned her eyes. *Tell me it's more than just one final night together!*

She listened to the regular tempo of his breathing, thought she should return to the house, but created a thousand excuses to stay with him, and fell asleep entwined in his arms.

Hours later, Savannah awakened. One of Travis's tanned arms was draped protectively across her breasts. She rolled over to kiss him and found that he was already awake and staring at her.

"Good morning," he drawled, his gray eyes delving deep into hers, and his fingers pushing the tousled black hair from her eyes.

Savannah smiled and stretched. "Good morning yourself."

She tried to toss off the covers and hop out of bed, but Travis restrained her by placing his hands over her wrists. "Where do you think you're going?" he asked.

"I realize that you're on vacation, early retirement, or whatever else you want to call it," she teased, "but the rest of us poor working stiffs have jobs to do."

He chuckled to himself. "Your father's back; you can relax."

"Not quite yet," she said, trying to wriggle free, but his hands continued to hold her down and she gave up with an exasperated sigh. "What's so important?" she asked.

"I think we should clear up a few things before you high-tail it out of here."

"Such as?"

"Like what we're going to do if you're pregnant."

Disappointment burned in her heart. There were no options as far as she was concerned; she would bear Travis's child and raise it—alone if she had to. Unfortunately, she didn't even have to worry. "I'm not."

He smiled seductively. "Too early to be sure?"

She did a quick calculation in her head. "Let's just say it would be highly unlikely, counselor."

"Oh?"

"I work with brood mares every day, remember? I think I can figure out when I'm able to conceive and when I'm not. Last night we were lucky."

"Lucky? Well, maybe," he said with a frown.

"Now, unless you have something that can't wait, I've got to get up."

"But that's the problem, don't you see?" he teased, still holding her wrists to her sides and sliding his naked body erotically over hers. "There is something that can't wait, something bothering me a lot."

Her breath caught in her throat. "Travis—"

He pulled her hands over her head and positioned himself over her, softly kissing her lips while rubbing against her.

Savannah found it impossible to think. The warm sensations cascading over her body made everything else seem unimportant.

"I really should go to work—"

"In time," he promised, dipping his head and kissing her gently on the swell of her breasts. He watched in fascination as her nipples hardened expectantly and the fires deep within her began to rage. "In time..."

TRAVIS HAD FALLEN back to sleep and Savannah was finally able to slip from the bed, throw on her clothes and head downstairs. It was nearly dawn, sometime after six, and Lester would be arriving at the farm soon.

As quietly as a cat slinking through the night, Savannah sneaked out of the room, through the studio, and down the stairs outside of the garage. The snow had quit falling, but the sky overhead was threatening to spill more powdery flakes onto the earth. She smiled when she noticed that the double set of footprints that she and Travis had made was nearly covered. Snow must have fallen most of the night.

Maybe we'll have a white Christmas this year, she thought with a smile as she pushed her hands into the pockets of her suede jacket and headed toward the stables. *Josh would love it!* This much snow was nearly unheard of in this part of the country.

Her spirits lifted as she walked through the backyard. Spending a night alone with Travis and listening to his words of love had made her think there was a chance that all would be right with the world. Perhaps loving him was the right thing to do, she thought. Even if his words of love had been whispered at the height of passion, he hadn't been forced to say them. So why fight it? She almost had herself convinced that the barriers of the past nine years had been destroyed in one night. Almost.

Humming to herself, she let Archimedes out of the back porch and started on her early-morning rounds. Archimedes bounded along beside her, romping in the snow and breaking a trail in the soft white powder.

Savannah's breath clouded in the air, and her boots crunched through the five-inch layer of snow. Intermittent flakes fell from the sky and clung to her shoulders and hair as she headed toward the stables.

The brood mares, their swollen bellies protruding prominently, snorted and nickered when she arrived. After checking the water and the feed of each of the mares, she walked back outside and crossed the parking lot to the brick path that led to the stallion barn. "That's odd," she thought, noticing the set of footprints leading to the barn from the front of the house. The prints were smaller than her own and softened by a fine dusting of snow.

"What is?" Travis's voice broke through the still morning air.

Savannah nearly jumped out of her skin and turned to face him. He was walking toward her from the direction of the garage. A Stetson was pulled low over his eyes and his hands were jammed into the pockets of his jeans. "Boy, I could use a pair of gloves," he muttered.

"I thought you were still asleep."

"I was, until someone rattled around and made so much noise that I woke up."

"What!" She'd been as quiet as a mouse. She looked into his eyes and saw the sparkle of amusement in his intriguing gaze. "Give me a break."

He leaned over and kissed the tip of her nose. "I missed you, Savvy."

Savannah's heart jumped. *God, how she loved this man.* "Good, I could use the company, as well as the muscle power. You can help me feed the stallions."

"I can think of better things to do."

Savannah laughed merrily. It felt good to throw off

the chains of the past. "Not right now, mister," she said. "I told you; I've got work to do." They walked together in the snow. "Speaking of which, are you going to tell me what you were doing in Dad's study last night? Wade nearly fell through the floor when I told him you were in the den."

"I'll bet," Travis muttered, hunching his shoulders against another blast of arctic wind. "I just wanted to do some checking."

"On what?"

"The books."

"Of the farm?"

He nodded and a shiver of dread slid down Savannah's spine. "Why?"

"Curiosity." He kept his eyes to the ground and noticed the other set of tracks in the snow.

"Whose are these?" he asked, then continued without pausing, "Lester's usually the first one around, but they're too small for him." He frowned. "And look at the tread. Definitely not boots. More like running shoes."

Savannah's heart nearly stopped beating. Snowflakes clung to her ebony hair, and her cheeks were flushed from the cold. Her blue eyes darkened with dread in spite of the light from the security lamps and the first hint of dawn.

"Like Josh's shoes?" she whispered.

"Like Josh's," Travis agreed as his eyes followed the arrow-straight path of the footsteps that led from the house to the stallion barn. The crease in his forehead deepened.

A premonition of disaster tightened Savannah's chest and made it hard to breathe. "But what would he be doing here this early?" she asked, as they approached the barn.

"That's what we're about to find out."

Travis opened the door to the barn, flipped on the lights, and began striding down the double row of stalls. Savannah walked more slowly, her eyes scanning the interior of the barn.

"Mornin', fellas," she said, patting Night Magic fondly on his nose as Travis walked down the parallel row of stalls. "It doesn't look like anyone's here," she said. "Just like yesterday morning. Lester heard a noise, but no one was there."

"Strange, isn't it?"

"Creepy," she agreed.

Several of the younger stallions snorted their contempt, while Night Magic whinnied softly. "You're a pushover, aren't you?" Savannah asked, petting the coal-black muzzle again.

Travis stopped at the far end of the stalls. "Where's Mystic?" he asked.

"What do you mean? He's here. The end stall—" The meaning of his question suddenly struck home and Savannah ran down the length of the barn, her boots clattering against the concrete floor, her heart thudding wildly in her rib cage. Once near Travis she stared into the empty box and fear took a stranglehold of her throat.

"Where else could he be?" Travis demanded.

"Nowhere…" Her heart thudding with dread, she slowly went down the double aisle and counted the stallions. All seven stallions and colts were in their proper stalls. Except for Mystic. He was gone, vanished into the night.

"Didn't Joshua say he could ride Mystic?" Travis asked.

Savannah had all but lost her voice. "But he wouldn't...couldn't take him." She leaned against the stall door for support.

"Why not?"

"He's just a boy—"

"An angry, humiliated boy."

Fear tightened her chest. "Oh, God. I don't think Josh would take off like that. Not in the middle of a snow-storm. Not on *Mystic*, for God's sake." But even to her own ears, her protests sounded weak.

"Wade pushed Josh into a corner last night," Travis said. "I know, I've been there myself." He started walking down the row of boxes again, his fists balled at his sides, his jaw jutted forward angrily, and Savannah was reminded of the rebel Travis had been as a teenager. "I'll kill him," Travis swore. "So help me, if that boy is hurt I'll kill Benson and be glad to do it!"

"Wait! Before we go to the house, I think we should check the other barns and the paddocks. Maybe Mystic got out by himself."

"Do you really believe that?" Travis asked, his anger flushing his face.

"Look, I just want to make sure, that's all," she said, nearly screaming at him. "You check the other barns and I'll call Lester."

Travis walked out of the building and headed for the main stables. Savannah used the extension in the stal-lion barn and dialed Lester's number. While it rang she tapped her fingers nervously on the wall and eyed the interior of the barn.

"Answer the phone," she whispered on the fourth ring.

"Hello?"

"Lester!" she said with relief.

"I was just on my way over," the trainer replied. "What's up?"

"It's Mystic. He's not in the stallion barn."

"What!"

"He's gone."

The old man whistled softly and then swore. "I locked him up myself last night."

"You're sure?"

"Course I am," Lester snapped.

Savannah's knees went weak and she leaned against the wall for support.

"Any other clues?"

"Just another set of tracks coming to the barn. Smaller ones. Maybe Josh might know something about this."

"Well, ask him."

"I will," she promised. *If he's here.* "I'll be over in about twenty minutes. Have you told Reginald what happened yet?"

"No. Travis is still checking to make sure Mystic didn't get in with the mares or yearlings by mistake…"

"I shut him up myself, missy. If he's gone, it's because someone let him out."

Someone like Joshua, Savannah thought miserably.

Travis came back into the barn just as she hung up the phone. His expression was grim, the set of his jaw determined. "No luck," he said, walking back to Mystic's stall.

"Lester locked him up himself."

"Then it looks like Josh took him." Travis slid open the door at the opposite end of the barn. It was used rarely, only for grain delivery. "And this confirms it." In the freshly fallen snow were two sets of tracks: those of a horse and those matching the tracks at the other end of the barn.

"Oh, God," Savannah whispered. Her small fists clenched when she saw the trampled snow and mud where the horse had shied. At that point, near the fence, the rider had to have mounted Mystic. And then the hoofprints became a single file that led through the gate, across the field and toward the hills. "He'll freeze," she whispered, tears beginning to build in her eyes and fear clenching her heart.

"Not if I can help it," Travis said. "Let's go."

After securing the stallion barn, they half ran back to the house. Savannah didn't bother taking off her boots as she mounted the stairs and raced to Joshua's room. She knocked quietly once and then again when there was no answer.

"Josh!" she called through the door.

Charmaine's door opened. Her dark hair was mussed, her eyes still blurred with sleep. "Savannah, what's going on?"

"I don't know," Savannah replied, her hand on the doorknob. Until she was sure of the facts, she didn't want to worry her older sister.

"Savannah?" Charmaine whispered, her eyes widening.

Ignoring her sister, Savannah opened the door to Josh's room and sank against the wall when she saw that the room was empty. The covers of the bed were strewn on the floor. A quick check in the closet indicated that Josh's jacket was missing, as were his favorite shoes and hat.

Charmaine walked into the room. "Where's Josh?" she asked, nearly choking with fear. "Where is he?"

"I don't know," Savannah admitted. Her shoulders slumped in defeat as she thought about the child braving the elements. "But we think he took Mystic."

"Mystic!" Charmaine leaned against the dresser for support and knocked over a stack of comic books. "What do you mean?"

"That's a good question," Travis said. "All we know is that Mystic is missing. There're small footsteps from the house to the stallion barn and then it looks like someone took Mystic from his stall, led him outside and rode him into the hills."

"Not Josh," Charmaine whispered, shaking her head. "He wouldn't have done that. He's got to be here on the farm somewhere. Someone else let the horse out of his stall or rode him away but Josh is here... He's just hiding..."

"He told me he could ride Mystic," Savannah said.

"What the hell is going on here?" Wade demanded, running his fingers through his unruly hair as he entered the room. "Where's the boy?"

"They think Josh is missing," Charmaine whispered miserably.

"Missing?"

"Gone, Wade." She gestured feebly toward Savannah and Travis. "They think he took Mystic."

"Josh took Mystic? That's impossible. That demon of a horse won't let anyone near him..." Wade's angry words died as he surveyed the tense faces in the room. "My God, you're serious, aren't you?" The sleep left his eyes.

"Dead serious," Travis muttered.

"I don't believe it. He's just here somewhere," Charmaine insisted, looking frantically around the boy's room. "Josh? Josh!"

Travis caught her by the arm. "We're pretty certain about this. Otherwise we wouldn't have alarmed you."

Charmaine jerked her arm free. "It's freezing outside. Josh wouldn't go out in the cold...not away from the house. And he wouldn't take the horse..." The reality of the situation finally caught up with her. "Oh, God, it just can't be." She moaned, letting her face fall into her hands and finally releasing the sobs she had been fighting since entering the room.

"Listen, I'll call the sheriff," Savannah offered.

"The sheriff!" Charmaine was horrified. "What good will that do?" Her pale face was terror-stricken and she lashed out at the first person she saw. "Savannah, if what you're saying is true, this is all your fault, you know. You're the one who took him riding, you're the one who planted all those damned horse-loving ideas in his head, you're the one who let him think about riding that horrible horse!"

Travis stood between Charmaine and Savannah. "We're not getting anywhere by pointing fingers! We've got to find Josh."

"We are talking about my son," Charmaine said, tears sliding down her white cheeks. "My son, dammit! He's gone!"

"This is insane," Wade said, shaking his head as if trying to shake out a bad dream. "Josh wouldn't take Mystic. Why in the world would a boy want a race-horse?"

"Maybe he thought it was the only friend he had," Savannah said, fighting her own hot tears.

"You're wrong!" Wade said, pacing the small room and rubbing the golden stubble on his chin. "Josh is probably just pulling one of his rebellious stunts. No doubt he's hiding somewhere on the farm and having a good laugh over this."

"He's only a nine-year-old boy," Charmaine wailed.

"That you mortified last night!" Savannah said, staring at Wade through tear-glazed eyes.

"Oh, give me a break," Wade mumbled, but he was sweating. "Charmaine's right, you know, Savannah. You've been filling that boy's head with all sorts of idiotic ideas. You should never have encouraged Josh to have anything to do with the horses. Especially Mystic. If anything happens to my boy, I'll hold you personally responsible!"

Travis's eyes glinted like newly forged steel. "And if anything happens to either Savannah or Josh, you'll have to answer to me, Benson," he threatened, his voice becoming ruthless. "Now let's quit arguing about it and get to work. Savannah, you call the sheriff. Charmaine will stay here with Virginia in case anyone calls. The rest of us will start searching the farm by following the tracks as far as we can."

"I'm coming with you," Savannah insisted, trying to pull herself together.

"Not on your life. You stay and wait for Lester and the rest of the hands. Someone's got to run the farm and take care of Charmaine. Besides, I want you to talk to that repairman, make sure that the broken wire was just a case of the alarm wearing out. If we get moving now, there's a good chance that we can catch up to the boy by noon."

Travis was walking out of the room and toward the stairs. Wade was only two steps behind him. Before Travis descended, he turned to Wade and his cold eyes bored through Josh's father. "I think you'd better tell

Reginald what's happened—that he's missing a valuable colt as well as his only grandson."

Wade nodded curtly and walked toward Reginald's room.

Savannah had followed Travis and Wade. At the top of the stairs she brushed her tears aside and held her chin defiantly while holding Travis's severe glare. "I'm coming with you," she announced. "Josh is my nephew."

"No way, lady."

"You can't talk me out of it."

Travis let out an exasperated sigh and hurried down the stairs. Savannah was on his heels. "Use your head, Savannah. You're needed here," Travis said.

"But I know Josh; I know where he might go."

"We'll find him. You stay with your sister. Whether she knows it or not, she needs you."

"I can't stay here! Not while Josh is out...wherever!"

Travis looked up at the ceiling. "Don't we have enough problems without you trying to add to them?"

"I only want to help."

"Then stay here and be sensible!" he snapped before turning to face her and seeing the tears in her eyes. He wrapped his arms around her and sighed. "Listen, Savannah, you're the only one on this whole damned farm that I can count on. Stay here. Help your mother and the police."

"But—"

"And quit blaming yourself! If Joshua left it was because of his father."

"I did encourage him to take an interest in the horses," she whispered, her throat raw.

"Because you're his friend." Travis's face softened.

"And right now, Josh needs all the friends he can get. So hang in here, okay? Help me."

The sound of Lester's pickup spurred Travis into action. He released Savannah and went outside. A few minutes later, Wade and a pale-looking Reginald, who was still stuffing his shirt into his pants, joined Travis and Lester. The men formed a search party on horseback and in four-wheel-drive vehicles.

It had begun to snow heavily again, showering the valley with white powder and making it impossible to see any distance. Finding a nine-year-old and a runaway horse would be difficult.

Savannah stood near the fence by the stallion barn, her arms huddled around herself. She felt absolutely helpless.

"I'll see you later," Travis promised as he climbed into the saddle on Jones. The chestnut gelding swished his tail and flattened his ears impatiently.

Travis's plan was to follow Mystic's footprints on horseback. Reginald and Wade were driving ahead in a Jeep, but Travis insisted on taking the horse just in case Josh rode Mystic through the trees and the vehicle was unable to follow the Thoroughbred's prints in the snow.

Lester and Johnny, one of the stable hands, were searching the other areas of the farm in a pickup. They were hoping to come across Josh's hiding place…if he had one.

Then Travis and the others were gone.

The sounds of engines rumbling up the hills made Savannah shiver inside and she said a silent prayer for the lost boy. *Come home, Josh,* she thought desperately. *Please come home!*

Savannah watched the tall man on horseback for as

long as she could. Travis rode past the stallion barn, through the enclosed field and up the hillside, carefully following the slowly disappearing tracks in the snow and the roaring Jeep.

Standing on the fence, Savannah squinted and stared after him until he finally vanished from her sight.

With cold dread settling in her heart, she climbed off the fence, turned back to the house and worked up the courage to face Charmaine and call the sheriff.

CHAPTER SEVEN

SAVANNAH LEANED ON her father's desk, closing her eyes while trying to hear the voice on the other end of the phone. Listening was difficult as the wires crackled and the background noise in the sheriff's department was nearly as loud as the deputy's voice. Deputy Smith sounded weary, as if he'd been on the job all night, and the words he gave Savannah were far from encouraging.

"It's not that I don't appreciate your problem, Ms. Beaumont," he said in a sincere voice, "and we'll do what we can. But you have to understand that the storm is causing a lot of problems for other people as well as you folks. Several cities are without power and I don't have to tell you about the conditions of the roads. We've got two trucks jackknifed on the freeway and traffic backed up for six miles." He paused for a minute and Savannah heard him talking in a muffled voice to another officer. He was back to her within a minute. "We'll send someone out to the farm as soon as possible."

"Thank you," Savannah said before hanging up the phone and feeling the energy drain from her body. *So Travis and the rest of the men couldn't count on anyone but themselves.* Travis. She should have ignored his anger and logic and gone with him. At least that way she would feel as if she were accomplishing something, doing something useful.

She picked up a cold cup of coffee, took a sip, frowned and set the cup back on the desk.

Taking in a steadying breath, she dialed all of the neighbors within a three-mile radius of the breeding farm. It was another waste of time. No one had seen Josh or Mystic.

"Well, what did you expect?" she asked herself after hanging up and staring through the window at the white flakes falling from a leaden sky. "Oh, Josh, where are you?" She stood transfixed at the window of the study and watched with mounting dread as the small silvery flakes continued to fall. Maybe it was a good sign that none of the neighbors had seen Josh. Maybe he was still on Beaumont property. *And maybe the neighbors were just too busy taking care of themselves in the snowstorm to notice the boy or his horse,* she thought grimly.

Pushing the hair from her eyes, she tried not to think about either Travis or Josh, but found it impossible. No matter what she did to try to keep busy, her thoughts always returned to Travis. He'd been in the storm on horseback for nearly two hours, following a mere shadow of a trail in the snow. The longer the snow continued to fall, the less able he would be to track Mystic. God, how long had Josh been braving the elements? Was he still on the horse or was he curled up in the snow freezing to death?

Tears pricked the back of her eyes, and she leaned her head against the cool panes of the window. "Use your head, sport," Savannah whispered, as if the boy were standing next to her instead of somewhere outdoors in the cold. "Use your head and come home."

Shaking off her fears and fighting back tears, Savannah went into the kitchen and made coffee. When she let Archimedes into the house from the back porch, she eyed the snow. The storm hadn't let up and white powder was drifting against the sides of the stables and garage.

Somewhere out in the near blizzard Josh was alone. And so was Travis. Savannah shivered as she came back inside. Archimedes, from his favorite position under the kitchen table, thumped his tail against the floor.

"You're not worried, are you?" she asked the dog, who lifted his head and cocked his ears expectantly.

She prayed when the lights flickered twice. If the power went out now, running the farm would be nearly impossible. She switched on the small black-and-white television in the kitchen. After listening to the news for a few minutes and discovering that the intensity of the storm wasn't about to let up, she snapped off the set, poured two cups of coffee, put them on a tray and carried them upstairs to Virginia's room.

Knocking softly on the bedroom door, Savannah entered. Virginia was sitting in the bed, her pale hands folded over her lap, her eyes fastened on the floor-to-ceiling window at the far end of the room. Through the glass was a view of the hills surrounding the farm.

"Any news?" Virginia asked quietly.

Savannah shook her head. "Not yet."

With a loud sigh, Virginia slumped lower into the mound of pillows supporting her back. "What about the police?"

"I called the sheriff's department. They're pretty busy right now."

"Yes, I imagine so," Virginia said distractedly. One of her hands lifted and she fingered a small cross hanging from a gold chain at her throat. "And the storm. Who would have thought that we'd get so much snow? It's unusual... Can't the sheriff come over?"

"The deputy said he would send a man over as soon as possible."

"For what good it will do—"

"Mom," Savannah gently reproached.

Virginia sighed before stiffening her shoulders. "I know, I know. And I haven't given up hope. Really. I… I just can't help but think about Josh and that horse lost in the mountains or God only knows where…" Her voice faded and she swallowed hard. "He's such a dear, dear boy."

"I won't argue with that," Savannah said kindly. "But you know that Travis will find him." Her own throat was nearly swollen shut and the conviction in her voice wavered, so she changed the subject. "Here, I brought you some coffee. What about something to eat?"

Virginia waved the cup aside. "Not hungry," she mumbled, shaking her head against the pillows.

"You're sure?"

"Yes."

"Okay. Suit yourself." Savannah left the cup and saucer on the night table near her mother. Then she took the remaining cup of coffee and stood. "I'm going to see how Charmaine is, and then I'll check on the horses. If you need anything, I'll be back in about an hour."

"I won't need a thing," Virginia whispered. "But as for Charmaine…" Pain crossed Virginia's eyes and she raised her hand in a feeble gesture. "Maybe it would be best if you let her alone—let her sort out her feelings."

"She still blames me," Savannah deduced, leaning a shoulder against the wall.

"She's not thinking clearly. Josh is the only thing she has in her life. Even Wade…" Virginia lifted her shoulders. "Well, it's different when you have a child of your own."

"I think I'd better see her."

"Just remember that she's under a horrible strain."

"I will." Savannah started down the hallway to Charmaine's room, but stopped when she came to the open door of Josh's bedroom and saw her sister. Charmaine, still in her bathrobe, was seated cross-legged on the braided rug and softly crying to herself.

"How about a cup of coffee or some company?" Savannah offered, setting the cup on the dresser before folding her arms over her chest and leaning a shoulder against the doorjamb.

"No, thanks."

"Charmaine, I know what you're going through—"

Savannah's sister took in a long, deep breath, as if trying to calm herself. "You know what I'm going through," she repeated incredulously. "Do you? You couldn't!" Charmaine lifted red-rimmed eyes and stared at Savannah as if she wanted to kill her. "How could you understand—you don't even have a child!"

Savannah felt the sting of the bitter words, but tried to rise above Charmaine's anger. "But I love Josh. Very much."

Charmaine's throat worked convulsively. "Too much. You treat him as if he were your child, not mine!"

"I just wanted to be his friend."

"Like hell!" Charmaine tossed her head back angrily and her dark hair fell around her shaking shoulders. "You tried to be his mother, Savannah. And you allowed him, *encouraged* him to hang around the horses."

"The same way we were encouraged when we were children."

Charmaine just shook her head, and tears tracked down her cheeks. "You don't understand, do you? Because you don't have a child. Those horses are dangerous, and Mystic... Mystic, he's so mean-tempered that even Lester has trouble handling him. And you let a boy, *my* boy work with him. Now look what's happened. He's out there, with that demon of a horse, probably hurt... maybe...maybe dead. All because you wanted to be his friend." She began sobbing again, raking her fingers through her hair in frustration.

"Have you ever thought that the reason Josh ran away was because of his argument with Wade?"

"Ran away!" Charmaine repeated, her face draining of color. "Ran away?" She shook her head. "Josh did *not* run away! Sure, he was mad at his father, but he just took the horse for a ride, that's all. He didn't have any intention of running away!" Charmaine's fingers trembled when they cinched the belt of her robe around her waist.

"I hope you're right," Savannah whispered, wanting to stand up for herself, but knowing there was nothing she could say in her own defense. Charmaine was beyond reason, too distraught to be comforted, and she was lashing out at the easiest target. In this case, the easiest mark was Savannah.

"Of course I am. I'm his mother... I... I understand him." She stood on quivering legs. "Now, just leave me alone." Looking around the boy's room, noticing the posters of football players, rock stars and running horses as if for the first time, Charmaine cleared her throat. "I can't stand being in this house another minute. If Travis or Wade gets back, or you hear anything about Josh, I'll be in the studio."

"You'll be the first to know."

Charmaine walked past Savannah without a glance in her sister's direction, and in a few minutes the door to her room closed shut with a thud that echoed in Savannah's mind.

Swallowing against the sense of desperation and fear that parched her throat, Savannah braced herself and walked out of Josh's room. Surely Travis would find Josh and within a couple of hours they would all be together again. It was just a matter of time.

Savannah looked in on her mother again and found that Virginia was sleeping. She removed the cup of untouched coffee from the night table, went downstairs, and placed the cup in the sink. Then, on an impulse, she dialed Sadie Stinson's number. The housekeeper lived several miles away in the opposite direction of Mystic's hoofprints, but there was a slim chance that Josh had sought solace with Sadie. The phone rang several times, but no one answered.

Trying to disregard a feeling of impending doom, Savannah grabbed her coat and continued trying to convince herself that everything would be all right as she walked outside and headed for the brood mare barn. There was work to be done, the first of which was to draw water and make sure that the reserve tank was full. Electricity the farm could do without, but water was another story altogether.

A DEPUTY FOR the sheriff's department, a young red-haired man with sober brown eyes and a hard smile, made it to the farm later in the morning. After several apologies for not being able to respond earlier, and excuses ranging from jackknifed trucks on the freeway to power outages all over the state, he took a statement from everyone at the house before following Savannah to the office over the foaling shed.

"So you don't think the horse was stolen?" he queried, his dark eyes searching Savannah's. She gave him a cup of coffee and sat at the table near the window.

"No, it looks as if Joshua took the horse."

"Any note from the boy?"

She shook her head and frowned into her cup. "None that we've found."

"And he didn't bother to say goodbye to anyone."

"No."

The young deputy lifted his hat and rubbed his head before scratching a note to himself on his clipboard. "Now, the colt: Mystic. This the same horse that won the Preakness earlier in the year?"

"Yes."

"So he's valuable?"

"Very."

"And insured?"

"Of course." Savannah impaled the young officer with her intense gaze. "What are you getting at?"

"Just checking all the angles. Would you say that this Mystic was the most valuable horse on the farm?"

"No doubt about it."

"And would it be easy for another person, say one that wasn't familiar with the farm, to recognize him?"

"You mean someone that didn't work with him?"

The deputy nodded and took a sip from his cup. "Right."

Savannah thought for a moment. "I don't know. He was pure black, that in itself is striking, I suppose. Most Thoroughbreds are bays or chestnuts."

"How about the other stallions?"

"We have one other black horse, Black Magic, but he's quite a bit older than Mystic; his sire, in fact."

The deputy looked up from his clipboard. "His what?"

"Black Magic is Mystic's sire…you know, father."

"Oh. But could anyone tell them apart?"

"Temperamentally the two are night and day. Black Magic is fairly docile and Mystic is difficult to handle. Magic is slightly larger and has one white stocking. Both horses are registered with the jockey club so their identifying numbers are tattooed inside their upper lips. Anyone who knew what he was doing could make sure that he had the right horse," she mused, "but I don't think we have to worry about that. Josh is missing; he loved the horse, and the boy had a horrid fight with his father last night."

"So you think he just took off in the middle of the biggest snowstorm we've had in fifteen years with the most valuable horse in your stable?" Deputy Smith was clearly dubious.

"He's only nine and he was angry, so, yes."

Scratching the reddish stubble on his chin the deputy stared at the broken wire on the security alarm. "Don't you think it's quite a coincidence that the horse would be taken just when the alarm appeared to be broken?"

"I don't know about that."

"Okay." He shoved the clipboard under his arm and took a final swallow of coffee. "Let's have a look at the barn where the missing horse was taken from."

Savannah led the officer down the path to the barn. Most of the footprints she and Travis had made earlier were covered with snow, just as Mystic's trail was probably covered.

Opening the door of the stallion barn, Savannah stood

aside while Deputy Smith peered inside the building, scrutinized every horse and continued to make notes to himself. After searching the barn completely, Mystic's stall thoroughly, and asking Savannah again why Lester thought he'd heard someone in the barn the morning before, he scoured the outside of the buildings. By the time he was finished with his search and was driving away from the house it was almost three in the afternoon, and Savannah felt bone tired and discouraged.

"You'd think they could do more than just poke around and ask a few questions," Charmaine said bitterly when Savannah walked into the kitchen. Charmaine had returned to the house when the young deputy sherrif had arrived, although she hadn't had much to tell him.

"He promised to watch all the roads and inform all the state and county officers about Josh and Mystic," Savannah said quietly, shivering slightly as she took off her coat and hung it on a hook near the door to the back porch. "And when they have more men free, they'll be back. I don't know what more they can do."

"I just thought Josh would be home by now," Charmaine whispered.

"So did I."

Charmaine bit at her lower lip and studied the floor. "I know I've been a bitch, Savannah. I really didn't mean to blame you."

"I know."

"I said some pretty awful things earlier."

"You always do when you get angry."

"So why do you put up with it?" Charmaine asked, her chin quivering.

"Because I know you're doing the best you can and you're sick with worry about Josh. And—" she hesitated, but decided to say what she felt "—and you don't want to blame Wade."

Charmaine closed her eyes. "You're right," she admitted, shaking her head and frowning. "Thanks for understanding."

Shrugging, Savannah forced a smile. "What are sisters for?"

Charmaine thought a minute. "Well, I don't think they were meant to be whipping posts and I'm sorry that I lost control."

"It's okay."

"We all owe you something for holding this place together today."

"Don't thank me yet," Savannah said, watching through the window as the wind buffeted the wires near the barn. "We're not out of the woods, not by a long shot." Savannah gazed out the kitchen window to the stallion barn and beyond. Her thoughts were with Travis and Josh...wherever they were.

TRAVIS STUDIED THE tracks in the snow again and cursed. Mystic's hoofprints had become less defined until they all but disappeared in a stand of birch near a frozen creek.

"Son of a bitch," he muttered to himself, dismounting and eyeing the ground more closely. After tying Jones to a tree, in order to keep the hoofprints from crossing, he slowly circled the area again. Keeping his eyes on the frozen earth and trying to imagine where the kid had decided to go, he walked carefully, oblivious to the icy wind that cut through his clothes.

The tracks had faded near the edge of Beaumont land. On the other side of the ridge the property belonged to the federal government, and Travis hoped that Josh hadn't been stupid enough to leave Beaumont property. Dealing with the government only meant more red tape and more time lost. "He couldn't have gotten over there," he told himself for the third time. "No gate, and Mystic is smarter than to attempt to hurdle a fence. At least I hope he is."

Frowning at the dim prints, he thought about the boy. By now Josh had to be scared out of his wits. "Where the hell are you?" Travis muttered, as if the boy could hear him.

Maybe Reginald and Wade had found Josh. Two hours ago, they had doubled back to the house, still looking for Josh. Lord, he hoped that the boy was already back at the farm. This was no weather for man or beast. The wind had picked up and the snow was falling in small, hard crystals, somewhere between sleet and hail. A nine-year-old kid wouldn't last long out here.

Travis rubbed the tired muscles of his back and thought about Savannah. He envisioned her beautiful face and intriguing blue eyes. Less than twelve hours before, she had been in his arms, naked, warm and filled with passion. She would be devastated if the boy wasn't found.

With a frown, Travis remounted and tried to pick up the trail again. "Josh!" he yelled, cupping his gloved hands over his mouth and listening as his voice echoed through the hills. "Josh!"

The only answer was the whistle of the wind. *Damn it all to hell,* he thought angrily and reined Jones in the direction that Mystic's hoofprints had taken. *If something's happened to Josh, Wade Benson is going to pay and pay dearly.* Travis's steel-gray eyes concentrated on the frozen earth and he tried once again to read the puzzle in the snow.

FOR SEVERAL HOURS Savannah tried to keep herself busy in the house. Fortunately, when Savannah had finally gotten through to Sadie Stinson and told her about Josh, the housekeeper had insisted on braving the elements and driving to the farm. Though Savannah had protested, the housekeeper hadn't been deterred. Now Savannah was glad that Sadie was in the house. Just the familiar sound of clattering pans and the warm scent of Irish stew filling the house relaxed her a bit.

"When that boy get's home, he'll be hungry," Sadie had said when she'd removed her coat and scarf and donned her favorite apron. "And the men, you can bet they'll expect something on the table!"

"You don't have to—"

"Hush, child, and do whatever it is you do around here," the housekeeper had said, shooing Savannah out of the kitchen with a good-natured grin. "And you, too," she'd ordered, when she had spotted Archimedes under the kitchen table. "The kitchen's no place for a sorry mutt like you." Then with a wink, Sadie had extracted a soup bone and handed it to the dog as she'd opened the door to the porch. Archimedes had slid through the portal with his treasure clamped firmly between his jaws.

"Now don't you worry, Savannah," Sadie had cautioned, when Savannah was almost out of the room. "Josh is a smart lad; he'll be all right. And Travis, you can count on that one. He'll find the boy and the horse."

Though Savannah knew the older woman's optimism was more of a show than anything else, she was grateful for the cheer. The gloom that had settled in the house was oppressive. She was glad for the familiar sight of Sadie's happy face and her constant off-tune whistling as she rattled around in the kitchen.

Savannah glanced outside and noticed that there was a slight break in the weather. *Maybe the storm is finally letting up,* she thought without much hope. The sky was still dark and foreboding, but at least the falling snow had eased. Deciding that it was now or never, she went to the barns and talked to the few hands left on the farm, instructing them to let the horses out of their stalls for a little exercise. "Just keep them in the paddocks close to the barns," she told one of the hands. "I want to give them all a chance to stretch their legs." She glanced up at the cloud-covered sky and frowned. "No telling when this will let up, and if it ices over the horses will be stuck inside."

And what about Josh? she wondered grimly.

Not daring to think about what was happening to the boy, she concentrated on the horses. Watching the yearlings as they came out of the barn made her smile. Most of the young horses had never seen snow before, and they pranced gingerly in the white powder as the stable boys walked them around the paddock. Savannah led a chestnut colt around the small fenced area, and nearly laughed when the sleek animal tried to shake the clinging white flakes from his eyelashes.

"Careful now," she cautioned, leading the frisky colt back to the barn as he tossed his head and pulled on the lead rope.

The sound of an engine splitting the silence caught Savannah's attention, and her heart squeezed in apprehension.

It had to be news of Josh and Travis, she thought, quickly instructing the stable hands to finish walking each of the horses as she sprinted over the snow-covered parking lot.

A silver Blazer was parked near the house. Savannah didn't recognize the vehicle, but it could belong to one of the neighbors. *Maybe someone had seen Josh!*

She nearly slipped as she climbed up the back steps. Quickly kicking off her boots and sliding into a pair of loafers she kept on the back porch, she hurried through the kitchen and down the hall following the sound of unfamiliar voices.

Her heart was in her throat by the time she rounded the corner by the staircase and walked into the living room. Charmaine was standing nervously near the fireplace, her thin face pale and drawn. She seemed relieved to see Savannah.

Two young men whom Savannah had never seen before were sitting on the couch. One of the men, the shorter blond man, had a camera. The taller man held a tape recorder in his hand.

Charmaine made hasty introductions. "This is John Herman and Ed Cook from the *Register*, Savannah." Both men stood, and John stretched out his hand. "My sister, Savannah Beaumont."

"How do you do?" Savannah responded automatically, her eyes narrowing as she shook the reporter's hand.

"Fine," the tall man replied with a grin. "And the pleasure's all mine, Miss Beaumont."

"They've heard about Mystic and Josh," Charmaine said, her voice barely above a whisper. She was leaning against the mantel for support.

"I don't think there's much we can tell you," Savannah admitted, offering what she hoped would appear a sincere smile. *What the devil was the press doing here and who had sent them?* "Not yet."

"But surely you can confirm the rumor that Mystic is missing," John suggested.

"That's true," Savannah stated, wondering why she felt so nervous. "He's been gone since sometime last night."

"And he was stolen—"

"He was not stolen," Charmaine interrupted. "It looks as if my son, Josh, took him for a ride."

John Herman arched his eyebrows skeptically. "In this storm?" Shaking his head as if he didn't believe a word she was telling him, he adjusted his recorder. "But you must be worried; otherwise you wouldn't have called the police."

"Sheriff's department."

"Yeah." He checked his notes and then looked straight at Savannah. "What's the real story?"

"That's about all there is to it."

"So where do you think your son would take a horse like that?" the reporter asked, turning to Charmaine.

"I have no idea."

"Was he running away?"

"No!" Charmaine said, the features of her white face pinching together angrily. She paced from the fireplace to the window, as if by staring into the dark afternoon she could bring Josh back.

"So who's out looking for him?" Herman asked.

"Some of the people here on the ranch. We've called the neighbors, of course, as well as the sheriff's office."

"Maybe we can help."

"How?"

"If you give us a picture of Josh, we'll run it in the paper. There's a chance that someone who's seen the kid will recognize his picture. As for the horse, we've got a lot of photos on file, don't we, Ed?"

Ed nodded. "Yeah, about thirty, I'd guess."

"Good."

John smiled crookedly. "It's a long shot, but worth it, don't you think?"

"Yes," Charmaine said. "I've got a picture of Josh— it's recent; his school picture. It's upstairs, I'll get it." Glad for an excuse to leave the room, and buoyed at the thought of another avenue to locate her son, Charmaine hurried up the stairs.

"I'd appreciate any help you can offer," Savannah said, relaxing a little.

"Good. Then maybe you can explain a few things."

"Such as?"

"Why is Travis McCord back here? This is where he grew up, right?"

Savannah's chest tightened. "He came to live with us when he was seventeen."

"And now he's back. There are a couple of rumors circulating about him."

Savannah felt cold inside and her eyes sparked angrily. "Are there?"

"People are claiming that he's dropping out of the race for governor."

"I didn't know that he'd even announced his candidacy," she replied stiffly, her fingers curling over the back of a velvet chair.

"He hadn't. Not officially. But there's some controversy there, too. A couple of people, especially one lady by the name of Eleanor Phillips, claimed they made contributions to his campaign."

"Even though he hadn't announced his candidacy?"

Savannah returned, her voice even, her heart cold with dread. "That doesn't sound too smart. Are you sure you have the story straight?"

The reporter slid her an uneasy smile. "I've got it straight, all right. But I sure would like a chance to interview Mr. McCord."

"He's not here right now."

"Then maybe you or someone else can tell us what the real story is. You know, why he came here from L.A. and threatened to give up practicing law as well as drop out of a primary that he might easily win."

"I can't even guess," Savannah lied. "And I wouldn't want to. What Travis McCord does with his life is his business."

"Here it is!" Charmaine announced, returning to the room and handing the man a picture of Josh. "I really appreciate the fact that you're trying to help," she said.

"No problem," the reporter replied, meeting Savannah's frosty stare. "And if you change your mind or have anything to add to the story…" He handed Savannah one of his business cards. "Tell McCord that I'll call him."

"I will," Savannah promised tightly as Charmaine escorted the two men out the front door. After the reporters were out of the house and Savannah saw the silver Blazer slide out of the driveway, she crumpled John Herman's card in her fist and threw it into the fireplace.

Charmaine paused in the archway of the living room before heading upstairs. "Do you think that running Josh's picture in the paper will help?"

"I don't know," Savannah said, "but it certainly couldn't hurt. Let's just hope by the time that the *Register* is on the stands, Josh and Mystic are home."

"Oh, God, yes," Charmaine whispered desperately.

"If he's not home by tonight…" She looked out the window to the darkening skies.

"He will be," Savannah promised, hearing the hollow sound of her own words.

LESTER AND THE stablehand arrived back at the house at nightfall to report that they hadn't seen hide nor hair of the horse or boy. As Lester checked on the horses, Savannah walked with him and explained about the events of the day at the house.

"Why didn't that blasted repairman show up to fix the security system?" Lester asked.

"Problems with the weather, or so he claimed when he called," Savannah replied.

"Just what we need. How's your mother takin' all this?" the grizzled trainer asked Savannah.

"Not well," she admitted. "Josh is pretty special to her."

"Ain't he to all of us?" the older man asked, and then scowled. "Except maybe for that dad of his. Y'know, I can't understand it, the way that man treats his kid. If I were Reginald, I'd—" He caught himself and the hard angles of his face slackened. "Well, I suppose your father knows what he's doing. Just because a man ain't much of a father doesn't mean he can't run the farm, and though I'd never have thought I'd admit it, Wade does a passable job."

"But not great. Right?"

Lester's jaw worked angrily. "Like I said, the man was an accountant, and a decent one, I guess. Just never thought he'd want to work with the horses, that's all."

He opened the door to the stallion barn and let out

a long sigh. "Why on earth did that boy take Mystic?" Lester wondered aloud.

"That's the sixty-four-dollar question," Savannah replied with a frown.

Lester slapped her affectionately on the shoulders. "Don't you worry about Josh. Travis will find him."

"I hope so," Savannah replied, close to tears again. She patted Vagabond's silken muzzle and stared at Mystic's empty stall. "I hope so."

An hour later Savannah was in the house, looking through the books of the farm and wondering what Travis had been checking into the night before. She never had been one to work with figures, and this day, while her mind was filled with worried thoughts, she couldn't concentrate on the balances. She slapped the checkbook closed and leaned back in her chair.

Just the night before she had slept in the protective circle of Travis's arms. Never had she felt more secure, more loved. And now he was searching the darkness for Josh.

She stood just as a distant rumble caught her attention. Recognizing the sound of her father's Jeep, her heart began to thud, and she grabbed her coat before racing through the kitchen and outside. It was late evening and the sky was dark, and in the distance she could hear the sound of the Jeep as it roared through the fields closer to the house.

Please God, let Josh be with them, Savannah silently prayed as she searched the night for the welcome beams of the vehicle.

Charmaine was standing on the back porch in an instant. "Oh, God," she whispered, just as the Jeep came into view.

"Oh, God. Is he with them?" Running out of the porch and down the slippery steps, she hurried to the garage.

Savannah was only a step behind her sister.

Reginald cut the engine and emerged from the truck. He looked exhausted. His weary eyes sought those of his elder daughter. "I guess this means that Josh hasn't shown up."

Charmaine nearly collapsed. "You didn't find him?" she asked, her face ghostly with anguish.

Wade got out of the passenger side of the Jeep and tried to place a comforting arm around his wife, but Charmaine backed away from him. Stiffening, he sent Savannah a silent glare. "Now I suppose you're blaming me," he said to his wife.

"I'm not blaming anyone," Charmaine whispered, her fists clenching as she pounded the fender of the Jeep. "I just want Josh home and safe!"

"What about Travis?" Savannah asked. Her heart was beating wildly with worry for her nephew as well as Travis. *Where were they and why hadn't Travis returned?*

Reginald just shook his head. "Last we saw of him, he'd had no luck. He was going to keep following the tracks as far as he could. We had to turn back when it seemed as if the horse had gone into a thicket of oak."

"I don't even think that was Mystic's trail," Wade said, pulling nervously on his moustache and looking scared. "The damned part of it is, Travis won't find him, not tonight. Those hoofprints were nearly invisible. Now that it's dark, searching any longer would be a waste of time. We'll have to call the police, ask for choppers in the morning."

"No!" Charmaine nearly screamed, shaking her head violently and impaling her husband with furious green eyes. "We've got to find him! Tonight! He'll freeze if he stays out there all night!"

Savannah couldn't help but agree. She was anxious to join the search herself. Travis and Joshua were somewhere in the wilderness, possibly hurt, and she couldn't wait through a long, lonely night just hoping that they would be safe in the morning. She kept her thoughts to herself and just told her father the important facts. "We talked to the sheriff's office earlier today," she said, once they were all walking back to the house.

"I think we'd better call again," Reginald thought aloud.

Once inside the house, Savannah called Deputy Smith and told him that the search party had returned without Josh or Mystic. Charmaine, trying to control herself, told Reginald and Wade about the reporters, the deputy, and the fact that Lester hadn't seen any sign of Josh.

"Where could he be?" Wade asked angrily, stalking to the bar in the living room and pouring himself a stiff drink.

"He's got to be somewhere on the farm," Reginald said.

"We searched every square inch of this place," Wade reminded him, tossing back his bourbon.

"Except where the Jeep couldn't go."

"The rest of it is up to McCord," Wade said, pouring himself another shot. "He and that horse will have to ride down the ravines and through the forests. Like I said, our only hope is police helicopters in the morning."

Savannah walked into the room and heard only the tail-end of the conversation, but she could see from the fear in Charmaine's wide eyes that nothing of consequence had been decided.

"I'd better go upstairs and talk to your mother," Reginald said, looking as if he dreaded the conversation. "How's she been?"

"Remote," Savannah admitted.

"Worried sick, I'll bet," Reginald muttered. "Well, hell, aren't we all?"

Sadie came into the living room and tried to liven up the crowd. "Dinner's on. Now, come on, all of you. We'll eat and make some plans about finding the boy. None of us can think on an empty stomach."

"I'm not hungry," Charmaine said, but Sadie only offered her a stern look.

"I've set the dining room table, including a place for Virginia. I think a hot meal would do all of us a world of good!" Sadie reprimanded.

After much cajoling on Sadie's part everyone sat down at the dinner table. The conversation was strained, and though the meal was superb, Savannah barely tasted it. Her thoughts were moving furiously forward, and she nearly jumped when she heard the grandfather clock chime nine o'clock, just as Sadie served an elegant lemon mousse.

Savannah spooned the light dessert into her mouth, but didn't taste it. She was too busy thinking ahead. If Travis didn't return within the hour, Savannah decided, she would go out and find him. Her father would be furious, of course, so she would have to leave the house behind his back and then argue with the security guard posted at the stables. But she couldn't stay cooped up in the house another minute. Come hell or high water, she intended to find Travis and Josh, and she intended to find them before morning!

CHAPTER EIGHT

AT ELEVEN O'CLOCK that night, Savannah was alone. The house was quiet as everyone had watched the ten-o'clock news and then gone to bed, but Savannah's thoughts were screaming inside her head.

Exhausted from the nerve-wracking day, she sat on the edge of her bed and considered trying to sleep, but she knew that despite her weariness she was too restless and worried. Her mind was turning in endless circles of anxiety about Josh and Travis.

Staring out the window, she silently cursed the snowfall then slapped her palm against the cool sill. She was tired of waiting, tired of worrying and had to do something before she went stark, raving mad!

With renewed determination, she walked to the closet, jerked on her warmest riding clothes and silently went downstairs. Once through the hallway she paused in the kitchen at the pantry and grabbed a box of matches, two flares and a flashlight from the small closet.

"What else will I need?" she asked herself and tapped her fingers on the open pantry door. "Lord only knows." With a frown she took a couple of candy bars and stuffed them into her jacket pocket. "So much for nutrition," she muttered wryly.

Going out in this weather is insane, she thought to herself as she pulled on her gloves and wound a scarf around her neck before slipping out the back door. The cold night air cut through her suede jacket as easily as a knife. *Travis will kill you if he catches you,* she cautioned herself, but kept walking, through the backyard, down the path past the garage and across the parking lot to the stables.

The wind whistled and howled through the trees, and the icy snow stung her cheeks, but she had her mind set. She had to find Travis and Josh and there was no time to waste. The news reports indicated that the storm wouldn't let up for several days. *It's now or never,* she thought as she marched through the snow.

"Wait a minute," a male voice called to her just as she reached for the handle on the door to the main stables. "What're you doing?" Johnny, one of the stable hands who had appointed himself security guard when he found out that Joshua and Mystic were missing, placed a hand on Savannah's shoulder. She whirled around to face him and saw the confusion cross his face in the darkness. "Miss Beaumont? What're you doing out here?"

"I'm going looking for Josh."

"Tonight? Are you crazy?"

"Maybe, but I can't stand being cooped up another minute."

The young man was obviously nervous. He dropped his hand from her shoulder and rubbed his jaw pensively. Johnny was used to taking orders from Savannah, but he couldn't believe that she actually planned to light out in the middle of a cold, wintry night like this one. "Reginald said that none of the horses were to leave the stables and no one was to go in."

"I know, Johnny, but Mattie is *my* mare."

Johnny's small eyes moved from Savannah to the

cold, dark night and the constantly falling snow. "I don't see that you can do any good out on a horse in the middle of all this," he said, gesturing helplessly at the frozen surroundings.

"As much good as I'll do if I stay in the house."

"Except that tomorrow morning we might have to send a search party after you."

"Tomorrow morning the storm is supposed to get worse."

"I don't know…"

"I'll be careful," she promised, reaching for the door.

"Really, Miss Beaumont—"

She offered him her most disarming smile. "You're off the hook with my dad. I'm taking full responsibility for my actions."

He was wavering, but didn't seem convinced. Savannah pushed a little harder.

"Look, I promise I'll stay on Beaumont land and if the storm gets any worse, I'll come right back. You know Mattie, she could find her way back to the barn in an earthquake."

"It's not the horse I'm worried about."

"Well, don't worry about me. I'm twenty-six. I can take care of myself, and I'll absolutely go out of my mind if I have to stay cooped up a minute longer."

The poor man looked caught between the proverbial rock and a hard place. "You're the boss," he finally admitted. "But I think I should tell Wade or Reginald."

"And worry them further?" she asked. "Because whether they like it or not, I'm going after Josh." Feeling less strong than her words, Savannah turned back to the door of the stables and walked inside the barn without any further protest from Johnny. *Maybe he will tell Reginald,* Savannah thought as she pulled down the saddle and placed it on Mattie's broad back. If Johnny went through with his threat, she'd deal with her father when Reginald came roaring out of the house.

The little bay mare snorted and stamped her foot at the interruption in her sleep and several other horses looked inquisitively at Savannah, their dark ears pricked forward expectantly.

"It's okay, girl," Savannah whispered, tightening the cinch and slipping a bridle over the nervous mare's head. "So far, so good."

Obviously Johnny had decided against waking Reginald with the news that his youngest daughter had her mind set on taking a cold ride through a snowstorm. Otherwise Reginald would already have come storming to the barn in a rage. *Thank God for small favors,* Savannah thought.

Leading the mare out the back door and through the series of paddocks surrounding the stables, Savannah braced herself against the rising wind. She walked Mattie past the stallion barn and heard the quiet whinny of one of the horses that had been awakened by the unusual noises in the night.

The snow all but covered the hoofprints that had been visible earlier in the day. Only the deep ruts of the Jeep remained in the crystalline powder, but even the double tire tracks were disappearing rapidly. Her lips tightening as she tried to read the trails in the soft snow, Savannah climbed into the saddle and pressed her heels into Mattie's warm flanks. "Let's go," she said encouragingly, then wondered if she was talking to herself or the mare.

Deciding to work on intuition rather than fact, Savannah ignored the direction of Mystic's tracks and headed the little mare to the lake. As Mattie slowly circled the dark water, Savannah scanned the darkness and called Josh's name.

No response.

Reining in the horse to a stop and straining to hear over the roar of the wind, she tried shouting again, but still there was no answer.

"Strike one," Savannah muttered to herself. With a deepening sense of dread, she circled the lake and skirted the center of the farm until she came to a field with an old apple tree and a tree house that Josh had constructed the previous summer.

Tying Mattie to the thick trunk of the tree, Savannah climbed up the makeshift ladder of loose boards nailed into the bark and trained the beam of her flashlight inside the rough structure. The interior of the tree house was deserted, snow covering the dirty floorboards as it slipped through the cracks in the roof.

Savannah directed the thin beam of light around the crude shack in the branches and then, from her perch in the doorway, moved the light to the snow-covered earth. Again there was no sign of the boy or his horse.

"Great," she muttered under her breath as she snapped off the flashlight. *This isn't getting us anywhere,* she thought with a sigh. How many times last summer had she had to track down Josh for dinner and found him in his favorite spot, hidden in the branches of the gnarled old apple tree? *But not tonight.*

As Savannah climbed down the ladder, untied Mattie and pulled herself into the saddle, another image crossed her mind. The picture in her mind was of herself as a seventeen-year-old girl, sitting upon a much younger Mattie under the umbrella of the protective apple tree while secretively watching Travis as he strung the wire over a broken fence.

Don't torture yourself, she reprimanded herself, but thoughts of Travis and Josh spurred her into action. She turned Mattie's head and urged the little mare toward the fields surrounding the stallion barn. Having checked all of Josh's favorite hiding spots, she decided to follow Mystic's almost nonexistent trail into the hills.

As long as the double ruts of Reginald's four-wheel-drive unit were still visible, Savannah was able to follow Mystic's path. The journey was long and cold, but she bent her head against the wind and kept riding, silently promising herself that if she ever saw Travis and Joshua again, she would never let them out of her sight.

Don't think like that, she thought angrily. *Be positive.* But the cold blast of the wind and the silence around her made the doubts in her mind loom like foreboding ghosts that couldn't be driven away.

TRAVIS SWORE UNDER his breath. *Not one damned sign of the boy!* Where the devil had he gone? Josh couldn't have vanished into thin air. Of course, there was the remote possibility that Josh had returned to the house, but Travis didn't think so. Reginald had promised to send off flares and fire a rifle shot three times in succession if the boy had been located. Neither signal had reached Travis and despite the fact that he distrusted Reginald's politics, Travis was certain the old man would be true to his word and let him know about Josh's safety.

Huddling against the wind, he scowled and considered stopping to build a fire. He was cold to the bone, his face raw from the bite of the frigid air, and Jones, game as the gelding was, needed a rest. Trudging through the snow with a two-hundred-pound man on his back had tired the horse.

"Well, let's see what we've got here," Travis said to himself. Dismounting, he let Jones drink a small amount of water from a near-frozen stream.

His eyes trained on the ground, Travis walked to the edge of the clearing, plowing through half a foot of snow. He stretched his legs and tired back muscles; it had been years since he'd spent so much time in the saddle, and his thighs and lower back were already beginning to ache and cramp.

To Travis, the rest of the night looked bleak. In the morning, he'd have no choice but to return to the farm. Both he and the horse would have to rest. Maybe the roads would be more passable and maybe in the light of a new day, the boy would be found.

The creases near the corners of his eyes deepened as he squinted through the darkened pines. A slight movement caught his eye and he focused all of his attention through the thick curtain of snow.

Nothing stirred. He wondered if he was beginning to imagine things in his desperation to find the child.

Where the hell was Josh? Travis had scoured every inch of Beaumont land and there had been no trace of the boy or the fiery black colt. When Travis had lost Mystic's tracks just before nightfall, he hadn't been able to find any clue as to Josh's whereabouts. He paled beneath his tan when he thought about what might have happened on the more rugged federal land that bordered the farm.

Was the boy lying unconscious somewhere with snow piling over him, or did the kid have enough sense to seek shelter for himself and his horse? The bitter thought that Josh might not be alive crossed his mind again. Travis's jaw hardened with renewed determination. The longer the boy was on his own in the wilderness, the slimmer were his chances of survival.

After walking back to his horse, Travis lifted his Stetson from his head, scratched his head and then replaced the hat. "Let's go," he muttered angrily as he swung into the saddle, lifted the reins and directed the horse across the slippery rocks of the stream before shouting Josh's name into the darkness.

Again he saw a movement through the trees. This time he didn't hesitate, but dug his heels into Jones's sides and took out after whatever was hiding in the shadows.

SAVANNAH'S TOES FELT as if they would fall off. Even though she was wearing riding gloves, her fingers were stiff. *Maybe Johnny was right,* she thought angrily. *Maybe riding out here was nothing more than a fiasco. If I'm not home by morning, Mom and Dad will be worried out of their minds!* Still, the idea of turning back stuck in her throat. At least she was trying to find Josh rather than lying in a warm bed hoping the boy was all right.

She bit at her lower lip as she studied the ground. For over an hour, since the point where the tire tracks had turned back in the direction of the house, she'd seen no sign of Josh or Travis. If there had been hoofprints in the snow, they had long been covered with the drifting white powder.

Travis. Had it only been last night that she had slept in the strength of his arms? It seemed like an eternity had passed without him. *God, where was he? Was he all right?*

Her voice was raw from shouting Josh's name over the whistle of the wind. Her own words echoed back to her unanswered and the silence filled her heart with dread. "Merry Christmas," she whispered sarcastically, tears from both the stinging wind and her tortured thoughts filling her eyes.

She shivered as she came to the clearing where she, Josh and Travis had cut down the Christmas tree only two days before. Urging Mattie forward, she ignored her pleasant memories of cutting the tree, the snowball fight, decorating the room and making love to Travis… It all seemed so long ago.

The storm continued to rage, and Savannah bent her head against the wind. Mattie was laboring through the drifts, and snow was falling so thickly that it was almost impossible to see.

Savannah was almost on the verge of giving up her search and starting back to the house when a slight movement in the surrounding trees caught her attention. Mattie shied and nickered nervously, and Savannah's skin crawled in fear before she recognized the big black colt.

"Mystic!" she cried, her heart leaping at the sight of him. "Josh?"

Then she froze as she realized Mystic's saddle was missing, and the reins to his bridle were loose and dragging on the ground. "Oh, Lord," she moaned, dismounting and tying an anxious Mattie to a scrub oak. "Josh! Josh, can you hear me?" *Please let him be all right.*

She approached the black colt cautiously, but Mystic sidestepped, rearing on unsteady hind legs and slashing in the air with his forelegs. He tossed his head menacingly and snorted. His dark eyes were wild looking;

rimmed in white from fear. As he reared he stumbled backward and let out an anguished squeal.

"It's all right, boy," Savannah whispered, knowing that the horse was more than frightened. It was obvious from Mystic's erratic behavior that he was in severe pain. She walked up to the colt confidently, hoping to instill some calm into the overwrought animal.

"Be careful!" a voice warned, and Savannah turned to see Travis, leading Jones, step out of the trees. Relief swept through her body at the sight of him. Both he and his horse looked past exhaustion.

"Thank God you're all right!" she whispered, running to Travis, throwing her arms around his neck and warming just at the feel of his arms around her. "I've been worried sick about you!" She couldn't help the tears of relief that pooled in her eyes as she clung to him and kissed his beard-roughened cheek. The smell and taste of him was wonderful, but the feeling of joy was short-lived. "Where's Josh?" she asked, when she felt the restraint in his embrace.

"I don't know," he said softly. "I haven't seen him."

Savannah's heart squeezed in fear. "But Mystic…"

Travis slowly released her and wearily rubbed the back of his forehead. "I know," he admitted, "I thought when I found the horse, I'd find the boy. But I didn't. And right now we've got to catch this one and calm him down." He fixed his eyes on the skittish colt while he tied Jones to a branch of a tree next to Mattie. "And you be careful around him," Travis warned Savannah, keeping his voice low and calm. "He's hurt and scared out of his wits. I've been following him for about a couple of hundred yards. There's something wrong with his right foreleg."

"No—"

"Shh..." Travis continued to advance slowly on the nervous horse. "Steady, boy," he whispered, slowly extending his hand toward Mystic's head.

The frightened animal bolted out of the clearing. "Son of a bitch," Travis muttered. "This is what happened when I came across him a couple of hours ago, but he can't go far..." Travis trained the beam of the flashlight onto the snow, displaying Mystic's tracks as well as bloody splotches where the colt had stood.

"Oh, God," Savannah moaned. "What do you think happened? Where's Josh?"

"I wish I knew," Travis replied, starting out after the horse. "Come on. Let's go."

Slowly, with the quiet determination and ruthlessness of a predator stalking prey, Travis followed the colt. Mystic was standing under a naked maple tree, his ebony coat wet with sweat, his glistening muscles shivering with apprehension. Wild-eyed and ready to bolt, he watched Savannah and Travis as they approached.

"It's all right," Savannah said to the horse.

The colt moaned, tried to rear and finally stood still as Travis, moving with quiet deliberation, took hold of the bridle and wrapped the reins firmly around his right hand.

"Oh, no," Savannah whispered, coming close to the horse and seeing the frozen lather clinging to the big colt's body. She held her breath while Travis ran experienced hands down Mystic's shoulders and legs.

When Travis's fingers touched a sensitive spot on Mystic's foreleg, Mystic reared and jerked his black head upward with such force that the movement nearly wrenched Travis's right arm out of its socket.

"Whoa," Travis ordered, wincing and forcing the colt's head back down in order to continue his examination. "Damn!" He felt the distinctive bump near Mystic's ankle when his fingers touched the horse's foreleg and Mystic tried to rear again.

"What?"

Travis sighed and shook his head. "I think it's broken. The leg's swollen and he's favoring it. When I touch the area over his sesamoid bones, he nearly jumps out of his skin."

Travis tied Mystic's reins to the nearby tree, then trained the beam of his flashlight on the wound. Savannah felt her stomach turn over at the sight of the bloodied gash. She examined Mystic's leg and swallowed back the urge to scream in frustration. "Maybe it's just sprained," she whispered hopefully.

"Maybe." Travis didn't sound convinced.

"So, what now?"

Travis's jaw hardened and his eyes flashed with determination when he turned them upon her. "First we find a way to get him back to the barn, then we find Josh, and then maybe you could give me a quick explanation as to why you're out here."

"There's no time right now," she hedged, eyeing Mystic.

Travis studied the big black colt and sighed when he realized that she was right. They had to work fast to avoid injuring the horse any further. And then there was Josh to find… "Okay, you win. For now. But when this is all over, you can bet your hide that I'll want an explanation from you and it had better be good."

"It will be," she said frostily, then turned her attention back to the horse. "I don't think he should walk any farther than absolutely necessary."

"Agreed." Travis ran a hand over his stubbled chin. "If you ride Mattie, it will only take an hour, maybe less, to cut through the fields and get back to the house." Travis studied the big colt with a practiced eye. "I'll stay here with him until you can get Lester or Reginald to drive the truck up the federal road... I think it cuts through the land on the other side of the fence, about four hundred yards north."

"It does."

"Then bring wire cutters. We'll have to cut open the fence to get Mystic through."

Savannah hesitated. "I don't want to leave you."

Travis managed a weary, but rakish smile. "Just for a little longer," he promised, "until we can get the horse back to the farm. Oh, and call the vet."

"I will."

"And bring up a fresh horse and a couple of rugs for these two." He motioned toward Mystic and Jones.

"Why the extra horse?" she asked, dreading the answer.

"Jones is tired."

"And you want to keep looking for Josh?" she surmised, not knowing whether to feel glad or worried.

"I found the horse, didn't I? The boy couldn't be far away."

"Only miles," she speculated.

"Not if he fell off when Mystic hurt his leg. I can't believe that Mystic would try to travel that far when he was in as much pain as I think he feels. Anyway, let's hope not, for Josh's sake."

There was logic to Travis's thoughts and for the first

time that night, Savannah felt a glimmer of hope that they would be able to find Josh and bring him home. *Unless he was dead,* she thought, her heart fluttering with panic.

"Don't think like that," Travis said, his gray eyes delving into hers as he seemed to read her morbid thoughts. "We'll find him and he'll be all right."

"Oh, God, I hope so."

Travis's arms surrounded her. "Come on," he urged, pressing his cold lips to her forehead and hugging her fiercely. "Don't lose the faith; not now. Josh, Mystic and I are counting on you."

"Okay," Savannah whispered, then sniffed, pushing her worries aside and bracing herself for what promised to be a long, tiring night.

"I knew I could count on you," Travis said, slowly releasing her.

She mounted Mattie reluctantly, unable to tear herself away from Travis. There was something in the cold night air that seemed to warn her that leaving him would cause certain disaster.

Travis noticed her hesitation and he looked up and forced a tired smile. "Buck up, will ya? It's only a little while longer," he whispered, reaching up and stroking her trembling chin with his gloved hand. "And then it will be over."

"And Josh?"

"I'll find him," Travis promised, hoping that he sounded more sure of himself than he felt. "I won't give up until I do."

His fingers wrapped around the nape of her neck, and he pulled her head slowly downward until his lips brushed hers. "Don't you know there's nothing that can keep me away from you?"

Savannah's raw throat went dry. "I hope so," she whispered as he kissed her chilled lips, and she realized how desperately she loved him. Her heart seemed to bleed at the prospect of leaving him.

"Now, go on. Get out of here," he commanded, once the kiss had ended. He squared his shoulders and looked directly into her eyes. "You'd better hustle because I'm going to give you about a forty-minute head start and then I'm going to fire rifle shots into the air. That should wake everyone up at the house. Then I'll send up my flares. By that time, you should be getting back and everyone will be ready to go. Have Lester bring the truck with the fresh horse."

"And the wire cutters."

"Right."

"I'll throw in a thermos of coffee and a sandwich," she said, and then as a sudden thought struck her, she dug into her pockets for the candy bars. "It's not much, but here." She tossed him the snack.

Travis smiled and caught the candy. "You're an angel of mercy."

"I doubt it," she said, her eyes scanning the darkened landscape as she thought about Travis staying up there alone. "Do you really think that staying out here tonight looking for Josh will do any good?"

Travis stared straight into her eyes, his face suddenly solemn. "I don't think I have any choice. Do you?"

"No, I guess not," she admitted, gazing longingly into his eyes before reining Mattie toward the farm.

Travis watched her leave the clearing before striding through the snow to Jones, taking off the horse's saddle and blanket and placing the blanket over Mystic's quivering shoulders.

"I don't know how much good this will do, old boy, but it's better than nothing." He patted Mystic and then walked back to Jones and frowned, rubbing the gelding's neck. "Hardly seems fair, does it? Unfortunately, that's the way life is."

SAVANNAH RELUCTANTLY LEFT TRAVIS, calling Josh's name as she started back to the farm. She listened but heard nothing other than the steady crunch of Mattie's hooves in the snow. The wind whipped at her face and pushed her hair away from her neck while her thoughts lingered on Travis standing guard over Mystic.

"Josh," she screamed again, cupping her gloved hands to her mouth. "Josh! Where are you?" There was no response other than the rustle of the wind through brittle leaves and the mournful cry of a winter bird disturbed from his sleep. *"Dear Lord, let me find him,"* she whispered to herself. Where was he? Was he still alive, or lying half-frozen somewhere nearby?

Mattie came to an unexpected halt and sidestepped.

Savannah's eyes pierced the darkness, but she saw nothing. Knowing it was futile, she called one last time to Josh and waited for a response.

Somewhere in the distance, she heard a faint reply, a small groan in the darkness. Savannah's heart skipped a beat, and she told herself that she was probably just imagining what she'd heard. As loudly as possible, she called again. Not daring to breathe, she waited. This time the reply was more distinct.

Her heart in her throat, she urged Mattie forward, following the sound of Josh's voice and calling to him continually. "I'm coming," she yelled over the shriek of the wind, praying silently that Josh could hear her. To her relief, she saw Travis riding Jones through the trees.

"I heard you," he said, "I would have been here sooner but I had to resaddle old Jones here." Then he shouted Josh's name as loudly as possible.

The boy's groans sounded closer.

"He's alive," Savannah whispered, tears of relief threatening her eyes as Mattie plowed through the snow until they came to the edge of a steep ridge and they could ride no farther. "Josh, where are you?" she called, her voice echoing in the snow-drifted canyon.

"Here…help me…" The boy's feeble voice came from somewhere below.

"I'm here, Josh," Savannah replied, nearly jumping off Mattie and racing to the edge of the ravine. *Oh, God, it was so dark and so far down.* She could barely make out Josh's inert form in the snow. "We'll get you out of there in no time," she said, with more conviction than she felt. "You just hang in there."

Travis was at her side, his narrowed eyes surveying the snow for the quickest path to the boy. "I think I'd better handle this," he said.

"But he needs me," she protested.

"And how're you going to carry him?" Without waiting for her response, he took a rope from his saddle bag and anchored it around the trunk of a sturdy pine.

"Let me go after him," she pleaded.

"Just this once, Savannah, do as you're told, okay? If I need help, I'll yell, but the last thing I need is to have you get yourself hurt trying to help the boy. Now, I don't have time to argue with you."

Gritting her teeth, Savannah backed down. "Just get him up here."

"I will."

After securing the other end of the rope around his waist, Travis carefully picked his way down the steep hillside. Savannah watched from the top of the ridge.

The boy was huddled under the relative protection of a small pine tree. "How're ya doin'?" Travis asked, once he was near enough to talk to Josh.

Josh didn't answer. His teeth were chattering, and he was shaking from head to foot.

"Come on, let's check you out and see if I can carry you out of here." Carefully Travis examined the boy, feeling for any broken bones. "I know this is going to hurt, Josh, but we've got to get you home. Can you make it?"

Josh nodded weakly, but he didn't attempt to stand.

Travis threw his coat over the boy and gently lifted him from the hard ground. He considered his options. Either he could take the boy out of there now, or wait until Savannah went for help. But that could take hours. "Look, Josh, I'm going to try and carry you out of here. Do you think you can make it?"

"Don't know," the boy admitted, and groaned as Travis shifted his weight.

"It won't be long now," Travis encouraged, starting up the steep hillside, the boy pressed to his chest.

Savannah watched as Travis slowly climbed up the snow-covered incline. It seemed to take hours. He slipped twice and she gasped as she watched him fall, then regain his footing, until he finally made it to the top of the ridge.

"Oh, Josh," she whispered, kissing the boy on the

head and crying softly. "Thank God you're alive." Tears were streaming down her face as she touched Josh's cold skin. "He's freezing."

"We've got to get him back, but I don't think he can ride alone, and Jones is too worn out to carry two of us. Can you hold him in the saddle with you?"

"Of course."

"Good." After Savannah mounted Mattie, Travis helped Josh into the saddle.

"Where's Mystic?" Josh asked faintly once they were moving. He was pressed against her body, quivering from pain.

"I've got him tied; we'll send a truck for him when we get down the hill," Travis assured the boy.

"Shh. Don't worry about Mystic," Savannah said, her voice soothing as she helped hold Josh in the saddle. "We'll get him home. You just take care of yourself."

The journey back to the house seemed to take forever. Savannah's arms ached from the strain of holding Josh while trying to balance on Mattie. Josh didn't talk, but only groaned during the ride.

Savannah could hardly take her eyes off Josh, and she held him until she thought her arms might break. By the time the buildings of the farm came into view, the first streaks of dawn were lighting the sky, and Savannah recognized Lester's pickup in the parking lot.

They had barely gotten into the paddock near the stables when Lester spotted them. His grizzled face spread into a wide grin, and he told Johnny to wake everyone in the house to let them know that Josh had been found.

"You're a sight for sore eyes, child," Lester said to Josh as he and Travis carefully got the boy out of the saddle.

Charmaine and Wade met the ragged party just as they approached the house. Charmaine was dressed in her nightgown, bathrobe and boots. "Josh," she called, tears streaming down her face. "Oh, honey, are you all right? Let me look at you."

"I think I'd better take him inside," Travis said.

"No. Give him to me." She took the boy in her arms and held him tightly to her breast before raising tear-filled eyes to Travis. "Thank God you found him!"

"You'd better call an ambulance," Travis replied. "He's hurt and nearly frozen."

"Oh, baby," Charmaine whispered, turning to the house. Josh clung to his mother as if to life itself. Charmaine was sobbing and Savannah felt her own tears tightening her throat.

"Let's get him inside," Wade suggested, unable to do anything other than appear worried. "What the devil were you doing out there?" he asked Savannah, but she didn't bother to respond.

"What about Mystic?" Lester asked.

"We've got to go back to get him," Travis said, watching as Charmaine walked through the back door with Josh. "He's hurt and it looks bad. Right foreleg, probably his ankle."

Lester scowled. "I'll get the truck." He was off in a minute.

Travis turned to Savannah. His countenance was grave, his silvery eyes narrowed with worry and shadowed from lack of sleep. "I've got to go back for the horse, but you take care of Josh. Make sure an ambulance is on the way, and don't forget to call the vet."

"I won't," she said, running to the house.

Slipping her boots off on the back porch, she entered

the kitchen and smiled at the sight of Archimedes under the table. "Sadie will skin you alive if she catches you," she murmured to the dog, who responded with a sigh.

The warmth of the house made her skin tingle, and she jerked off her gloves with her teeth and set them on the counter.

Rubbing her hands together, she walked through the kitchen and down the short hallway to the den. Wade was just hanging up the phone.

"Ambulance?" she asked.

"It's on its way."

"Good. What about Josh?"

Wade frowned. His blond hair was stringing over his eyes and his skin was white with worry. "Charmaine's got him upstairs in his room. He...he doesn't look all that good," Wade said nervously.

"He was thrown from a horse, fell down a mountainside and spent over twenty-four hours outside in a snowstorm the likes of which we hardly ever get around here. He probably feels terrible!"

"I hope he'll be all right."

Savannah's eyes narrowed on her brother-in-law, and all of her anger and frustration exploded. "He'd be a lot more 'all right' if you'd treated him like your son, like you care about him, instead of acting like he's just one big bother!"

"I try—"

"Bull!"

"I don't relate to children very well."

"He's your son, dammit. Don't give me any excuses, Wade, or college buzzwords like 'relate.' Just give the kid a chance; that's all he wants. The bottom line is he needs your love!"

"I know, I know," Wade admitted, his fingers rubbing anxiously together. "But I can't help it if he gets on my nerves."

"My God, you almost lost a child and all you can say is that he gets on your nerves. That's disgusting, Wade. Think of what he's been through! Maybe it's time you showed him some compassion!" Savannah's cheeks were flushed, and she didn't bother to hide the rage and loathing she felt for her brother-in-law.

Wade paled slightly but didn't move. He had no response to her outburst. "God, Savannah, this is no time to get angry. What about Mystic? Where is he?"

"Still on the mountain. Travis and Lester are going to get him." She turned away from Wade in disgust, grabbed the telephone receiver and punched out the number of the local veterinarian, Steve Anderson. When he answered, Savannah explained about Mystic's condition and the vet assured her that he'd be over as quickly as possible, considering the conditions of the roads.

Just as she hung up, Reginald entered the room. He looked as if he hadn't slept all night. "What's this I hear about you taking off last night?" he asked.

"I couldn't sleep."

Reginald paled and ran his fingers over his head. "I was just up in Josh's room with Charmaine. That boy's been through hell and back. And you, taking off in that storm; that was a foolish thing to do. Good Lord, Savannah, we could have lost you, too!"

She shook her head and waved off her father's fears. "But you didn't and Josh is safe."

"Thank God. I think I need a drink."

"Me, too," Wade agreed, starting for the liquor cabinet.

"Why aren't you with your son?" Reginald demanded.

Stopping dead in his tracks, Wade turned to face his father-in-law. "I just got through calling the ambulance."

"Hmph."

Wade's back stiffened. "I'm as worried as you are about Josh, but I thought it would be better if he spent a little time alone with his mother."

Savannah didn't want to hear any of Wade's feeble excuses. She sighed and faced Reginald. "Travis and Lester are going to get Mystic."

"I'll go with them," Reginald decided.

"You should know something first," she said quietly. "Mystic's injured, Dad."

Reginald went ashen at the grim expression on her features. "Seriously?"

"I don't know, but it's his foreleg, around the ankle… well, you can judge for yourself. I've already called the vet."

"The horse will be all right," Wade said, looking to Savannah for support.

"I hope so," she replied, before walking toward the foyer. "I want to see Josh before the ambulance gets here."

"And you'll look after your mother, won't you?" Reginald asked, as he walked into the foyer, grabbed his coat from the closet and placed a warm cap on his head. "She's been worried sick about the boy."

"Of course."

"Tell Josh that I'll be up in a minute," Wade said, following Reginald. "I just want to see that they've got enough men to get the horse."

"Sure," Savannah said with a weary sigh. *Put your kid last again,* she thought as she hurried up the stairs to Josh's room. He was lying in bed, Charmaine huddling over him.

"How're ya feelin', sport?" Savannah asked.

Josh tried to smile, but couldn't.

Savannah's heart wrenched for the child. "The ambulance will be here in a minute. They'll fix you up, good as new. I promise."

Josh's worried brows drew together and when he spoke his voice was only a rough whisper. "What about Mystic?"

"Grandpa and Travis are going to get him right now," Savannah said. "Now don't think about him, you just take care of yourself, okay?"

Josh turned away from her and closed his eyes, letting exhaustion carry him away.

Am ambulance arrived a little later, and two attendants put Josh on a stretcher before carrying him downstairs. Savannah watched as Wade nervously paced the foyer between the den and the living room.

"Aunt Savvy?" Josh whispered to her as the attendants stopped in the hallway.

She walked over to the stretcher and took hold of the boy's hand. "What is it?"

"Will you come with me?"

"Of course I will," she answered, but Wade held up his hands in protest.

"No dice, Savannah," he whispered loudly. "I want you to leave Josh alone. If you hadn't encouraged him to ride that horse in the first place, we wouldn't be in this position, would we?"

"Dad—"

Savannah gave Josh a silent glance that warned him to be quiet. "I only want what's best for Josh."

"Please," the boy begged, his voice cracking. "Come with me."

Swallowing back the urge to cry, Savannah looked at Josh's drawn face and shook her head. "I'll come visit you later, but right now I think I'd better made sure the vet gets here to check on Mystic."

"Is he hurt?"

"We don't know, but he's had a pretty wild twenty-four hours. I promise to let you know how he is, okay?"

"Okay," Josh replied with obvious effort, wincing at a stab of pain.

"Good. And the minute you get home, we'll have Christmas."

"But Christmas is tomorrow."

"We'll wait for you," Savannah said.

"Promise?"

"Promise!"

She let go of Josh's hand and fought her tears.

"We'll be at the hospital," Charmaine told Savannah as she came hurrying down the stairs with an overnight bag. "I'm riding with Josh, and Wade will bring the car."

"Not alone, he won't," Virginia stated from the top of the stairs. She was dressed and holding on to the banister as she slowly descended. "I'm coming, too."

"You don't have to be there," Charmaine said.

"I know I don't, but Josh is my grandson and I intend to be at the hospital with him."

"Lady?" One of the attendants prodded Charmaine.

"I'm coming," Charmaine replied. "You two fight this out," she said to Wade and Virginia, as she followed the attendants outside and shut the door behind her.

"There isn't going to be a fight and that's that," Virginia stated evenly.

"Mom?" Savannah asked, but saw the look of defiance in Virginia's proud stare.

"Are you sure you're up to this?" Wade asked skeptically. "I think you should rest—"

"I'm going to the hospital. I think this is a good chance for you and me to have a little talk about your relationship with Josh."

"I don't think—"

"That we have much time," Virginia finished for him. "Let's go."

"All right," Wade said tightly, but turned his eyes to Savannah. "I want you to call me when the vet examines Mystic."

"And I'll expect the same from you when the doctor checks Josh."

Wearing a pained expression, Wade walked briskly out the door after Virginia, leaving Savannah to wait for news of Mystic.

TRAVIS AND LESTER returned within the hour.

Steve Anderson, the local veterinarian for the farm, was already waiting in the office over the stables when the big truck slowly drove into the stable yard.

"Well, let's see how bad it is," the vet said, getting up from the table and setting down his coffee cup. He and Savannah quickly put on their jackets before going outside to meet the truck.

Travis was the first man out of the cab, and from the expression on his face, Savannah guessed that returning Mystic to the farm had been more difficult than expected. The strain was obvious in his eyes.

"It doesn't look good," Travis admitted, placing a strong arm around Savannah's shoulders for support.

"Lester agrees with me; he thinks Mystic's broken his sesamoids."

"Maybe not," Savannah said hopefully, but grim lines deepened beside Travis's mouth.

Lester and Reginald had opened the back of the truck and were attempting to lead Mystic outside.

The horse was in a state of shock. Wild-eyed and flailing his hooves at anything that moved, Mystic tried to bolt when the veterinarian bent to look at him.

"I think he's broken his leg, sesamoid bones," Lester said as Steve tried to examine Mystic's ankle. The vet frowned at the sight of the frenzied animal's wound.

"Maybe." He shook his head and worked to place an inflatable cast on Mystic's leg, but the frightened colt tried to thwart all Steve's attempts to help him.

Savannah felt her insides shred at the sight of Mystic. Unless the veterinarian was able to calm him, the horse would be his own worst enemy and wouldn't survive the effects of the anesthesia.

"We'd better take him right to the hospital," Steve thought out loud. "I'll need X-rays and I'll probably have to perform surgery—unless we get lucky."

"He's not stable enough for surgery," Savannah said.

Steve nodded. "I'll sedate him and maybe we'll get lucky and nothing'll be broken. But I think that's being optimistic. It looks like Lester is right."

Savannah felt herself slump, but Travis's arms tightened around her shoulders.

"We'd better get moving," Steve said.

"Then let's do it," Reginald replied, looking at the agonized colt and shaking his head. "Travis, can you drive the truck?"

With a frown, Travis nodded. "Sure."

"I'm coming, too," Savannah said firmly. "This time you're not leaving me here alone."

"Don't you think you'd better get some rest?" Travis asked.

"No."

"You have to stay here," Reginald pointed out.

"Why?"

"Don't ask foolish questions," her father said irritably. "You need your rest."

"I'm fine!"

Reginald's face flushed with anger. "Okay, so you played the heroine and helped find Josh; now let it lie. You're needed here. Think about it. What if Charmaine calls about Josh? He's not exactly out of the woods yet, you know. Won't you want to take the message?"

Savannah looked helplessly from her father to Travis and then to Mystic as Lester led him back into the truck. "I suppose so," she agreed reluctantly. "But this has shades of a conspiracy, you know."

"Nothing all that sinister," her father assured her. "I just need someone I can depend upon to stay here and look after things. As soon as we know Mystic's condition, we'll call."

Steve was already walking to his van. Reginald and Lester had climbed into the cab of the truck.

Travis looked dead tired and his eyes held hers in silent promise. "I'll be back," he promised, "and soon."

She forced a weary smile and caressed the stubble on his chin. "I'll be waiting."

Managing a smile he said, "That makes it all worthwhile, you know." Then, as if to make up for lost time, he climbed into the truck, started the engine and drove out of the frozen stable yard to follow the path of Steve Anderson's van.

Savannah watched as the truck rumbled out the drive, and she felt more alone than she had in years. Josh was on his way to the hospital with the rest of the family, Travis and Lester were taking Mystic to a fate she didn't want to think about and she was left with the responsibility of the farm.

Shivering, she walked back to the house and let Archimedes inside for what little company he could provide. "Well," she said, making a cup of hot chocolate, "I guess all we have left to do is wait."

Looking out at the early-morning light she shook her head sadly and silently wished for the strength of Travis's arms.

CHAPTER NINE

TIME HAD NEVER moved so slowly for Savannah as she waited for word on Josh and Mystic. It was nearly dark when the phone finally rang. Savannah answered and heard the exhaustion in Charmaine's voice.

"Josh will be all right," Charmaine assured her.

Savannah sank against the wall of the kitchen in relief. "Thank God!"

"But he has to stay here a few days. He's got a broken collarbone and several fractured ribs, as well as a lot of cuts and bruises. Fortunately there's no evidence of internal bleeding or damage to any of his organs. He should be out of the hospital in two or three days."

"I'm just glad it wasn't any worse," Savannah said.

"My sentiments exactly." Charmaine hesitated and then sighed. "So...have you heard anything about Mystic? Josh keeps asking about that damned creature."

Savannah winced at Charmaine's harsh words, but managed to hold her tongue. Charmaine was under a lot of strain. "There's nothing to tell him yet. The vet was here and he took Mystic to the equine hospital near Sacramento. Everyone, including Steve, seems to think that Mystic may have broken the sesamoid bone in his right foreleg."

There was a pause at the other end of the line and Charmaine sighed. "What bone? I think you'd better talk in layman's terms, okay? Even though I've lived on the farm all these years, I've tried to avoid most of the talk about horses—especially when it came to anatomy," she admitted. "How serious is it?"

"Serious."

"I see," Charmaine whispered. "But he will pull through, be all right even if he can't race again, right?"

"I don't really know. Lots of horses do," Savannah thought aloud. "It all depends upon the horse, his mental condition at the time of the surgery, the skill of the vet and luck, I guess. The problem is that Mystic's temperament is against him and he was overwrought before the surgery. That's not good."

"But surely they can save him," Charmaine persisted.

"I hope so, for all our sakes," Savannah said, knowing that if Mystic didn't survive, Josh would be devastated with guilt.

"I guess we can only hope for the best. Look, I'll call you if our plans change," Charmaine said. "But at least for tonight, Wade and I are staying in town."

"How's Wade taking it?" Savannah asked.

"Not too good. Josh admitted that he took the horse because he was angry with his father. He also said that he had intended on running away. And, oh, that's how the security wire broke. Josh was using a key he had 'borrowed' from his father one morning when he wanted to see Mystic, and the wire snapped."

Savannah let out a weary sigh. Josh had managed to dig himself into a deeper and deeper hole of trouble.

"And now Josh is petrified that Wade will punish him—not let him see Mystic again. It's a horrible mess."

"Is there anything I can do?"

"Not now."

"I'll call Josh in the morning, when he's feeling better," Savannah said.

"He'd love it."

"How's Mom doing?" Savannah asked.

"Fine. She's staying here with us."

Savannah thought about her mother's frail health. Worrying about Josh and Mystic wouldn't help Virginia's condition. "How's she taking all this?"

"Like a trooper. Hard to believe, isn't it?" Charmaine replied, and then she rattled off the name and number of the hotel in which she and Wade were staying. "Call me if you hear anything about Mystic."

"I will," Savannah promised. "And give Josh my love."

After hanging up the phone, Savannah glanced at the clock. Four-thirty. She'd spent the past six hours making sure that all the horses were comfortable and cared for, especially Mattie and Jones, and that the stalls had been cleaned, the water was running and the heat was working.

Exhaustion had finally taken its toll on her. Even a quick snack of cheese and crackers didn't give her the energy to stay on her feet.

Worried about Mystic and Josh, she went upstairs, took a long, hot shower and then tumbled into bed and fell asleep just after her head hit the pillow.

WHEN SAVANNAH AWOKE it was completely dark. A glance at the bedside clock told her that another four hours had passed. Still tired, she forced herself out of bed and was about to call the veterinarian's number when she heard the sound of familiar voices drifting up the stairs. Travis's low voice made her heart leap expectantly. *He's home! Maybe Mystic was already in the stallion barn!*

Shoving her arms through the sleeves of her robe, Savannah hurried down the stairs, through the hall and into the kitchen, where Travis and Lester were talking. Both men looked as if they hadn't slept for over a week.

Travis was sitting on the counter, his long legs dangling down the cupboards, his elbows supported by his knees. The lines of strain on his rugged face had become deep grooves and his gray eyes had lost their spark. His wrinkled shirt was stretched tautly over his broad shoulders, which were slumped in defeat, and his jaw was dark with his unshaven beard. All in all he looked completely worn out.

Lester, too, appeared fatigued. The wiry little trainer seemed bent with age as he sat at the kitchen table slowly sipping coffee and smoking a cigarette. His eyelids folded over disenchanted dark eyes and his cheeks were hollow. Gray smoke curled lazily to the ceiling.

Instinctively, Savannah prepared herself for the worst.

"How's Mystic?" she asked without preamble as she walked over to Travis and stood next to him.

The men exchanged worried glances and then Travis looked at her with pained gray eyes. "He's gone," he said. "Never had a chance." With a sound of disgust, he lowered himself from the counter and angrily tossed the dregs of his coffee into the sink.

"Gone?" she echoed blankly but she knew exactly what he meant. Steadying herself against the refrigerator she fought the dryness in her throat. "Oh, no..."

Lester stared into the black liquid in his cup. "Your father had him put down, missy. It was the only thing to do." Taking a drag from his cigarette, he blew out the smoke and then crushed the cigarette out in disgust.

"But why?" she asked, slowly sinking into one of the chairs at the table and staring at the little old trainer.

"It wasn't anyone's fault, and Steve, he tried his damnedest to save Mystic's leg," Lester said, rubbing his chin and fishing into his jacket pocket for another crumpled pack. "I thought he'd do it, too, but…" The old man shook his head and lit up again, blowing smoke through his nose. "Mystic, he just couldn't handle it."

"What happened?" she asked, though it really didn't matter. Mystic was dead and that was that. But the thought of the proud black colt brought tears to her eyes. Mystic had been the finest horse ever bred at Beaumont farms. A hellion, yes, but also a gallant Thoroughbred with the speed and endurance of the best. Savannah had to clear her throat against a painful lump that blocked her voice.

Travis stretched his shoulders and rubbed his hands over his dark chin. "The way I understand it, the operation on his ankle was a success. After Mystic had been sedated, Steve had been able to clean the wound, remove some of the bone chips, repair the torn ligaments, set the bones and put a cast on the leg."

"Then what went wrong?" Savannah asked, but knowing Mystic's high-strung temperament, she had already guessed the answer.

"Mystic was in a frenzy when he came out of the anesthesia," Lester explained, drawing on his cigarette and staring through the window into the black night. "We couldn't control him."

"He was frantic, kicking and rearing. No one could hold him down. He managed to kick off his special shoe as well as his cast and he even landed a blow on Lester's thigh."

Lester just shook his head and stared blankly through the window.

"So couldn't Steve have set the leg again, put him in a sling? They do wonderful things these days."

"Maybe," Lester admitted, "but your dad, well, he did the most humane thing possible. The horse was out of his mind as it was; more anesthesia and surgery would have been too traumatic for him. It was doubtful if he would have survived a second operation. It's a shame," Lester said softly. "A goddamned shame."

Fighting the constriction in her chest Savannah stared at her hands. "So what about Josh? What're we going to tell him?"

"I don't know," Travis said. "Your father went straight from the equine hospital to Mercy hospital, where Josh is, but I don't think he's going to tell the boy about Mystic until Josh is on the mend."

"Do you...do you think that lying to him is a good idea?"

Travis took the chair next to her and took hold of her hands. "I wish I knew. I've been asking myself a lot of questions today, and I haven't had much luck finding any answers."

"Well," Savannah said, taking in a steadying breath and telling herself not to grieve for the big, black colt. At least Mystic was out of pain and there was nothing she or anyone else could do for him now. And Josh was going to be well. She explained about Charmaine's phone call to both Lester and Travis. As she told the men of Josh's condition and prognosis, both Travis and Lester relaxed a little. "Now, how about something to eat?" she asked, forcing false cheer into her voice. "I made some soup earlier."

"Not for me, thanks," Lester said, stubbing his cigarette in an ashtray on the counter. "It's been a long day. I think I'll go home."

"You're sure?"

"As sure as I am about anything, missy." He reached for his hat, which was sitting on the corner of the table, pushed it onto his head and walked out the back door. A few minutes later his pickup rumbled down the drive toward the main road.

"What about you?"

"I'm starved," Travis admitted, gazing affectionately at her. But his gray eyes were clouded with a silent agony. "I just hope I don't have to go through another day like this one," he admitted, stretching his tired back muscles. "There just wasn't a damned thing anyone could do to help the horse."

"Then it's over."

"Except for Josh."

"Except for Josh," she repeated hoarsely. "It won't be easy for him."

Seeing the defeat on her soft features, he squeezed her shoulders and then placed his larger hands over hers. "Well, we'll just have to help him through it, won't we? Now, didn't you promise me something to eat?"

"Oh. Yes. It'll only take a few minutes to warm."

"Do I have time for a shower?"

"Sure." She tried to shake off her black mood and offered him a tentative smile.

Still holding her hand in his, he pulled her closer to him, so that his face was just a few inches from hers.

"It's been one helluva thirty-six hours," he said, his voice low, a finger from his free hand reaching forward to the point where the lapels of her robe crossed. The finger brushed her skin and her heartbeat accelerated rapidly.

His eyes lowered to the seductive hollow of her breasts. "And throughout it all, the one thing that kept me going was the thought that eventually, when it was all over and the smoke had cleared, I'd be with you."

The lump in Savannah's throat swelled. "I've been waiting a long time to hear just those words, counselor," she admitted with a weary sigh.

His hands drifted downward to the belt cinching the soft velour fabric together, and his long fingers worked at the knot.

Savannah's breath caught in her throat as his fingers grazed the sensitive skin between her breasts.

"There's one thing I'd like better than a hot shower," he admitted, his voice rough, his eyes meeting hers in a silent, sizzling message.

Savannah's blood was already racing through her body in anticipation. "And what is that?"

"A hot shower *with you.*"

The robe slid open to reveal Savannah's scanty silk-and-lace nightgown, and Travis, his teeth flashing beneath the dark stubble of his beard, smiled wickedly. "Looks like you were expecting me."

She laughed unexpectedly at the seductive gleam in his eyes. "You're flattering yourself."

"I deserve it."

Smiling shyly and observing him through the sweep of dark lashes, she had to agree. "Yes, I suppose you do," she said, gasping when his fingers slid downward to outline the point of her nipple beneath the pink silk.

His other hand slipped upward, behind her neck, and his strong fingers twined familiarly in the black silk of her hair as he gently drew her face closer to his.

Savannah's heartbeat quickened. When his warm lips

molded to hers hungrily and a gray spark of seduction lighted his gaze, she felt warmth spread through her body in rippling waves of desire that started deep within her and flooded all of her senses.

Travis groaned and buried his rough chin against her neck as the breast in his hand swelled, and the firm dark peak pressed taut beneath his palm. He felt Savannah quiver beneath his touch. His loins began to ache with the need to make love to her, the desire to wipe away the strain of the past two days by burying himself in the soft, liquid warmth of her and the yearning to be comforted by her tender hands.

He squeezed his eyes tightly shut and kissed her almost angrily, as if by releasing his leashed fury in passion he could forget that he had just spent two days in the wilderness to save a boy and a horse and that he had failed.

"Just love me, sweet lady," he insisted, wanting to think of nothing other than the yielding woman in his embrace, the smell of her hair, the feel of her pliant muscles, the taste of her skin. "Make love to me until there's nothing left but you and me."

Her answering moan was all the encouragement he needed. Without another word, Travis picked her up and carried her lithely up the stairs to her bedroom.

Then he placed her on the bed and stared down at her with night-darkened eyes that studied every curve of her body.

The pink silk shimmered in the semidarkness. Beneath the fragile cloth, dark nipples stood erect. Her tousled ebony hair splayed against the white pillow, framing the oval of her face in billowing, black clouds. A soft flush colored her creamy skin and her deep blue eyes, glazed with longing, delved deep into his soul.

A powerful swelling in Travis's loins pressed painfully against his jeans as he watched the gentle rise and fall of her breasts. It was all he could do to go slow, take it easy, draw out the sweetness of making love to her.

"I couldn't forget you," he admitted roughly, slowly unbuttoning and removing his shirt only to let it fall onto the floor.

She watched in fascination as he started on the wide buckle of his belt.

"I tried, y'know," he admitted, as if remembering an unpleasant thought. "For nine years I tried to tell myself that you were just a summer fling, one night in a lost world that didn't really count." He slid the jeans off his hips and kicked his boots into the corner of the room. "But I couldn't. Damn it, I couldn't forget you."

"And you regret that?"

A crooked smile slashed white across his face. "Never!" Sliding next to her on the bed, his fingers fitting familiarly around her waist, he let out a long, ragged breath. "We should have stayed together; it would have saved everyone a whole lot of grief."

"We're together now," she whispered.

"And that's all that matters," he said with that same wicked smile, his fingers inching upward to stroke the underside of a breast through the lace and silk.

"You're so right," she agreed with a sigh as she arched upward, fitting her body against his and kissing him passionately, her tongue slipping familiarly between his teeth.

Travis moaned and slid one hand under the hem of her nightgown as he moved against her. "About that shower?" he asked.

"Later…" she whispered, listening to the thudding of his heart and feeling the wiry hair of his chest brush against her cheeks. "Much later."

VAGUELY AWARE OF someone saying something to her, Savannah woke up. She rolled over in the bed and groaned before she felt a warm hand reach over and brush her hair away from her cheek.

"Merry Christmas," Travis whispered.

Opening her eyes and blinking as she stretched, Savannah smiled into Travis's silvery eyes. "It is Christmas morning, isn't it?"

"Christmas afternoon."

Savannah's groggy mind snapped, and she levered herself up on one elbow in order to see the clock on the nightstand. Twelve-thirty! Without another thought she swung her legs over the side of the bed. "Oh, my God! The horses—"

Travis's long arm encircled her waist. "Hold on a minute, will ya? Lester's already been here and looked in on them. Everything's fine. Even Mattie and Jones survived without you. Lester said he'll be back later this afternoon."

"And I slept through it?" she asked, unbelieving.

"Like a baby."

"I can't believe it!" She pushed the hair out of her eyes and let out a sigh. "I haven't slept like that in years."

"Nine years, maybe?" he asked softly, nuzzling her ear.

She remembered back to that morning long ago. She had woken late and learned that Travis was going to marry Melinda without even offering an explanation. The old needle of betrayal pricked at her heart and she had to ignore the painful sensation. "Maybe," she admitted, her voice rough.

"Well, lady, you'd better get used to sleeping in, I guess," Travis said with a twinkle in his eye. "Because I never intend to let you get away from me again and I expect that last night was just a preview of what's ahead."

She blushed a little as she thought about the shameless passion that had overtaken her just hours before. Her hunger for Travis had been all-consuming to the point that she had finally fallen asleep from sheer physical exhaustion.

Looking at him lovingly and affectionately stroking his chin, she asked a question that had been in the back of her mind for the past two days. "What is ahead, for you and me?"

"Before or after we're married?"

Her heart nearly stopped beating. *Married? To Travis?* It was almost too good to be true.

He nibbled at her ear, but she pushed him away. She needed to clear her mind and force him to become serious.

"Both," she finally replied, thoughtfully.

"You're no fun," he accused. Then when his thoughts revolved back to what had occurred between them just hours before, he grinned roguishly. "At least you're not much fun this morning."

"And you're ducking the issue."

"Make me some breakfast and I promise to confide in you," he suggested, burying his face in her hair and playfully running his fingers up her spine. "Or maybe you have a better idea..."

She laughed as his fingers slid against her skin, tickling her lightly. "Okay, okay, I guess it's the least I can do," she muttered, realizing that he hadn't eaten much for the better part of two days.

She slid out of bed and started dressing in front of the bureau, aware that his eyes never left her as she took her clothes out of the drawers. Though she was facing away from him, she could see his reflection in the mirror. After tugging her sweater over her head and pulling her thick hair out of the neck opening, she shook the black strands away from her face and arched a brow in his direction. He was still draped across the bed, the sheets covering only the lower half of his body.

"I'm not about to bring you breakfast in bed, you know," she pointed out.

"Like I said, 'no fun in the morning.'" He reached behind his head, grabbed one of the plump pillows and hurled it across the room.

Savannah sidestepped, managed to dodge the soft torpedo and laughed merrily. "Watch it, buster, or you'll end up with dry toast and water instead of crepes and salmon pâté," she warned.

He arched a thick, dark brow and smiled. "Thank God."

"You'll be sorry," she warned.

"I don't think so. As long as I'm here with you, I really don't care." His gray eyes were serious.

"Give me a break," she muttered, but smiled all the same as she left the room.

A half hour later, the kitchen was filled with the tantalizing scents of sizzling bacon, warm apple muffins and hot coffee. Travis was pulling a sweater over his head as he walked into the kitchen. He eyed the table with a Cheshire-cat-sized smile.

"For me?" he asked, looking at the small table decorated with brass candlesticks, a Christmas-red cloth and dainty sprigs of holly.

"For you, counselor," Savannah admitted, pouring two glasses of champagne and setting them on the table near the plates before lighting the candles.

"Champagne?"

"It's Christmas, isn't it?"

"Maybe the best one of my life," he thought aloud.

She was standing at the sink cutting fresh fruit, when he came up behind her and rested his chin against her shoulder, his long arms wrapping possessively around her waist, his fingertips pressed against her abdomen. "I love you, you know."

Savannah felt tears of joy build behind her eyes. "And I love you."

"I can't think of a better way to spend Christmas than with you," he said, his voice low, his clean-shaven cheek warm against her skin. "Domesticity becomes you."

"Does it? I'm not sure I like the sound of that."

"It's a compliment, and you'd better get used to it," he suggested. "I think I want to wake up with you every morning to pamper me."

"I'm not pampering you." She slid him a sly glance, but grinned at her obvious lie.

"No?"

Smiling, she thought for a minute. "Well, maybe a little. But I really just wanted to say thanks for finding Josh. If you hadn't been out there looking for him…" Her voice drifted off and she shivered.

Travis's strong arms tightened around her. "But I was," he remarked. "I just wish we could have done something to save Mystic."

"So do I," she whispered, thinking of Josh and how devastated the boy would be when he learned that Mystic had been put down.

She'd called Charmaine with the bad news while Travis was still upstairs. Charmaine had been adamant that Josh wasn't to be told about Mystic, at least not right away. When Savannah had spoken to Josh, she'd found it difficult to side-step the truth about his beloved horse. Josh had sounded tired, but anxious to come home to celebrate Christmas and see Mystic. Savannah had hung up with mixed feelings.

Now, she frowned and pushed those unhappy thoughts aside. It was Christmas, she was alone with Travis and she wouldn't let the rest of the world intrude. Not today. "Come on, let's eat and then I intend to put you to work."

"That sounds interesting," he drawled, kissing the back of her neck.

"Not that kind of work," she quipped. "I'm talking about the back-breaking work on the farm."

"Even on Christmas?"

"Especially on Christmas. No one else is here."

"Precisely my point," he said, his lips brushing her ear sensually.

She trembled beneath the gentle assault of his tongue on her ear. He smelled so clean and masculine and the feel of his fingers moving against the flat muscles of her abdomen started igniting the tiny sparks of passion in her blood all over again. It was all she could do to concentrate on the apple she was slicing.

"Travis," she whispered huskily, "if you don't stop this, I might cut myself…or you."

"Spoilsport," he accused with a soft chuckle, but kissed the top of her head and finally released her.

The meal was perfect. They ate in the kitchen and finished the bottle of champagne in the living room between a warm fire and the decorated Christmas tree.

"Two nights ago I never thought I'd be warm again," Travis said, setting his empty glass on a nearby table. He was lying on the thick carpet and lazily watching Savannah.

"And I wondered if I'd ever see you again."

"Well, that's behind us," he said, propped on one

elbow near the tree and staring up at her as she sat on her knees and adjusted a misplaced ornament. "And now you'll have one helluva time getting rid of me."

"Promise?" she asked.

"Promise!" He leaned closer to her and kissed her neck until she tumbled willingly into his arms.

They spent the rest of the day taking inventory of the feed and supplies in the barns. It was tiring work and, coupled with the usual routine, Savannah was dead tired by the time she returned to the house.

Sadie Stinson had come by earlier in the day and put a stuffed goose in the oven, a platter of cinnamon cookies on the counter and a molded salad in the refrigerator.

"It's not much," the older woman had said as she was leaving.

"What do you mean? It's a feast and it'll save my life! I didn't have anything planned," Savannah had replied.

"Well, I'd rather have stayed and helped."

"Forget it!" Savannah had waved off the older woman's apologies. "I won't hear any excuses! You have your family to worry about. It's Christmas!"

The housekeeper had finally agreed and left with a gift from Savannah tucked under her arm and a promise to return and fix "that child the best beef Wellington this side of the Rocky Mountains" when Josh was released from the hospital.

"I'll hold you to it," Savannah had replied, waving as Sadie drove carefully down the snow-covered lane.

Now, hours later, as Savannah opened the door to the kitchen, the scent of roasting goose filled her nostrils. "Thank you, Sadie Stinson," Savannah murmured to herself while kicking off her boots and walking through the kitchen in her stocking feet.

She dashed upstairs for a quick shower and hurried back down to the kitchen to put the finishing touches on the meal just as Travis returned from the barns.

"I'd forgotten what it's like to work with the horses," he said, raking his fingers through his hair. "I've spent so many hours behind a desk or in the law library that I can't remember the last time I cut open a bale of hay."

"And how did it feel?"

"It felt good," he admitted with a bemused frown as his eyes searched hers. "But maybe that was because of the company. What do you think?"

"I think you're addled from overwork, counselor." She laughed.

Travis built a fire in the living room while Savannah set the table. They ate by candlelight in the dining room and finally had brandied coffee in the darkened living room. The flickering fire and lighted Christmas tree cast colorful shadows on the walls and windowpanes.

Savannah sat with Travis on the floor, her back propped against the couch, Travis's head resting in her lap. He had taken off his shoes and was warming his stockinged feet by the fire while her fingers played in the dark chestnut curls falling over his forehead.

"I want you to marry me," he said at last, moving slightly to get a better view of her face.

She arched a slim, dark brow. "Just like that?"

He chuckled. "This isn't all that quick, you know. I've known you most of my life—well, at least most of yours," he said with a smile. "I don't think we're exactly rushing into it, do you?"

"No..."

"But?"

"A lot of 'buts,' I guess," she admitted.

"Name one."

"Melinda."

Savannah felt the muscles in Travis's back tighten. "Melinda's gone," he said, his jaw clenching and anger smoldering in his eyes.

"But if she were still alive?"

"That's a tough one," he admitted, rolling over and sitting up so that his eyes were level with hers. "And it's not really fair. While she was alive I tried to be the best husband I could to her. Maybe I failed, but I damned well gave it my best shot. Now it's over. She's gone. Don't get me wrong, I didn't wish her dead, but I can't bring her back, either."

Savannah's throat felt raw. "You loved her."

"Yes," he admitted, his eyes seeming distant as he gazed into the fire. "I did. It was a long, long time ago. But I loved her very much."

Even an admission that she had expected tore a hole in Savannah's heart. She tried to tell herself that what happened in the past didn't matter; it was the future that counted, but doubts still nagged her mind. Loving Travis as much as she did, she couldn't bear the thought of him having cared for another woman.

"But I fell in love with you," he said, his lips twisting downward at the corners as if he had read her thoughts. "I think I fell in love with you on the very day I saw you riding Mattie in the fields. You were watching me from under the apple tree and trying to look very grown up and sophisticated. Remember?"

How could she ever forget? "I remember."

"From that day on I couldn't get you out of my mind." He turned his solemn gaze in her direction, and his eyes caressed the soft contours of her face. "You have to believe that I would never have married Melinda, never, except that I believed she was carrying my child. I couldn't very well marry you knowing that Melinda was going to have my baby, could I?"

"I suppose not. But Dad seems to think… Oh, I guess it doesn't matter."

He became rigid and his back teeth ground together in frustration. His thick brows drew downward over his eyes. "Of course it matters. Tell me, what does Reginald think?"

"He warned me to stay away from you, that you weren't the man for me, that you've always loved Melinda and she'll always be between us."

Travis's face hardened. "Do you believe that?"

"No…"

"Then?" he snapped.

"I just wanted to be sure."

"Good Lord, Savannah," he said with a loud moan. "Haven't you heard a word I've said this past week? Don't you know that your father is still trying to manipulate us both?"

"That, I don't believe. My father is only concerned about my happiness."

"Is that why he didn't tell you that he knew about our affair?" he argued.

Savannah's temper flared. "You mean our one-night stand, don't you? It was only once, by the lake, remember?"

Travis softened a little. "Oh, I remember all right. That night has haunted me for the past nine years, and for the first time since then I'm going to do something about it. I'm going to marry you, lady, and you're not going to come up with any more excuses."

The argument should have ended there, but Savannah couldn't let it lie. Instead, she got to her feet, walked to the fireplace and turned to face him. "Suppose we do get married Travis. What then?"

"We'll move to Colorado."

"Colorado!" she repeated. "Why Colorado?"

"I have some land there; my parents left it to me. I thought we could make a clean, fresh start away from everything and everyone."

"You're talking about running away and dropping out, right?"

The corners of his mouth twisted downward. "No. What I mean is that we could raise horses, if that's what you want to do. But we wouldn't have Reginald looking over our shoulders, and I'd be rid of the law practice for good."

She could feel her stomach quivering, but the anger in his eyes gave her pause. "Is that what you want?"

"What I want is you. It's that simple. I've got enough money to get started somewhere else and I want to get away from lawsuits, political schemes and the past." He looked her squarely in the eye. "I'm not running away from anything, Savannah, I'm running *to* a home, a private, safe place for my wife and my children and I'm asking you to come with me."

"I want to, Travis, but I have a family here, a family that I love very much. My mother's not well, my father depends on me, my sister needs me and then there's Josh. He's more than a nephew to me, he's almost like my own son."

"I'm not asking you to give them up, not entirely."

She raised her hands in the air and let them fall to her sides. The argument was futile, but couldn't be ignored. "I understand that you're dissatisfied with your work and your life, but I'm not. I love it here. It's my home. Working with the horses is what I do. I tried working and living in the city once and it didn't work out. This house, this land, these horses..." She gestured around the room and toward the windows. "They might belong to Dad, but they're mine."

"You're not coming with me, are you?" he asked.

She felt the tears threatening her eyes. *Why was she arguing?* All she ever wanted was to be with Travis, and he was offering her a lifetime of love, if only she could give up the family that meant so much to her. "You know that I love you," she said. "I always have. But I need a little time to think about all this."

"I can't wait forever," he said slowly.

"And I wouldn't expect you to." She shrugged her shoulders and tried to think clearly. "Would it be possible for you to stay here on the farm?"

"Live here with your family?"

"Yes."

"No," he replied tersely. "I'm not about to live my life like Wade and Charmaine. I want my own place, my independence, my own home. I came here to cut the ties with Reginald, Savannah, and I still mean to do it."

A slow burn crept up her cheeks at Travis's ingratitude to her father. "You're going to forget that he raised you?" she asked, sarcasm tainting her words. "When no one wanted you because you were such a problem, my father gave you a home!"

Travis pushed himself upright and his shoulders bunched angrily. "I'll always owe your father a debt, no doubt about it, but I'm not paying for it with my life. I'm going to try and forget that he's tried to run my life— to the point of going behind my back with my partner, Henderson. I'm not about to be anyone's pawn, not even Reginald Beaumont's!"

"You'd better watch it," she snapped, her blue eyes sparking. "Or that chip you're wearing on your shoulder might just fall off and create another Grand Canyon!"

"Cheap shot, Savannah."

"But true."

A glimmer of revenge flickered in his eyes. "Then while we're taking shots…"

"Be my guest."

"At least I'm not afraid to face the past or take a chance and be my own person. I'm not tied like a calf ready for branding to a father and mother because I'm afraid of stepping out on my own for fear of failure."

"I haven't failed!"

"Because you haven't even tried. We all fail, Savannah."

She was so angry her fingers curled around the edge of the mantel. "The only time I've ever failed was when I trusted you nine years ago," she said, shaking with raw emotion. "I trusted you and loved you, and you made a mockery of that love. And you! You were such a coward that you didn't even bother saying goodbye before you married another woman!"

Stripped of all pretenses, alone in the house, Travis walked over to Savannah and gripped her shoulders. His eyes were bright with challenge, his jaw hard with anger. "I made a mistake," he said between clenched teeth. "And I'll be damned if I'll make another. I've lived with the love I felt for you burning my skin, ruining my wife's self-worth, and I've paid over and over again. Now I'm through paying and lying, and so are you. You can hide from me, Savannah, but I'll find you, and sooner or later you're going to have to face the fact that the past is dead and gone. Buried, just like Melinda and Mystic. We've got a future, damn it, and we're going to have it together."

He pulled her roughly to him and kissed her angrily, his lips hard and bruising, his tongue plundering. She tried to resist but couldn't. Traitorous desire burned brightly in her breast, and she leaned against him and let her tears of frustration run down her cheeks.

"Tell me you love me," he demanded, his hands spreading on the small of her back, pushing her tight against the hard evidence of his desire, possessively claiming her as his.

"You know I do—"

"Say it!"

"I love you," she whispered, her voice catching.

His glittering eyes softened a little. "Then don't let all the bullshit get in our way. I love you and I'm not about to let anything or anyone stand between us!" His shoulders slackened a little as the fury seeped from his body. "Oh, Savannah, we've come too far to turn back and hide. We're going to face the future and we're going to face it together!"

He kissed her again, more gently this time, and she wound her arms around his neck. And then, by the warmth of the fire, with the colored lights from the tree winking seductively, he slowly undressed her and made love to her long into the night.

CHAPTER TEN

FOR THE REMAINDER of the week, Savannah and Travis lived with an unspoken truce. The subject of the future was pushed aside while Savannah concentrated on keeping the farm running smoothly.

The snow had finally begun to melt the third day after Christmas, and life on the farm returned to a more normal schedule.

Travis seemed to thrive on the physical labor of the farm, and Lester was pleased to have him around. From time to time, Savannah caught the trainer smiling to himself and nodding as he watched Travis working with the animals.

Saturday afternoon, Lester was watching Vagabond and a few other other colts stretch their legs in the paddock when Savannah and Travis joined him. Only a few patches of snow remained on the ground, and the horses were making the most of their freedom.

Vagabond, his tail and head held high, raced from one end of the field to the other while snorting and bucking.

"Sure beats all that Perry Mason law business, doesn't it?" Lester remarked, watching the frisky colt's easy strides.

Travis threw back his head and laughed aloud. "If only my cases were as interesting as Perry's. If they had been, I might not have given up law." He leaned against a fence post and rubbed his cramped shoulders. "Most of the time I was in the library reading decisions regarding corporate law."

Lester's older eyes sparkled. "Not exactly your cup of tea."

"Not exactly," Travis commented dryly, his lips thinning as he watched the animals romp.

"But you've got a way with the horses," Lester pointed out.

"That's right," Savannah added, smiling slyly in Travis's direction. "You've got Vagabond eating out of your hand."

"That'll be the day," Travis replied, cocking his head in the direction of the bay colt. "Just yesterday he tried to take a piece out of my arm."

"He's a little temperamental," Savannah admitted with a teasing smile.

"High-strung," Lester added.

"Temperamental?" Travis echoed. "High-strung? I'd call it downright miserable and mean," Travis said before chuckling to himself.

"But you've got to admit he's got charisma," Savannah said.

"And speed," Lester added, watching the bay colt kick up his heels in the west pasture. The bay's smooth coat and rippling muscles glistened in the pale morning sunlight. "Let's just hope he has a little luck as well!"

"That, we all could use," Savannah agreed.

Later in the morning Charmaine called to say that Josh was about to be released from the hospital. Reginald and Virginia as well as Wade, Charmaine and Joshua would be home late in the afternoon.

"Worried?" Travis asked, resting on the handle of the

pitchfork in the hayloft over the stallion barn and staring into Savannah's troubled blue eyes.

"A little," she admitted. "These past few days I'd forgotten about all the problems, I guess." She smiled faintly and climbed down the ladder to find herself standing in front of Mystic's empty stall. It had been cleaned and now was waiting for another one of Beaumont Breeding Farm's colts to claim it as his own. She felt empty inside at the loss of Mystic.

"And now all the trouble is coming home?" Travis followed her down the ladder and hopped off the final rung.

"Yeah, I guess."

"Don't worry about it," he suggested with a patient smile.

"Easier said than done." Leaning over the gate to Mystic's stall, she thought about the magnificent black colt.

"You can't bring him back, y'know," Travis said softly.

Savannah sighed and nodded. "I know, but I can't help but worry about Josh and Wade..."

"Wade is Josh's father."

"Unfortunately," she whispered. "I wish to God that I could take that kid away from Wade Benson."

"He's the boy's father whether you like it or not."

Her throat ached and her frustration made her angry. She turned around to face the tenderness in Travis's eyes. "Is it as simple as all that?" she asked. "Is the law so cut-and-dried that a man who should never have become a father in the first place can browbeat a child until he has no self-esteem left?"

Travis tugged pensively on his lower lip. "Unless you can prove abuse—"

"Physical abuse, you mean," she snapped, her jaw jutting forward angrily. "But it doesn't matter what kind of mental cruelty a child like Josh is put through."

"That's Charmaine's problem," Travis pointed out, steadying Savannah with his hands by placing his palms firmly over her shoulders.

"According to the law! But I feel responsible for that child. It's just so damned unfair!" She crossed her arms over her chest and tried to turn away from him.

"Hey, slow down. Come into the house… I'll buy you a cup of coffee. Josh will be home soon and you can shower him with all that pent-up auntly love."

"Auntly?"

"That's what you are, aren't you?" he asked, pulling on her shoulders and hugging her body next to his before kissing her tenderly on the top of the head.

She had to smile despite her anger. "I suppose so."

"And I'd guess that you bought out the stores with all sorts of those ugly creatures and robots that he likes."

"Not quite."

Travis laughed. "Then buck up, will ya? Josh's coming home tonight and you promised him that we'd celebrate Christmas together. So you'd better put on one helluva show or you'll disappoint that nephew you love so much. I've got to run into town for a while, so you can fiddle in the kitchen with Sadie."

"She'd kill me. When she's here, the kitchen is her domain. Even Archimedes isn't welcome."

"Then go and string popcorn, hang mistletoe, sing carols or whatever it is you do around this time of the year, and while you're at it put a smile on that beautiful face."

"Sing carols?" she repeated, laughing a little. "I don't think so."

He sobered slightly and squeezed her shoulders. "Just be happy, love; that's all."

The depth of her feelings for him was reflected in her eyes as she forced a small grin. "And where will you be?"

He winked broadly. "I'm gonna get Josh a present that will knock his socks off."

"Are you?" Savannah was delighted.

"You bet."

"So who's going to take care of the horses while I'm, uh, singing carols?"

"I will, when I get back."

"You?"

"Sure, what's wrong with that?"

"Nothing," she said with a wicked twinkle in her eyes. "You're on." She chuckled as she handed him a bucket and a brush. "First you can clean the stalls and then—"

Setting the tools aside, he glared at Savannah in mock anger. "And then I'll come into the house and show you who's boss."

"Promises, promises," she quipped as she slipped out of his arms, through the door of the stallion barn, running back to the house with Travis on her heels.

"I thought you were going into town," she laughed when he caught up with her and jerked her roughly against him.

"I am, but when I get back..." He pressed warm lips to hers and held her as if afraid to let go.

"What?" she coaxed with a knowing smile.

"I'll deal with you then."

"I can hardly wait." She extricated herself from his arms and heard him swear under his breath as he started toward the pickup in the parking lot.

SAVANNAH, HER HEAD bent while tucking a pin in her hair, started down the stairs. After helping Sadie in the kitchen, she'd spent the past hour showering, dressing, pinning her hair into a chignon and wondering when Travis would return. Josh would be home any minute and Travis hadn't come back from town.

The doorbell caught her by surprise.

"I'll get it," she called downstairs toward the kitchen, where Sadie was still fussing. She hurried down the remaining steps and across the foyer.

Jerking open the door, Savannah found herself face to face with the reporter from the *Register*. Her heart nearly stopped beating and her smile froze on her face. *Not now,* she thought wildly, *not when Josh is due home within the hour!*

"Good afternoon," John Herman said, extending his hand.

"Good afternoon. What can I do for you?" she asked warily.

"I'd like to talk to you about Mystic, for starters," the reporter responded, a full smile sliding easily over his face. "I'd like to do a story about a great horse, you know, from the time he was a foal to the present."

She blocked his passage into the house and met his inquiring gaze. "I thought the *Register* already ran an article on Mystic."

"Right, but I'd like to do a bigger piece on the horse. You know, more of a human-interest story. I'd need to find out where he was raised, who worked with him, interview his trainer and the jockey who rode him, bring up all of his races, especially the Preakness, and slant the story for the local readers."

"I don't think so."

"It could be good publicity for the farm," John Herman persisted. "We'd be glad to include anything new, say, about the other horses. You've got another horse, a—" he checked his notes "—Vagabond, isn't it?"

"Yes. He's a two-year-old."

"I've heard people compare him to Mystic."

"The same temperament," Savannah said, forcing a tight smile. "But that's about it. And, as for Mystic, I'm not ready to give you a story about him, not yet, anyway." *Not until Josh is told the truth.* "I'm sorry you made the trip for nothing, maybe next time you'll call," she apologized, when she heard the sound of a pickup coming down the lane and realized with a sinking feeling that Travis had finally returned.

"Then maybe I could speak to Mr. McCord," the reporter persisted.

"He's…he's not here at the moment."

The screen door to the back porch banged shut. Savannah heard Travis walk through the kitchen and toward the hall.

"I'll tell him you were here to see him," she said hurriedly.

"Savannah," Travis called out, stopping when he walked into the hall and saw her wedged between the door and the doorjamb. "What the devil?"

"Mr. McCord!" John Herman said with enthusiasm, looking over Savannah's shoulder and smiling broadly.

There was nothing she could do about it. Reluctantly Savannah let the man inside. It was obvious from the spark of interest in John Herman's eyes that the main purpose for his visit to the farm had been to question Travis.

"John Herman," the reporter said, extending his hand. Travis took the man's outstretched palm, but didn't hide his skepticism. "I'm a reporter for the *Register*."

"I see." Travis smiled cynically. "Why don't you come into the living room where we can talk?" He glanced at Savannah and mildly inquired, "Savannah?"

Stunned at Travis's polite reaction to the press, Savannah realized she had completely forgotten her manners. "Yes, please come into the living room and I'll get some coffee." Casting Travis a I-hope-you-know-what-you're-getting-yourself-into look, she went to the kitchen, grabbed the blue enamel coffeepot and several empty cups and quickly explained to Sadie what was happening.

"Lord have mercy," Sadie prayed, rolling her eyes to the ceiling before preparing a tray of cookies. "Just make sure that reporter is gone before the boy arrives. His folks haven't told him about the horse, you know."

"I know," Savannah muttered angrily.

Sadie noticed Savannah's trembling fingers and placed her hand over the younger woman's wrist. "You go in there and keep Travis out of trouble. I'll bring the coffee in when it's brewed."

"You're sure?"

"Go on...go on."

"All right," Savannah replied as she walked out of the kitchen.

There was something about John Herman's attitude that rankled and unnerved her. The reporter tended to write a biting column that was filled with sharp wit, a smattering of truth and more rumors than fact.

Don't worry, she told herself as she started back to the living room, *Travis can handle himself. He's a lawyer and was almost a politician. He can deal with the press.*

"So you really are dropping out of the race?" Herman asked, his tape recorder poised by his side on the arm of the couch.

Travis, looking calm and nearly disinterested, leaned against the fireplace. Only the tiny muscle working in the corner of his jaw gave any sign of his inner tension. "I was never in it."

"But you did take contributions?"

"Never."

Herman's mouth tightened and he quickly scanned his notes. "There are several people who would dispute that. One of the most prominent is a Mrs. Eleanor Phillips. She charges that she gave you five thousand dollars."

"She didn't give me a dime," Travis replied. "And I wouldn't have taken it if she'd tried to give it to me."

"She claims she has a cancelled check to prove it."

"If so, I've never seen it."

John Herman held out his hand, as if to prevent Travis from lying. "Mr. McCord—"

"There may have been a few people working for me who were…overzealous in thinking that I would run. And they may have taken contributions in my name, but they did it without my knowledge, and I've instructed them to return the money with interest."

"So you're saying that you can't be persuaded to run for governor."

"That's right."

Flipping his notebook to a clean page, and making

sure that his recorder was working properly, the reporter turned to Savannah just as Sadie brought in the coffee.

"Now, what can you tell me about Mystic?" he asked, while accepting a cup of coffee from a cool Sadie.

"Nothing you don't already know."

Herman wasn't about to be dissuaded. "We got the official story from the veterinarian, Steve Anderson, but we'd like to know exactly what happened to the horse to cause the break in his leg."

"I really don't know," Savannah replied.

"Well, how did he get out? Did the kid really take him?"

"Joshua took him," she admitted.

"But why? Where was he going? Did he have an accomplice?"

"I think that's enough questions," Travis cut in, the smile on his face deadly. "Josh took the horse out for a ride and got caught in the storm. Subsequently, Mystic was injured and unfortunately couldn't be saved. It was a very unfortunate and tragic situation for everyone involved."

"Yes, but—"

"Now, if you'll excuse us," Travis said calmly. "Ms. Beaumont and I have work to get done."

Begrudgingly taking the hint, John Herman stood from his position on the couch, shut off his recorder and stuffed it, as well as his notepad, under his arm.

"It's been a pleasure, Mr. McCord," he said and nodded curtly to Savannah. "Thank you, Ms. Beaumont."

"You're welcome," she lied.

Travis escorted the reporter to the door and Savannah sank into the cushions of the couch.

"Vultures," Travis muttered once the reporter was

gone. Taking a cup of coffee from the table, he balanced on the arm of the couch and patted Savannah on the knee. "The good news is I don't think he'll be back."

"Impossible," Savannah replied, threading her fingers through Travis's strong ones. "You know what they say about bad pennies?"

Nodding, Travis waved off her worries. "Well, we can't be too concerned about John Herman; he writes what he wants to. We'll just have to hope that the editor of the *Register* makes him stick to the facts." He cocked his wrist and checked his watch before finishing his coffee. "Everyone will be home soon and we still have Christmas to celebrate."

"Speaking of which, what did you get Josh?"

A broad smile crept over Travis's face. "Something that he'll positively adore."

"I hate to ask."

"Then don't. I'm going to get cleaned up and then I have some work I have to finish in the den," Travis said.

"Again?" Savannah's fine brows drew together in confusion.

"It wont take long," he promised, kissing her lightly on the check.

"What is it you do in there?"

"Accounting," he replied cryptically.

"Why?"

His smile grew. "For peace of mind."

"I don't believe you."

"You asked," he said, standing and stretching, "and I told you. Now, why don't you get this couch fixed up for Josh? That way he can be down here with the tree before we have to put him in his room for the night."

"That's a good idea, even if you only offered it because you wanted to change the subject."

"Stick with me," he said, his eyes gleaming seductively and his voice lowering as he touched her cheek. "I've got lots of good ideas, some of which I'll be glad to personally demonstrate later."

She laughed in spite of herself. "That's a terrible line, counselor," she said, chuckling. "It's a good thing I love you or I'd never let you get away with it."

Deciding to bring down warm blankets and a thick quilt for Josh, she left the room and smiled to herself. The love in her heart swelled until she could almost feel it.

JOSH LOOKED SO SMALL. He was pale and in a brace that covered most of his upper body. His usually bright eyes were dull, and his hair had lost some of its sheen.

"You look like you've been to the wars and back," Savannah said as she finished tucking the blankets around the cushions of the couch.

"I feel like it, too."

"Tell me about it," Savannah suggested, helping the boy onto the sofa and tugging a Christmas quilt around his slim pajama-clad legs.

"I'm okay, I guess," he said bravely looking at the room full of adults.

"Are you ready for Christmas?"

"You bet," he replied, his eyes dancing a little and color coming back to his cheeks.

"Good. Just wait here, and I'll move this table in front of the couch, and you can eat right in here."

"Will you eat with me?" he asked shyly.

"Wouldn't hear of anything else," she agreed, smiling fondly at the boy and pulling up a chair near him.

While the rest of the family changed for dinner, Savannah spent her time spoiling Josh. "I missed you around here," she said, once the small table was covered with more food than an entire battalion of soldiers could eat.

"Really?"

"Really."

"I missed you, too," Josh admitted. "And I missed Mystic. Do you think you can take me out to see him?"

Savannah had thought she'd prepared herself for the question, but her carefully formed response felt like the lie it was and it stuck in her throat. She forced herself to meet Josh's worried gaze. "No, Josh, I can't. You know that. You've got to stay in the house and rest. At least until the brace is off."

"That might be weeks," he whined.

"Well, for the time being the stables and the stallion barn are definitely off limits." Turning to her plate, Savannah made a big show of starting the meal, hoping Josh would follow her lead and quit asking about Mystic.

Josh studied the platter of food before him but didn't touch it. "I think something's wrong with Mystic," he finally said.

Savannah's palms had begun to sweat. "Wrong? Why?"

He eyed her speculatively, with the cunning of a boy twice his age. "Everyone gets real jumpy when I talk about him."

"It's just because we're worried about you."

He shook his head and winced at a sudden stab of pain. "I don't think so," he said paling slightly. "Dad and Mom, even Grandpa, they act like they're hiding something from me."

"Maybe they're just sharing Christmas secrets."

"Aunt Savvy?"

Here it comes, she thought.

"You wouldn't lie to me, would you?"

Savannah felt her heart constrict, but she managed to meet his concerned gaze. "I wouldn't do anything to hurt you, Josh."

"That's not what I asked."

"Have I ever lied before?"

He was quiet for a moment. "No."

"Then why would I start now?"

"Because something bad happened. Something that nobody wants me to find out about."

Savannah forced a smile. "You know what I think, don't ya?"

"No, what?" Earnest boyish eyes pierced hers.

"That you've been lying in that hospital bed with too much to think about and too little to do. Well, sport, we're about to change all that right now. Eat your dinner and we'll open some presents, what do ya say?"

"All right!" Josh exclaimed enthusiastically, but slid a questioning look through the window toward the stallion barn.

JOSH WENT TO bed early, and he was so besotted with the cross-breed cocker spaniel puppy that Travis had given him, he didn't ask about Mystic again.

The evening had been strained and Savannah was grateful that it was over. *But there's still tomorrow and the next day,* she thought angrily to herself. *Sooner or later someone will have to tell Josh the truth!*

Savannah and Travis were just pushing the used wrapping paper into a cardboard box when Charmaine came back down the stairs. She was dressed in her bathrobe and slippers and she looked tired enough to drop through the floor.

"I just came down to say good-night," she explained, leaning one shoulder against the archway between the foyer and the living room. "And to say thanks, Travis, for the puppy."

"I figured that Josh might need a special friend when he finds out about Mystic."

"I know, I know," Charmaine said, shaking her head. "I should have told him before now, but I just couldn't. Strange as it was, he loved that foul-tempered horse. It'll kill him when he finds out that Mystic's gone."

"He'll know sooner or later," Travis said. "Reporters were here earlier today. There's bound to be another story in the paper. Even if that doesn't happen, one of Josh's friends might call and ask him about the horse."

Charmaine paled. "You're right, of course, but it's just not that easy."

"It's better if he hears it from you," Savannah said, pushing the last piece of paper into the box before straightening. "That way the lie will seem smaller."

"Maybe we'll tell him tomorrow," Charmaine said. "I just can't think about it right now, I'm too tired." She smiled sadly and left the room.

"Someone's got to tell him," Savannah said, crossing her arms over her chest.

"But not you, remember?" Travis reminded her. He took her hand and pulled her into the archway. "That's a job for his parents."

"Then they'd better do it and soon."

"I've got no argument with that," Travis said, "but let's trust Charmaine and Wade to handle it their way. Like it or not, you're not his mother."

"So you keep reminding me. But I am his aunt and his friend, and I can't stand lying to him."

"Then don't. Just avoid the subject of Mystic."

"That sounds like a lawyer talking," she said caustically. "And even if I do avoid the subject, it won't matter. Josh can read me like a book."

"Come on, lady," he cajoled, unplugging the Christmas tree and then pinning her against the wall with the length of his body. "You can worry about that tomorrow. Tonight you've got enough on your hands just keeping me happy."

"Is that so?" she asked.

The darkened room cast intriguing shadows over Travis's handsome features. His eyes stared deep into hers, and the kiss he gave her made her insides quiver. "There is something else I've been meaning to discuss with you," he murmured into her ear.

"Such as?"

"Something I've wanted to do for a long time." He reached into his pocket and extracted a white-gold ring with a large, pear-shaped diamond. The exquisite stone shimmered in the firelight, reflecting the red and orange flames. "Merry Christmas," he whispered against her hair.

Savannah stared at the ring and fought the urge to cry. "But when did you get this?"

"It came with the dog."

"Sure." She laughed, tears gathering in her eyes.

"Honest."

"I never dreamed…" she whispered.

"Dream. With me." His lips brushed over hers and his slumberous gray eyes looked past her tears and deep into her soul. "Just know that whatever happens, I love you."

"What's that supposed to mean?"

"Just that the fireworks are about to begin."

She swallowed hard. "You're going to confront Dad again, aren't you?" she accused. "Oh, Lord, Travis. What is it? What have you found out?"

"Nothing," he said. "Nothing yet."

"But you expect to."

"Just trust me." He placed the ring in her palm and gently folded her fingers around it. "I'm giving this ring to you because I love you and I want you to marry me. No matter what else happens, remember that."

"You act as if you're going to leave," she said.

"I am, for a little while. But I'll be back."

"And then?"

"And then I'll expect you to come with me."

"To Colorado," she guessed, feeling a weight upon her slim shoulders.

"Wherever. I really don't think it will matter."

Savannah sensed that things were about to change, that all she had known was about to be destroyed by the one man she loved with a desperation that took her breath away. "What're you going to do?" she asked, her fingers clutching his shirt.

"Bait a trap," he said with a sad smile.

"And you're leaving tonight?"

"In the morning." Travis saw the anxiety in her eyes and kissed her forehead. "Don't worry. I'll be back, and when I am, you'll be free to come with me."

Ignoring the dread that feathered down her spine, she

responded to the gentle pressure of his hands against her back and the warmth of his lips over hers.

"We only have one night together for a while," he murmured. "Let's make the most of it." Without waiting for her response, he gently tugged on her hand, led her through the kitchen to collect their coats, and out the back door, to the loft.

As she had worried it would, Savannah's life changed drastically the next morning.

"What the hell is all of this about?" Reginald roared as he kicked off his boots on the back porch. He'd already made his rounds and had come back into the kitchen with the morning paper tucked under his arm. Seeing Travis and Savannah together obviously made his blood boil.

He slapped the open paper onto the table. Bold black letters across the front page of the *Register* made Travis's withdrawal from the governor's race official.

"I told you I wasn't planning on running," Travis said, a lazy grin slanting across his face.

"But I thought you'd change your mind. A man just doesn't throw away an opportunity like this! We're talking about the governorship of California—one of the most powerful positions on the West Coast! Why in God's name wouldn't you want it?" Reginald looked stunned and perplexed, as if Travis were a creature he couldn't begin to understand.

"I explained all that before."

Reginald slid into the nearest chair and Savannah poured him a glass of orange juice. "I thought you'd change your mind, that you just needed a change of scenery to recover after the Eldridge case as well as Melinda's death."

"I haven't and I won't."

"You should have waited before you told the press," Reginald said dejectedly.

"No reason."

"But there's a chance you will reverse your position."

"No way. I'm out." Travis finished his glass of juice and reached for a cup of coffee.

"So what do you plan to do? Willis Henderson said you wanted to sell your half of the law partnership to him."

"That's right. I'm going back to L.A. today to sign the papers and tie up a few loose ends."

"And then?"

"And then I'll be back. For Savannah." The smile on Travis's face hardened around the corners of his mouth. "I've asked her to marry me."

"You what!" Reginald paled. He slumped lower in the chair and sighed before looking at Savannah. "You're really not seriously thinking about marriage are you?"

Savannah laughed. "I'm twenty-six, Dad."

"But your feelings for him are all turned around. They have been since that summer that he came back to the farm." He rubbed a tired hand over his face and then impaled Travis with his cold eyes. "And after the marriage, what then?"

"Colorado."

"Colorado? Oh, God, why?"

"A new start."

Reginald reached into his jacket pocket for his pipe. "Well, I can't say as I blame you, I guess," he said wearily. "From the looks of this," he tapped his pipe on the paper, "you'll need one."

Savannah picked up the paper and her stomach twisted as she read the article. Though most of the facts were accurate, the slant of the report was that Travis was leaving the race because of a reported scandal in which he had been accused of taking contributions for a non-existent campaign.

Later in the article it was mentioned that Travis may have been involved in the controversy surrounding Mystic's death.

Savannah, white and shaking after reading the article, lifted her eyes to meet the concerned gaze of her father. "What controversy?" she asked.

"There are those who think Mystic could have been saved," Reginald said. "I heard about it when I stayed in Sacramento to be near Josh."

"But Steve did everything possible."

"There are always some people who will second-guess." Reginald studied his pipe. "I considered another surgery on the horse, but it just didn't seem fair to Mystic. The odds that he would have survived were minimal and we—Lester, Steve and I—agreed it would be best to put him out of his agony. I explained that to the press, but of course, other people, including some in the racing industry, disagreed."

"So what does that have to do with Travis?"

"Nothing, really," Travis explained with a grimace. "But right now it makes for an interesting story, especially since I've been staying here at the farm and was involved in finding Mystic."

"You should stay here and fight," Reginald said, his face suddenly suffusing with color. "You should run for the governorship and win, damn it. That would stop all the wagging tongues...."

Travis took a seat opposite Reginald at the table. "But that's not what you're worried about, is it? You have other reasons for wanting me involved in politics."

"Of course I do."

"Name one."

"I think it would be a great accomplishment for you."

"I said, 'name one' and I meant a real reason."

Reginald's eyes flickered from Travis to Savannah and back again. "You know it would be a feather in my cap," he said nervously.

"How?" Travis leaned forward on his elbows and stared straight at Reginald with a look that could cut through steel.

"I practically raised you as my own son and—"

"And that has nothing to do with it except for the fact that you've always tried to use me." He pointed one long finger on the table and tapped it against the polished wood. "Now, give me specifics."

"I don't have any."

Travis frowned and settled back in his chair, crossing his arms over his chest. Then he smiled cynically and his eyes remained cold.

"What's this all about?" Savannah asked, surveying the confrontation between the two men with mounting dread.

"I think it all started with a piece of property just outside of San Francisco."

"You mean Dad's land?" Savannah asked, noticing that Reginald's stiff shoulders fell. "I don't understand."

"You would if you snooped through his office and did some digging in the checkbook."

"Oh, Travis, you didn't," she murmured.

"Why don't you let your father explain?"

Reginald's thick brows lifted. "Wade was worried that you'd been looking where you shouldn't have."

"He had good cause to worry," Travis said angrily.

"What's wrong with the property?" Savannah asked.

"Nothing. Not yet. But plans are already being made."

"What kind of plans?" she asked, leaning against the counter and staring at her father with wide, disbelieving eyes.

"It's not all that big a deal," her father said with a frown. "You know, I've always thought that Travis should go into politics."

Savannah nodded and Travis's eyes narrowed. "Go on," Savannah coaxed.

"Two years ago I had this opportunity to buy some land near San Francisco at a good price. The company that owned it was going bankrupt. I heard of the distress sale and bought the acreage. It was just a case of being in the right place at the right time. Anyway, I had it surveyed and decided that I'd want to build a racetrack, a kind of memorial to myself and the horses we've raised, name it Beaumont Park." His eyes slid to Travis. "There's no crime in that, is there?"

"I didn't know this," Savannah said incredulously. "So what does that have to do with Travis?"

"Red tape," Travis explained. "The land was zoned all wrong and there was bound to be some protest from the farms bordering Reginald's land if he decided that he wanted to build a racetrack."

"But Travis wasn't even elected," she said to her father.

"I know. It was kind of a long shot, but when I couldn't get a straight answer from Travis, I talked to

Melinda and she told me that he was setting his sights for the next governor's race. I knew that as governor he could be influential and help me build the park."

"As well as make a ton of money," Travis cut in.

"That, too, of course."

"Of course," Travis repeated. "You know, Reginald, that's taking a helluva lot for granted. Especially since I hadn't announced any intention of running."

"But I knew Melinda and how influential she was in your life." Reginald looked at his daughter. "She managed to get you to marry her, when you were attracted to Savannah, didn't she?"

Savannah felt her face color in the ensuing silence.

"And she held on to you, helped you make career decisions as well as personal ones. I knew that you relied on her judgment, Travis, and if she said you were going to run, it was good enough for me."

"All behind my back."

"You were busy."

"So what happened when Melinda died?" Travis wanted to know.

"There was the Eldridge case, which you won with flying colors. You were the hero of the hour after winning that decision against the drug company..."

Travis glared at the older man. "What if I had run and lost? That was a distinct possibility, you know."

"Not according to the pollsters."

"A lot could have happened between now and then; besides, the public does happen to change its mind on occasion."

"I'd considered that," Reginald admitted. "I could still sell that land at a substantial profit. But of course, it would be a lot less than I'd make if I sold to a consortium of investors who were interested in building Beaumont Park."

"I don't believe this," Savannah said.

"There's more," Travis thought aloud. "You expected me to appoint you to the board, didn't you?"

Reginald frowned thoughtfully. "I'd hoped," he admitted.

"You expected one helluva lot, didn't you?" Travis said, swearing angrily. "Good God, man, not only did you bet that I'd win a race I wasn't running in, but then you wanted personal favors from me as well." Travis's face colored as he became more incensed. "I just want you to know here and now, for the record, if I ever decide to go into politics, I'll never owe any man anything!"

"This is insane," Savannah thought aloud. "Travis hadn't even announced his candidacy!"

Reginald offered his daughter a humbling grin. "I still have dreams, you know, dreams I haven't fulfilled, and I'm running out of time. I'm not the kind of man who can just retire…." He lifted his palms, hoping she would understand.

"But you don't have to."

Lighting his pipe, Reginald shook his head. A thick cloud of scented smoke rose to the ceiling. "I'm afraid I do. I need to move your mother into town, so she's closer to the things she likes to do. She needs to be near a hospital, but I'd be bored to death in the city. You know that."

"Yes," Savannah replied, remembering her own brief career in San Francisco. All the while, she'd been itching to return to the farm. Working outside with the horses was in her blood, as it was in her father's.

Reginald stood and walked to the door. "Then try and understand and be patient with me."

She watched in disbelief as Reginald, attempting to straighten his shoulders, walked out the door. "So you were right," she whispered to Travis. Through the window Savannah watched her father walk through the wet grass toward the stables. Archimedes was tagging along behind him.

"Does that change things?" Travis asked.

She offered a faltering smile. "A little, I guess."

He looked down at her hand and the diamond sparkling on her finger. "Come with me to L.A."

"I can't." She shook her head and smiled. "Too much is unsteady here at the farm. Josh is still laid up, Charmaine's worried, Dad's still despondent about Mystic and Wade..."

"Yeah, I've noticed. He's holed himself up with a bottle every night." Travis sighed wearily and looked deep into her eyes. "So what happens when I come back for you? Will you be able to leave with me?"

"I hope so," she said, her eyes sliding over the familiar rolling hills and fields that were so dear to her.

"But you can't say for sure."

"No, not yet."

"I was afraid it would come to this, but maybe I can help you make up your mind." His smile became hard. "Like I told you last night, I'm going to L.A. to bait a trap, and when I come back, maybe this whole mess will be straightened out."

"I don't see how," she whispered.

"Trust me," he said, kissing her softly on the lips. "I told you that I wasn't about to let you go again and that's a promise I intend to keep!"

CHAPTER ELEVEN

TRAVIS HAD BEEN gone for over a week, and Josh was beginning to heal. So far, Charmaine had been able to screen Josh's friends' calls, and no one had let Josh know that Mystic had been destroyed.

Savannah was more on edge with each passing day, afraid that she or someone else on the farm would experience an inadvertent slip of the tongue around the boy. She'd even tried to talk to both Wade and Charmaine, but no amount of persuading could convince Josh's parents to tell their son about the dead colt.

She missed Travis more than she thought was humanly possible and reluctantly agreed that he had been right all along. It was time for her to make a life for herself, a life with him. But walking away from the family she loved and the farm she held dear would be like tearing a huge hole out of her heart and leaving a dark empty chasm in her life.

"Don't be foolish," she'd told herself, but couldn't fight the pangs of regret she was already feeling.

She walked slowly from the main stables toward the stallion barn and wondered when Travis would return. Though he'd called once, their telephone conversation had been brief and stilted.

The engagement ring around her finger continued to sparkle and remind her that soon, after so many years apart, she would be Travis's wife, able to start a new life, perhaps have a child of her own. *Travis's child.*

With that warming thought she hurried to the stallion barn but stopped dead in her tracks when she saw Josh near the barn door.

"Hey, sport," she called, and Josh jumped and whirled to face her. "What're you doing out here?" she asked softly. "I thought you gave up your early-morning rounds."

"I just wanted to see Mystic," Josh replied, turning earnest eyes upward to meet her loving gaze.

"Does your mom know you're here?"

Josh pushed his toe into the mud. "No."

"Or your dad or grandpa?"

"No one but you, Aunt Savvy. You're not going to tell on me, are you?"

Savannah shook her head and smiled. Bending her head to be on eye level with the boy, she winked at him. "I wouldn't dream of it."

Josh took advantage of her good nature. "Then you'll let me into the barn?"

She leaned a shoulder against the door and weighed the alternatives. In another week Josh would get his brace off and would be returning to school. He needed time to adjust and grieve for the horse he'd loved before he faced his friends.

"I'd be in big trouble with your folks," she said.

"They'll never know," Josh pressed.

"They'd know." Her smile slowly fell from her face.

"How?" His question was so innocent. It ripped through her heart.

Breathing deeply, she placed a comforting hand on Josh's shoulder. "First of all, let me explain something."

"Why?"

"For once, you just listen, okay?"

The boy swallowed and stuck out his chin. "Okay."

"You know that we all love you very much." When he tried to interrupt, she held up her hand and kept talking very quickly. "And everything that we've done is to protect you and keep you safe."

"Like what?"

"Josh, I really don't know how to tell you this, but I wish I'd done it a long time ago. Come on." She pushed open the door to the barn. It creaked on old hinges and let a little daylight into the darkened interior. Several stallions nickered softly as Savannah snapped on the lights and braced herself for Josh's despair.

"What's wrong?" Josh asked, his gaze wandering to Mystic's empty stall. "Where's Mystic?"

"He's gone, Josh," Savannah said softly, touching the boy on the shoulder.

"Gone?" he repeated, his face pinching with fear as he twisted away from her. "Gone where?" The boy raced down the aisle and stood at Mystic's empty stall. "Where is he?" he asked, tears in his eyes. "Grandpa didn't sell him did he? He wouldn't!"

"No," Savannah said calmly. "But Grandpa did have to have Mystic put down. He was hurt and the vet couldn't help him."

"Hurt!" the boy screamed, losing all of his color, his eyes widening in horror. Several of the horses began to shift warily within their stalls. "What do you mean?"

"His leg was broken," she said as calmly as possible.

Josh's small features contorted in grief, and tears drizzled down his cheeks. "Because of when I took him away from here during the storm, right?"

Savannah's stomach knotted painfully. "That's when it happened."

"Then it's all my fault!"

"Of course not." Slowly she advanced toward her nephew, offering him an encouraging smile as well as her understanding gaze.

"How can you say that?" Josh demanded, his voice cracking. "I took him, didn't I? I rode him when I wasn't supposed to! Oh, Aunt Savvy, I killed him! I killed Mystic!"

"Mystic hurt himself. It was an accident."

"Then why didn't anybody tell me?" Josh asked, wiping his eyes with his sleeve.

"Because the doctors were afraid that you'd be upset. Once you got home it was difficult to tell you about Mystic because you loved him so much."

"I should never have taken him," he said, sobbing.

"That's right, you shouldn't have. But it happened and you can't blame yourself for the accident. You loved the horse; no one blames you for his death. Now, come on. Let's go into the house and I'll fix you some breakfast."

"No!" Josh stepped away from her and angrily pushed her arm away from his shoulders. "You lied to me! All of you lied to me! You let me think that Mystic was alive and all the time he was dead!"

Josh began to run from the barn.

"Josh, wait!" Savannah yelled after him, and watched as he disappeared through the door. "Damn!" Her fist balled and she slammed it against the top of the gate to Mystic's stall. Vagabond snorted and tossed his head, but Savannah, her thoughts centered on her nephew, ignored the horse. "You made a fine mess out of this,

Beaumont," she chastised herself before running after Josh to the house.

When she walked into the kitchen, she found that the entire household was awake.

"You told him about Mystic, didn't you?" Wade demanded. He was sipping from a cup of coffee and impaling her with his cruel eyes.

"Josh was already at the barn. What else could I do?"

"March him back here and have him talk to me. I'm his father."

"Then I suggest you start acting like it and quit lying to the kid. You had plenty of opportunities to talk to him about Mystic."

"And since I didn't you took it upon your shoulders to handle the situation."

"Don't push this off on me, Wade. Face it, you blew it." She started through the kitchen in an effort to go up to Josh's room and try to console him, but Wade's hand restrained her.

"Stay away from him, Savannah. He's with Charmaine. She'll handle him. As far as I'm concerned you can leave my boy alone and just butt the hell out of my life."

"I love Josh, Wade."

"But he already has a mother." He dropped her arm and ran an unsteady hand through his hair. "And as for Travis McCord, you can tell him to leave me alone as well."

Savannah bristled. "What's Travis got to do with you?"

Eyeing her speculatively, Wade pressed his fingers against his temples as if trying to forestall a headache. "Nothing. Forget it."

"Forget what?" she asked. "Have you talked to him?"

"Of course not!" Wade snapped.

"Then—"

"I said, 'forget it,'" Wade grumbled, taking his coat from a peg near the back door and storming out of the house toward the garage.

"What was that all about?" she whispered to herself as she watched Wade walk angrily to his car. A few minutes later he drove away from the farm at a break-neck speed.

Knowing that something had happened between her brother-in-law and Travis, she tried to dial Travis's apartment in L.A. Though she let the phone ring for several minutes, Travis didn't answer. "Where are you?" she wondered aloud, hanging up the receiver and realizing just how much she depended upon him.

Taking a deep breath, Savannah climbed the stairs and found Charmaine walking out of Josh's room.

"I let the cat out of the bag," Savannah admitted.

"I know. It's all right. I should have told him when it first happened," Charmaine said with a weary smile. "He just wants to be left alone for a while."

"Do you think that's okay?"

"Yeah. He's okay. And Banjo's with him."

"Thank God Travis gave him the puppy."

Charmaine slid a conspiratorial glance in her sister's direction. "I had to do some fast talking to get Wade to agree to the dog," she admitted.

"I imagine. Wade just left."

"I heard," Charmaine said as if it didn't really matter one way or the other.

"How're things…between you two?"

"No worse than they ever were, I suppose, but it's

hard to say. He's been a basket case ever since Travis showed up here a few weeks ago, and I'm about ready to call it quits." She ran a trembling hand over her eyes.

"Charmaine—"

"I'm okay. Really. I just don't understand Wade anymore. And his reaction to Travis...it's scary, he almost acts paranoid."

"Because of the governor's race?"

Charmaine shook her head and bit pensively on her lip. "There's more to it than that, I think. I just don't exactly know what it is." Looking Savannah squarely in the eye, she said, "But the whole thing scares me; it scares me to death."

"Why?"

"I don't know. I feel like Wade is worried about something—something big. But he won't confide in me."

"Maybe you're just imagining it," Savannah offered. "We've all been on edge ever since the accident with Mystic."

"I wish I could believe that was all it was," Charmaine replied grimly. "But I don't think so."

TWO DAYS LATER Travis returned to the farm. Savannah was standing near the exercise track with Lester when she heard footsteps behind her. She turned and found Travis, his eyes sparkling silver-gray in the morning light, walking toward her.

"I was beginning to think that you'd changed your mind," she accused with a laugh.

"About you? Never!" Travis took her into his arms and twirled her off the ground. "God, it's good to see you," he said, lowering his head and capturing her lips with his.

"You could've called," she accused.

"Too impersonal. I didn't want to waste any time. The faster I got done in L.A., the quicker I could get back to you!" He kissed her again, and this time the kiss deepened, igniting the dormant fires in her blood and sending her senses reeling.

Savannah blushed when she looked up and saw Lester staring at her.

"Don't mind me, missy." Lester grinned. "I always knew you two were right for each other."

"How?"

The older man grinned. "I was younger once myself, y'know. Had myself a wonderful lady, but things didn't work out."

Savannah was dumbfounded. "Why not?"

The older man smiled wistfully. "Turned out that she was married. And to a good man, too." He shrugged. "Water under the bridge. But with you two, that's a whole other story."

Vagabond finished his workout and Lester studied the colt with narrowed eyes. "This one, he might just do it this year."

"Do what?"

"Win 'em all!"

Savannah laughed and shoved her hands into her pockets. "That's what you said about Mystic."

"Ah, well, some things just don't work out as ya would have liked, don't ya know?" he said wistfully.

Lester walked over to the horse, and Travis and Savannah turned back to the house.

"You think you can ever really leave this place?" Travis asked suddenly.

"With you? Yes."

"But you wouldn't be happy." It was a simple statement and one Savannah couldn't really deny as she looked at the wet, green hills and the carefully maintained buildings of the farm. In a few months the brood mares would be delivering their foals and the spindly-legged newborns would get their first breath of life on the farm.

"I'll miss it," she admitted.

"Even if we start again?"

"In Colorado?"

"Wherever."

She angled her head and looked up at him. Light from a wintry sun warmed her face. "This farm is special to me. For you it represents my father and the fact that he tried to mold you into something he wanted. So, to you, it's a prison. But to me, it represents freedom to do exactly as I please."

"Which is work with the horses."

"And be near my family."

"I see," he said tersely, his teeth clenching together just as they reached the back porch. "I think it's time I talked to Reginald in person."

"Oh, God, haven't you quarreled enough already?"

"That's behind us."

"I don't understand."

"Oh, but you will. I've been doing a lot of thinking lately and I've talked to Reginald every day."

"You called here and didn't talk to me?" she demanded, confusion clouding her eyes. *What was going on?*

"Guilty as charged," he conceded with a rakish smile.

"I'll get you for that, you know."

A grin sliced across his tanned face. "I can't wait."

They walked into the den and found Reginald, his glasses perched on the end of his nose, sitting at his desk and carefully making marks on invoices as well as ledger entries.

"So you finally got here," Reginald said, all the old animosity out of his voice.

"Just a few minutes ago."

"You knew he was coming?" Savannah asked in surprise.

"Didn't you? Oh, I see." Reginald pushed the papers on his desk to the side and motioned for Savannah to take a seat in his recliner. "Well, I thought you'd want to know that I've decided to retire."

"Right away?"

"Yes. As soon as possible."

"What!"

He tapped a pencil to his lips and smiled at his daughter. "I've given a lot of thought to it, ever since the tragedy with Mystic and then with what Travis has discovered, it just seemed like the right time to turn over the farm to you."

"To me?" Savannah repeated, stunned. "Wait a minute. What about Wade?"

Reginald frowned and looked at Travis. "So you haven't told her anything, have you?"

"I figured it was your responsibility."

"What responsibility?" Savannah demanded. "What's been going on?" Then Travis's cold words came back to her. *I'm going to bait a trap.* What had happened?

"I've decided to sell that piece of property near San

Francisco, take your mother and move to a warmer climate, somewhere south near San Diego, I think."

"But why now?"

"I told you that your mother needs to be closer to town and a hospital, and I'd been giving some thought to retiring anyway. When Travis discovered that Wade had skimmed money from the farm, I double-checked. Unfortunately, he was right. In the past six years, Wade has taken Beaumont Breeding Farm for nearly a quarter of a million dollars."

Savannah blanched and dropped into the nearest chair. "No!" But the expression on her father's face remained grim.

"Yes," Travis interjected. "Also, much to my partner, Willis Henderson's, embarrassment, Wade has been skimming money out of the law firm with phony invoices and receipts."

"Same here," Reginald said, gesturing to a stack of bills. "Dummy companies, who supposedly charged us for anything from paper clips to alfalfa to stud services." Reginald picked up his pipe and began cleaning the bowl. "I guess I'm getting too old to oversee everything. A few years ago this never would have happened. I would have caught it." He sighed heavily. "I just can't afford to make mistakes like that, not even for my own son-in-law."

"I can't believe any of this," Savannah whispered, but Travis's stony gaze convinced her that it was true. *Wade? A thief?*

"So I'm counting on you to keep the farm going," Reginald said with a sad smile. "Charmaine has no use for the horses, but you, you've had a feel for them ever since you were a little girl."

Savannah looked from her father to Travis. "You knew all about this, didn't you? And yet you let me think we were still going to Colorado."

"Just checking," he replied, his eyes lighting mischievously. "I had to know that you were serious about marrying me."

"Nothing will ever change my mind," she vowed, standing next to the man she loved with all of her heart.

"What the hell's going on here?" Wade demanded, bursting into the room. His face was flushed, his eyes wild and he was shaking from head to foot. "Charmaine just gave me some cock-and-bull story about you retiring and leaving the management of the farm to Savannah."

"That's right," Reginald said quietly.

"But—" His voice dropped when he saw the stack of invoices on the corner of the desk.

"I think you'd better call a good lawyer," Reginald said. "We've found you out, Wade."

"And don't bother contacting Willis Henderson," Travis added. "He's on to you."

"What's that supposed to mean?"

Travis sighed loudly. "Give it up, Benson," he suggested, his voice cold. "Not only do we know about the phony receipts and how much money you've embezzled to the penny, but we also know about the gambling debts that you've had to repay."

Wade blanched and stumbled backward, leaning against the wall for support. "Lies," he choked out. "All a pack of lies."

"I don't think so."

Gesturing wildly, Wade pointed a condemning finger at Travis. "And I suppose you've spread all these lies to Charmaine, haven't you! Haven't you?"

"She knows all about it. If you want, you can try and explain your side of the story," Travis said. "But she's got all the facts and figures."

Wade's eyes narrowed and his fist curled at his side. "This is all your fault, McCord. You've spent the last few weeks of your life trying to destroy me. Well, I'm going to fight it. Tooth and nail. Just because you're a big hotshot attorney, you're not going to force me into going to jail for something I didn't do!"

He stomped out of the room and thundered up the stairs.

"Well, that's that," Reginald said wearily. "Can't say that I like it much." He lit his pipe and sighed as the smoke billowed around his face. "It will probably kill your mother."

"She's stronger than you think," Savannah whispered.

"I hope so." Reginald shook his head and put his hands on the desk to rise to his full height. "Oh, and Savannah, you may as well know that I told Travis I expect him to help you with the farm."

"That's right," Travis said. "The old man is still trying to manipulate me."

"And you let him?" Savannah asked.

Travis's smile stole from one side of his face to the other. "Maybe it's because he told me he wanted us to fill this house with his grandchildren."

She lifted her confused eyes to her father. "Wait a minute. Are you saying that after all your warnings you *want* me to marry Travis?"

Reginald snorted. "I would have preferred him to become governor; I wouldn't even have opposed having a daughter who's the first lady of this state, but I guess

I'll just have to settle for a son-in-law who will run this farm with care and integrity."

"And what about Wade?" Savannah asked.

"I don't know," Reginald said, obviously tired. "But he's made his own bed; now he'll have to lie in it." Reginald walked out of the room and trudged up the stairs to talk to Virginia.

"So what happens to Wade now?" Savannah asked.

"I suppose Wade will be prosecuted, if Willis Henderson and your father have their way," Travis replied.

"And Charmaine?"

"She's taking it in stride, but she could probably use a little support from you."

Savannah's heart twisted and her voice was only the barest of whispers. "And what about Josh?"

"Charmaine's already talked to him. The boy seemed to handle it fairly well. Remember, he and his father didn't get along very well, anyway."

"He and Charmaine have become a lot closer since Mystic's death," Savannah said.

Travis leaned against the desk with his hips and drew Savannah into the circle of his arms. "The way I figure it, we'll live here until we can build a house of our own. And your father has promised not to try and run our lives."

"I can't believe you've buried the hatchet."

"Face it, the man is your father. I'm stuck with him and he's stuck with me. Because of you, we're trying to work things out."

"Unbelievable," she murmured. "Now, tell me what's wrong with this house."

"Nothing, except that it belongs to Reginald and Virginia. Charmaine and Josh will probably stay here."

"So what was all this song and dance about filling up this house with children?" she asked, turning to face him, a sparkle lighting her blue eyes.

"Just that. The house I intend to fill with children will have to be twice this size just to hold them all."

"You're out of your mind, counselor," she said, but tossed her hair away from her face and laughed at the thought.

"Only with love for you." He pulled her closer, so that her ear was pressed to his chest and she could hear the steady pounding of his heart. "Don't worry about anything, we can have it all."

"And Wade?"

"He'll probably be sent to prison, and I think that's a good place for him. He won't be around for the next few years, and by the time he gets back, if Charmaine doesn't decide to divorce him, Josh will be old enough to stand up for himself."

"You've got it all figured out, don't you?"

"Except for one thing."

"Oh?" She lifted her head and traced the seductive curve of his lips with her finger. "What's that?"

"How I'm going to get you to marry me before tonight."

"Impossible."

"Reno's not that far away...."

She laughed merrily. "Oh, no, you don't. I'm not settling for a quick ten-minute speech in front of some justice of the peace I've never met before. You're going to have to go the whole nine yards on this one. You know, big church, long white gown, stiff uncomfortable tuxedo and at least four attendants."

Travis squeezed her. "You're really out for blood, aren't you?"

"I've waited a long time."

"And it was worth it, wasn't it?" Without waiting for a response, he pressed his hungry lips to hers and deftly swept her off her feet. "Don't answer that question," he whispered against her ear. "We have much more important things to do right now."

Without a word of protest, Savannah stared into his eyes and locked her arms around his neck. "And for the rest of our lives," she added.

Travis smiled and carried her out of the den, down the hallway and into the kitchen.

"Hey, where are you taking me?" she asked.

"To some place where we can be alone." He crossed the parking lot to the garage and climbed the stairs to his loft. Once inside, he set her on the floor, kicked the door shut and locked it. "Now, Ms. Beaumont," he said, with a twinkle in his eyes. "I think it's time we spent the next few days locked away from the rest of the world."

"Is that possible?" she asked.

"Probably not, but we can try." Grinning wickedly, he extracted a gold key from his pocket and dangled it in front of her nose. "Face it, lady, you can't get away from me."

"I wouldn't have it any other way," she agreed, as he folded her into his arms and carried her into the bedroom.

* * * * *